THE OASIS MAGE

THE OASIS MAGE

THE SPRITE SAGA — BOOK TWO

ZAID HASAN

ISBN 979-8-9914467-2-3 (Paperback)

First Edition: May 2026

Published by Zaid Hasan
www.hasanfantasy.com
contact@hasanfantasy.com
Instagram: @hasanfantasy

To my wife and our fur babies,

It is you who gives me inspiration each and every day, my love. Who fills me with purpose when I can't seem to find it on my own.

And to Abid Rafi Siddiqi (1931 - 2024),

By the grace of Allah, he lived an incredible life truly worthy of an epic adventure novel. And his experiences battling Alzheimer's disease in his final years formed the foundation for one of the more emotionally-driven subplots of this novel.

Baba, even though you didn't remember us, we will always remember you.

If you feel so inclined, and if you can afford it, there are a number of organizations working to research cures, to provide resources, and to raise awareness for neurodegenerative illnesses, who could use your support.

Alzheimer's Association
alz.org

Alzheimer's Disease International
alzint.org

Alzheimer's Foundation of America
alzfdn.org

Cure Alzheimer's Fund
curealz.org

Dementia Society of America
dementiasociety.org

A Note to the Reader

Dearest Reader,

I thought long and hard about what the subtitle of this novel should be. Eventually, I landed on, "Rise of the Three Deaths," but a part of me truly felt compelled to go with, "The Journey Continues." Had I settled on the latter, it would've only partially been alluding to the continuing adventures of our main characters: Unisa, Rafael, Kyoko, Salessa, Naina, and Saila. But the other allusion, and perhaps the more meaningful one, would've been to my journey as an author.

You see, this is the second book of the series, and while in some ways the process of writing and publishing it was easier, in so many other ways, it was more difficult. The easier parts of this were mostly technical, in service of publishing. The harder parts were mental. Hurdles, like imposter syndrome, that needed to be overcome. I've yet to overcome them, but I'll let you know if I ever get there.

Anyway, the point that I'm (quite poorly) trying to make is that my journey as an author continues in this novel, and if you've picked it up, you've presumably read The Ore Monger and have decided to continue this journey with me. For that, I'm grateful in ways I'm unable to articulate.

Similarly to The Ore Monger, injustice is a powerful theme in this novel. And there would be no greater injustice than ending this note without relaying to you the Trigger/Content Warnings of the novel. They're listed below my signature at the end of this note, and I do urge you to read them. My aim in including graphic content is never to upset or offend anyone.

Thank you again, and I truly hope this sequel exceeds your expectations.

Yours,
Zaid Hasan

Content Warnings

Graphic violence and bloodshed throughout, dementia and neurodegenerative disease, caring for aging loved one, death of aging loved one, non-graphic discussion of sexual abuse and grooming of minors, non-violent sexual assault, manipulation and coercion (sexual and non-sexual), cults and organizations/institutions of control, frequent nudity in non-sexual contexts, incest and incestuous sexual assault, pregnancy loss due to medical complications, graphic scene of death during childbirth, blood exchange, discussion and depiction of enslavement, strong/heavy discussion on many socio-political topics, including, but not limited to, reproductive rights, racial supremacy, capital punishment/the death penalty, and discriminatory policies based on sexual orientation

THE KNOWN CONTINENTS OF THE ALL-SPHERE 1628 DG

Eloa
BEAUTY'S DOCKS
Small Beauty
River
SunSide
Anairda Village
CereCenters 45 to 56
OLD SUNSIDE DOCKS
Nivyan Hollow
NEW SUNSIDE DOCKS
SEABED
Lily Beach
Ardev Ocean
FlatHat Empire
FeatherKnife Mts.
Nysabaan Desert
PANAERTH DOCKS
The Canopy

PANAERTH

AERTHOMNI
LIBRARY DOCKS
BROTHEL DOCKS
Smith
Courtesan
THE LIBRARY
Dissolved Nations
Cobbler
Merchant
Bard
Red-Lo River
Northern Hills
PeakHaven Mountains
Eloa
BEAUTY'S DOCKS
CereCenters 4 to 22
Small Beauty
Ona's River
SunSide
Anairda Village
Luila
CereCenters 41 to 44
Evic
Lahu
ADERA
CereCenters 1 to 3
Gerontocratic Villages
MoonSide
Soil King
CereCenters 45 to 56
OLD SUNSIDE DOCKS
Ward's Fall
PEAKHAVEN
Salta
Kinara
ARLUN
Guardleaf Grove
CereCenters 23 to 40
LARSO
PeakHaven Pass
Deepweed
INNKEEPER'S RANCH
Meradil
Pyari
DORUH DOCKS
West Wine
Agrarian Townlets
Nivyan Hollow
The HearthBark
EVEREMBER DOCKS
WEST DOCKS
EVEREMBER
NEW SUNSIDE DOCKS
SOUTH DOCKS
Balyan Ocean
SEABED

Lily
Beach
FlatHat
Empire
Ardev
Ocean
FeatherKnife
Mts.
Nysabaan
Desert
The Canopy

PANAERTH

PROLOGUE

"IMPRISONED"

Continent of Panaerth *The Great Sprite Empire*
Date *2160 EN (3368 Years Before the Everlasting Journey)*

FEW SIGHTS ARE MORE FRIGHTENING than a torn sky, crimson and inflamed like a fresh wound. Few sounds are more harrowing than the staggered final breaths of those surrendering to death's embrace. Few smells are more intimidating than the stench of burning flesh and pungent brimstone, as it needles into the nostrils.

Vala pushes every godforsaken sensation to the back of her mind as she strides forth, higher and higher to the black stone ridge upon which Kova and Elva stand. Thick beads of sweat scurry past her temples, as exhaustion batters her muscles. Wounds burn open along her arms, chest, shoulders, and wings. With every step, she feels the weight of the clay pot hanging about her waist, swinging back and forth under her tattered robes.

The peak approaches and she sees them, her former husband and his sister. With all her might, she represses a gasp; what have they become?

A second pair of arms extrude from their ribs. Their once-sparkling teeth have been replaced with monstrous fangs, and the colorful plates of their shimmering butterfly wings have disintegrated into nothing more than skeletal loops.

The demons with which they've merged, the ones they've invited to the All-Sphere, have disfigured them entirely. They wear the lush robes of the Sprite Empire, but all evidence of the Sprite blood in their veins has been wiped clean. The Kova and Elva she once knew, the ones she still cares deeply for, are already gone. These beasts are all that remain.

No remorse for what she is about to do exists in her heart.

The disfigured siblings' red pupils find Vala when she steps up onto the ridge. Elva's lips part and a powerful spell trickles from her serpentine tongue, forming a protective barrier, an invisible shield, against Vala's incantations.

Kova chants the next hex, blasting beams of hot energy from his chest, through the barrier, toward Vala. She has the quickest tongue in the Empire. Her incantation deflects the blast into the skies.

His sister's next attack opens the stone beneath Vala's feet, nearly swallowing her. Vala's lips part again and she hovers over the dark hole until it forms into solid ground again.

The Empress of the Sprites takes a deep breath and interrupts another attack from her former husband. "I'm sorry, Kova!"

Kova falls silent mid-incantation and moisture develops in his eyes. He raises one of his four mighty arms, sweeping it across, gesturing at the battlefield from which Vala came. "Your apologies will not bring back your soldiers any more than they will heal a broken heart."

A tinge of sadness envelops Vala and she speaks sincerely. "I never wanted to hurt you, Kova. I never meant for either of you to become"—she steadies her tone—"what you are now. What have they done to you?"

"They cured me." The tightness of his throat strains his voice. "While you sentenced me to death. I woke up each day praying for a trace of your scent. I bathed in the tender rays of your voice each blessed morning. You were the reason I breathed."

"I seek atonement," Vala responds, hoping to break through the walls between them.

"The great Empress shows humility," Elva spits. She bows grandly and facetiously. "We are not worthy, Your Majesty."

Vala keeps her gaze locked on her former husband. "I remember every flower you ever gave me. Every moment we spent wrapped in each other. I remember every single time you told me you loved me. I want to fix this and go back to how we were."

Kova swallows hard and speaks after a long pause. "There is not a shred of surprise in that, Vala. Now that we and our demon allies have brought the mighty Sprite Empire to its knees, you come to us begging for mercy. *Now*, you offer me the attention you deprived me of." He steps forward. "It is too late."

Vala nods. "You're correct, Kova. You and your demon army have won. Please, end this battle and ease our suffering. Now that you've conquered your disease, and the Empire, let us be together again."

"And what of our suffering?" Elva demands. She raises all four arms and gestures to her body. "Look at what we've had to do, had to become, just to cure my brother's ailment and take back what you stole from us. We had an agreement, Vala, and you turned your back on it."

"I was wrong," Vala admits. "If you end the bloodshed now, turn the demons back to the plane from which they came, I will return what is rightfully yours. Both of you will enjoy the respect of being Emperor and Empress."

"And?" Kova asks.

Her next words, and the tone on which they're conveyed, will have to be believable if she is going to survive this conversation. She breathes deeply, then speaks. "And I will surrender myself to your custody. Punishment, banishment, imprisonment. Whatever you want."

"You don't care what we want," Elva taunts her. "When you discovered my brother and I in bed, you called us deviants. Depraved. When it was you who put us there."

"I was negligent, I understand that now."

"Now, now, now." Kova rolls the word around in his mouth. "Now is too late."

Vala speaks the words with conviction. "It doesn't have to be. I know you don't love me the way you did when we were married, and it is my fault for driving you into Elva's arms. But you can still have the Empire." She gestures to the battlefield. "But not if you raze it."

She swallows and steps forth courageously until she is chest-to-chest with her former husband. "You don't have to forgive me. But you can't lead a community that is extinct. Send these demons away and claim what is yours."

Her hand rises and falls delicately onto his cheek, pushing it to the side softly until his eyes lock onto the Sprite Empire below the ridge. Slowly, she backs up and allows Elva to join Kova as the siblings stare out at what could be theirs.

Vala draws all her energy to her lips and whispers, *"hydronda kuronda."* An ancient spell found buried in dusty texts earlier that morning. If it works, the Empire is saved. If it doesn't, it is doomed.

But it was doomed anyway. She had to try.

Elva's eyes widen when the spell reaches her ears, but it's too late. Vala pulls the clay pot from her waist and removes the lid, revealing a small amount of water inside. Elva and Kova attempt to bring the barrier back up, but their feet have already begun to shatter into the molecules which form them.

Vala chants the incantation, again and again, in regular intervals, tone stagnant. With every repeated spell, the demonic siblings grow weaker. Atom-by-atom, Kova and Elva are pulled into the clay pot and bonded to the water within.

"We trusted you, Vala!" bellows Elva as her head disintegrates and plummets into the clay pot.

Kova looks down at his four dissolving hands, then he meets Vala's gaze. Droplets trickle from the corner of his eyes. "Vala, I..." He swallows. "I love—"

He becomes dust. Nothing remains of him when Vala replaces the lid of the clay pot, imprisoning the siblings.

Lightning races across the sky and the demon soldiers are plucked, one-by-one, off the ground and tossed back through the tear from which they entered the All-Sphere. The last of them returns to their plane and the wound in the sky heals instantly, turning crimson to star-speckled nightfall once again.

Vala breathes a deep sigh as her fingertips caress the flame designs etched into the outer rim of the clay pot. Her chest tightens and she battles the urge to weep. Not for the demon who stood before her, but for the husband she lost to him. And for the sister she once cared for as her own.

"I love you, too, Kova."

She steps up onto a tall stone outcrop that overlooks the battlefield, expending every remaining drop of energy in her body to raise the clay pot into the air. Those who survived the battle spot her.

The field erupts into cheers so loud they rattle the stone beneath her feet. Chants of Vala's glory proliferate into the air, as swords rise to the skies in her honor. Comrades weep and embrace as they celebrate the victory of their courageous leader.

"All praise to the Empress!"

"Blessings to the great leader!"

"Cheers for Vala, the Protector!"

And finally, "Long live the Oasis Mage!"

CHAPTER 1

"An Uphill Struggle"

Theocracy *SunSide*
Date *21st Day of Month 6, Year 1629 DG - One Year After the Halving of SunSide*

RED-LO'S BEDCHAMBER DOOR CLOSES with a soft click, and he turns to face the four-post bed in the center of the room. Grasping the head of his cane tightly with wrinkled fingers, he hobbles slowly toward it.

Clack. Step. Clack. Step.

His hunched back and stiff knees throb sorely and he reminisces about the ease with which he once strode. Inflexible fingers rise to sweep through long gray hair, moving it out of his face.

SunSide's beloved MegaMother sits in the bed, her back against the headboard, a blanket draped over her legs. On a small table over her lap rests a modern retelling of a faerie folktale, and in her hand is a device she uses to magnify the print for her deteriorating eyesight.

"The MegaFather requests a few moments of attention before he falls victim to slumber," Red-Lo states coyly when he reaches the bed. He groans as he sits, then pulls his legs up onto the bed and under the blanket.

Drof-Fa smiles and moves the small table to the floor beside the bed, placing the magnifying device next to it. "As you wish, my liege."

Red-Lo laughs. "In sixty years of marriage, I don't think I've ever heard you call me that." He shifts his body lower on the bed and places his head down on the pillow before turning to face Drof-Fa.

The MegaMother tenderly kisses his lips, then mirrors him on her side of the bed, head on the pillow facing him. "I certainly wouldn't get used to it now."

As they lie together, Red-Lo's cheeks warm and a deep sense of love bubbles in his chest. He raises one hand and places it affectionately on Drof-Fa's cheek, taking in the softness of her skin and her familiar lavender scent.

"What are you thinking, Red?" she questions him.

Memories light up his mind; visions of the decades he sat on the throne, serving the kingdom, uplifting and empowering his faerie brethren, raising his children to value the strength of their bloodline and the work of their forefathers.

Above all, the soft, quiet moments he spent cherishing his queen. It was all for her, always for her.

"I am so proud of this life we've built together," he says. "And now Tha-Lo can carry on our legacy. We've given her the knowledge, experience, and tools she needs to assure the longevity of the faerie clan's rule."

Drof-Fa laughs. "Don't speak as if this is the end, my love. You still have some years in you."

"I don't want another day," Red-Lo admits. He buries his head against Drof-Fa's chest and wraps his arms around her.

She kisses the top of his head. "What do you mean?"

"I love you, my darling," Red-Lo professes to his wife. "This is how I'd like to leave this world: buried in your arms."

He can feel the smile radiating from her.

"I love you more," she whispers.

Wrapped in each other, this is how the MegaMother and MegaFather of SunSide die. Peacefully, warmly, lovingly.

Red-Lo's eyes open again and reality comes into focus. He isn't in bed with his wife, dying peacefully of old age. He's trapped in his descendant's body, filth and grime matting his hair, the stench of rat feces and defeat clinging to him.

For a year, he's sat with his back against the cold stone wall of an underground cell, withered and underweight, his once turquoise skin now nearly as gray as his eyes. Every inch of his body aches and he is constantly nauseous and light-headed.

The warm embrace of the MegaMother, the tender voice in his ears, the eternal tranquility of their simultaneous demise, it's all a cruel stunt; a reminder of what could have been had he simply left the Sprites' cavern when Drof-Fa tugged at his elbow eight centuries earlier.

Or had he never dragged her onto the Everlasting Journey in the first place.

Just beyond the bars of his cell stands Saila, her eyes glowing, blood trickling from her nostrils. Flanking her is the crimson-skinned nymph, Kruga, whom Saith nearly killed a year earlier.

"That's enough," Red-Lo grumbles.

The Facilitator's daughter is unaffected, her eyes continuing to glow as the warmth of Drof-Fa's chest against Red-Lo's cheeks burns a hole into his heart.

"I said enough, Saila!"

The glow of her eyes dies and she wipes her nose clean. "This is a future you can still have, Red-Lo. Tell us where and when to expect the Three Deaths, and I'll take you to her myself."

Red-Lo sighs. "Taunt me all you want with these visions, my answer will not change. I know nothing more than this: we are four months from the twenty-first anniversary of the last essence transfer. By then, the Sprites will know I have no essence to provide to them. Catastrophe will strike, at the latest, when this realization dawns on them."

"Where?" Saila pushes.

Cold, hard stone against his back and buttocks distracts him. Even after a year of sitting in one corner of the cell, he yearns for the soft seat of his throne; he longs for the warm adulation of his followers, the heavy comfort of a full belly, and the soft caresses of a faerie in his bed.

"I asked you a question," Saila interrupts his wallowing. "Where will the Three Deaths—"

"Do you simply *never* tire?" Red-Lo blurts out. "Surely after a year of listening to me admit my ignorance, you're exhausted."

The corner of Saila's lips curves up slightly. "I could never tire of asking you the same question, over and over again, knowing what a torture it is for you."

"Torture," Red-Lo scoffs. "How do you raise your legs to walk around with so much unwarranted self-importance weighing you down?" He closes his eyes and leans his head back against the wall behind him. "The only torture you bring me is the memory of watching you burn your innocent father alive."

"Innocent?" Saila questions facetiously.

Had he the strength, Red-Lo would've leaped to the bars between them, reached through, and wrapped his fingers tightly around the ungrateful pixie's throat. Instead, he weakly separates his eyelids again to meet her gaze. When she comes back into focus, he speaks.

"You know as well as I do how much your father loved you. As much as you disappointed him, as much shame as you brought to your family, he never stopped hoping you would come around."

"Come around to what, exactly?" Saila questions. "A pixie family that aided in the subjugation of our clan for centuries? Empowering a dynasty that battled Doruh Liberation and occupied MoonSide?"

"You sound just like her," Red-Lo responds, memories of a long-forgotten MegaMother flooding into his mind.

"Like whom?"

"Picana. She insisted her clan had been *subjugated* and *oppressed,* and held the faeries back from our ambitions. She removed my father from his position in her ministry, along with so many other faeries who wanted to uphold the legacy of our forefathers. When they couldn't take it anymore, the Faerie Empowerment Forces were born."

"Is there a point to this history lesson?" She taps her foot.

Red-Lo smiles, revealing a brown film covering his teeth. "The point, you ungracious little bitch, is that your beliefs are the same kind that led Drof-Fa to remove Picana's head from her shoulders. Your father, and other family members who served the crown, understood—"

"My father is dead."

The words are no surprise to Red-Lo, yet they strike him nonetheless. A pain erupts in his chest as he remembers every moment Saith stood by his side, from the day the pixie lost his arm trying to save Red-Lo's life, to the day Saila murdered him.

"I wouldn't be here, in this cell, had he survived."

"Had he survived, he'd be here in this cell with you. I just needed an opportunity, and he gave it to me the moment Alba was killed."

"Ah, yes," Red-Lo says. "A dead Librarian on SunSidian soil. You wanted the monarchy gone, didn't you, Saila? Now the theocracy rules. Tell me, how are you dealing with this situation? Has the Prime marched his army of Librarians through the Pass yet? Do you know how to prevent war?"

"It's already taken care of."

Red-Lo's expression betrays his astonishment. "I am"—he pauses—"impressed. Have you handled *all* matters that come with governance, with the same proficiency?"

There's a long pause before Saila responds, her tone weak, her volume low. "I have."

Red-Lo smiles again. "You're lying. Ruling is not as easy as you thought it would be, is it?"

"We're done here," Saila says sternly, turning on her heels.

Red-Lo raises his volume as she and her crimson companion depart, hoping his words echo through the dungeon and strike her heart. "You're a failure, Saila, just as your father always predicted you'd be. You may have prevented a war with the Library, but you'll never rule like I did. I was a natural fit for the throne. Do you hear me, Saila? Your father was right about you!"

As the Chief Member reaches the door leading out of the dungeon and up to the main level, Red-Lo shouts a final statement. "Alba and Sonali would be so disappointed in you."

Her strides stop and she remains still for a moment as her fingers blanket the doorknob. Red-Lo thinks she might turn around and blast him with Radiant energy, but the crimson nymph leans forward and whispers something to her.

Saila nods and continues through the doorway, closing it behind her, leaving the faerie to his solitude amongst the insects, rodents, and decay.

***

Her throat tightens further with every step she climbs. The faerie's words sting and burn her deeper and deeper the more they linger in her ears.

Alba and Sonali would be so disappointed in you.

He's arrogant and insidious. Corrupt and cunning. He's rotting in a cell deep underground; a cell she put him in with her own hands.

But he's right. When one problem is stamped down, another drops into her lap. The Chief Member of the Assembly of the Radiance knows nothing about governance. Her ineptness and inexperience are on full display. She covered herself in shimmering new robes, granted herself a title, held elections to fill the empty seats of the Assembly, and did all she could to usher SunSide into its new era…

But none of that makes her a good leader. Red-Lo was a supremacist and an oppressive dictator for eight centuries, but he was beloved by his followers. Every citizen now looks to Saila for direction, they seek her guidance, but they do it out of necessity, not love. Not admiration. Not respect.

"I hope you've cast his words into the gutters where they belong" comes Kruga's steady tone to break her from her thoughts.

She chains her tongue.

"Don't listen to him, Saila," Kruga urges her.

Again, she keeps her lips sealed tightly, swallowing hard to break the tension in her throat. *Why does this staircase feel so much longer than when we descended?*

His fingers wrap gently around her wrist and she stops climbing, turning to face him.

The nymph repeats himself. "Don't listen to him."

"Is he wrong?" Saila questions.

"Yes," Kruga responds quickly, assertively. "Unequivocally, he's wrong. He didn't know Alba and Sonali the way you did. He has no idea how they would feel if they were here watching you right now."

"Neither do you," Saila challenges him. "You never met Alba and you only knew Sonali through her correspondence with the Revolution. How are you so sure he's wrong?"

Kruga pauses, then shrugs. "You're right, I didn't know them."

Saila's chest tightens. She was hoping for some profundity from the Counsel to the Chief Member, but he appears to concede on their back-and-forth.

Until he speaks again. "But you did. You knew both Alba and Sonali better than anyone on the All-Sphere. You tell me: would they be disappointed in all you've accomplished?"

Saila searches deep in her heart and memories for an answer and comes up short. She shakes her head. "I don't know. I haven't accomplished much in the past year that I've been Chief Member."

"That's not true. So much of the ore has been dismantled and shipped back to EverEmber for their funerals. Every day, more and more faeries get relocated from the settlements in MoonSide, to Larso."

"Causing overpopulation and a housing crisis," Saila responds. "Everything I've decreed seems to have created more problems than it's fixed."

"Cities aren't built overnight, Saila. These are natural problems that will be sorted as soon as the new cities—"

"The new cities will never be completed if I can't get control of Tund-Ra and the Bravers United."

Kruga sighs. "The Bravers United are a problem, but not an unexpected one. We're holding the former MegaFather captive in a cell underground. Generations of Bravers pledged their fealty to this dynasty, they weren't going to disappear quietly into the night. But the New SunSidian Guard is nearly eighty percent Revolution warriors, and the remainder are former Bravers themselves. They'll take care of Tund-Ra and his resistance."

"They'd better. The new Members won't stop interrogating me about it."

"Good."

"Good?" Saila raises an eyebrow.

A soft smile spreads across Kruga's lips and he nods. "Good. The new Members were elected by the citizens because they're willing to fight and advocate for the concerns of those they represent. Let them voice those concerns. Acknowledge them. The whole point of an Assembly is for all of you to work together. You're not alone."

It is moments like these where Saila is reminded that she is, in fact, not alone. The edge of her lips curl into a half-smile.

"Thank you, Kruga. For agreeing to be my Counselor."

Kruga's smile deepens and he bows respectfully. "You honor me, Chief Member."

Saila cannot restrain her laugh at his formality. She turns up toward the stairs that remain, then back to Kruga. "They'll be waiting. We should continue the climb."

Kruga nods. "It looks steeper than it is. An uphill struggle always does."

As Saila moves to ascend, Kruga captures her attention again.

"I forgot to say this earlier, but I know today must be difficult for you."

Saila is completely taken aback, jaw slack, nearly shocked into silence. "I-I didn't think anyone remembered."

"It's exactly one year since you lost Alba, and only days since I lost Symin. I don't think any of us will ever forget. But no one wanted to mention it to you in fear of causing you further emotional distress. I thought I would take the chance and let you know, again, as your Counselor, that you aren't alone in your grief."

"As my Counselor?" Saila challenges him, an eyebrow raised.

Kruga smiles. "Somewhat as your Counselor. But mostly as your friend."

Saila opens her arms out to him and he leans forward to embrace her. "Thank you, Kruga."

The Chief Member and her Counselor turn and conquer the ascent together.

CHAPTER 2

"The New SunSidian Assembly"

Theocracy *SunSide*
Date *21st Day of Month 6, Year 1629 DG*

IT WASN'T UNTIL SALESSA LEFT that Naina truly realized how many innate gifts her sister possessed. She knew Salessa was studious and personable and diplomatic and mature, but now that her twin isn't by her side, for the first time in their lives, the wolf feels the pressure of having to make up for those gifts alone.

There isn't any resentment in Naina's heart toward Salessa. No indignation, no anger. She knows how important it was for Salessa to search for the author of the note.

Come find me.

Those three words had haunted the falcon until, a few weeks prior, Naina insisted she begin the quest. Hesitantly, she did, promising to write to Naina as often as she could with updates.

Had Salessa been sitting here with her now, in the Forum with the rest of the Members of the Assembly of the Radiance, she might have filled the awkward silence with friendly banter or light conversation. Instead, eight Members sit at the rotund wooden table in the center of the room in shimmering robes, lips tightly pressed, eyes wandering with boredom.

I wish you were here, Lessi. But maybe I can try to be more like you.

Naina rises to her feet, capturing the attention of the other Members. With every eye on her, she suddenly feels a discomfort she wasn't expecting.

This is a terrible fucking idea. I'm not Lessi, I don't have her charm. What do I even say? They're all staring at me. I shouldn't have stood up. Well, now I'm standing, I have to say something.

"Is there something you'd like to say, Member Naina?" inquires a young angi Member named Aissa. Her natural, coiled hair springs down her deep mahogany cheeks in twists, her silver-feathered wings tight against her back.

The question isn't posed antagonistically, yet Naina can feel a sweat break out near her hairline. *Alright, here goes.*

"I know all of the Members value their time, and I appreciate that everyone was punctual in their arrival." *Doing well, I think.* "So perhaps we can begin and the Chief Member will join us when she arrives."

The Members exchange uncertain glances, trading confusion until one speaks up. He is an elderly pixie with lavender skin, and as he speaks, the tips of his pointed ears shake with disapproval. "Are you the Chief Member?"

Naina clears her dry throat, confused by the question. "I'm sorry, Member Vinino?"

The pixie continues. "Who gave you the authority to start the meeting without the Chief Member? Are you under the impression that because you were appointed and not elected, you have some power over us?"

"I don't believe Member Naina intended to imply such a thing," Aissa comes to her aid.

Naina passes gratitude to the angi with her expression, then turns to Vinino. "I wasn't implying that at all. I only meant that since the Chief Member hasn't arrived, and we're well past our meeting's start time, maybe we should—"

The thick, towering doors of the Forum creak open and Saila storms through with Kruga at her side. Guards close the door behind them and Kruga announces, "Rise for the Chief Member of the Assembly of the Radiance! Glory to the Quad Gods."

"Oh, thank the Twins," Naina breathes. Member Vinino shoots her a glare and she adds, "And the Four, of course."

The eight seated members join Naina on their feet, and all nine raise four fingers to their foreheads to salute the arriving Chief Member and her Counselor.

Saila's robes glitter with the gems embedded in the floor beneath her. She walks quickly, but confidently, and returns the salute to the Members at the table, then asks them all to take their seats.

"Thank you all for waiting," Saila starts. "I apologize, sincerely, for my lateness. I was in another interrogation."

"Has any new information come about?" another elderly Mega, Member Hemmar, inquires.

Saila hesitates, then speaks in a low, even tone. "There are many matters of business to discuss at today's meeting. If it's alright with the Members, I'd like to discuss my interrogations of the MegaFa—" She pauses. "Of the former king at the end of the meeting."

The Members exchange glances again, then a handful nod and Saila continues, turning to a new face at the other end of the table. She smiles and her tone warms. "Welcome to the Assembly, Member Faolan. We're delighted that you've joined us."

Member Faolan, a young nymph the color of reddish autumn leaves, excitedly folds his hands on the table. "Thank you, Chief Member. It's an honor to be elected to represent the villages of the north in the Assembly."

"Has it been much of a culture shock for you, moving to Larso? Small Beauty is not far from Eloa, where I grew up. I remember how strange city life was to me when I first moved here."

Faolan shakes his head. "Oh, not at all. My aunt and uncle live in Larso. I spent many summers visiting them as a child."

"Excellent," Saila responds before turning to the other Members. "Well, with the election of Member Faolan to represent the northern villages, every seat in the Assembly is now filled. Perhaps you can all take a moment to introduce yourselves, in order of election."

Member Rayga, a pink pixie, raises her hand first, grabbing the room's attention. "The middle villages held their elections first, and I was chosen to represent them. Member Rayga of Ward's Fall."

Aissa speaks next. "Member Aissa, representing the inner districts of Larso."

After the angi is a faerie named Member Pyr-Sa, representing the outer districts of Larso, followed by the two elderly Members, Hemmar and Vinino, both representatives of the communities in Nivyan Hollow.

Saila then gestures to Naina and the orange, armor-clad Mega next to her. "This is Member Naina, one of our liaisons to MoonSide, and beside her is Member Ovida, the General of the New SunSidian Guard."

"They were not elected," Vinino grumbles.

Saila turns to him with a frown. "I didn't quite hear you, Member. What was that?"

Vinino speaks louder. "I was clarifying to the child that Naina and Ovida are appointed Members, not elected."

"Child?" Member Faolan's cheeks grow redder than they already are. "Sir, I'm seventeen, and I was elected just the same as you were."

"Indeed," Saila agrees. "Regardless of age or the manner of your employment, you're all Members of the theocracy now. You will be treated with the same—"

"But we are not treated the same," Vinino continues. His wrinkled finger rises to point to the empty seat next to Naina. "None of the elected Members are permitted to disappear for weeks on end. We're here to contribute to the theocracy and to governance."

A growl emerges in Naina's throat. "Salessa has done more for the Assembly, and for SunSide, than—"

"Then where is she?" Vinino challenges.

At this moment more than any other, Naina wishes she had Salessa's voice in her head telling her to calm down and ignore the grump.

"Member Salessa had dire personal matters to attend to," Saila explains. "Member Vinino, if something were to ever come about in your personal life requiring extended leave, I wouldn't hesitate for a moment to grant it to you, as I have for Salessa."

Vinino nods with a huff and turns away from the table.

"We don't doubt it, Chief Member," Rayga jumps in. "Your leadership has always proven fair. Though, I do recognize that our *elected*

Members"—she glances at Naina and Ovida—"aren't followers of the Four. I'd like to initiate a motion to rename this council, from the Assembly of the Radiance, to the New SunSidian Assembly, in line with our military, the New SunSidian Guard."

"I second the motion," Aissa concurs. "This will open us up to act as a secular parliament."

"I'm not in favor," Hemmar objects. "We were chosen to sit on a council of theocrats to govern by the will of the Four. We should not change those aims because non-clergy were appointed to that council without our knowledge."

"I understand both sides," Saila interjects diplomatically. "The motion is"—she pauses—"partially approved. Member Rayga, I agree with the idea of a fresh name for the council. I'll decree that, henceforth, we shall be known as the New SunSidian Assembly."

She turns to Hemmar. "However, even our appointed Members have agreed to enforce laws by the will of the Four. Their personal spirituality is irrelevant as long as that is maintained. The New SunSidian Assembly remains a theocracy. Do we all have an understanding?"

The Members nod their approval. Saila exhales and continues. "Alright, with introductions complete—"

"Sorry to interrupt you, Chief Member," Faolan pipes up, "but the Member seated to your right hasn't introduced himself."

Kruga laughs. "I'm actually not a Member. My name is Kruga and I'm the Counselor to the Chief Member."

Faolan's eyebrows meet his hairline. "Oh, I've never heard of such a position before. I've researched the Assembly's history and don't think I've ever come across this title in my readings."

"It's a new position," Saila explains. "When we were a Theocratic-Monarchy, the MegaParents had Facilitators. Now that we are a sole theocracy, I thought it would be appropriate to appoint a Counselor."

"Forgive me, Chief Member and Counselor Kruga," says Pyr-Sa. "I mean no disrespect by asking, but I don't recall you ever mentioning, what your qualifications are as Counselor to the Chief Member?"

Saila turns to Kruga, who smiles. "I have extensive experience in a range of sciences, from biochemistry and medicine to physics and engineering."

"Again, forgive me, Counselor," Pyr-Sa continues, "you're obviously quite qualified as a scientist or salver, but I'm failing to see how this qualifies you to Counsel the leader of the nation."

Kruga swallows and silence fills the room. He seems unsteady, unsure of how to respond.

Ovida speaks up. "None of you knew Symin." The Members turn to her. "The Facilitator was a threat to everyone who wasn't a faerie. And when there was no one left to face him, Symin stood, giving his life fearlessly for the cause. He was brave, he was powerful, and he was a fierce leader."

She raises her finger to Kruga. "The nymph who sits at the Chief Member's side spent more than a decade at Symin's, learning what it means to lead and to advise and to guide. To give everything you have for something bigger than yourself. I don't think there's anyone on this planet I'd trust more, to counsel the Chief Member, than Kruga."

"I agree," Naina says, speaking up for the first time without hesitation or discomfort. If there's anything she can attest to without uncertainty, it's Kruga's competency.

Kruga nods to the appointees gratefully and Pyr-Sa folds her hands, saying, "That answers my question. We can move on."

Saila turns to the sky through gargantuan windows to ascertain the positions of the Four. "We should address our orders of business now, the meeting has run quite late. Member Naina, may we begin with you?"

Uneasiness grows in the pit of Naina's stomach as she rises to her feet and withdraws a piece of paper with Salessa's notes on it. Her twin has always spoken for them, often volunteering to be the first to present. Now, Salessa's dedication has become the wolf's damnation.

Naina clears her throat and tries to steady the quiver of her fingers on the page. "The settlement walls northwest and southwest of Arlun have all been dismantled, and settlers from each of these locations are almost entirely relocated to the temporary shelters in Larso and Nivyan Hollow. Salessa met with local leaders in Lahu and Kinara prior to her leave, and confirmed that they will assist in facilitating the elections for the new Alphocracy. Once she returns, she intends to hold these elections at—"

"What are you reading from?" Vinino interrupts her.

Naina breathes deeply to control her irritation, but fails. "My sister's notes."

"Why? Are these your sister's accomplishments? Are they *her* updates? Where are yours? What have you done?"

"Member Vinino." Saila steps in. "It's completely inappropriate to—"

"To question a public servant about how much service they contribute? Accountability is a cornerstone of politics. At least, it should be, shouldn't it?"

Saila tightly presses her lips together.

Vinino turns to Naina again. "I appreciate that your sister made some progress on her assignments prior to her disappearance, but what have you done in the past month?"

"Look"—Naina's skin reddens with anger—"the whole political diplomacy thing is not something I'm good at, alright?"

"We're well aware of that," Vininio spits with a venomous chuckle. "But what exactly *are* you good at?"

"That is enough!" Saila says, rising to her feet and slamming her palms onto the table. She turns to Naina with a pleading expression and the wolf realizes her canines have elongated and a muzzle has started to grow.

I know exactly what Salessa would be saying right now.

She takes a few more deep breaths and allows her heart rate to slow, as her face and teeth return to their human forms. She takes a seat calmly.

"Thank you, Member Naina," Saila says, taking her seat as well. "Member Rayga, any updates on the residential city construction?"

Rayga stands next, her pink fingers interlocked, her tone even. "Some residential complexes have been completed in City One, located on the northern outskirts of Ward's Fall. Additionally, a site has been selected for City Two: southwest of Small Beauty, just across Ona's River."

"That's great progress," Saila commends her. "Why do you appear unsatisfied?"

"Chief Member, if we continue at the rate we're going, it'll be a decade or more before both cities are constructed and ready for occupancy."

Saila frowns. "We don't have a decade, Member. I'd like to see at least one of those cities occupied by this time next year."

"I understand. Which is why I'd like to request we halt plans on the construction of City Two. We've gotten a good head-start on the project by selecting the site, but we should now shift those laborers to the City One project to have it completed, at best, in the next two or three years. If you'd truly like to see City One completed by this time next year, I'll need a vast improvement in the workforce assigned."

"I don't have any more workers to give you," Saila responds. "I need them here in Larso to continue dismantling the ore and shipping it out. I promised to have all of the ore removed and on EverEmber's shores by the end of the year, or we're going to end up in a war we can't afford."

Rayga nods. "I understand. Two or three years, then." She takes a seat and Ovida stands next.

"I wish I had a more positive update for you all," she explains glumly. "But the Bravers United are still underground. We've searched relentlessly through the former Revolution chambers and tunnels but they don't appear to be using our abandoned resources. They're hiding somewhere else and we haven't been able to root them out. They appear suddenly, sometimes in the day, sometimes under nightfall, and the attacks on civilians are growing more violent and more deplorable."

"The New SunSidian Guard is almost entirely made up of former Revolution fighters and reformed Bravers," Aissa remarks. "How is it possible that the Bravers United can hide for this long from them?"

"Their leader is"—Ovida pauses.—"experienced. Tund-Ra may be a supremacist of vile character, but he was also a revered assassin who reported directly to the former Braver General in their hidden legions. He's taught the thousands of Bravers United fighters how to commit these acts of unrest and disappear without being caught."

"Then what, exactly, is your plan to capture or execute this supremacist assassin?" Vinino hisses.

"A weak link in his armor," she says. "I have warriors posted without uniform in taverns and brothels in the outer districts, and as servants in the homes of those in the middle and inner districts. As soon as one of them reports back to me with information on a high-ranking target of the Bravers United, I'll take them into custody and root out Tund-Ra. Without him, this war is over."

"Your plan is approved," Saila says to the General. "Keep me updated on your progress."

Ovida nods and takes her seat again.

Saila takes a deep breath and continues. "I believe that concludes all matters we had to discuss, outside of my interrogations of the former monarch." She turns to the newest Member. "Faolan, there are some facts about the former MegaFather's deposition, and the abolition of the monarchy, that have been kept out of public knowledge. Only those of us in this room, and some of our trustworthy associates, know the truth. I have to ask that the information I'm about to share with you is kept tightly guarded."

Faolan nods and the Chief Member explains everything to him about the former monarch's true identity. About how he has lived through forty-five descendants over nearly eight-hundred-and-twenty years. And about the ancient Sprites he serves, who will undoubtedly rain catastrophe over the world when their arrangement with Red-Lo goes unmet.

Faolan's jaw hangs so low; Naina thinks she may have to find a salver to reattach it.

"Surely, this is a prank on the newcomer," Faolan finally mutters.

"Oh, how I wish it were," Saila responds. "But it's all true. Over the past year, I've been interrogating Red-Lo in the hope that he will reveal when and where the Sprites will attack. He denies knowing and, strangely, I believe him."

"Preposterous," Vinino huffs. "You believe the immortal dictator who sacrificed the souls of his own progeny to live through their bodies?"

"I do," Saila reasserts. "What I mean is, I know the information is there, in his head, somewhere, but when he says he doesn't know, I think he's telling the truth. He doesn't know how to get that information. All he's been able to do is give his best guess as to *when* the Sprites will come, which he believes to be sometime within the next four months."

Vinino mumbles, "Perhaps we need someone who is better at interrogating."

Something clicks in Naina's mind. Vinino's prior question pops into her ears again. *What exactly are you good at?*

"I'll interrogate him," she volunteers. The Members all turn to her. "You said the information is in his head somewhere, right? I can get it out of him."

Saila raises an eyebrow. "How?"

A scheme unfolds as she speaks. "By going in for it. Send me into his head and I'll bring the information back out with me."

The Chief Member shakes her head quickly. "Out of the question. Going into his head is what killed Saimiza. Anytime I go in, I come out with a pounding headache and a nosebleed."

"No disrespect to your dead auntie," Naina responds, "but I have two things she didn't: youth and so much Radiant energy in my body that I'm practically one of the Four." Vinino gasps at the blasphemous statement, but Naina ignores him. "Your father's machine pumped me full of everything he'd stored for decades."

Saila hesitates. "You don't understand, Naina. Time works differently on a mental plane. For some, they'll feel as though a year has passed, while they've been there for a minute. For others, it feels like an hour, but they've been there for a decade. Not only is it impossible for me to assure your survival, there's no way for me to pull you out, even if you do survive. You'll have to find your own way out and there's no telling when that will be. You could come out ninety seconds after you went in, or ninety years."

"This is the only option. If there are Members here"—she shoots Vinino a look—"who believe I'm not contributing enough, then let this be the response. I'm potentially sacrificing everything for this: my life, my youth, who knows what else."

Again, Saila shakes her head, enunciating as she speaks. "It's. Too. Dangerous."

"Look, Saila. Lessi's gone on her quest, Feathers is taking care of her mother, Kyoko and Ana are translating the Sprite texts for clues, and Rafael's been training with Kruga. This is my contribution." She raises her hand. "All in favor, raise your right hand."

Saila's and Ovida's hands are the only ones that remain stationary.

The wolf grins. "You're outvoted, Chief Member."

Saila looks around the room at the raised hands, then sighs. "I'll post guards in shifts to monitor your body here in the physical plane at all times." She makes firm eye contact and her tone hardens. "For the record, I don't approve of this."

"Noted."

"When do you want to go in?"

Naina considers the question. She could wait until Salessa returns, but the falcon has been gone for weeks, with no clear indication of when she would return. Naina could enter Red-Lo's mind, ascertain the information they need, and return in a few minutes. Salessa wouldn't even have to know.

Or, Naina could enter Red-Lo's mind, and return with the information to Salessa having passed of old age. The entire idea is dangerous and risky and challenging.

And that is exactly what Naina is good at.

She smiles, revealing a wide, toothy grin and says to the Chief Member, "Now."

CHAPTER 3

"SILENCE AND SOLITUDE"

Alphocracy *MoonSide*
Date *21st Day of Month 6, Year 1629 DG*

SOME NIGHTS ARE SO COLD, even the dead must shiver.

Clad in a light pink shalwar kameez, a white dupatta wrapped around her head and over her shoulders, Salessa steps cautiously between headstones and grave markers, clutching a bouquet of bright red roses to her chest. A thin breeze of brisk air wraps around her, intensifying her involuntary trembling. She wonders if anyone below the ground shivers where they lie.

With only the delicate starlight to guide her, she squints in the darkness to read the names etched into stone. The smell of fresh grass and affectionately-laid flowers builds a warmth in her chest; it reminds her that the Doruh lying under the soil aren't forgotten. They aren't a distant memory lost to time. They're loved ones that live on in some visitor's heart.

Even here in the cemetery, they're not alone.

Alone. Exactly as Salessa has felt for weeks on end. How many times has she done or said something, then waited for a snarky, sarcastic remark from Naina in her head, but nothing came. She's heard people beg for silence and solitude; the overstimulated who need a break from the world, from children, from the demands of others.

She'll never understand them. Living without a voice in your head is torture.

It takes some time before Salessa finds what she's looking for. Three grave markers stare up at her; one reads "Kamal" another "Sonali" and the third "Maahi." All three have the image of a bald-faced hornet on them; it's customary for Doruh graves to depict the decedent's animal form on their marker or headstone.

Salessa lays the bouquet of roses down at Sonali's grave, then turns to find a withered bunch of lilies on Kamal's marker. She removes it, cleans off any fallen petals, and then divides the bouquet she brought between Sonali and her father.

"Sorry, Uncle," she says, addressing Kamal the way any young Doruh would an older man. "This visit was short notice and I wasn't prepared. I promise, I'll bring you a full bouquet of your own next time." His silence conveys forgiveness.

Maahi's marker shows considerably less wear than the other two, having been laid there only a couple months prior.

"I told you I would visit you here, Aunty," Salessa reminds her. "It was a pleasure to have met and spoken with you the few times I had before you"—she pauses—"started your rest. Saila misses you dearly."

Salessa turns to Sonali with a polite smile. She treads in discomfort for a few moments before speaking. "It's a bizarre feeling to hold so much love and gratitude for someone I've never met. For someone who never even knew I existed, but gave her life for me and for all Doruh anyway."

Her fingertips dance along the "S" on the marker. "The day after you left this world, Naina and I left MoonSide. We were"—she sighs—"so close to meeting you. Your sacrifice that day saved us all. You probably watched it all happening from wherever you are, but in case you didn't, I just want you to know that. I want you to know that you saved the Doruh."

Another breeze envelops her and she clutches her dupatta tighter against her chest, continuing. Some chilly winds won't deter her from paying her respects.

"I feel like I know you so well. Saila recounts your bravery daily. She lost the two people closest to her within days of one another, yet, she carries herself with such dignity and poise. You'd be so proud of what she's accomplished in the past year. I know I am. I should probably tell her that more often."

Salessa arrives at a perplexing crossroads where she no longer has much to say, but doesn't want to say goodbye yet. She opts to sit quietly, taking in the crisp night air and the calm sobriety circulating about her. It's been some time since she's found a tranquil spot to rest, after weeks of jostling from one village to the next, bustling marketplace after bustling marketplace.

Her thoughts drift to the small note in her pocket and she withdraws it, unfolding it to read the words she's been staring at for a year: *I'm waiting for you on Lover's Plateau. Come find me.*

She turns the note around to show Sonali, then speaks again. "I came to MoonSide to find Lover's Plateau. But I think it's time for me to head back to SunSide. I've been passed around from one village to the next for weeks. Somehow it's led me here to the Northern Hills. 'Talk to this elder!' Or 'Talk to that one!' Half the elders think Lover's Plateau is a myth. The others believe it's an ancient ruin somewhere, lost to history."

She traces the fading letters of the note. "How can someone be waiting for me at a place that doesn't exist anymore, or that never did in the first place?" Her eyes find the grave marker and she smiles, her cheeks turning red. "I'm sorry, Sonali. I know you don't have the answers for me and probably just want to rest quietly. I'm sure you're enjoying your silence and solitude."

A rustling near the trees behind her catches her attention, but when she doesn't see anyone, she turns back.

"I'm heading back to SunSide tomorrow morning. It may be some time before I can come visit you again. I think some of the other Members were unhappy with my leave. I can think of one in particular who will have some unkind words for me when I get back. If Naina hasn't bitten his head off, yet."

She laughs at the thought, then moves to her knees and bends forward to affectionately kiss the marker. "Thank you again for everything you did for us. Saila says you wouldn't care for it, but I've made plans to have them erect a monument in your honor once Alphocracy Hall is properly set up in Arlun. They have monuments in SunSide for their saviors. Why shouldn't we have them for ours?"

The rustling of the trees behind her grows louder and when she turns, the branches are shivering, but not from the cold.

"Is someone there?" she calls out into the darkness.

Slowly, a face emerges from within the leaves as a man climbs down from the branches and says, "Yes."

Salessa's heart pounds against her chest as she finds the mountain of a man approaching her in this graveyard, the only light coming from the moons above.

May the Twins protect me.

She breathes deeply, trying to calm herself, but as the coat-wrapped giant approaches her, uneasiness sets in. Not just because of his size, or because of the darkness, or even because of the fact that she's alone with him in a graveyard—though that doesn't make her feel any safer—but because of his peculiar appearance and the way he's dressed. The man appears to be actively holding himself between his human and his animal forms.

He has his human eyes, forehead and slick brown hair, yet the entire lower half of his face is a feline muzzle. His mighty, muscular arms are exposed, as his coat is sleeveless, displaying the rosette pattern of a leopard on his skin. Below his wrists, Salessa finds heavy, thick paws.

His coat hangs open, revealing a loose, black shirt which is unbuttoned at the top. His strong chest, tapered torso, and thick legs appear to be entirely human with nearly no indication of his other form.

When the man gets within a few feet of Salessa, she instinctively clutches her dupatta to shield her face and rises to her feet, taking a few steps back.

The man quickly moves into a defensive, non-threatening posture, bending his knees slightly, hunching forward, and raising his paws to reveal the wide, leathery pads underneath. "Please, don't be alarmed. I'm sorry, my intention wasn't to startle you."

"Regardless of the intention, that's what happened," Salessa responds.

"I was in the tree before you came," the man explains. "I didn't know how long you'd be here, so I was just trying to climb down, silently without you noticing, so I can leave you alone. Clearly, I didn't do a very good job." He chuckles weakly.

"What were you doing in the tree?" Salessa asks.

"Just resting. I came here looking for someone"—he gestures to the grave markers—"but I didn't find her. I got tired from searching, so I decided to rest in the tree. It's where I'm most comfortable." He waves his paws loosely in the air. "Leopard."

"I see," Salessa responds. She considers whether or not to bring up his appearance, curiosity burning a hole in her thoughts. Naina is the only Doruh she's ever met who's been able to maintain a half-form for this long.

As if he can read her mind, the leopard-man says, "This is just how I'm most comfortable. I know I look strange, but we can't help what we feel, can we?"

Salessa's curiosity turns to guilt. He's right, who is she to judge what makes him comfortable? Who is she to find him strange?

"Sorry, I didn't mean to stare," she apologizes.

The leopard-man shakes his head. "That's quite alright. I've grown used to it now. Not many Doruh walk around comfortably in a half-form. Particularly not at six-and-a-half feet with a sleeveless coat. It's almost as if I *want* the attention." He smiles and Salessa finds something warm about it.

"Do you?" Salessa asks him. "Want the attention?"

"I certainly don't mind it," he responds with another weak chuckle.

Salessa realizes that, as they've been conversing, the man's come quite close to her and she's no longer clutching her dupatta to her face. She feels comfortable until she realizes what Naina would be saying right now if she were able to reach her thoughts: *Don't trust the man-panther. Get out of there.* Her hand rises to clutch her dupatta again.

"It was nice speaking with you, but I'm going to leave now." She turns to follow the path to the exit when the leopard-man speaks again, drawing her attention to the graves.

"You came to see Sonali?" he asks.

Salessa raises an eyebrow. "I did. You knew her?"

"No, I didn't. I was actually in Larso, a few days after her execution. My sister and I went to SunSide and walked into the middle of a war.

We hid out for a week, then we came back home after the new Chief Member's speech."

Salessa opens her mouth to mention she was there, on stage, for Saila's speech, but the faux-Naina in her head tells her not to draw attention to herself unnecessarily.

The man continues, "I learned later about who Sonali was and what she did for us all. I wasn't eavesdropping, but I heard what you said about monuments. I think that's a noble thing; for you to arrange one for Sonali outside Alphocracy Hall. She deserves it."

Salessa drowns out faux-Naina and smiles widely at her new acquaintance. It's the first idea she's had in a year that's been praised.

"Thank you," she says. "I'm sorry, I never asked your name."

"Afzal," he responds. "And yours?"

"Salessa."

"It's very nice to meet you, Salessa." He bows respectfully.

Salessa returns his bow. "I really should be leaving."

"Will you be in the Northern Hills for long?" he asks abruptly.

Salessa's smile fades. The question makes her uneasy. "No, I'll be leaving in the morning and heading back home."

LEAVE, LESSI, faux-Naina urges her.

"Maybe next time you're here, I'll see you again."

"It'll be some time before I'm able to come again, but maybe." She takes a few steps backward. "Take care, Afzal."

"Take care, Salessa."

She conveys a final goodbye and steps onto the path toward the exit. When she's left the leopard-man far behind, walking along the dirt road leading back to the inn where she's staying, she finally feels safe again. It's quiet, and there's no one around, but at least she doesn't feel like there's anything lurking in the dark, or on the branches of the trees.

Perhaps now she understands those who enjoy their silence and solitude a little better.

CHAPTER 4

"THE SERPENT"

Alphocracy *MoonSide*
Date *21st Day of Month 6, Year 1629 DG*

KNOCK. KNOCK. KNOCK. KNOCK.

Salessa's eyelids spring apart and she rises to a seated position. Was it a nightmare? It's been months since she last had one.

Knock. Knock. Knock. Knock.

Pounding rattles the door, as her eyes dart to the moons. *It isn't even midnight. I've paid until midday. What kind of inn kicks paying guests out in the middle of the night?* She quickly realizes the one who knocks wouldn't be the innkeeper. He would've announced himself already, and he certainly wouldn't be knocking so hard.

Knock. Knock. Knock. Knock.

The falcon breathes deeply as the hammering in her chest matches that which woke her. She slowly places her feet onto the floor and swallows her nerves as best as she can. Passing the chair where she absently hung her robe the night before, she grabs the garment and pulls it on, tying it quickly at her waist.

Knock. Knock. Knock. Knock.

She reaches the door and inhales deeply, pouring as much conviction into her tone as possible. Even if she can't convince herself she isn't terrified, maybe she can convince the one beyond the shattering hinges.

"Who's there?"

There's a long pause in which Salessa thinks the knocker may have left. Nothing joins her in the dark of night but silence.

And then he speaks. A terrifyingly familiar voice. "It's me, Salessa. Afzal. From the graveyard."

Her heart drops so quickly she thinks it may have hit the floor. *He's here? Did he follow me? What could he want?*

Salessa's awake, but she's living a nightmare. Twirling quickly on her heels, she removes her robe and her nightgown by the time she reaches the open window, ready to shift into a falcon and fly off to safety. A cool burst of frozen night air strikes her bare body. Her arms move from the frame of the window to wrap around her chest.

How is Naina so comfortable shifting? I'm freezing. She gives herself a shake, blows into her hands, and rubs them together. *I can do this, I can do this.*

Just as she steps up onto the window sill, a beak forming on her face, another voice calls out to her from the door.

"Salessa! Open up, please." It's a woman's voice.

Salessa sits there for a moment on the window sill, naked and confused, wondering who this woman is and where she came from, when she abruptly remembers something the leopard-man told her earlier.

My sister and I went to SunSide and walked into the middle of a war.

Is this woman Afzal's sister? What is she doing here?

A flurry of questions strike Salessa at once. Does the sister's presence change anything? Should she still shift? Where will that lead her? To a foreign part of MoonSide, completely naked?

Another part of her mind is oddly curious as to why the leopard-man brought his sister along. Are they dangerous? Is it something important?

"Salessa, it's me."

It's who?! I don't recognize the voice.

She climbs down from the windowsill and gets dressed, a battle raging in her heart between curiosity and caution. Slowly, she steps forth and finally reaches the door again. If Naina were here, by her side, she'd never allow Salessa to open the door. In fact, Naina would've had them back in SunSide by now. She never would've spent *weeks* on this journey.

But that's exactly why it was so important for the falcon to go alone. Salessa needed an experience in which she behaved the way Salessa would; an experience in which she made decisions that Salessa would make. Not the ones Naina would want her to make.

She places her hand firmly on the doorknob and turns, opening it just enough for her field of vision to break through.

Standing inches from her, his girthy arm resting on the top of the door frame, the hood of his sleeveless coat up over his head, is the man she met in the graveyard. He looks exactly as she remembers, human above the eyes, leopard below them. Instinctually, she takes a step back—he's far closer to her now than he ever was at the graveyard—but when this reaction opens the door further, she resumes her position closer to the doorway.

"What can I do for you?" she asks, keeping her tone sharp. The falcon wants to look around and try to find the individual whose voice sounded feminine, but she also knows better than to take her eyes off the giant breathing the same air as her.

"We were hoping to speak with you," Afzal says.

"We?" Salessa asks.

The man nods and steps aside, revealing his female companion. She dons a black shalwar kameez; a sinuous design embroidered with red threading winds down her sleeves from the shoulders and around the unbuttoned placket on her chest. Her sleeves are rolled up, revealing her forearms, and her dupatta is wrapped around her shoulders and over her head, exactly as Salessa wears it.

She's a foot shorter than Afzal, almost equal in height to the falcon. She also appears locked between her human and animal forms. Much of her face is human, though there are noticeable patches of serpentine scales all over her forearms and the visible part of her chest, just below her neck. Her forked tongue whisps past her lips rapidly even when they appear closed.

When Salessa meets her eyes, a forceful shiver runs deep through her bones, despite a lack of wind at the doorway. Her breath catches in her throat, and every fiber of muscle in her body freezes. One look, and the woman under the black dupatta has retrieved all the damage

Salessa had long-since buried in the graveyard of her worst memories. The last time she saw this woman, Naina had torn her to pieces and left her for dead.

"Hello, Salessa." The words slither off of her serpentine tongue. In all these years, her voice hasn't changed at all. This voice is a prison and it's holding the falcon captive. Salessa kicks herself for not recognizing it sooner, or for not shifting and flying away when she had the chance.

I should never have opened the door.

Salessa faces her for the first time in three years. "Lexona."

Lexona smiles, revealing two short fangs in front of her human teeth. "It's been so long."

Salessa is sixteen again, madly in love for the first time in her life. The elders all said she was too young, that she didn't know what love was. The falcon challenged them, kissing the girl she loved openly and rhapsodically. Who were they to tell her that age was a prerequisite to understand what's in one's own heart?

That heart shattered the day she found out they were right.

Salessa is eighteen again, having lived the two most glorious years of her life in those warm, protective arms. Naina told her to be careful. Reminded her not to trust too easily. But surely, she was just jealous. She hadn't found anything nearly as powerful, with a man, that Salessa had with Lexona.

She wanted to prove to Naina how wrong the wolf was. So, excitedly, she revealed their plans to the girl of her dreams.

"We're leaving MoonSide!" she had exclaimed under the cooling shade of *their* tree. Away from the Bravers, away from any judgmental eyes.

"When?" Lexona had asked, her face contorting with concern.

"I don't know. We still have a long way to go, but we've started a fund to save money. Naina's been fighting in the Pit. She comes home exhausted and injured, but she's earned more stones in a few nights than we've ever had in our lives."

Lexona's eyes had widened as she suggested, "I should also contribute! Then the three of us can leave together. Tell me where you're keeping the fund and I'll put some money in."

Salessa had never felt such unbridled joy. The idea of them all escaping together, Lexona spending her life with Salessa in a safe corner of the world, protected by their love. It felt like some kind of fantasy, an epic folktale.

As it was.

Naina had left the Pit early one night. That innocent change in routine altered the course of Salessa's life. When Naina arrived home, she found Lexona in their hiding spot, withdrawing all that they had saved and stuffing it into pouches.

The wolf didn't hesitate for a second. She didn't wait for an explanation. She didn't have to.

Salessa walked in while she was tearing the serpent to shreds. When the snake shifted back, Lexona's limbs were strewn on one side of the hut, her torso was on another, her head was in a corner, and her blood coated every inch of the floor, walls, and ceiling.

Salessa begged for answers and Naina simply pointed to the hiding spot. The falcon refused to believe, she couldn't accept that someone she cared so deeply for would betray her trust in such an abhorrent manner.

But it came down to a simple question: Had Lexona betrayed her? Or was Naina lying?

The answer was as simple as the question. From that day, to this very day, standing in the doorway of an inn, miles and miles from her new home and her sister, the answer has never changed.

Naina doesn't lie to Salessa. The falcon would believe that the sky has turned green, and the grass blue, before she believes that Naina is a liar.

"Salessa?" Lexona raises an eyebrow and waves a hand in front of Salessa's face, trying to break her from the journey through time. "I said it's been a long time."

"I heard you," Salessa responds when she can find her voice again. "How?" She finds it difficult to articulate the question. "How did you survive?"

Lexona inhales and then exhales deeply, as if she is about to unburden a great secret. "The same way Naina survived the Pit night-after-night."

"Naina is strong. *You* should know that."

The words clearly sting Lexona. "I do know that. But it isn't just her strength keeping her alive, it's the Twins'. The same strength that kept me alive."

Salessa's eyes widen and her heart bursts against her chest. "This is another trick. A lie." Her breaths sharpen as the panic slowly creeps up. "It can't be."

"It is. Do you remember the resurrection prophecy?"

Salessa nods.

"Say it."

Salessa hesitates, as if reciting the prophecy will make Lexona more real than she already is. She takes a deep breath to quell the light-headedness. *"One from the land, one from the sea. One from the skies, one from the trees."*

Lexona nods. *"Two sets of twins will be conceived.* And the four Doruh will join together to resurrect the Twins."

Salessa's gaze darts from Lexona to Afzal and back to the serpent. When she speaks, her voice is barely louder than a whisper. "Impossible. We were together for two years, and I never knew you had a twin?"

"*I* didn't even know I had a twin," Lexona admits. "But I do now, thanks to Naina."

"Naina?"

Lexona nods. "After Naina"—she pauses—"attacked me, I healed. Salvers couldn't believe it. I couldn't believe it. But my parents—those who raised me—weren't surprised at all. I begged them for answers and that's when they told me: they weren't my birth parents. I was born to a family of leopards who realized what my brother and I were when we shifted into two different animals despite being twins. They were fearful that the prophecy would bring unwanted attention to their family, so they gave me to their friends, the serpent couple who raised me."

The world starts to spin around Salessa. Her knees buckle and she grabs the door frame for support. Lexona reaches forth to grasp Salessa by the elbow.

"DON'T TOUCH ME," Salessa yells, louder than intended. She takes deep breaths and steadies herself as Lexona steps backward. "Naina and I are the land and the skies mentioned in the prophecy. The wolf and the falcon. That leaves the sea and the trees. But you're a snake."

Lexona shakes her head. "Technically, I'm a sea serpent."

Salessa turns to Afzal. "Trees?"

Afzal nods, sheepishly. "It'll make sense when you see how much of my day is spent napping on branches."

"I'm not seeing anything," Salessa growls. "I want nothing to do with either of you. Stay away from me."

She attempts to slam the door, but Afzal's mighty paw stops it.

"I sent you the note, Salessa," Lexona admits.

Another revealed truth crashes down on Salessa like a towering wave. "You called me here."

"I called you to Lover's Plateau. Which is not far from here. In the morning, we can—"

"We?" Salessa's shock turns to a lupine rage. She channels Naina. "What do you think is about to happen? I'm just going to forgive and forget and accompany you to some ancient ruin? Did your brain not grow back when the rest of you did?"

Lexona sighs. "Salessa, please, you have to listen."

"I don't have to do anything." She turns her gaze to Afzal. "Move your *fucking* paw."

He moves the paw without hesitation.

Salessa turns to Lexona for, what she hopes, is the last time.

"If I see your face again, I'll make you wish you had called Naina instead."

"Salessa, wait—"

"Fuck you, Lexona."

With these words, Salessa slams the door shut. She waits, biting her lip, and once she hears their footsteps fade out of the hallway, she drops to the ground and wraps her arms around her knees.

And the falcon weeps.

CHAPTER 5

"THE IGNI AND THE MARI"

Theocracy *SunSide*
Date *21st Day of Month 6, Year 1629 DG*

THERE ARE FEW REMEDIES TO exhaustion as effective as returning to a home filled with loved ones. With each descending step into the Bunker, Rafael swims deeper into an ocean of tranquility. He's greeted with familiar smiles, from those seated at the wooden table in the middle of the room.

Nothing can comfort him after a long, tiring day quite like this.

He removes a quiver of arrows from his back and places it, along with his bow, next to the narrow, straw cot where he sleeps. Marching toward the table where Kyoko and Ana sit, he holds out a hand and extends Radiant energy from his fingertips the way Kruga taught him. The invisible force wraps around a peach on the table and drags it through the air back to Rafael, who catches it in his palm.

He sinks his teeth into it ravenously and juice congregates on the edges of his mouth before descending into his scruffy facial hair. Ana keeps her gaze affixed on the many ancient texts in front of her, while reaching over them to push a stack of napkins toward him. "Gross. Wipe your face."

Rafael smiles, takes a seat, and does as he's told. "Sorry, I have the manners of a shark when I'm hungry."

"Have you had a proper meal since you left for work this morning?" Kyoko asks him.

Rafael shakes his head. "There's no time to eat at work."

"There would be if you didn't schedule classes back-to-back."

"It's the only way I can accommodate every student."

Kyoko sighs. "I know you have a hard time turning applicants away, but you have to start considering what you can handle."

Rafael's gaze swallows the shimmer of both her mighty stone exoskeleton and her soft eyes in the light. He gestures to her shoulder, changing the subject. "How was your session today?"

The igni raises her right arm laterally as far as she can, not quite parallel with the ground.

"That's excellent!" Rafael cheers. "A few months ago it was stuck there at your side."

Kyoko smiles, but the sadness of her expression remains. Rafael understands, without her saying a word. The mari reaches forward and places his hand over hers. "The salvers said it would be a long road. I can't imagine what you're feeling—"

"No, you can't," Kyoko stops him. "Vy-Ro took more from me than anyone can imagine."

Rafael pulls his hand back and nods.

Kyoko's expression softens. "I'm sorry. It's been a long year for all of us."

"Exactly a year," Rafael notes. He turns to Ana and leans in to grasp her attention from the Sprite texts in which she's buried herself. "How are you feeling today?" And then back to Kyoko. "Both of you."

Ana pulls her face out of the tattered tomes and exhales deeply. "You remember." Relief floods her expression. It's clear she didn't want to bring it up herself.

"Of course I remember," Rafael responds, a wave of sadness pushing down on him. "This is where we found out. The next day." His fingertips run circles along the wooden table. "Unisa was sitting here with Naina and Salessa."

Ana forcefully slams the delicate book shut, burying her fingers deep in her lofty, dark curls. "One year since Alba's death and I've accomplished nothing."

Rafael sighs. "You expect too much of yourself. Poring into box-after-box from Red-Lo's library without a break."

Ana keeps her fingers firmly tangled in her hair as she mumbles a response. "The Three Deaths aren't taking a break. Neither will I."

"Ana," Rafael begins, before Ana slams her fist down on the table and meets his eyes.

"No! We know nothing of when or where they'll come. Saila hasn't made any progress with Red-Lo in a year, and she's asked me to find the answers in these texts." Her volume increases slightly, as she enunciates her next words. "The *leader* of an entire *nation* asked *me* for answers."

"We'll figure this out," Kyoko attempts to reassure her.

"Me," Ana responds with mounting frustration, jabbing a finger into her chest. "Not 'we.' Me. I'm the Nysabaani expert here. My career, my credentials were built on translation."

Rafael pulls one of the texts toward him and, from what little he can translate, it appears to be a text in which the Sprites had cataloged recipes. "You're not to blame if the information doesn't exist in what you're translating. What will recipes tell you about the Three Deaths?"

"They haven't all been recipes. I've read Sprite texts on politics, spirituality, sexuality, geology, trigonometry, arts, culture, sporting events…" Her voice quivers. "What if Alba died believing I'm something that I'm not?"

"Alba knew you better than perhaps you know yourself," Kyoko counters. "She would be so proud to witness your bravery, leaving the Library—the only home you've ever known—to venture out into an unfamiliar world. That's all she wanted for you."

Ana shakes her head. "Stepping onto an empty battlefield with a sword doesn't make someone brave. Wielding it against monsters does." She taps the text in front of her. "I have to find the monsters to prove my bravery. Then, and only then, will I allow you to tell me how proud Alba would be of me."

She rises to her feet and picks up a text in each hand, her forearm fins slicing through the air wildly. "For now, I'm going to sit in my bedroom and translate the Sprite's unquestionable wisdom of"—she examines the book in her right hand—"tribal governments and"—then the text in her left—"environmental science."

She strides quickly to the bedroom, clutching the two texts to her chest, and slams the door behind her, leaving Rafael and Kyoko alone at the table.

"She hasn't slept well in months," Rafael says.

"I know," Kyoko responds with a nod, her eyes lowered. "And today she's reminded of all that she's lost."

"You lost Alba, too."

She raises her gaze. "I did, and I can understand how she's feeling, but it's not the same. I loved Alba, you know that, but Ana's never accomplished anything other than for Alba's approval. Without that, she's drowning." She turns to Ana's bedroom door. "She's lost her way."

The severity of Ana's strain unleashes a fog of solemnity around them; a gravity that weighs both former Librarians down, as they struggle to save her from the pressure of this mission. Rafael recognizes the discomfort it causes between him and Kyoko, even when Ana isn't there.

But he also recognizes that only sunshine can disperse fog.

"We will help her find her way again," he says, offering Kyoko a reassuring smile. "That's what Alba wanted. For Ana to find her own path."

Kyoko nods. "You're right. It's up to us to help her." She lowers her head, attempting to hide a yawn breaking through slightly parted lips.

"You should sleep," Rafael suggests.

Kyoko raises her head again, cheeks aflame at being exposed. "I will, but I wanted to run upstairs first and get you something to eat from the inn." She rises from her seat and begins the trek to the stairs, but as she passes Rafael, he gently takes hold of her wrist. She stops walking and turns to him, and he's suddenly aware of the softness of her skin and the warmth of her gaze.

"I'm not hungry, Kyoko, I promise," he lies. "Get some rest."

She flashes a half-smile and he finds his gaze lingering longer than he intended. A year of close proximity and emotional familiarity, of nightly dinners and morning discussions, of shared confidences and mutual respect…

A year of her smiles and her scents, of her eyes and her exoskeleton, of her thoughts and ideas and hopes and goals, has driven the igni and the mari to a common intimacy that somehow doesn't reach the physical, yet extensively surpasses it.

Long after Ana has gone to bed each night, Rafael and Kyoko have remained awake, sometimes speaking with their words, and sometimes with their eyes. And then each morning, she's been the first person he sees when he wakes.

For a year, his day has begun with Kyoko and ended with Kyoko, and he no longer wishes to live a day in which this is not the case.

"Good night, Rafa." Kyoko's silvery tone delicately flows through the air between them. She leans down and they perform the traditional mari kiss on each cheek.

"Good night, Kyoko."

CHAPTER 6

"TIME TO COME HOME"

***Sub-Oceanic Stratocracy** SeaBed*
***Date** 48th Day of Month 2, Year 1620 DG - 9 Years Earlier*

THE MARI HAVE EVOLVED TO withstand the frigid temperatures of the ocean floor. Where others would freeze, the ocean-dwellers thrive. And yet, somehow, Rafael shivers.

He's never been to the surface in all fifteen years of his life. SeaBed's temperatures typically offer him comfort. Why is he feeling so cold?

The boy wraps himself tighter in the blanket, hoping to placate the chill, but it does little good. He exhales deeply and a puff of hot breath floats out of his nares and mouth, a mist of evidence that the freezing temperatures aren't in his head.

The unbearable smell is worse than the cold. Are the prisoners held in these cells allowed to wash? Where do they relieve themselves? Will he have to do it in a corner?

Will he even be alive until his next bowel movement?

His throat tightens and moisture develops in his eyes. Memories flood the boy's mind. A doting father who raised him amongst the olive groves. A protective sister who put a bow in hand and confidence in his heart.

A mother who…

What can be said about his mother? He'd always heard about the warmth of motherhood, but his own had always been colder than this cell. She woke him in time for school, assigned him chores, governed his posture, offered him nutritious meals. Rafael had to assume that these were the ways in which she showed love.

Because she rarely verbalized it.

He knows she loves him, vocalized or not. That's apparent now more than ever, as he awaits her return. She could've abandoned him. Damned him to an execution out of anger for allowing her beloved daughter to be slaughtered on a battlefield.

A tear breaks loose from Rafael's cheek and a light sob bursts into the air. His cheeks grow wet as images of Joaquina's cold body at the funeral, wounded by an igni blade, appear before him.

It's their fault. The boy thinks. An igni exoskeleton flashes through his mind, turning his anguish to rage.

The clang of the lock on the cell door grasps his attention. Rafael swallows and wipes his tears before turning to see his mother enter the cell. She holds a lantern up to get a better view, then steps into the small space and closes the doors behind her. A long cloak embraces her, with the hood down, revealing dark tresses dancing on her shoulders.

"What did they say?" Rafael asks her, hopefully.

General Sofia pauses for a beat. An eternal beat in which Rafael thinks they've denied her request and he will face execution. But then she nods and responds, "They've agreed. I begged for mercy."

A weight lifts off of Rafael's shoulders. He won't die, not tonight. But the weight returns quickly when he notices his mother's expression doesn't settle.

"What's wrong?" he asks.

"Rafa," she says, moving closer. "Son." When she's only a few feet from him, he realizes how red and swollen her eyes are. She's distraught.

"Mother, what happened? Tell me. You said they agreed to mercy. When are we going home?"

Slowly, General Sofia shakes her head. "You aren't coming home, Rafa."

Rafael's mouth falls open as confusion sets in. "If I won't be executed, and I'm not going home, what's going to happen to me?"

General Sofia swallows hard and replies in a whisper, "You're being exiled from SeaBed."

The world stops. Time sits completely still as the weight of her words falls on his teenage shoulders. "I'm leaving? Forever? I can't come home?"

Slowly again, the General shakes her head, and without another word, Rafael drops to his knees in heaving sobs. The truth of his situation becomes clearer and clearer; he must leave everything he knows, everyone he loves, behind, as punishment for his mistake. For allowing Joaquina to take his place.

He feels an arm wrap tightly around his shoulders and his instincts kick in. He launches himself into his mother's arms and buries his face in her chest, allowing his sobs to break free.

When he's able to speak again, he weakly asks her, "Where will I go?"

"I've arranged for passage to the Library. The Prime Librarian, Alvaro, is mari. I've written him a letter asking for him to accept you under his guardianship. My hope is that he'll feel some degree of cultural and national connection, and he'll take you into the city."

"And if he doesn't?" Sobs threaten him again. "What are they going to do to me if he doesn't agree?"

General Sofia shakes her head and places a hand on Rafael's cheek. "Everything will be fine. I raised you to conquer any challenge that comes your way."

They sit a little longer in this way, a son wrapped in his mother's embrace for the final time before he has to say goodbye to her.

"I'll never see you again?" he asks, knowing the answer but asking anyway.

General Sofia shakes her head.

"I will," Rafael asserts with conviction.

The General looks down at him. "You can't come home, Rafa."

"You always called Joaquina your pearl, and you called me your little salmon." He looks up into her eyes and takes in the icy blue they offer. "Salmon always come home, Mother. Regardless of how far they go, how long they travel the ocean, they always come back home. One day, I will know it's time to come home."

General Sofia's lower lip curls as she breathes out in agony. "Not this time. You must never come back. Promise."

"But we don't know what the future holds, Mother. Maybe they'll let me come home if it's for something important."

"They will not show mercy twice, Rafa. Promise me, you'll never come home."

After a few seconds of suffering, Rafael nods. "I promise."

"Good." She reaches down to the silver bracelet with the blue gems on Rafael's wrist and unclasps it, then slips it into his pocket. "If they see you wearing it, they may not let you keep it. Take care of it as your sister did."

"You should keep it," Rafael offers. "Joaquina asked me to take care of you before she left. I promised her I would, but I won't be able to anymore. Why don't you keep the bracelet so she can be with you?"

"I can take care of myself. I just want you to be safe." She leans down and gently kisses the top of his head.

"I love you, Mother."

She places her finger under his chin and tilts his head back until their eyes meet. "If you truly love me, you will remember your promises. You will remember all that I've taught you. Keep your head raised every second that you breathe. Conquer every challenge. Never forget who you are. You are the son of General Sofia."

He nods and buries himself into her again, as they sit together, mother and son, waiting for the soldiers to come and take him away. Waiting in silence before they have to say goodbye.

And as they wait, Rafael's words echo in his ears. *One day, I will know it's time to come home.*

Theocracy *SunSide*
Date *21st Day of Month 6, Year 1629 DG - Present Day*

BATHED AND DRESSED IN HIS sleepwear hours later, Rafael lays down on his cot with a belly full of peaches and water, grateful that Kyoko keeps the fruit bowl on the table stocked.

Before slumber seizes him, he reaches into a bag of his personal belongings kept under his cot and withdraws an envelope marked with the seal of SeaBed's Council of Generals. Every night for weeks he's read the letter held within, and every night before he reads it, he twirls the envelope back and forth, examining it as if the formality of the words on the front will change.

"Official Correspondence of the City of SeaBed," it states at the top, followed by, *"From General Sofia,"* below it.

He smiles. There's something comforting in the fact that she hasn't changed. It's been nine years and she's still less mother, more General.

As he removes the letter from the envelope, he considers the risk she took in sending it. It isn't illegal to write to an exile, but there is nothing more frowned upon in SeaBed. Particularly as a government leader, his mother risks compromising her credibility with her colleagues *and* the citizens, if they found out.

She risks being accused of allowing her emotions as a mother to outweigh her duties as a General; an accusation with which SeaBed's society salivates to mar women's reputations. Perhaps, Rafael thinks, he should be more understanding of her desire to be formal and duty-bound, even with her own son.

Perhaps emotionless formality is the most natural shield against society's accusations of emotional informality.

The letter opens with a greeting and well-wishes, similar to those one would send to a colleague or a distant relative. She then writes that she's "come to know" of his departure from the Library.

Thanks, Uni, he thinks.

He reads the letter twice, and then a third time, in its entirety, but the words he's desperately seeking never appear. Not once does his mother mention she loves or misses him. Rafael folds the letter again and places it back in the envelope.

He's wanted to tell Kyoko about it since it arrived weeks prior. And about his mother's position on the Council of Generals that governs SeaBed, and why it was so brave for her to send the correspondence. He's wanted to share his experiences as an exile, forced away from his home.

About the lingering idea floating around his mind since he was fifteen; that, despite the illegality, a day would come when it was time for Sofia's little salmon to return home.

But she wouldn't understand. No one could. He's been through something extraordinary and there's no one on the All-Sphere who could see it from where he stands. She would try to stop him from going home. Try to protect him from the inevitable punishment that would follow.

Exiles who return to SeaBed are brought before the Generals, and then executed. But if the reason is important enough, Rafael is willing to take that risk. Kyoko would never allow it.

After putting the letter back in the bag under his cot, he stares up at the ceiling while running his fingers along Joaquina's bracelet. As if his sister is in the room with him, he speaks to her.

"I know I promised you I would take care of Mother, but I can't."

"You didn't know you were going to be exiled when you made that promise," her voice echoes around the Bunker. He feels juvenile for imagining what she might say to him if she were actually there.

Rafael's fingertips dance along the blue gems in the bracelet links. "I should've given her your bracelet before I left."

"You tried. She didn't want it."

"She wanted me to keep it so I wouldn't feel alone. Last year, when I spoke with your essence, I got my closure. She's the one who's alone now."

Silence.

"Joaquina?"

"Yes, Rafa?"

He swallows hard. "I miss you."

Silence.

And then a scream thunders through the room. His eyelids burst apart, surging with searing Radiant energy. His vision is entirely red, as he battles the burn of the Radiance around his sockets. Flipping off the cot and onto one knee, he scans the room for the source of the screech until he finds Ana excitedly scurrying toward the main table, the two Sprite texts again clutched to her chest.

"Get up! Get up, get up, get up, get up..." She reaches the table and turns toward Rafael, noticing the red glow of his eyeballs, ready to blast energy through the air. "Turn that off and come over here!"

Rafael closes his eyelids tightly and grunts as the heat makes its way out of his eyeballs, back through his optic nerve, and dissipates into his body. He's grateful for Kruga's training, but it will take time to get used to the temperature that accompanies Radiant energy.

Kyoko's bedroom door swings open violently and she stands in the doorway, sleepwear thrown on haphazardly, hair reaching for the stars.

Rafael has never found her to be more enchanting.

The igni mumbles through gritted teeth. "What. The. Fuck. Ana."

Rafael makes his way to the table, where Ana is fervently flipping through the texts, seemingly searching for specific passages. Kyoko joins them and Rafael turns to her. "I think Ana's found something valuable."

"I have," Ana says. "I found what I was looking for."

Kyoko yawns loudly, massaging her injured shoulder. "It couldn't have waited until morning?"

Ana ignores her and places her finger on a passage in the first book. "This is the text on the Sprites' tribal government political system."

"Tribal governments?" Kyoko asks. "The Sprites had an empire."

Ana shakes her head. "That was much later. Before that, they were separated into many different tribes. The largest and most powerful of these tribes was led by a pair of siblings, who were"—she pauses, looking between Rafael and Kyoko dramatically—"lovers!"

Rafael is bewildered at her excitement to have discovered a case of millenia-old incest, but Kyoko's eyes widen.

"The Ancient Ones," she says. "The TreeKeeper mentioned they were"—she pauses, struggling to continue—"intimate upon release from imprisonment."

Ana continues, her smile reaching both ears. "These two tribal leaders had an obsession with ritualistic sacrifices."

"Sacrifices to whom?" Rafael inquires.

"Demons." Her eyes return to the page and she translates as she scans. "It doesn't say what, exactly, but they needed the demons' help with something, so they opened a portal between our world and theirs." Her gaze returns to the former Librarians. "The two tribal leaders would sacrifice their followers in an effort to maintain a connection to the demon plane. Now, listen to the best part."

Rafael leans over to Kyoko. "Should we be worried about her enthusiasm for incest and sacrifices?" Kyoko covers her mouth, stifling a laugh.

Ana continues. "There were three very specific places where the siblings would make these sacrifices. *Fulosa, haamik,* and *troma.*"

Rafael looks to Kyoko who shrugs, then turns back to Ana. "We know basic Nysabaani, Ana."

"*Fulosa* means 'mountain's peak.' *Haamik* means 'ocean's floor.' And *troma* means—"

"Volcano's mouth," Kyoko completes the thought.

Ana nods. "Sound familiar?"

Rafael catches on and the realization collapses on him like cut timber. "The Three Deaths are coming to PeakHaven, SeaBed, and EverEmber." A memory ignites in a dark alcove of his mind. "One from the sky, one from the soil, one from the sea. That's what the TreeKeeper told us. This is what she meant."

"And they're coming from this demonic plane," Ana confirms. "That's why the Sprites needed centuries of essences from Red-Lo. They're trying to build their connection to the demon plane again. It's not just about regaining strength. It's about reconnecting to an entirely different dimension."

Kyoko locks eyes with Ana. "You did it."

The mari woman drops into a seat and exhales, allowing the accomplishment to toss the weight of expectations off her shoulders. "I did it."

"What do we do now?" Rafael asks Kyoko.

Kyoko's gaze falls to the table and Rafael can see the wheels in her mind turning. "Saila should send emissaries to the three cities and warn them of what's coming."

Rafael builds on the suggestion. "Saila should send *us*"—he gestures to those around the table—"as emissaries."

"Why us?" Ana asks, leaning in.

"These are human cities. PeakHaven and SeaBed would categorically disregard a warning from a Mega emissary. And after the revelation of the ore, EverEmber would start a war as soon as they saw pointed ears approaching. The only humans who know about the Sprites are the three of us in this room, Uni, and the one human Member of the Assembly: Aissa."

After a tentative pause, Ana nods. "If Mega suddenly start showing up at human doorsteps, unannounced, with vague warnings, they won't even be allowed into the gates. But *we* might be."

"We should split up," Kyoko proposes. "To deliver the warnings as quickly as possible. I'll go to EverEmber, Ana can visit SeaBed, and

Rafa…" Her mouth hangs open slightly as the realization appears to strike her.

"None of us can breathe at PeakHaven's altitude," Rafael reminds her. "We need an angi."

Ana and Kyoko exchange a glance, then turn to Rafael, a request in their eyes.

He shakes his head. "Absolutely not. I will not ask Uni to leave her dying mother's bedside."

Kyoko nods. "Saila can ask Aissa to go to PeakHaven then."

"What about SeaBed?" Ana asks. "Last time I was there, I was an infant. To them, I'm just another citizen of the Library. They won't care about anything I have to say."

"They certainly won't take me seriously," Kyoko responds, raising her palm to display her exoskeleton.

Rafael's ears inundate with his own words. *One day, I will know it's time to come home.*

For nearly a decade, he's known a day would come when it was time for Sofia's little salmon to return home. If the reason were important enough. Warning SeaBed of the impending cataclysm will allow the city time to defend itself. It will allow him to save his mother's life.

What reason is greater than that?

Rafael speaks deliberately, seizing the opportunity fate has presented. "They'll take both of you seriously if"—he swallows—"you walk in with an exile."

Kyoko's expression hardens with a rage he's never seen before. Her tone cuts through him as she speaks. "Out of the question. I don't want to hear that suggestion again."

Rafael inhales deeply and releases. "Kyoko, if I don't come with you, they won't listen. I understand what they could do to me, but you need me. SeaBed needs me." He pauses. "My mother needs me."

"Saila will send someone else," the igni argues.

"Saila asked us to keep the Sprite situation under control. She doesn't want this spreading until she has answers to all of the inevitable questions that come with it. If her citizens demand responses she doesn't have, it'll make her look incompetent. There is no one else."

"They will execute you, Rafa." Kyoko's eyes nearly brim with tears.

"The Three Deaths can come at any moment. *They* cannot be talked out of killing me."

Kyoko's head swivels sharply to Ana. "Tell him we won't allow it."

Ana lowers her gaze and steps back, a cowering mouse facing a lioness. She speaks so softly, Rafael has to lean in to hear her. "He makes a valid point, Kyoko."

Kyoko's fist slams the table and her cheeks burn red. "NO." She turns to Rafael. "We can't. We won't. I won't."

Rafael cautiously places his hand on hers and gently squeezes her fingers. "We will all walk into SeaBed together, and we will leave together. We can head to EverEmber after."

Kyoko pauses, breathing deeply. "Can you promise that?"

A thick hesitation settles between them as Rafael considers her question. He cannot guarantee his safety. In fact, simple probability would prove a far greater chance that walking into SeaBed will be the last action he ever takes.

But there must be something so much more powerful than coincidence offering him the opportunity to walk back into his homeland. The opportunity to save his mother. Or to say goodbye.

Sofia's little salmon forces a smile, and lies. "I promise."

CHAPTER 7

"SUPREMACIST LIES"

Theocracy *SunSide*
Date *Unknown*

WHAT TERRORS LIE IN THE mind of a monster? What creatures scurry, fly, or slither in the perverse psyche of pure evil? What greenery can be expected beyond the vicious vines that vandalize virtue?

This isn't what I was expecting. Naina parts her lips, but no sound crosses her tongue. The words project out from her thoughts. As she stands still in a peaceful white void, clad in a white kurti and shalwar, clear glass bangles on her wrists, her throat is only capable of silence.

There's no speech in a mental realm, echoes Saila's voice around her, *unless the realm or the memory is yours.* Naina spins quickly around, looking for the pixie, but finds nothing but the endless white expanse in every direction. *Only Red-Lo's memories are able to speak in his mind. You and he will be communicating with your thoughts.*

Where is he? Naina asks into the emptiness. *I was expecting to find him sitting on a throne of ash and fire, surrounded by a kingdom of death and destruction, licking blood off the corpses of the innocent.*

Saila's voice rings out again, hitting her from all sides as if the glowing void itself speaks. *You're not in his mind yet. This is a holding area, where you're still safe, and time still moves in tandem with that of the physical world. It's the only place I can still communicate with you before you enter.*

A plain wooden door appears before Naina.

Once you walk through that door, I lose you. Remember what I told you before: for some, a decade passes in a minute, while for others, it's the opposite. There's no telling, once you cross over into his memories, what you'll experience.

Can you give me an idea of what I might find? Naina wonders, growing frustrated with the vague statements.

Every door you open will lead to a new memory of Red-Lo's life. He'll be there, guiding you. Memory-to-memory, door-to-door. Gather the information you need and then find the door that lets you back out into our world.

Naina's heart drops. *I'm just supposed to keep opening doors until I find one that frees me?*

I told you this was dangerous. My nose is already bleeding out here in the physical realm from the strain of holding you in the void. Frankly, I'm surprised you're still alive. This is your last opportunity to back out, Naina.

If the wolf didn't know any better, she'd think the distortion of time had already begun. She contemplates for moments, but it feels like several eternities. Her mind cycles to Rafael, Kyoko, and Ana, hard at work translating the Sprite texts. Then to Saila, who bears the greatest burdens with such integrity and grace. To Feathers, who's dropped everything to care for her mother in her final days, taking on the responsibilities of someone much older in her early twenties.

And finally, to Salessa.

Naina could return to a world that's moved decades past her. Return to a body that's grown gray and frail. Will Salessa ever forgive her if she can't find the door that releases her?

What good is a home if its days are numbered? she thinks. *I can save it.*

You can, Saila agrees. *But what are you willing to risk for it?*

Naina takes a deep breath to settle the ache in her chest. *Everything. Please, Saila, tell Lessi I love her.*

Just so you're aware, I still don't like this pla—

Naina turns the knob and enters Red-Lo's mind, allowing the door to fade behind her. There is truly no way out now, but forward.

Her gaze drinks in the surroundings. The whiteness of the void has dissipated to reveal the cold stone of a small bedroom. Moonlight and starlight trickle in through grimy windows, while small lit torches adorn the walls.

The room smells of unwashed sheets and old bottles of ale, though she doesn't see any. The stench permeates every inch of the air, leaving Naina struggling not to gag. At the other end of the room—which is not very far—are two small beds sitting side-by-side, at the foot of which, on the floor playing, are two children.

A Mega boy with turquoise skin and a girl with magenta.

They appear to be around the same age, both under ten. They giggle in hushed tones as they spin tops in a circle drawn on the stone floor with chalk. Naina wonders how they can be playing so cheerfully amidst the odors and grime.

You don't notice it when you live with it everyday, comes a somewhat familiar voice from the entrance of the bedroom. Naina finds another turquoise-skinned Mega leaning against the doorway, wearing a plain undecorated version of the MegaFather's gown, in a pristine white that matches Naina's outfit. It takes a moment before she recognizes him from the images in history texts.

Red-Lo, she states matter-of-factly. *The real you.*

The only me, he corrects her as he steps away from the doorway and strides to the corner of the room where she stands. *Surely you didn't think I'd appear in my own mind as Zar-Lo, or any other descendent in whose body I've resided for the last eight hundred years.*

He stands next to her and turns to face the scene around them. *I'm glad you're here, pup. There's so much I'd like to show you in my memories.*

My name is Naina, she responds, narrowing her eyes. *This isn't a tour. I'm going to get through this as quickly as I can, until I find the information I need, and then I'm leaving you to rot in your cell.*

The faerie chuckles. *Is that what you think, wolf? That you're somehow in control?* A smile curves his wicked lips, sending a chill down Naina's spine. *You don't leave until I give you permission. You see, and hear, and smell everything that I want you to. You taste and feel what I feed you. And then when I'm done, perhaps I'll allow you to go.*

Naina swallows hard, turning to the memory around them. *What are you showing me here?*

Nothing yet, Red-Lo sighs.

That's you, she points to the boy, then the girl, *and that's...*

Drof-Fa. His tone drips with sadness. *Her parents fought alongside my father in the Faerie Empowerment Forces.*

A supremacist cult, Naina responds. She can feel the red-hot rage steaming off of Red-Lo's skin. *I may not know as much about history as Lessi does, but I know who was on the wrong side of it.*

A liberation military. Her parents died in the battles against the Mega-Mother's guard shortly after we were born. My father took her in and raised her alongside me. Here, he gestures to the scene of the two children before them, *we're around seven years old, so this would be 755 DG.*

Twelve years before you assassinated MegaMother Picana and usurped her throne.

Assassinated. Usurped. Red-Lo growls the words. *I took what belonged to the faeries. You'll learn true history while you're here with me.*

Naina opens her mouth to respond, but something catches her eye. The children drop the tops and their smiles fade quickly as a low, rhythmic stomp grows louder and louder, rattling the stone floor. The children turn toward the doorway, unbridled terror pooling in their eyes.

What's happening? Naina asks, but no response comes. She looks up at Red-Lo and realizes he has the same terror in his eyes that the children do.

He's coming, the former MegaFather whispers.

An adult turquoise-skinned Mega appears in the doorway. The lines of his face betray his age; perhaps he's in his sixties. His skin is thin, sickly, and the deep, dark circles under his eyes tell a story of a person who hasn't slept in years.

A seething scowl etched onto his frown makes him appear even older.

The children back away from the doorway, cowering together, as the adult Mega slowly drifts into the room. He's carrying a book in his hands.

"I found this," he says, raising the text. "In your belongings."

The children clutch each other, knees trembling.

"Speak!"

Child Red-Lo goes pale. "It's from school! They made me read it, Father."

"*Made* you?" His father tosses the word around in his mouth. "Are they forcing you to read this filth?"

Child Red-Lo nods shakily. "Yes, they're forcing me."

"Are they threatening you? How are they forcing you?"

Child Red-Lo opens, then closes his mouth.

"Speak, Red-Lo!"

The boy's voice continues to tremble. "No, they're not threatening me, but it was an assignment. I have to read it or they'll fail me."

"You have already failed *me*!" The father's volume erupts. "This is exactly what our clan has been fighting against for decades." He shakes the book in the air. "The rewriting of our history!"

He steps forward, too quick for Child Red-Lo to evade him, and grasps the hair on the back of Red-Lo's head tightly. "Let me show you true history." He drags the boy out of the room, followed closely by Drof-Fa, pleading and crying for the older faerie to let go.

Naina stands in stunned silence, processing what she just witnessed. Of all the emotions she thought she'd feel in Red-Lo's memories—anger, hatred, disgust—sympathy wasn't one of them.

She looks up at the dictator standing next to her and wonders how the cowering little boy turned into the monster.

Red-Lo steps forward toward the doorway and, when he reaches it, he turns back to address Naina over his shoulder. *Come quickly, pup. Or you're going to miss the rest of it.*

An anxious steel ball sits in the pit of Naina's stomach. She doesn't want to see what's next. She wants to leave. But, turning around to see the door-less wall behind her, she remembers that the only way out now is forward.

She exits the bedroom and follows adult Red-Lo to a family room. At the center is a wide fire pit, flames dancing over coal. The stench is far more visceral in this chamber, and empty bottles of ale lie scattered around the ground.

Next to the fire pit stand Child Red-Lo and Drof-Fa, facing Red-Lo's father, who paces back and forth, thumbing through the text and mumbling to himself.

"Do I have *no* say in what is taught to my children? These are lies. All lies. This *cunt* thinks she can change SunSide?"

Naina's blood boils. *Who did he just call a cunt?*

Picana, Red-Lo responds. *I know you think my conquering of the throne was unwarranted, but before I took her head, Picana and her dynasty had spent decades removing hard-working faeries like my father from their positions within her administration, only to replace them with nymphs and pixies.*

Your father was a supremacist, Naina reminds him.

Red-Lo nods. *Of all the things he was—a drunk, an abuser—a supremacist is the only thing I'm actually proud of.*

You cannot be serious.

I promise you, pup, I am. Now, watch.

Red-Lo's father stops pacing and turns to his frightened son. He forcefully shoves the book into the boy's hands, nearly knocking him back, and says, "Go ahead, then. Read it."

The boy holds the man's gaze. When he speaks, his quivering voice is little more than a whisper. "Father, I'm sorry, I don't want to—"

The father holds his hands out and glowing blue Radiant energy stretches out from his fingertips. It extends into a long shape, then hardens and becomes a wooden rod. The man raises the rod into the air, but before he swings it, Child Red-Lo is already flipping the pages open to read from it.

The boy clears his throat and speaks as loudly as he can under the circumstances. "The chapter I last read says, 'It's important to see biological equality in our friends and neighbors. But even more so in those who may be employed in our homes. Science created species, but it didn't create blood or diseases or attributes that are specific to one species over another. Individuals and nations and kings created those distinctions, which don't truly exist.'"

Child Red-Lo looks up to meet his father's rage.

"So these are the lies they teach our children in schools now?" His tone is somehow both frozen and burning at the same time. "That there is no biological difference amongst the species? I'll teach you the truth." He whips his head around, pointed ears flapping side-to-side, and bellows, "Sarfaraz! Get in here!"

Who is he calling? Naina asks.

Red-Lo faces the wolf. *One of our slaves.*

Naina's heart drops into her stomach. The Doruh man enters the room clad in nothing but a small garment tied around his waist that barely extends to his knees. His shoulders, arms, legs, and torso are littered with bruises and small wounds. He takes small steps toward Red-Lo's father, keeping his expression stoic and his chin raised.

Red-Lo's father snatches the book from the boy's hands and tosses it into the fire pit, allowing the flames to devour it.

"*Employed* in our homes?" He says the word with venom, then points to Sarfaraz. "This animal, this beast is not in our employ. He's our property, we own him." He brandishes the rod before the children and yells, "Say it!"

Together, the two children repeat, "He's our property, we own him."

Heat explodes from Naina's heart. Hearing the faerie call this innocent Doruh servant a "beast" and an "animal" drives visceral rage through her body.

"Good," the father approves. "*Science* created species? Is that true, Red-Lo?"

Child Red-Lo slowly shakes his head, his eyes locked on the wood in his father's hand.

"Then who created species? Drof-Fa?"

"The Four," Drof-Fa responds quickly.

"Correct. The Four created us all, which makes them our gods. Who created the beasts?"

Drof-Fa responds again. "The faeries."

The father smiles. "Our forefathers used the Radiance to create these animals for our servitude. Now, if the Four created us and they are our gods, what does that make us to those *we* created?" He pokes Child Red-Lo's chest with the end of the rod.

"That makes us their gods," the boy speaks, his gaze low.

Naina clenches her fists, fury flowing from her.

Easy, pup, adult Red-Lo says. *This memory happened centuries before your parents crawled into bed together. There's no point in allowing it to anger you.*

This is humiliating.

It's just the way it was, Red-Lo responds flippantly.

"The most egregious claim of them all," the father continues, "is that there are no attributes distinct to one species over another. Hogwash!" He points to Child Red-Lo. "You've been able to read since you were four." His finger shifts to Sarfaraz. "This animal, in the prime of his life at twenty-five years, cannot read."

The heat reaches Naina's face and burns against her cheeks. *He can't read because he was never taught.*

That's not the point, Red-Lo replies. *There is an intellectual distinction between the species.*

"But despite his obvious stupidity, there are tasks for which he is useful." The father turns Child Red-Lo around, and back to face him again, examining the child. "Your body is meant to be nourished, so you can rule over others."

He turns quickly and presses the tip of the rod against Sarfaraz's chest. The Doruh man winces.

No! Naina shouts from her mind.

They can't hear you, pup.

"*His* body"—the father brings his face close to Sarfaraz's—"is a tool for our use. That is the biological distinction. He works the fields with these arms"—he squeezes Sarfaraz's bicep—"he carries heavy items with these legs"—he slaps Sarfaraz's thigh with the rod—"and he makes more servants for us with *this*."

Red-Lo's father pulls the garment around Sarfaraz's waist to the side, baring the Doruh man, and wraps his fingers tightly around the organ between his legs. He squeezes it and Sarfaraz cries out.

NOOO! Naina screams and bounds forward toward Red-Lo's father. Her instincts beg her to shift; to take the faerie's head into her jaws and tear it from his shoulders. But no matter how hard she tries, she remains in her human form.

You can't shift here, Red-Lo calls out.

Naina ignores him. She releases a guttural bellow from her mind and swings a flurry of punches at the memory of Red-Lo's father, but her fists phase through him. He stands there, smiling as he clutches Sarfaraz, displaying him to the two children, and Naina can do nothing to stop it.

She tires herself out trying to hit him, eventually dropping to her knees and dissolving into sobs. She weeps not only for Sarfaraz, but for every innocent Doruh that was ever treated as a faerie's property. For every man, woman, and child that was told they were unequal, bound and shackled, because of distinctions that a society created.

For an entire species that was forced to build and create and benefit all others but themselves, and who was later tormented and ridiculed for it, and told to "get over it" after they were liberated.

Red-Lo steps forward until he's standing in a pool of Naina's tears. When she looks up and meets his gaze, he kneels down beside her.

I told you before, pup: you aren't in control here. You don't leave until I give you permission. You see, and hear, and smell everything that I want you to. You taste and feel what I feed you. Here, I am the master.

The supremacist snaps his fingers and the world around them dissolves back into the white void. A door appears behind Red-Lo.

And you are the slave.

CHAPTER 8

"THE PATH FORWARD"

Alphocracy *MoonSide*
Date *22nd Day of Month 6, Year 1629 DG*

AT SOME POINT IN THE night, Salessa found the bed again. She lay awake, staring at the stars through the window, begging the Twins to grant her the gift of slumber.

No such gift came.

Her eyes, crimson and swollen, burn with every blink. When the first of the four suns makes its appearance over the horizon, she rises from the bed, enters the curtained-off bathing area and finds a bucket of water.

She splashes her face with it. Repeatedly. Violently. As if punishing herself for opening the door. For trusting Lexona all those years before.

For falling in love in the first place.

She trembles from the cold wetness dripping from her chin and hair. Once dried, the falcon packs her belongings into her traveling sack. She searches her pockets before exiting the inn to make sure she hasn't forgotten anything and her fingertips brush a piece of paper.

The note that spawned this godsforsaken journey. Lexona's note. It burns her fingertips as if it were made of lit coal, yet it freezes her heart as if it were made of ice. With haste, she crumples it in her fist and tosses it out the window, into the soil behind the inn.

It should rot here in MoonSide.

The falcon steps into the warmth of the morning suns. There are many paths leading out of the Northern Hills, but the only one to grasp Salessa's attention is the one heading southeast. Back to SunSide. Back to her life.

Back to Naina.

Salessa trembles again as she realizes the wolf will be furious when Salessa tells her Lexona's alive. She may even set out to hunt the serpent down.

As the falcon treads the path southeast, she wonders if she should hide the truth from Naina. Tell her she never found the author of the note, and that Lover's Plateau is a ruin that no longer exists. Or it never did in the first place.

But what if Lexona and Afzal show up in SunSide. He mentioned in the graveyard that he and his sister had been there. Evidently, it wasn't hard for them to get through the Pass and find Salessa. She's a public figure now, a politician. They can find her again.

Perhaps Naina and Salessa were better off when they were in hiding, when the world didn't know they existed. Now their names will be etched into history books. Generations from now, young SunSidians will learn about the dawn of the new iteration of the theocracy.

In the same fashion that Salessa taught history during the day at the local orphanages and schools of Evic, some educator centuries away will teach about her and her sister.

Despite the warmth of the suns, a chill runs down Salessa's spine.

She pulls out a map to plan her route through MoonSide, back to the Pass. It's now mid-morning and she hasn't gotten very far on the dirt path. She's walking slower than she intended and wishes there was a way to get home quicker.

As if the Twins hear her prayers, the rattling of a wooden cart and the pattering of a horse's hooves come from behind her on the path. A small smile breaks out on her lips, and she folds the map and returns it to her bag.

The falcon turns around to greet the traveler, to request a ride to the Pass, but when she sees who sits atop the carriage, her heart nearly stops.

Perhaps the Twins haven't heard her. Perhaps she's being punished instead.

Lexona sits with leather reins in hand, steering the horse toward Salessa. Behind her, Afzal leans back against one of the rear seats, the hood of his sleeveless coat covering his face, his thick arms crossed over his chest. Salessa can hear him snoring lightly.

The serpent is clad in the same black and red shalwar kameez she wore the night before. When she sees Salessa, she smiles, but the falcon simply turns her back to the travelers and continues down the path as she was.

She *despises* herself for the sickening thought festering in her mind: despite the serpent scales on her skin, despite the fangs and forked tongue, despite the duplicitous, loathsome individual she is…

She is still beautiful.

Salessa shakes her head and pushes the thought as far back in her mind as she possibly can. No amount of superficial beauty can expiate the serpent's sins. The sounds of wood and hoof get closer until the cart rides beside Salessa on the dirt path.

"Salessa," the serpent calls to her.

The falcon ignores her, keeping her eyes on the path ahead.

"Salessa, please, wait," she continues, to no avail. There's a deep sigh and she continues again. "Salessa, I'm sorry."

"Don't." Salessa's finger is raised and pointed directly at Lexona, though her feet keep moving her forward. She brings her finger down and turns back to the path ahead. "I don't want to hear apologies or excuses."

"I won't give you any excuses. Nothing can excuse what I did."

Salessa nods. "Correct."

"But things are different now. We're not eighteen anymore."

"We're twenty-one," Salessa scoffs. "How much could you have changed in three years?"

"Have you not changed in the past three years? Have you not learned and grown and corrected behaviors you're deeply ashamed of?"

Though she keeps moving forward, she admits silently that Lexona may have a point. She has changed in the past three years; she isn't the same person she was at eighteen…thanks to Lexona.

Salessa turns to her and makes steady eye contact. "All of my shame comes from ever having loved you."

The expression on Lexona's face is one she never thought she'd see. The color drains from the serpent's cheeks, and beads of tears appear at the corners of her eyes. Very quickly, Lexona looks more hurt than she had the day Naina caught her stealing.

She wipes her eyes with the back of her hand and clears her throat. "I deserve that, Salessa, I know I do. There's nothing I can say to change what's happened. But right now, I need you to look at the future."

Salessa turns back to the path ahead. "My future is in SunSide, with Naina. Good luck surviving her a second time."

"It isn't," Lexona responds. "Please, Salessa, come with me to Lover's Plateau."

"For what?" Salessa demands. "Why did you call me here?"

"You know why. The prophecy—"

"The prophecy speaks of *four* Doruh who will resurrect the Twins. Not *three*. Why did you call me here alone? You need Naina, too. If this were truly about the resurrection and the prophecy, you would've called us both."

"How could I call you both? Naina would've split me in half before I could say a word."

Salessa chuckles lightly. "So you're afraid of her."

Lexona pauses. "Of course I'm afraid of her. Naina doesn't have the maturity to put her emotions—"

"If you want me to listen, this is a *very* poor start," Salessa warns. "Insulting my sister will plug my ears quicker than you realize."

"I'm not insulting her, Salessa. I'm stating a reasonable fact; you are the only one who...I had *hoped* would listen. Despite everything that happened, you're mature enough to realize that there is a mission to complete and our history cannot be a hindrance to that mission."

"The mission is already being completed in SunSide, Lexona. The prophecy states that we will resurrect the Twins to prevent a great catastrophe. I have friends who are hard at work, as we speak, to uncover the timing and location of that catastrophe so they can prepare for it."

"How?" Lexona challenges her. "How will they prepare?"

Salessa hesitates before she responds. "They will find a way."

"Will they?"

Salessa doesn't have a response. There's no way for her to know how successful Kyoko, Ana, or Saila will be in finding the information they need, or in acting on that information once it's found.

Lexona continues, "The battle to come isn't theirs, Salessa. It's ours. There is something so much more powerful than coincidence at work here. Fate has brought us back together."

Salessa shakes her head and strengthens her resolve. "I won't come with you."

Lexona sighs again. "There is something so much bigger than you and me coming for this world, Salessa. Tell me: how are you going to feel when the skies fall and the mountains crumble on innocent men, women, and children? Will you be smiling, thinking to yourself, 'At least I didn't go with her?' Or will you wish you had?"

For the first time since she left the inn, Salessa's feet stop moving forward. This time, Lexona definitely has a point. Innocents shouldn't suffer because she was too stubborn to put the past behind her and do what was needed to save them.

She turns and makes eye contact with the serpent.

Lexona softens her tone as she speaks. "I will never ask you to forgive me. I will never ask you to forget. I will never ask you to trust me. But I am asking you to do what you were born to do. Come with us. Unleash the Twins. Save this world, Salessa."

Salessa sighs, allowing one thought to roam free. *Naina is going to kill me.*

Lexona reaches her hand down from the cart, offering to help Salessa up onto it. The falcon turns to the path southeast. She can keep walking. She can go home and hope to figure out a solution with Kyoko, Ana, Rafael, Saila, and Naina. Or she can prepare for the inevitable battle.

She turns back to meet Lexona's expectant gaze. After a long, fraught breath, she hoists herself up onto the cart, ignoring the serpent's outstretched hand.

CHAPTER 9

"THE ONE MYTH"

Alphocracy *MoonSide*
Date *22nd Day of Month 6, Year 1629 DG*

SALESSA NEVER BEFORE REALIZED THE direct correlation between the degree of awkward silence filling in the air and the pace of the suns' journeys overhead.

There were questions. A statement or two. But outside of single-word responses and some Naina-like grunts, Salessa has kept a stone wall of silent tension up between her and her fellow travelers.

It's made the day pass excruciatingly slowly.

Most egregious amongst the interactions have been Lexona's weak attempts at bringing up some of her *fond* memories of their time together as teenagers. Memories that have grown sour for the falcon. That leave nothing but a bitter taste on her tongue and an ache in her heart.

Some time after midday, they stopped for Afzal to relieve himself. Salessa dismounted from the cart, stretching her legs and distracting herself from the sound of fluid hitting the ground just beyond the tree line. But shortly after the dripping died, another sound caught her attention: scraping on the dirt. It took some seconds before Salessa realized the half-feline was on all fours, using his back legs to kick the soil back and cover the urine spot.

During this stop, she looked into the eye of the horse leading them and recognized the dual essences within, discovering another shifter on the journey. There's an inexplicable discomfort that erupts from abruptly finding out that there's another traveler, hiding in plain sight, listening to your conversations. Their name, age, gender, everything is concealed until they shift, and by then, they could know so much more about you than you know about them.

When people become adept at deception, there's so much more to fear than just a fly on the wall.

By the time the suns dip, and the stars dance, and the moons bloom, they've traveled through the Northern Hills and started trekking the paths up the PeakHaven Mountains. The range is vast, traveling the entire width of the continent between SunSide and MoonSide, and then cutting quickly northwest to outline the northern coast, ending at Red-Lo River. It would take days to reach the city of PeakHaven, if they were traveling to the other end of the range. Salessa feels the distance from home now more than ever.

Not SunSide.

SunSide isn't her home.

Naina is.

"Tired?" Lexona asks after Salessa yawns involuntarily.

"Mmhm," Salessa responds tersely, keeping the walls between them raised.

"When we get to Lover's Plateau, I'll have the O'Raha prepare your room, so you can rest."

The name sets off a bell of recognition in the back of Salessa's mind, compelling her to crack the stone barriers of her silence with a genuine response. "The O'Raha?"

Lexona nods. "The devotees, who've pledged themselves to the One Myth."

"What's the One Myth?"

Afzal stretches his arms over his head, waking from a catnap, and responds. "It's what the O'Raha call the resurrection prophecy. There's more to it than just the rhyme, you know."

"A lot more," Lexona explains. "The rhyme we all grew up learning in temples is just a small portion of what the O'Raha have documented. They've shared their texts with me and Afzal, and will share them with you and Naina, as well."

"I thought the O'Raha were long dead. How did you find them?"

Lexona smiles. "*They* found *us*. After I healed from Naina's attack, and my adoptive parents revealed the truth of my lineage, I began my search for my birth parents. Their last known residence was in the Northern Hills. When I arrived, I learned they had passed, but Afzal was still there."

"We became inseparable almost instantly," the leopard-man adds, but his expression conveys no joy or love; he simply states it as a fact. "It's hard not to when someone shows up at your door and you can communicate with her through your thoughts."

For the first time, Salessa can relate to him. Connecting with another's thoughts, day in and day out, living in their emotions, it's impossible for them to feel anything less than a part of you.

Afzal continues. "People around the Northern Hills learned about Lexona's return, and why she was separated from me at birth. They guided us to the O'Raha, who refused to believe our story. It took some time before we were able to successfully convince them that we were one set of twins from the One Myth."

Lexona adds, "Once they believed us, they asked us to allow them into Lover's Plateau."

"*Allow* them in?" Salessa's eyebrows scrunch together. "They can't just walk onto a plateau? Why would they need to be allowed in?"

Afzal takes over. "'Lover's Plateau' is a misnomer. Intentionally inaccurate to mask its location. It's a city, and it's built"—he gestures to the stone walls around them—"within the mountain. The Twins housed the O'Raha there, but they enchanted the entrance with their divine energy. So after they died, the O'Raha were locked out."

Lexona pulls her dupatta tighter against her face, bracing against the chill of a nighttime breeze. "Centuries later, we were asked to reopen it. Using clues in the texts their ancestors left behind, we located the entrance, and felt..."

"Felt what?" Salessa asks, leaning in.

Afzal and Lexona exchange glances before the leopard speaks. "The divine energy that opened the entrance of Lover's Plateau. We absorbed it, breathed it, drowned in it. It ran through our veins and penetrated our blood."

Lexona continues. "And that's where we've been the past two years. Living in Lover's Plateau with the O'Raha, reading the texts, learning about the One Myth and the resurrection of the Twins."

Salessa's gaze darts between the leopard and the serpent. Deep in her core, despite the open dialogue, something holds her back from accepting their words as reality. A question.

"How did you find me and Naina?"

"There was an O'Raha member at PeakHaven Pass when you crossed through to SunSide," Lexona explains. "He recognized you from my descriptions, then informed us. Afzal and I traveled to Larso, unaware of the unrest that had broken out the night before our arrival. We sheltered at an inn throughout the Halving of SunSide, then began our search for you and Naina. After a week without success, we were ready to head back, until we found out about the speech at the Temple Complex. We decided to stay for it."

Afzal smiles. "And there you both were on stage. Lexona wrote the note, passed it to a child to hand off to you, and then we left. We've been waiting for you since. When we caught wind of a young shifter walking around the Northern Hills asking about the location of Lover's Plateau, we knew you'd come."

"So you lied to me," Salessa responds abruptly, challenging him. "When we met in the graveyard last night, you told me you didn't find the person you were looking for. You never mentioned you were there for me."

A rosy glow ignites around Afzal's feline muzzle. "How receptive would you have been to a shifter of my size, approaching you in a graveyard in the dead of night, admitting he was looking for you? I lied because I was trying to introduce myself without alarming you."

"I'm a woman. I was alone with a man I'd never met, who kept stepping closer as we spoke. I promise you, there *was* no way of introducing yourself without alarming me. Why didn't you wait for another opportunity?"

Afzal pauses for a moment with a creased forehead. "I suppose, after all I'd read in the O'Raha texts, I couldn't resist meeting you."

Salessa's eyes widen. "The O'Raha texts mention me?"

"Not specifically," he clarifies. "They describe elements of the One Myth that aren't common knowledge. One of those elements is the relationship of the four Doruh who will resurrect the Twins. It's written that all four shifters will form a bond stronger than that of siblings. When I saw you last night, I just couldn't stay in the tree."

A single thought races through Salessa's mind. *They must be wrong.*

If these texts do indeed claim that the four resurrectors will share a bond more powerful than that of siblings, then they must be wrong. Her eyes drift over to Lexona. Vines of betrayal wrap tightly around her throat, suffocating her as if no time has passed at all.

The falcon could never love this person again.

"What do you want from me?" Salessa asks them, exhausted. "Why did you call me in the first place? What do you expect me to do here?"

"The same thing Afzal and I have been doing for two years," Lexona says. "Study. Learn."

"Learn what?"

The serpent turns to her and smiles, her forked tongue slipping through sharp teeth in rhythmic bursts. "How to resurrect a deity."

The silence resumes. Salessa's mind aches, attempting to digest so much information at once. She battles her exhaustion, forcing her eyelids apart to maintain watch on the travelers. Just as she starts to slip into slumber, the horse stops.

It's an arbitrary spot atop a level section of the trail. There's little more than a foot of space between the sides of the cart and the jagged, towering stone walls on either side.

"We're here," Lexona says, dismounting into the thin space.

Salessa looks around. "Here? There's barely enough room for the cart between these walls. Where is Lover's Plateau?"

"In there." Afzal points to a crevice in one of the stone walls, blanketed by the darkness of nightfall. Lexona turns her body sideways and slips into the slit, barely making it through.

Afzal reaches into the traveling sack at his feet and withdraws what appears to be a petite woman's shalwar kameez suit. The leopard dismounts from the cart, shuffling through the narrow space to where the horse stands, and releases the shifter from her harness. Salessa follows, watching as the horse shifts back into a young Doruh woman in her late twenties.

"How are you feeling?" Afzal asks the woman, his tone soft and warm.

She smiles and places one hand on his shoulder. With the other, she reaches down and massages her bare feet. "Nothing a foot massage won't cure."

Afzal clears his throat and his volume drops. Salessa can barely make out a few words of what he says to the horse. "If you…we get back…foot massage…be happy to."

The woman's cheeks grow pink and she nods, then she looks in Salessa's direction and her jaw drops open. The falcon turns to look for what's prompted the woman's astonishment.

The horse shifter steps forward, approaching Salessa quickly, and then drops down onto her knees on the stone trail. She places her hands onto the ground and then her forehead as well, entirely prostrating at Salessa's feet. She does it so quickly and forcefully that Salessa has to step back.

"What are you doing?" Salessa demands.

"I am Zoya of the O'Raha, Great Falcon Goddess," she says, forehead, palms, and knees still pressed into the mountain beneath them. "I am your humble servant, devoting my life to worshiping and serving you."

Salessa could search the entire All-Sphere, for her whole lifetime, and she wouldn't be able to find the words to articulate her discomfort.

"Please, Zoya, stand up," Salessa asks her.

Zoya rises to her feet. "As you command, Great Falcon Go—"

"Just call me Salessa."

Zoya nods with a smile, then brushes the pebbles and specks of blood off of her knees. Afzal hands her the outfit he removed from his bag and she steps away from the narrow part of the trail to get dressed.

Salessa approaches Afzal. "You're one of the resurrectors, too. Why didn't she react that way with you?"

"I put a stop to it a long time ago. Every O'Raha you meet will want to do the same thing, so you'll have to ask them to stop getting on their knees when you walk by."

"Has Lexona asked them to stop as well?"

Afzal chuckles. "The Great Serpent Goddess? You've known her much longer than I have. What do you think?"

The answer is clear. If someone dropped to their knees and called Lexona their goddess, years ago or today, she would have stood there and basked in her own glory.

The leopard uses his girthy, muscular arms and chest to push the cart, alone, to the wider part of the trail beyond the walls, guiding it to a dirt patch off-road. Zoya, now dressed, joins them, and the three travelers slip through the opening to join Lexona.

Afzal barely fits.

They're in a warm, wet cavern, lit by small torches. At the far end is another stone wall, this one unnaturally smooth. Lexona places her hand on it, then turns to the falcon. "This is it, Salessa. When you touch this wall, you'll feel the divine energy flowing through you, and it'll allow you to enter." She closes her eyes, breathes deeply, and then steps forward, through the smooth stone as if it were made of mist.

Salessa rubs her eyes, mouth agape. Afzal and Zoya step forward next. He puts one hand out between them, which she takes, and the other on the wall. Eyes closed, a deep breath, and then they step forward through the wall together, disappearing behind it.

The falcon turns around, facing the entrance to the cavern. Again, she finds herself wondering whether this is the moment she should turn back and return to her new life in SunSide. To Naina.

Has she come too far to turn back?

Salessa remembers all the innocents who will perish if she doesn't step through stone to resurrect the Twins. This is the precipice of a journey she is meant to be on. She presses one fingertip to the stone. Then five. The ten. Then two whole palms.

Nothing. There's no divine energy. She closes her eyes and breathes deeply. She remembers Naina and immediately, she feels the buzzing of her telepathy, as if Naina has entered her mind again. It's a feeling she hasn't felt in weeks.

Naina, are you there?

Silence.

The feeling grows, expanding out of her mind and covering her entire body. The divine energy of the Twins has spread from its usual location—concentrated in her mind to provide her and Naina with their telepathy—to blanketing her entire body. It's a thrumming along her skin that raises her hair and tingles every inch of her.

The stone wall beneath her fingers softens, then becomes fluid, and then like fog.

Before she takes a step forward, she uses the divine energy for one last attempt to reach out.

Naina, if you can hear me, I need you to stop me. I'm surrounded by people I don't trust. Her throat tightens. *Tell me we'll find another way to save the world and I'll walk back to SunSide. Right now.*

She begins to sweat, and a trickle of blood gathers on the tip of her nose, as she forces the divine energy out as far as it can go. It surges like an ocean, covering the mountains, until she hears…

Nothing but deafening silence.

Salessa nods. *I understand. I love you, Naina.* She steps forward and passes through the stone wall, like she's passing through a cloud, and when she emerges on the other side, she finds Afzal, Zoya, and Lexona standing on a ledge.

Salessa's eyes widen as she looks around. Hundreds of feet above her, all around her, everywhere she can see, is hollow space. The entire mountain is empty.

"Come here, Salessa," Zoya calls her forth to the edge. "Let us show you."

Salessa obliges and joins them at the top of a cliff that leads straight down into a valley. On the floor of the valley are hundreds of stone buildings, clustered together in an expansive city, lit up enchantingly with the glow of a thousand torches. Homes, roads, paths, farmland, jungle, it's all visible, comprising different parts of a small city.

"Welcome to Lover's Plateau," Zoya says to the falcon. "Your new home."

There are innumerable shifters, in both animal and human form, scurrying about, so small that Salessa can barely see them.

"The O'Raha," Salessa deduces.

Lexona nods. "These are our people, Salessa. They've devoted their lives to serving us." Salessa's discomfort grows, and it must be apparent in her expression, as Lexona continues. "I know it's going to be an adjustment for you. But, I promise, you will learn to appreciate the devotion and servitude that divinity brings."

We were already a people who served others, and were liberated. Why would I want to shackle our people again?

"Down there, Salessa, is where they keep the scripture that holds the answers to our destiny."

Salessa scoffs. "What do the O'Raha, and some old texts, know of *my* destiny?"

"So much more than you do," the serpent responds.

"It's time to descend," Afzal says, pointing to a trail that leads down to the city.

Salessa takes another long look at the glowing buildings, the statues and monuments, the jungle and the farmland. It's more than a city; it's an ecosystem. And it's no wonder it remains hidden. Explorers search for a plateau atop a mountain. Not for the bustling world within it.

As they descend to the city in the valley, Salessa moves towards her new home.

And *much* farther from her old one.

CHAPTER 10

"Never Forget"

Sovereign City-State *The Library*
Date *23rd Day of Month 6, Year 1629 DG*

UNISA STANDS WITH HER FINGERS wrapped tightly around the doorknob for far longer than she intended. It's supposed to be a routine visit with her mother before she heads off to work, but she's stood outside the door, clutching the knob, for long enough that she might actually be late.

What am I waiting for?

Nothing. She's not waiting for anything. She's simply steeling herself for the reality that lies beyond the door. She hasn't seen her mother in four days. For a healthy individual, four days apart is a short trip, where little changes.

But when a loved one's wits are in rapid decline, four days can turn them into someone completely new. Four days could be the difference between "How are you?" and "Who are you?" When a loved one's time is dwindling, the "Goodbye" before a four-day trip could be the last.

With a long exhale, Unisa turns the knob and steps into the apartment, hoping she's ready for whichever Ora she might meet. Hoping her mother is still there at all.

The medical bed sits at the opposite end of the chamber, beyond the kitchen, under the warm light of the suns pouring in through the window. She sleeps soundly, a soft smile on her face as her nymph salver unpacks the equipment from her bag.

When Unisa closes the door behind her, the azure-skinned salver peeks out at the positions of the suns through the window. "Shouldn't you be on your way to work by now?"

"I should," Unisa agrees, "but I just wanted to see her before I go."

The salver nods. "Of course. I can step out if you'd like privacy."

"That's alright, I won't be long."

As Unisa passes her, she gently places a hand on the angi's shoulder to get her attention. "Remember what we talked about. Just say *anything*. It doesn't matter what it is. Talk about work, or a date you've been on, or a memory you share with her. Just, whatever you do, remember that she's still here. Don't treat her as if she's already gone."

Unisa nods, breathing deeply to steady the ache in her chest. She's heard the advice before, a number of times, and tries her hardest to follow it, but there's difficulty in not feeling alone when having long one-sided conversations.

She steps to the chair next to the bed and sits. Gently, affectionately, she takes Ora's cold, stiff fingers into her hands, softly pressing them to warm them as much as she can. The odors of gowns, medications, and the elderly strike her nostrils, but she ignores them.

"Hi, Mom," she begins, trying to keep her voice strong, though it falters almost immediately. "I missed you. I've been gone for four days. I had to go to the Agrarian Townlets for work. The Soil King got into another spat with the Headman of Deepweed. Juhi and I were sent there to negotiate another treaty, though I hardly see the point. The Soil King will violate this new one, as well, eventually, and we'll be back to where we started."

Ora stirs a bit in her bed, and Unisa thinks she might be waking up, but her eyes remain closed and she starts to breathe loudly again.

Unisa continues. "It's a strange feeling, being the one to lead a mission. I've never supervised anyone before, but Juhi is reliable and educated and resourceful. I couldn't have asked for a better Vice. You must have supervised some Gatekeepers when you were a Recorder. I wonder if you appreciated being in charge, or if you felt as much discomfort with it as I do."

Her rambling feels dry and tedious. She isn't sure if Ora would want to hear about her travels or work, so she tries to switch to a shared memory. These are the hardest to talk about, but she tries anyway. It's all she can do.

She swallows through the tightness in her throat and speaks. "Remember that time you took me to Plucky Park for a picnic? I was six and had just started having my nightmare. The night before was the first time I had it, so you kept me home from school and took a day off of work. We made sandwiches right there"—she turns and points to the dining table beside the kitchen—"and then walked to the park. It was such a beautiful day. Autumn, your favorite time of the year. 'Blue skies and red leaves,' you would say.

"You let me jump in leaf piles for hours. Never stopped or reprimanded me. Never told me it had been enough and it was time to go. I must have jumped into that pile of leaves two hundred times, and you laughed, enjoying my childhood innocence every single time."

Unisa brings Ora's hand to her lips and kisses it, as a tear breaks free from the corner of her eye.

"And then that couple walked by and gave us *the look*. We hated that look and I think this was one of the first times we got it. I remember you charging up to them and asking what their problem was. I thought you were so brave. Even when they seemed angry and asked where my *real* parents were, you never backed down. Who cares if you had gray eyes and celadon skin, and could connect to the Radiance? Who cares if I had braids and wings and was human? I was still your daughter."

She clears her throat, pushing out a strained voice as best as she can. "I *am*. I am still your daughter, Mom. And I love you so much. I just want you to know that you were the best mom I could have asked for. Everything I am, everything I will be, is because you took me in and loved me. I've heard the stories of Librarians taking in children for the youth education program, and then putting them in a corner until it's time to release them. But you never made me feel anything but the love of a devoted parent. I owe my whole life to you, Mom."

She rises and places her forehead against Ora's, closing her eyes and pouring her heart out through her words, as if they're the last ones Ora will ever hear. As they very well may be. "If someone offered me the chance to go back in time, to live my life again in a world where my birth parents never sent me to the Library, where you never adopted me, I wouldn't do it. I hope you know that. I would never choose a life in which you weren't my mother."

Her eyes open and she wipes them dry, finding the suns out of the window. "I have to go to work now. But I'll be back this evening to see you."

Ora's eyes slowly open and she turns to Unisa. The angi's heartbeat quickens, awaiting some indication that her mother is there, behind the glassy expression. She softly pushes Ora's hair back.

"Mom? How are you feeling?"

Ora smiles, but there's no response. Her speech has become limited.

"Are you alright? Is there something I can get for you?"

The pixie continues to smile, a blankness in her eyes. It appeared there some months ago, coming and going periodically, though now it's remained for days without interruption. The angi's heart drops as disappointment sets in. Her mother is not there today.

Unisa leans forward and kisses Ora's cheek. The elderly pixie says something. Her voice is frayed and weak, but a sound drips from her lips. Unisa's heart quickens again at the thought that Ora might be trying to communicate with her again.

"What is it, Mom?" She leans in to put her ear closer to Ora's mouth.

"Nira," the pixie says.

Unisa's eyes grow moist again.

Nira is Ora's sister's name; another celadon-skinned pixie, who lived in the Gerontocratic Villages. She visited Unisa and Ora a few times during the angi's childhood, but passed away when Unisa was around sixteen years old.

Unisa shakes her head. "It's me, Unisa."

Slowly and weakly, Ora raises her finger and points. Unisa looks over her shoulder to see the salver standing behind her.

"Nira," Ora repeats. "Where is father, Nira?"

The salver steps forward. "Father is in his study, Ora. You can go back to sleep for now, I'll call you when mother finishes making dinner."

Ora nods and closes her eyes again. She doesn't acknowledge Unisa.

"I'm not sure if it's the right thing to do," the nymph admits. "But I think it helps her feel comfortable when I play along."

Unisa forces a smile and wipes her eyes dry. She clears her throat before speaking. "Then you should play along. Keeping her comfortable is the best we can do now. Thank you, I'll see you in the evening." She takes a last long look at her mother before she turns and exits the apartment.

Ora may not remember her, but Unisa remembers every single moment she's spent with the pixie throughout her life. She remembers the smiles, the wisdom, the laughs, and all of the love.

And she will never forget.

CHAPTER 11

"FULLY BONDED DISCIPLE"

Sovereign City-State *The Library*
Date *23rd Day of Month 6, Year 1629 DG*

THE FIRST DAY BACK AFTER a work trip is always a bit jarring.

Unisa's become quite comfortable with the fluid flow of the top floor; a river of Librarians charging around the room, working diligently and paying no attention to anything but their work. But returning from a mission is like standing on the riverbank and trying to match the current as you dive in.

You have to swim well or be swept away.

The angi Ambassador's desk is a mess. Papers strewn about, manuals piled in a corner, two old food containers that once held toasted corn bowls and vegetable stew from Kura's Kitchen sitting over her calendar; Unisa can't decide if she should be glad to see everything as it was when she left, or embarrassed by the state of it.

She takes a moment to organize, disposing of the old containers, stacking papers neatly together with the most recent documents at the top, and putting the manuals away in a drawer. It's her one attempt at tidying per month. She finds a framed picture of Ora in the drawer and places it in the corner of the desk.

The documents sitting at the top of the pile are Juhi's reports from their most recent mission to the Agrarian Townlets. The Vice Ambassador must have been on time for work this morning and left them on Unisa's desk. Unisa always gives her a week to submit her reports, but Juhi is diligent, even when they arrive late in the night and have to be at work the following morning.

When does she sleep? Unisa wonders.

The angi thinks back on the relationship she's built with Juhi in the year they've been partnered together. The first two missions were somewhat uncomfortable, but once Juhi—a hawk—started to shift more frequently in front of Unisa, they started spending most of their travel time in the air. Despite having to carry both of their travel bags as she flies, Unisa appreciates the relief of not having to walk for long distances.

And being in the air with a hawk reminds her of Salessa. Though hawks and falcons are not the same, the similarity quells the ache of missing her friend.

Another friend doesn't give her the opportunity to miss him. Rafael writes to her so frequently, she often receives a second letter from him before she's had the opportunity to respond to the first. She's grateful that he keeps her updated on the efforts to translate the Sprite texts.

As she's perusing Juhi's reports, a messenger arrives to deliver another letter from Rafael. Unisa thanks the pixie, who distractedly nods and moves on to the next desk, holding a stack of envelopes. She smiles, letting her fingertips flow over Rafael's handwriting. Perhaps she misses him more than she lets on.

Before tearing the envelope open to read, she peeks over her shoulder and around the room. The fluid flow continues, every eye looking down at some paper or book. Behind her, the Prime's door is closed and his new Gatekeeper is nowhere to be seen.

It's safe.

The angi is surprised to find that the letter is far shorter than any of Rafael's previous correspondences. She usually expects two or three pages to pop out of the envelope, but only one does this time:

Feathers,

I have something important to tell you, but first: I hope Mother remains comfortable and steady. Remember to keep talking to her. Just say anything. You have no idea how much I wish I were there to speak to her, as well. To hold your hand through this time. Though it may not mean anything to her anymore, please remind her how much I love her.

The important news is that Little Sister has recently had a breakthrough in our mission. We're going to be informing Jade Leader of our findings soon, hoping she will authorize our travel to the theorized locations. Mountain, ocean, volcano. Estimated countdown is: under four months. I know it's a lot to take in, but it's all developed quickly, and I don't have time to tell you much more.

Please, don't worry about me, I will be fine. I'll write to you as often as I can, as I always do, but we intend to meet with Jade Leader a week after the composition of this letter, and we'll likely start our travels shortly thereafter. As soon as I get the opportunity to report again, I will.

I'm just relaying this so you're informed. I know how you feel about remaining in the nest while we fly, but Mother needs you now more than ever. She should come first while you still have her. We can take care of everything else.

Speaking of mothers, I received a letter from the General stating she's become aware of my situation. No doubt you had a hand in that. You'll be surprised, as I am, that I've already forgiven you. If I am to be part of the upcoming journey, I may have a chance to interact in person.

Again, don't worry about me, I'll be fine.

All my love,

Fins

P.S. Falcon still not back from quest.

Unisa reads the letter three times with eyes wide, taking in all of the information it presents. Not because of Rafael's meticulous use of coded language—though he's quite committed to it—but because he seems to be telling her he's going to do something immeasurably idiotic, and his persistent request for her not to worry about him confirms this is the case.

He's going back to SeaBed?

She blinks hard, hoping the words will change, or that she's deciphering it incorrectly, but when they don't, her heart dips into her stomach.

"Little Sister has recently had a breakthrough in our mission." Great job, Ana!

"Mountain, ocean, volcano." They're going to ask Saila to authorize trips to the human cities. That must be where the Three Deaths are coming. In under four months.

"We'll likely start our travels shortly thereafter." He's going with them to SeaBed? There's no way Kyoko is allowing this.

"If I am to be part of the upcoming journey, I may have a chance to interact in person." There is no way…

"We intend to meet with Jade Leader a week after the composition of this letter."

Unisa checks the date on the letter. Twenty-First of Month Six. Today is the Twenty-Third. There's time to send out a letter before they leave for their journey if they aren't meeting with Saila until the Twenty-Eighth. She pulls a blank page out of her desk drawer and writes the shortest letter she's ever written:

Fins,

Let Little Sister and Stone Skin go alone. Give my love to them, Jade Leader, and Wolf.

Hope Falcon returns soon.

Feathers

She folds the paper, slips it into an envelope and seals it. As soon as she's on her feet, ready to find a messenger to whom she can pass it off, she's knocked back into her seat by a sturdy chest behind her.

"I'm so sorry!" Andres cries, rubbing his chest where Unisa's chin made contact with it. "Are you alright?"

Unisa massages her jaw, sore from the impact, then stands again, this time slower and more carefully. "Yes, I'm alright. I was lucky you were facing me and not turned the other way, or I would've run into a spine fin."

Andres laughs. "Where were you running off to in such a hurry?"

"I think a better question is why the Prime's Gatekeeper was hovering over my shoulder while I was writing a personal letter."

Andres's cheeks glow red. "I'm sorry, I didn't read anything, I promise. I'm just here because the Prime has asked to see you in his office."

Unisa's smile dissolves and her chest tightens, a common reaction anytime she has to have a face-to-face interaction with the Prime. Ever since her promotion, since her return from SunSide on that first godforsaken mission, things have changed.

She's become the new Alba for him. His Fully Bonded disciple. She understands Alba's need to escape so much better now. He's suffocating, and nauseating, and terrifying. And she has to play along as she secretly works to enact Alba's final plan.

To burn down this iteration of the Library. To build the city anew with the values on which it was originally founded.

Andres holds his hand out. "Why don't you give me your letter, and I'll pass it off to a messenger?"

Unisa hesitates and holds the letter tightly against her chest. "I can do it, Andres, thank you. There must be a messenger still around somewhere."

Andres reaches forward and grips the corner of the envelope tightly, his knuckles grazing Unisa's chest. "You don't want to keep *him* waiting, do you?"

He may not have intended it this way, but his tone feels too sinister for Unisa's comfort. She nods and allows him to take the letter from her. The mari walks around her desk and, presumably, takes it to a messenger, while Unisa turns and heads for the black door behind which the Prime works.

The reception area where Rafael used to sit feels empty. Not only because Andres isn't behind the desk, but because Rafael's smile no longer fills the room. With five long strides, she's standing in front of the Prime's door. She takes a deep breath to prepare herself for the way in which he likes to be greeted when they're alone, then knocks.

The door opens and the eyes she despises most in this world appear before her; as always, they are somehow warm and cold at the same time. He smiles down at her, the lines of elderhood streaking across his face, the sleeves of his black tunic rolled to his elbows to reveal his forearm fins.

Only a year ago, Unisa worshipped this man. Every book on her shelf was written by him. Her personal time was spent listening to his speeches. And now, she stands before him everyday at work, trying to figure out his weaknesses. The cracks in his shield that will allow her to break through.

"Welcome home, Unisa," he says, stepping to the side to allow her entry. As much as her mind and heart beg her to retreat, her feet pull her forward obediently. They know she must keep up the ruse. The Prime closes the door behind her and, once they're alone, he steps in front of her, leans down, and presses his lips to hers.

It's over in a moment, but it hasn't gotten any less repulsive in the year they've been doing it. She swallows back the bile rising into her throat and forces a smile. When the Library burns, those lips will burn with it.

"Please, have a seat." He gestures to the chair on the other side of his desk. Unisa sits at the edge of it. She hates this seat, where Alba sat during Unisa and Rafael's sentencing. "So how did your mission go?"

"Very well, Great Prime. The Soil King has agreed to Deepweed's new terms. He will no longer encroach on their land, and they will reduce pesticide emissions by thirty percent."

"Any chance he'll stick to it, this time?"

Unisa shakes her head. "Unlikely. He hasn't stuck to any of them in the past fifty-eight years."

The Prime groans. "Will the Soil King join the soil already, so his son can take over? The Soil Prince won't spend so much energy fighting for the environment."

"It may be some time before he takes over, Great Prime. The Soil King is in excellent health for his age."

"We all wither eventually," the Prime notes. "Speaking of, how's Ora doing?"

The words strike her in the chest, but she keeps her smile up. "She's doing as well as she can be in her condition. Thank you for asking."

"And the salvers have been doing well to care for her, yes?"

Unisa swallows hard, uneasy at the direction of the conversation. "Yes, they have."

"Excellent." The Prime stands and walks over to his door. He opens it and calls to Andres, who steps forward from his desk to the door. "Andres, do me a favor, send word to Ora's salver that she's to immediately pack her things and leave the apartment."

Unisa rises to her feet, sweat breaking at her temple. "Great Prime, what are you saying?"

The Prime turns to her. "Is there a problem?"

Unisa pauses, stunned. "You...you know I need her to care for Ora while I'm at work."

"Oh." The Prime feigns surprise. "I thought you were caring for Ora yourself now and that's why you were late this morning."

His game dawns on her. It's punishment.

The Prime's expression hardens and his tone becomes venomous. "The Library will not provide an attendant and equipment and long-term care if you are not going to take your work seriously."

"I am, Great Prime. I will never be late again." Her tone has grown frantic.

"No, you won't. If you want to spend your morning with your mother, when you're supposed to be working, you can spend your afternoons and evenings with her as well."

"I won't be late, I promise." Her voice trembles.

The Prime steps forward and places his hands on her shoulders, lowering his volume and softening his tone. "Shh. shh. Everything is alright, Unisa. Andres knows I wasn't serious."

Andres's eyes are wide with astonishment, but he slowly nods and steps away, closing the door to the office again.

When they're alone together, the Prime holds powerful eye contact with Unisa and says, "Always remember what the Library has given you. What I have given you."

"I will," Unisa says, promising herself as much as she promises him. "I will never forget."

CHAPTER 12

"The Recruits"

Sovereign City-State *The Library*
Date *23rd Day of Month 6, Year 1629 DG*

LONG AFTER THE TOP FLOOR of the Center has emptied, Unisa remains at her desk, completing the day's work. The other Ambassadors and top-floor Librarians, even Andres and the Prime, have gone home for the day.

Her final task before beginning the trek through the Loops is to review the calendar on her desk and make sure it's updated. Of the fifty squares on the page, each representing a day of the month, one in particular stands out, with thick red writing on it. The Thirtieth of Month Six, displays "Prime Palace."

The Prime doesn't live in a palace, though the estate of the Prime Librarian, built centuries prior, was dubbed with the name upon construction. It is larger than most of the homes in the Library, but the name certainly adds a grandeur to the residence that isn't there.

At least, from what Unisa has seen in pictures, it doesn't *appear* as grand as the name would imply. Next week will be her first time actually stepping foot into the Prime's home. It'll be her unofficial induction into the Prime's Inner Catacomb.

Unisa first heard the term from Kyoko, who had relayed it from her sister. Kanako had been one of a small circle of young women and girls who are given preferential treatment, affection, and attention from the most powerful man on the continent. In return, they...

The angi doesn't want to think about what happens to the girls in order for them to remain in his grasp. Likely the same thing that happened to Kanako years ago. Unisa has followed every command, carried out every order, allowed him to kiss her at every greeting, played the part of the perfect Fully Bonded Disciple in order to get close enough that he would invite her to join.

If she's going to follow through with the mission that Alba set upon her shoulders before she died, she'll have to get into the Inner Catacomb and start tearing it apart from within. She'll have to free all of those young women and girls. Alba's mission must succeed for them as much as for Unisa.

Prior to her most recent mission to the Agrarian Townlets, he called her into his office and bestowed the honor of the Inner Catacomb on her. Until that offer, she had thought the mission was failing. That *she* had failed Alba. But with the offer to join the Inner Catacomb, she knows it's working. The time to act has come.

Unisa realizes how long after sunsdown it is and quickly packs her bag. She was already late for work and she'd rather not be late for her nightly appointment as well.

Walking the streets from the Center to the Loop Network station, Unisa remains acutely aware of the eyes that watch her from dark corners. Had someone told her a year prior that, as she walked through the open streets of the city, she would be surveilled by the Prime's loyal shadow forces—the undercover faction known as the Cicada Librarians—she would have thought them paranoid.

But reality is far from paranoia. The Cicada's fingerprints cover the Fully Broken; those who are hauled off to an alleged "rehabilitation" that doesn't exist. Alba once told her the truth.

Under the city, you'll find equal parts books and bones.

The journey through the Loops is quick. It always is when Unisa's mind is occupied and not focused on flying.

Time flies when you're distracted.

There are fewer Cicada eyes on her during her walk from the Loops to the claystone building where she lives. For a faction of undercover shadow Librarians, she's learned quite well how to spot them.

Up the steps to the second floor, she heads to Ora's apartment. Unisa hasn't been to her own in weeks. She remains where she's needed.

The salver's gone home for the day, following strict orders from the Prime. She doesn't want to disobey them anymore than Unisa wants to disobey her own. The back of Ora's bed has been shifted upright for dinner time.

Yuki, a young igni neighbor, sits by the bed, slowly spoon feeding Ora some pureed vegetables; typically food that is made for infants.

"I'm sorry I'm late, Yuki," Unisa apologizes.

"Don't apologize," Yuki responds with a smile, her exoskeleton shimmering in the starlight falling through the windows. "Ora and I were just having dinner."

Unisa reaches into her pocket and pulls out a pouch, from which she withdraws two red triangular stones and quietly places them into Yuki's bag sitting on the dining table. Yuki catches her out of the corner of her eye.

"Uni, please."

Unisa shakes her head. "I can't thank you enough, but I can pay you."

"I'm not here for money, Uni. I'm here for Ora"—she turns to the elderly pixie and then back to Unisa—"and for the mission."

"The mission thanks you, but you're a twenty-year-old who's here feeding my mother when you could be out partying with your friends."

Yuki rolls her eyes. "First of all, it's a work night. Secondly, I've never partied a day in my life. All I do is study." She points to the open books on the dining table next to her dinner. "Which I do here anyway until you get back home from the nightly meetings. Speaking of which, aren't you late?"

Unisa sighs and approaches Ora's bed. "I am, but I'm not going to leave until I've seen my mother first." She reaches the bed and leans down to kiss Ora's forehead. The elderly pixie gazes up at her, making glassy eye contact, displaying no recognition.

"Hi, Mom. It's me, Unisa. I hope you had a good day today. I love you."

Ora's blank expression and soft smile lingers. She doesn't respond.

"I'll be back in a little while, alright? Yuki is here to take care of you again."

"She's eaten a few bites, but I don't think she wants any more," Yuki explains. "She keeps closing her mouth when I bring the spoon near."

"The salver said not to force her. If a few bites is all she wants, that's good enough. We just want her to be comfortable now."

Never has a word caused Unisa as much discomfort as the word "comfortable" does now. It's an odd situation, to be told by salvers that comfort is all you can give a loved one because medication and love will no longer help.

Comfort is all that they can recognize.

Unisa takes Yuki's hand and squeezes it affectionately. "Truly, thank you."

"Stop thanking me and go to your meeting! The others must be waiting."

Unisa starts walking toward the door. "I won't be long, I just want to update them, and then I'll be back. Is your apartment door unlocked?"

"It is," Yuki confirms. "Tell them I said hello."

"I will."

Unisa closes Ora's door behind her, a weight lifting off of her shoulders. Yuki's volunteering to care for her while Unisa's at her nightly meetings provides the angi with a relief she can't describe. Yuki is young, but she's sharp-witted, fiercely protective, and a warrior for those in need.

Ora had introduced Yuki to Unisa shortly after her return from her SunSide journey. Yuki lives on the first floor of the apartment building and a messenger had accidentally delivered a letter for Ora to Yuki's apartment. Yuki came to return the letter, the two started talking, and Ora fell in love with the young woman's idealistic philosophies and sense of determined justice.

The pixie was doubtless in her belief that Yuki could make an excellent Prime Librarian.

It was almost too easy a decision, when the time came for Unisa to recruit for Alba's mission, to divulge the truth to Yuki and ask if she wanted to participate. Yuki hesitated at the thought of wielding a weapon and marching into battle, which Unisa understood, having the same reservation. But caring for Ora while Unisa meets with the other recruits is as much participation as Unisa needs from the young igni.

That and the entrance to the underground tunnels they built into Yuki's apartment floor.

Unisa descends the stairs to the ground floor and, as Yuki said it would be, her apartment door is unlocked. She closes and locks the door behind her, marching to the glass table in the middle of Yuki's sitting room. Unisa moves the table first, then the rug under it, and grabs a broom to sweep away the thick layer of sand on which the rug sat. Under the sand is a wooden door, identical to the one Unisa used to enter the SunSidian Revolution's tunnel system under Larso with Salessa.

With the help of a pixie on her team, Unisa has built an identical tunnel system under the Library, weaving around the Catacombs. She's even gone so far as to build a replica of the Bunker that Zakia built, calling it "the Nest."

The angi descends into the tunnel system, closes the wooden door behind her, and heads for the Nest. The room is built under the Center, so Unisa flaps her wings and takes flight in the tunnel, hoping to quicken the journey. When she arrives, one member of her team is already there, waiting at the table in the center of the chamber, while the other hasn't yet arrived.

The angi breathes a sigh of relief that, while she is late, she's not the last to arrive.

"Did you get my reports?" Juhi asks when Unisa lands in the Nest and folds her wings against her back. The Doruh wears a black shalwar kameez suit with her dupatta draped over her shoulders and around her head, in the same fashion that Salessa wears it.

Maybe that's why I've been missing Salessa so much, Unisa thinks as she takes a seat across the table from her Vice Ambassador.

"I did, but can we talk about anything but work?"

"Sure," Juhi says. "You made sure they weren't following you?"

Unisa nods. "Before I got into the Loops, I saw a few of them watching me, but there weren't any around here after I started my walk home. Maybe he's pulling back on them."

Juhi shakes her head. "The Prime? Pulling back on the Cicadas? You give him too much credit."

"She's right," comes a voice through the darkness at the opposite end of the chamber. The third member of their group—fourth, counting Yuki—is an indigo-skinned pixie named Konni, who'd been friends and colleagues with Alba for many years. In fact, Alba was once Konni's Vice Ambassador.

She was the second addition to the group, after Yuki. Unisa had written in a letter to Rafael that she was having difficulty recruiting for her mission, and a week later, Konni showed up at her door with a letter in Kyoko's handwriting, asking her to join the cause. Konni was enthusiastic to oblige, mentioning that she is thrilled to put her combat and weapons training to use against the Cicadas.

Juhi made a similar statement when Unisa had recruited her, after they had started to grow close during their missions together. Long personal conversations on lonely nights of traveling are a surprisingly favorable time to mention recruitment for an underground military with which one intends to demolish the political structure of the city.

"The Cicadas will never stop following you," Konni says as she sits at the table.

"Do you think he suspects something?" Unisa asks her.

"I don't think he suspects"—she gestures to the chamber around them—"*this*. But is he unsure if he can trust either of you? Absolutely. He still hasn't caught on to my involvement, perhaps because of my age. When you're as close to retirement as I am, people tend to think you don't want to be involved in things."

"We're lucky that's not the case for you," Juhi says. "I hope I'm as much of a badass when I'm fifty-eight, as you are."

"Fifty-six," Konni corrects her. "Alvaro and I are about the same age."

"It's still bizarre to me that he lets you call him that," Juhi mentions.

"I was his colleague long before he assigned Alba to be my Vice. I've known him longer than most of the people in this city have."

There's a long pause in which Juhi attempts to convey something to Unisa with her gaze, though the angi fails to pick up on her intention.

Frustrated, Juhi scoffs. "Fine, I'll ask her."

"Ask me what?" Konni raises an eyebrow.

"I have no idea," Unisa admits.

"Did you and the Prime ever..." Her eyebrows slam against her hairline over and over again until both Unisa and Konni understand what Juhi means.

Unisa slaps Juhi's shoulder. "Why would you ask that?!"

"You weren't wondering?" Juhi challenges her.

"Absolutely not. This is important, we aren't here to ask about romantic histories. This is so inappro—"

"Yes, a few times, when we were younger," Konni admits. Silence fills the room as both Juhi's and Unisa's mouths have fallen open. "But it didn't last long. He was selfish and didn't know what he was doing."

Juhi raises her hands with her palms nearly touching and slowly begins to move them further apart. "Tell me when to stop."

"Can we *please* focus and stop talking about this?" Unisa asks, feeling her dinner coming back up from her stomach.

Juhi nods. "Let's talk about recruitment. I may have someone; I'm testing him to see if he's a good candidate or not. Give me a few days and I may be able to get him on board."

"Great," Unisa approves. "Konni?"

Konni frowns. "No one yet. I've tested a few people, but anything I say that comes across as not supportive of the Prime, the Library, or our allies, they back away."

Unisa's heart sinks. "It's been a year. How are we going to complete Alba's mission with three people?"

"Four people," Juhi corrects her.

Unisa shakes her head. "I don't want to get Yuki too involved. She's young, and doesn't have any combat or weapons training."

"We're all young," Juhi says, and Konni clears her throat. "What I mean is, her youth is exactly what we need for this. I'll train her to fight."

"Not until she agrees that she wants to fight."

"What about Maksi?" Konni asks. "Any progress?"

Unisa slowly shakes her head. "Maksi is going to be the hardest to recruit."

"Then why are you still wasting time on him?" Juhi questions her. "It's been months. Find a different recruit."

"I need to know," Unisa replies. "I need to know if this can even be done. Maksi is my test. If I can break Maksi, the most Fully Bonded Librarian I know, I can break anyone."

"But you haven't broken him," Konni reminds her.

"I'm close. Give me just one more week. I have my first visit to the Inner Catacomb on the Thirtieth. That night, I'll bring Maksi here, and we break him together. I've made some small progress, but maybe it'll take all three of us to recruit him."

"I like that plan," Konni agrees.

"Fine," Juhi says. "Next week, we break Maksi. But *only* if he is going to be willing to fight for this cause. No more recruits who aren't willing to pick up a weapon."

"There's more to this than the battle," Unisa says. "We need salvers and all kinds of non-combatant recruits. I can find them, since I'm also a non-combatant."

Juhi sighs and pinches the bridge of her nose. "Uni, we've talked about this. When you recruited me, you said, 'the Prime isn't a problem that can be solved without violence.' I joined for that ideal."

"I meant it. But that doesn't mean I have to be the one engaging in that violence. I can lead. I can do so much more without sacrificing my values."

Juhi and Konni exchange a long look before Juhi speaks again. "Uni, I'm Doruh. Do you have any idea what a mission like this means for me? The Library has actively perpetuated the oppression of my species for centuries. I need justice."

Unisa nods. "I understand. And I want to help you attain it, but I'm just not willing—"

Juhi lifts a hand. "Then become willing. If we could do this without ever lifting a sword, I'd still be an enthusiastic participant. But that's not possible. For any of us. I'm ready to give my life for this cause."

She takes a long pause, seemingly measuring her words carefully. "And if I am going to die for it, I need to know that the people by my side are willing to kill for it. That I won't die for nothing." She holds steady eye contact with Unisa as she speaks her next words.

"That I will be avenged."

CHAPTER 13

"MAYHEM AND MASSACRE"

Theocracy *SunSide*
Date *23rd Day of Month 6, Year 1629 DG*

THE FOUR IGNITE THE SKY with hues of orange and purple and pink galloping across the horizon. It captures Saila's attention long enough that Kruga begins to tap his foot.

"Chief Member!" he calls to her from the other end of the city block. "May we continue now?"

Saila sighs. "How often do we get to stand in the tranquility of the Four as they retire?"

"There's no tranquility for those who serve."

"No truer words have ever been spoken." She turns back to the towering ore plate covering the side of a stone building that houses a bank on the first level, a brothel on the second and third, and a residence on the fourth.

Saila channels the Radiance through her arms to her fingertips and places them onto the ore surface, allowing the energy to flow through the metal. She steps backward and as her fingertips separate from the cold surface, it follows, pulling away from the wall, revealing the stone beneath.

When she claps, Radiant energy covers the hovering ore wall and it folds in on itself. She claps a number of times again until the once towering wall becomes a metal cube, ten feet on each side. The energy emitted from her fingertips guides the cube onto the back of a long, flatbed trailer attached to the back of a cart, which a group of laborers guides down the street toward the docks. A ship waits there to transport it to EverEmber.

The farther the trailer packed with ore gets, the wider Kruga smiles. His gaze falls to his tightly-clenched fist. "I can feel it. For the first time in so long, I can feel the natural Radiant energy in Larso flowing again."

Saila crosses her arms over her chest and leans back against the stone wall, eyes on her feet. "We're amongst the lucky few with a connection to the Radiance strong enough to feel *anything* yet. Most are waiting for us to complete the removal. To relieve them of The Ore Monger's aftermath."

Kruga steps forward and leans on the wall next to her, as if there's a mirror between them, and he is her reflection. "We can continue southeast in the morning. By next week, this quadrant will be complete."

Saila sighs. "There's still so much ore left. Red-Lo stamped every square inch of the city with it."

"We're doing the best we can, Saila. This is a substantial task, it's going to take time."

"I don't have time. You heard Rayga at the meeting. Until I can free up some laborers to send to the residential city construction projects, we're stuck in a housing crisis. I can't let over half the city sit in shelters for the next two years. I need to find workers, fast."

Kruga frowns. "You're putting a lot of pressure on yourself. Have some—" He stops abruptly. "Ovida."

"Have some Ovida?" Saila turns to him, an eyebrow raised.

He lifts a finger and points over Saila's shoulder. She turns to see the General of the New SunSidian Guard, as well as four other warriors, hastily charging toward them in a cart led by two pronghorn antelope.

She's hopped out before it's even fully stopped, her concerned expression igniting anxiety in Saila's chest. The General leans in close to Saila and Kruga. "I need to speak with both of you urgently. Is there somewhere private close by?"

Saila scans the surroundings, but they're standing in a heavily commercial area. A private location will be hard to find. Her eyes rise and an idea comes to her. "The roof." She turns to Kruga. "I'll take Ovida up first, and then I'll come back and get you."

The nymph shakes his head and returns his gaze to his fist. "No, I think I can teleport again. Let me try." He turns to the General. "Coming with me, Ovida?"

"While you *try* to teleport?" She raises an eyebrow. "Not a chance. I'll go with the flier."

Saila wraps an arm around Ovida's waist, while the General holds tightly to her shoulders, and together they float up onto the stone building delicately, two feathers dancing in the wind. Kruga joins them a moment later, scans his body, and then smiles when he realizes he's arrived in one piece.

"Is it the Bravers United?" Saila deduces from Ovida's urgency.

The General nods. "One of my spies picked up whispers at a minister's home. His son is a warrior, high in their ranks. Next attack is coming."

"When?"

Ovida hesitates. "In less than an hour. At the Temple Complex."

Saila's heart sinks into her stomach. Sacred grounds. Filled with worshippers. "We have to go. Now. It'll take us at least twenty minutes to get there, and then we have to get into position."

Mind focused, she starts to rise into the air when Ovida's fingers wrap around her wrist and grab Saila's attention. The pixie, still airborne, turns back to face the General.

"He'll be there this time." Ovida's tone hardens with clarity.

Saila knows exactly what she means. Tund-Ra will come out of hiding for this attack.

"This is it, Saila. We can't lose him. Again."

Saila nods and doesn't say anything further. Ovida is right; if they miss this opportunity, and the leader of the Bravers United gets away again, after attacking the theocracy's most hallowed community, it'll not only put the kingdom at further risk, but it'll make the Chief Member, her General, her administration, and the entire SunSidian Guard seem incompetent to citizens.

And it'll exalt Tund-Ra from a common criminal to an unstoppable demon. It'll ravage any sense of safety amongst SunSidians.

Just as Frona, the last of the suns, touches the horizon, Saila arrives at the vast compound of shrines, ablution fountains, stone tilework, and shimmering golden monuments.

"Ovida, Kruga, you're with me," she instructs them, marching through the complex. "The ore has been stripped away from the area; you and the Guard should all have access to the Radiance here. How long until they arrive?"

Ovida looks to Frona. "Less than half an hour."

The SunSidian Guards enter the shrines and temples, clearing out any worshippers and taking their places to await the Bravers United attack. Saila leads Ovida and Kruga into the tunnels that the food hall workers use to transport meals and kitchen carts.

The three Mega discuss the plan of attack until they reach a circular chamber with six exits leading in different directions.

"I think we should take the north exit to the ablution fountains," Ovida suggests. "The city opens up there. That's their attack point."

"No, it isn't," Kruga argues. "The southeast corridor is where the most worshippers enter and the Bravers United have been growing more violent in their unrest. We need to protect the southeast or there will be casualties."

Saila opens her mouth to interject, but before she can produce a sound, something catches the corner of her vision. It happens so fast, she reacts purely on adrenaline. She doesn't even realize her hand is raised until the dagger soaring through the air makes contact with her palm, which is alight with the Radiance.

The dagger touches her skin and disintegrates into dust. Originally headed straight for the back of Kruga's head, it now flows away in the wind, a stream of sand. Instinctually, Saila has pulled him behind her protectively.

Ovida unsheathes two long swords, one from each hip, while Kruga's palms glow with energy as well. The three Mega get into formation, back-to-back-to-back, until they're circling around the chamber taking in the sight. In each of the six tunnels leading to the surface, Saila can count at least fifty Bravers United warriors closing in on them.

The three officials face a horde of well over three hundred.

"I thought we had half an hour," Kruga whispers to Ovida.

"They knew we were coming. It's an—"

"Ambush." Saila completes the sentence.

As soon as the word slips from her lips, the daggers fly again. Hundreds of them from all directions. Quickly, Saila balls her fists and raises them to the ceiling. A shimmering barrier of purple light rises and the daggers slam into it like birds on a washed window, then clank down onto the ground just outside of it.

After a few moments of failure, the Bravers United charge forth and attempt to break through the barrier with their weapons. The pressure of their attacks mounts, as Saila struggles to keep the walls of light up.

"Pick it up from me, Kruga," she murmurs through gritted teeth.

Kruga obeys, raising his own barrier of energy so Saila can lower hers and take a deep breath.

After a moment to think, she signals to Kruga to drop the barrier and he does. The opposing forces charge forth, swords and axes and maces raised overhead. Saila spins and blows at them, exhaling every ounce of air in her lungs with ice crystals streaming from her throat and freezing the first two rows of warriors in place, as Kruga and Ovida duck to avoid the frigid air.

Kruga slams his fist into the ground and a circular shockwave of energy blasts outward, shattering the icy warriors into tiny pieces as if they were made of glass. The ones in the rows behind step over the fragments of their fallen comrades' bodies to continue the charge.

Ovida surges green Radiant energy through her arm and into her blade. She throws the weapon as hard as she can, sending it circling around the three officials, mowing down warriors like blades of grass.

As the General's blade circles them through the air, Saila and Kruga pull energy into their eyeballs and, ignoring the sear in their nerves, blast the energy out of their eyes as beams of burning light. It pierces through the rows of oncoming warriors, a hot knife through butter, until another dagger soars through the air toward them. Saila blinks to stop the eye beam and tries to catch the dagger, but misses. It speeds past her and hits Kruga in the shoulder, knocking him backward.

At the same time, another warrior knocks Ovida's circling sword out of the air and charges at her with a battle cry. Many follow and within seconds, Ovida is facing a legion of former Bravers alone, cornered into a wall.

Saila looks around and acknowledges how dire the situation is. Kruga on his back, armed warriors pouncing on him; Ovida against the wall, the Bravers closing in. Two hundred more inches from the Chief Member herself.

Time slows as she reacts to the mayhem and the massacre. There's no survival in extreme circumstances without extreme measures. She channels all of the Radiant energy in her body to her palms, releasing it into a dense glowing ball between her hands. Tighter and tighter, she adds more pressure to it until it's ready to detonate with the heat of the suns.

And then it explodes.

The energy, pressurized and superheated, discharges in every direction. The force is so powerful it rattles the world. The warriors closest to her are immediately incinerated into ash. Those a few feet away melt, leaving puddles of their organs behind. And those further away scream as they ignite into flames that quickly consume them.

Saila drops to her knees, the world spinning around her. Every single warrior who walked into the tunnel is now dead, leaving Kruga and Ovida in stunned silence.

Sweat drips from Saila's temples, as blood runs from her nose. Ovida places her hand on the Chief Member's shoulders and helps her stand. Her knees buckle. She's too weak to stand on her own, so she leans on Ovida for support. They start to make their way out of the tunnel, wading through a sea of blood and bodies, with Kruga following closely behind clutching his wounded shoulder.

When they get out of the tunnel, through the haze of her exhaustion, she finds more bloodshed. The SunSidian Guards she had ordered to secure the temples and shrines must have walked into ambushes as well. Much of the military lies dead around the Temple Complex with Bravers United warriors hovering over them, celebrating joyously.

Saila has never, in her life, felt such overwhelming defeat.

"There," Kruga says, pulling her attention from the battle in the Complex to an escaping group of warriors beyond its gates.

"Why are they running when they're winning?" Ovida asks.

Saila recognizes the violet-skinned warrior escaping. "Because Tund-Ra is a coward."

"He's too far now, Saila," Ovida responds. "We have to finish the battle here in the Complex or we'll lose more Guards."

"I'm finishing this everywhere," Saila says. Collecting what little energy she has left, she pushes Ovida away then rises into the air. Her consciousness begins to fade as her flight begins to waver.

Come on, she wills herself. *Almost there.*

When she gets high enough that she believes her plan will work, she turns around and flies straight back down towards the ground. Saila knows how to use the Radiance to paralyze an individual. Perhaps even two or three at a time. But in order to accomplish what she hopes to, she'll need an impact that will spread her energy out in all directions.

She gathers all the Radiant energy in her body into her fist, aimed at paralyzing every Bravers United warrior, and Tund-Ra, where they stand. When she reaches the ground again, she strikes it as hard as she can.

The tiles of the Templex Complex shatter as the punch forms a crater under the Chief Member. From the epicenter, her paralysis magic races out of her fist and expands until every Bravers United warrior is stilled in place.

Kruga leaps down into the crater beside Saila.

"Arrest them," she whispers as her vision starts to darken, and she falls into Kruga's arms.

He channels the Radiance into his larynx and when he speaks, his voice echoes throughout the city. "Guards! Arrest Tund-Ra and the Bravers United. By the will of the Four, the Chief Member commands you!"

The surviving Guards step forth and either shackle the former Bravers at the wrist, or sever them at the throat.

By the time her vision completely goes dark, by the time her senses fail, the Bravers United warriors are either dead or cuffed. The last thing Saila hears before she loses consciousness are Kruga's whispers.

"You did it, Saila. You got Tund-Ra."

CHAPTER 14

"And What Did You See?"

***Theocracy** SunSide*
***Date** Unknown*

GET UP, PUP.

Red-Lo towers over Naina and commands her. The wolf remains seated in the white void, her knees to her chest, arms wrapped around them. Her swollen eyes release despondent droplets with every blink, as her thoughts remain on Sarfaraz, the Doruh servant who, centuries before she was born, was subjected to the horrors of bondage.

Horrors familiar to all Doruh. Sarfaraz was just one of so many; a heartbreak from which the shapeshifters now, generations later, still feels the pain.

You have to get over it and we have to move on.

Get over it? Naina looks up and her gaze travels with flaming rage. *What kind of egomania gives a perpetrator the right to tell someone to 'get over it?'*

Red-Lo shrugs. *It's just the way things were.*

And? Did they not come to learn that shackling other humans and treating them as property is a moral failing? She stands. *You want me to get over a history that faeries can't forget. There are still monuments up in Larso displaying your heroes, those who owned Doruh as property.*

And so many more of our monuments have been replaced, erasing faerie footprints from SunSide. My tongue burns every time I say Nivyan Hollow. That forest was first named after a great faerie warrior. And then a pixie Mega-Mother renamed it.

Naina reaches deep into her memories of the few conversations she's had with Salessa on SunSidian history. She wishes now she had paid more attention, but she presents what she remembers.

Nivyan was a minister, wasn't he? He designed the legislation that eventually became Doruh Liberation.

Red-Lo nods.

Naina's thoughts float back to the Mega of Nivyan Hollow. Symin's family and loved ones and the unbridled joy of their communities, protected amongst the Radiance of the forest.

She steps toward the door behind Red-Lo. *His name still shelters the pixies and nymphs from you. We will get over it, Red-Lo, the day we are bathed in justice. But while our lands are occupied, while we are subjected to both literal violence and the rhetorical violence of your monuments, we will always remember.*

She wraps her fingers around the doorknob and turns, entering the next memory of Red-Lo's mind. *And we will remind you, too.*

Red-Lo follows her through the door and when he shuts it behind him, it vanishes. They now stand on a crowded street in Larso.

When is this? Naina asks.

Eight years after the first memory, 763 DG.

That would make you fifteen?

Red-Lo nods.

Where are you? And why have you brought me here?

Red-Lo gestures at the crowd amassed ahead of them, more Mega joining by the minute. They congregate at the foot of a makeshift stage. *This is another core memory for me. I'm somewhere in the crowd and Drof-Fa is standing next to me. We're waiting for my father to speak.*

A knot thickens in the pit of Naina's stomach. *Your father is the last person I want to hear from.*

I've told you before, pup. You're not in control here. You'll stand and you'll listen.

My name is Naina.

I don't care.

Red-Lo's father appears at the head of the crowd, turquoise arms raised, clad in armor with a sword slinging from his waist. The crowd chants for him, "Zif-Lo! Zif-Lo! Zif-Lo!"

"My brothers and sisters! My faerie countrymen! Where we stand now, here in this spot"—he gestures widely to the street below their feet—"once stood Rom-Ap the Citizen." Cheers erupt from the crowd at the named faerie. "SunSide's first MegaParent after the institution of the monarchy, was a faerie. The theocracy knew that such a magnificent responsibility could only be borne by the mighty shoulders of our kind."

So the egoism is genetic, Naina comments to Red-Lo, who ignores her.

Zif-Lo continues. "Do you know why they called Rom-Ap, 'the Citizen?' He was truly a faerie of the populace. He listened and elevated and empowered. Rom-Ap was a shining example of the power of a faerie's heart, as much as of his body."

More cheers from the crowd, more nausea for Naina.

"But now a time has come when the monarchy is in the hands of a pixie." The crowd erupts into jeers. "Picana doesn't value all citizens equally. She doesn't want us to remember Rom-Ap the Citizen, or any of our heroes. She wants to erase faerie footprints from our schools, our cities, our landmarks and monuments."

Naina shakes her head. *All of this because she removed a supremacist from her administration?*

My father fought for so much more than himself. Picana replaced countless faeries in the social and political structure. She made it so that more pixies and nymphs were accepted into universities than faeries.

Naina scoffs. *How many faeries were gifted enrollment into universities for generations before that because their wealthy parents donated a building?*

Nonsense. Faeries earned the right to attendance, many continuing generational legacies. Nymphs and pixies were handed enrollment based on clan, not merit.

Naina raises an eyebrow. *How do you know that? You researched this?*

It was a well-known fact.

Amongst whom?

A frown plays on his lips. *Everyone. But mostly our kind. No other community cared about the injustices against us.*

Naina pauses, hoping to frame her next statement in a way that Red-Lo might be receptive. *Injustice to anyone is an injustice to everyone. But perhaps what your clan saw as an injustice, wasn't that at all.*

Then what was it, pup?

Some semblance of balance, correction, in an unjust world where not everyone is born into generational legacies. Because their ancestors weren't given the opportunity to form such.

Red-Lo turns to her. His expression remains blank, void of emotion. He doesn't agree with her, he doesn't smile, he doesn't in any way give an indication that her words stuck with him, or that he is contemplating the depth of her statement.

But he doesn't discount her either.

Naina's attention is drawn back to the squawking sermon of the supremacist on the makeshift stage.

"We will not allow Picana and her so-called *progressive* ideals to erase the true history of our clan. The faeries built SunSide, and the kingdom has thrived on our shoulders. We will not be replaced!"

Naina watches, eyes wide, disgust brewing in her chest, as the faeries in the surging crowd raise their fists and chant in unison, "We will not be replaced! We will not be replaced!"

Here it comes. Red-Lo raises a finger to a narrow alleyway from which warriors of the royal SunSidian Guard flow with the current of a river.

Zif-Lo unsheathes his sword and yells, "First lines! Attack!"

A long row of Doruh men and women, young and old, tall and short, clad in servant rags, step forward through the crowd, terror and dejection painted on their expressions.

Naina's heart sinks deeply and powerfully. *No.*

The Doruh shift into their animal forms, tearing through their clothes, and charge forth at the SunSidian Guard, the warriors of the MegaMother who was fighting to liberate them. But there was no other choice available. They were still shackled and the command had been delivered.

The smaller animals—the snakes, the capybara, the wolverines, the otters—are slain indiscriminately with haste. The larger ones—the lions, elephants, the stags, the wolves, the buffalo—face groups of warriors who take a few minutes to slaughter them.

None of the Doruh survive. They were commanded to their deaths and while they fought, the faeries got their opportunity to either flee, hide, or strategize their next move. The Doruh servants had been sacrificed, protecting those who viewed them as property, from a monarch who knew they were people.

How could your father do that to them?

Red-Lo pauses, taking a deep breath as he watches the Doruh being cut down. *He was the commander of the resistance. Battle strategy was his expertise, and acting as living shields was the greatest duty the beasts could serve.*

Naina shakes her head. Her mind refuses to accept the scene her eyes digest. The faeries occupied her home for centuries, and justified it by spreading the lie that the Doruh resistance fighters in MoonSide were using civilians as living shields.

But it wasn't the Doruh who committed such unforgivable crimes, it was the faeries themselves.

This is what the faeries accused us of. Bravers raided our villages and massacred our children. And then told everyone they were being used as living shields. Her heartbreak manifests into tears. *But we didn't do that. You did.*

Red-Lo doesn't turn to her. His eyes remain focused on the battle, his lips pressed tightly together.

You have nothing to say? You're just going to stand there and call them beasts and sacrifice them as if they don't matter.

They… He pauses. *At the time, we didn't think they mattered.*

And what about now? Naina's tone hardens as she swallows and clears her throat before addressing him. *Watching this back eight centuries later, do you see it any differently?*

She turns to look out at the battle ahead of them and finds fifteen year-old Red-Lo in the crowd, smiling as his face and body are splashed with the blood of the SunSidian Guard.

I know that bloodthirsty fifteen-year-old didn't think the Doruh mattered because his hateful, supremacist father taught him that they didn't matter. But you've lived through forty-six generations now. Tell me you see it differently.

There's a long pause in which Naina truly believes that Red-Lo will not respond to her. But then he exhales deeply and whispers, *I've never looked into their eyes before.*

And what did you see?

Another long pause as Red-Lo's expression contorts as if he's in pain. Then, he shakes his head and finally turns to the wolf. *Nothing. I saw nothing. And we're done with this memory, it's almost time to move on.*

Naina's tongue refuses to move. She can't imagine how a being who's lived forty-six lives, through eight centuries, can refuse to accept that he may have been wrong about something. Doesn't humility come with age? Don't wrinkles shatter hubris?

The former MegaFather snaps his fingers and the scene around them changes slightly. The four suns jump forward in their arc, casting brilliant shades of purples and pinks and oranges across the horizon. Warriors of both the SunSidian Guard and the Faerie Empowerment Forces go from bellowing battle cries and charging into battle, to laying severed across the city streets, bleeding into the drains.

In the center of it all, fifteen-year-old Red-Lo sits, drenched in crimson from hair-to-toenail, cradling his father in his lap. The boy rocks back-and-forth, as his father raises a hand and places it on his cheek. An open wound is visible on Zif-Lo's side, bleeding out onto the ground profusely. When he speaks, his voice is so strained, Naina has to lean in to hear him.

"You lead now, son," he says to Red-Lo.

The boy shakes his head, tears streaming down his face. "I can find a salver, Father. I can get help, just wait here."

"Shhh, quiet, Red-Lo. Have I taught you nothing? Dying for faerie empowerment is the most honorable way to make your Radiance-Return. Stop crying and promise me something."

Red-Lo nods through his sobs. "An-anything, Father."

"Do not let the faeries be forgotten. Do not let us be erased or replaced." He vomits blood, coughs and continues. "Who are we?"

"The ma-master clan. We are to rule over others as we were born superior. We are conquerors and we will have our justice."

Zif-Lo's head falls slack and he dies smiling. The legacy of faerie supremacy lives on.

A snap of Red-Lo's fingers ends the memory and draws Naina's attention away from the scene. They are in the white void again, between memories. A door to the next alcove of Red-Lo's consciousness appears behind them. Without a word, the faerie reminds the wolf that he is still in control.

But when Naina looks up to his face, she realizes his cheeks are as slick as those of the fifteen-year-old Red-Lo who held his dying father in his arms. There was so much in this memory that Red-Lo wanted

Naina to see. There was a perspective that he wanted to show her, but it appears that, by the end of it, he has seen something he wasn't expecting to as well.

As he turns and reaches for the doorknob into the next memory, poorly trying to hide his tear-stricken face from Naina, she starts to wonder for the first time since this journey began.

How much control does Red-Lo truly have?

CHAPTER 15

"SALVATION"

Alphocracy *MoonSide*
Date *23rd Day of Month 6, Year 1629 DG*

CAN YOU HEAR ME, NAINA?

Salessa reaches out with her mind again, touching the inner walls of the hollowed mountain with her consciousness. It doesn't reach the world outside, and it certainly doesn't reach SunSide, but Salessa is desperate now for her sister's thoughts. For the wolf's voice and tone and personality joining her mind, connecting with her.

The divine energy that coursed through her veins when she touched the entrance to Lover's Plateau no longer extends the reach of her telepathy.

I wonder how you're doing without me. Do you miss me as much as I miss you? She scoffs. *Probably not. When I get back, I'll probably find you sharing a chai with Kruga after work, and you won't even remember my name.*

She pauses. *Alright, now I'm being dramatic. Naina, don't be angry with me for going with Lexona. I haven't forgotten what she did to us. I'll never forget or forgive. But this isn't about us. It's about the innocents who deserve to be—*

A knock at the bedroom door interrupts her thoughts. Salessa springs up to a seated position and peeks at the clock hanging on the wall: a metal square with four circular panels displayed on it. Only one panel is lit, indicating only the first of the suns has risen. It's still quite early in the morning. She'll have to rely on this technology to know what time it is, unable to verify the positions of the suns herself within the mountain.

"Coming," she responds to the knock. The falcon struggles to rise from the cloud of a bed. Soft, in the most uncomfortable way.

Her strides across the room are long and quick, and it still takes a few seconds before she gets to the door. The bedroom could've held the entire hut in which they lived in Evic. There's no one in the hallway when she opens the door. She leans her head out and looks in either direction, but it's empty.

"Is the Falcon Goddess ready to be bathed?" the high-pitched voice asks.

Salessa nearly jumps from her skin when she hears it, until she looks down and finds two young girls, teenagers, sitting on their knees in the doorway. The one on the left is wearing a plain, dark green shalwar kameez, while the other is wearing a light brown outfit, the color of chai.

"Please, get up," she begs them. The girls stand. "You don't have to do that."

They appear confused and the one who spoke earlier, in the dark green, asks, "Do what, my Goddess?"

Salessa sighs. "You don't have to get on your knees, and please just call me by name."

Light Brown nods. "Alright, Salessa. Are you ready for your bath?" She lifts up a bucket with two sponges in it.

Salessa forces a polite smile onto her face. "I can bathe myself, thank you."

The cheer in their expressions melts away. They exchange a confused glance and then Dark Green responds, "I'm certain you *can*, Godde—" She pauses. "Salessa. But why would you?"

Now it's Salessa's turn to battle confusion.

Dark Green elaborates. "Our parents have been members of the O'Raha their whole lives, as our grandparents and ancestors were. As we are. Most of the Doruh who moved to Lover's Plateau after Afzal and the Serpent Goddess reopened the entrance have been raised under the expectation that if the four Doruh of the One Myth were to be born in our lifetime, it would be our duty to serve them."

She takes the bucket and sponges from Light Brown and holds it up, displaying it for Salessa. "Why would you bathe yourself when we have been waiting to bathe you every moment for the sixteen years of our lives? Generations of our ancestors came and went from this world, praying that you would be born in *their* lifetimes so they could serve you. It would be an honor to complete my duty."

The weight of the girl's words are not lost on the falcon. The Twins died in 71 DG, fifteen hundred years before Lexona and Afzal reopened Lover's Plateau and allowed the O'Raha to return. In all those centuries, the group went into hiding in MoonSide, but they never stopped believing. They never stopped passing down the One Myth. These families have waited generations to serve the ones who will resurrect the Twins.

They've waited over a thousand years to serve Salessa.

Her breath catches in her throat, as heat rises to her cheeks and her chest tightens. She inhales deeply to quell the rising discomfort. "I think I need to sit down," she whispers.

The teenagers' expressions contort with concern and they step through the doorway and into the room, helping Salessa to her bed.

"Would you like us to come back and bathe you later?" Light Brown asks.

Salessa shakes her head. "I appreciate your"—she pauses, feeling crass just saying the word—"devotion, and the thoughts you shared with me, but I'd like to bathe myself. Please, just leave the bucket and you can go."

She feels guilty when she sees their expressions dim, but regardless of how it disappoints them, there was no world in which she would allow two teenagers, or anyone for that matter, bathe her. The girls leave the bucket, then bow respectfully and exit the room, leaving Salessa to wrap her head around the candor of the information they offered.

Everyone she meets here at Lover's Plateau will be a member of the O'Raha. She'll be telling hundreds of people each day to get up off of their knees and to call her by her name. A wave of uneasiness drowns her. Never before has she felt a need to escape as strongly as she feels now. Her chest tightens again and she forces breaths. Lightheadedness clouds her mind as the room blurs.

I'm alright, I'm alright, she repeats, rubbing her chest until her heart relaxes.

Another knock echoes throughout the room.

Oh, great. What now?

Slowly, she rises to her feet and, when she feels stable on them, she moves to the door and opens it. A familiar face finds her on the other side. Zoya looks the falcon up-and-down, then frowns.

"I'm so sorry, Salessa," she apologizes. "I had asked Mehek and Laila to come help you with your morning bath, they should've been here already. I'll go find them and—"

"They came," Salessa tells her, and relief washes over the mare's expression. "I asked them to leave."

Zoya raises an eyebrow. "Were they not doing it well? Shall I take their place?"

Salessa raises her hands. "No, please! I just want to bathe myself."

"Is everything alright, Salessa?" Zoya asks, her expression darkening. "You're looking pale, and you're sweating. Here let me help you." She takes Salessa's arm and helps her back to the bed. "Are you unwell? Shall I get the salver?"

Salessa shakes her head. "I'm not unwell, I've just fallen out of the boat without knowing how to swim."

"What do you mean?"

Salessa hesitates, unsure how to articulate her discomfort.

"Zoya, until last year, the One Myth didn't matter. I mean, it *mattered,* and it has for a long time, I understand that. But once Naina and I escaped the Facilitator and went into hiding, we just continued our lives. We went to school, we got jobs, we had dinner together while she was recovering from a fight, slept on our hard cots, and we shared some laughs as we talked about our day. We were—" She struggles to complete the sentence.

"Not bathed by anyone," Zoya assists her with a soft smile.

Salessa nods and her breathing finally becomes regular again. "Yes. We were not served, and I don't think I want to be. I'm just Salessa."

Zoya laughs. "You are 'just Salessa' for you. But for them"—she gestures to the door—"you are so much more. It's not about *who* you are. For them, it's about what you represent."

"Resurrection?"

"Salvation. The resurrection is a means to that salvation, but what you truly represent is the key to the Twins' triumph in the battle to come. The triumph that will save us all."

Somehow, the weight on Salessa's shoulders grows heavier with these words. The triumph of saviors, a battle between good and evil, the resurrection of powerful deities, all rest on the wings of a four-pound falcon.

Zoya frowns. "I apologize. I was trying to make you feel better, and I think I've failed miserably."

Salessa shakes her head. "It's not you. It's everything here. The pressure, the people."

"Everyone here means well, Salessa, they're just excited that this is happening in their lifetime."

"That's the worst part," the falcon groans. "I know they aren't *trying to* make me feel uncomfortable, but how can I be comfortable with people serving me? When the Twins dictated the One Myth to the original O'Raha, and they talked about the four Doruh who will resurrect them, did they ask the O'Raha to treat us like deities?"

Zoya nods. "Oh, yes."

"I don't remember ever hearing or reading about that."

The mare smiles. "There's more to the One Myth than what you've heard about. Much more. The original O'Raha, our ancestors, recorded decades of visions that the Twins had throughout their lifetimes about their resurrection, and about the four Doruh who would resurrect them. What was passed down in oral tradition is a fraction of what we know, and how we were instructed to serve you when the time comes."

"I can't do it," Salessa says, burying her face in her hands. "After our people spent so long in shackles. I can't have Doruh serving me. We served others for too long."

"Bondage is very different from worship, Salessa."

Worship. The word nauseates her.

Zoya continues. "The Doruh didn't choose to be subjugated by the faeries. They didn't choose to be herded by the walls of occupation." She gestures to the bucket and sponges by their feet. "But when I told those girls they had been selected to assist you with your morning bath, they wept in gratitude. They felt the weight of all the generations of their ancestors who had lived and died praying that they would one day be able to serve you in some capacity."

Salessa pulls her hands from her face and meets Zoya's gaze. "Would it—" she hesitates. "Would it be horrible if I asked them all to stop treating me this way while I'm here? To see me as another resident of Lover's Plateau and not to look at me as anything more than myself?"

Zoya pauses, and her eyebrows scrunch with strain, as if she's having trouble articulating her thoughts. "May I speak freely?"

"Please. I would appreciate that very much."

Zoya breathes in and exhales deeply. "People will search for gods and goddesses in all kinds of things. In the suns, in a temple on a mountaintop, in the heart of a volcano, in a young Doruh woman who can shift into a falcon. But when they look for that divine spirit, they're all simply searching for the same thing."

Salessa leans closer. "What are they searching for?"

"The answers to the questions that scare them. Why does thunder strike? What happens after you die? Why has this hardship or that struggle befallen me?" She smiles again and holds firm eye contact with Salessa. "Who will save us?"

Salessa's understanding of the O'Raha perspective mounts. She can relate to a fear of the unknown, as, she believes, most individuals can, regardless of clans or species.

Zoya continues. "There are two things that spirituality provides to those who seek it out: the answers to their questions, and a community to share those answers with. Surely, you can understand what it means to search for a community."

Memories are brought to life in Salessa's mind; a tall, pink nymph with a beard knocking on her door in the middle of the night and offering her exactly what she needed. Exactly what the O'Raha need.

A community. And something to bring that community together. The way Symin did for her and Naina.

"Believing in me has kept these people together for generations," Salessa responds, feeling the connection to the O'Raha she was missing.

Zoya nods. "It has. Please don't take that from them." The mare stands. "I can't ask you to transgress your comfort zone to appease them. But maybe I can ask you to consider their dogma, and their long-standing desire to uphold it, when you see them bow or ask to assist you in some way."

Salessa smiles and nods slowly. "A bow is better than kneeling."

"I'll send word out throughout Lover's Plateau, for the O'Raha to tame their kneeling, and to resist the urge to act on their duties as best as they can." She starts to exit, but when she reaches the door, Salessa calls out to her and the mare turns back around.

"Thank you," Salessa says. "I'm sorry for my resistance, this is just very new to me. But the conversation has helped me feel a little better."

Zoya returns her smile. "It's been my honor to serve you," she responds with a short, respectful bow, then winks and exits.

Salessa remains on the bed for a few minutes, staring at the bucket and sponges. Perhaps Naina would've been more comfortable here than Salessa is. Then again, Naina would've never followed Lexona here at all. But Salessa has, and now she has to make the most of her time here; has to live as fate ascribed. She picks up the items and takes them to the tub.

And the Goddess bathes herself.

CHAPTER 16
"BROKEN HISTORY"

Alphocracy *MoonSide*
Date *23rd Day of Month 6, Year 1629 DG*

THE BATH IS WARM AND refreshing. Salessa cleanses herself of the grime of travel and the night's perspiration. She pulls down the towel draped over the curtain rod, dries her body, and then wraps her wet hair as she steps back out to the main bedroom.

Zoya is sitting on the bed. She hears Salessa approach and takes to her feet, as Salessa realizes she isn't alone and jumps back. The falcon quickly pulls the towel down from her hair and wraps it around her body.

How are you so comfortable with being naked all the time, Naina? She knows there won't be any response, but she asks out of habit and imagines how her sister would respond, mimicking Naina's tone in her head. *What do I have to be ashamed of?*

"I didn't mean to startle you, Salessa," Zoya says with an apologetic bow. "The Serpent Goddess had some new clothes pressed for you and she asked me to deliver them, before you join her and Afzal for breakfast."

Salessa responds as she steps closer to Zoya. "Afzal, Salessa, and"—she pauses—"the Serpent Goddess?"

"We adhere to the wishes of each deity individually. You and Afzal both requested we use your names; however, the Serpent Goddess has made no such request."

Salessa nods. "I know, Afzal told me yesterday. I just can't believe she wants you to call her that."

"We are most honored to oblige to her wishes. Speaking of wishes, I've relayed your desire for bowing to replace the kneeling to the O'Raha elders. They will make it known to all."

"Thank you," Salessa says, reaching the bed. A fresh outfit is laid out over it: a golden silk saree shimmering with intricate floral patterns embroidered throughout. The garment is delicate and glamorous and elegant and...

Not Salessa.

"It's a saree fit for a queen."

"It is," Zoya agrees. "But it is also just fabric, like any other clothing."

"I brought my own clothes for my travels. Can't I wear those?"

Zoya laughs. "You are a goddess. You can wear whatever it is that you like. No one can tell you what to wear, or what not to." She looks down at the exquisite outfit. "Perhaps the Serpent Goddess thought you would appreciate the gift."

"The Serpent Goddess cannot buy atonement."

Zoya frowns. "I'm sorry?"

"Nothing, sorry." Salessa shakes her head. "You can tell Lexona I'll join her and Afzal for breakfast shortly. Don't say anything about the saree, I haven't decided what I'm going to wear yet."

Zoya bows respectfully again. "As you wish."

She exits the chamber leaving Salessa alone with the scintillating saree. The longer she stares at it, the harder her heart beats. Donning this magnificent garment brings her another step closer to the divinity she's actively been avoiding. What good is it to end the kneeling if she's still dressing and acting like she's above everyone?

She breathes deeply and reminds herself: *It's only fabric. It's only fabric.*

"It's very expensive and shiny fabric," she whispers to herself. With her eyes locked on it, the decision becomes clear to her.

Everything is long and large at Lover's Plateau. Inside a hollowed mountain, there is plenty of room. Salessa's bedroom is large, the hallway to the main atrium is long, the atrium itself is vast, and it opens up to a wide dining room, in the middle of which rests a grand table with twenty or more chairs. There's a plate and utensils resting at each spot, though only one seat is occupied: the one in which Lexona sits.

Rows of candlesticks in elegant candelabras sit in rigid formation along the table, lit and inviting. A number of O'Raha members, including Zoya, stand at the edges of the chamber, their hands folded before them. They appear ready to take any commands that Salessa or Lexona might give. As the falcon passes each of them, they bow their heads respectfully toward her.

They got the message.

Salessa approaches the table and finds Lexona in a sophisticated navy blue saree, her hair flowing down her shoulders, a soft, charming red color on her lips, and kohl decorating her eyes. Neither the patch of scaly serpentine skin on her cheek, nor the fangs or the flicking tongue, take an ounce of Lexona's beauty from her.

This is the woman who, only three years prior, shattered Salessa. Attempted to steal her escape funds. The woman who Naina left in pieces and, had she not been divine, wouldn't have survived. *Should* never have survived.

And yet, despite everything that happened between them, despite the hatred she knows she should feel for the serpent, seeing her this way lights a warmth deep in Salessa's core. She swallows hard and shakes her head, trying to rid herself of the thoughts and feelings brewing inside.

Lexona watches Salessa enter and her eyes trek from the falcon's hair to her toes. She frowns when she notices Salessa wearing her own clothes and not the lavish saree that was pressed and laid out for her.

"You didn't like the saree?" Lexona asks as Salessa takes the seat at the opposite end of the table. Their seats span the entire length of it, yet, it somehow still feels too intimate.

"It was stunning," she responds honestly.

Lexona smiles. "Perhaps you can change into it later, if you'd like."

"If you remembered anything about me, you'd know that I absolutely would not like."

Lexona's expression melts again. "I'm sorry, I know it isn't your style, but—"

"You don't know anything about me, Lexona. Not anymore."

Lexona stares blankly at her in stunned silence, her jaw slack. She clearly wasn't expecting breakfast to be served with a piping hot side of hostility. Salessa almost feels guilty for the way she's speaking to her former lover.

Almost.

Lexona turns to Zoya, tone rock solid, fangs clenched. "Where is Afzal?"

Zoya's cheeks glow red as she responds. "He was up early this morning, hunting in the jungle. Now, he's resting on his favorite branch."

"Go get him," Lexona hisses between tongue-flicks. "Tell him breakfast is ready."

Zoya bows deeply and says, "Yes, Serpent Goddess." Then turns and exits down the long hallway, leaving the falcon and the serpent in a room full of O'Raha onlookers and tense silence.

Salessa breaks it with venom. "I see you haven't asked them to stop calling you, 'Serpent Goddess.' You're relishing in the control. The attention. The power."

"I see you haven't accepted your place in the Doruh hierarchy. You're *afraid* of the control. The attention. The power."

Salessa's blood boils over. "There is no Doruh hierarchy."

"The Twins created a hierarchy. It died with them and has been reborn with us."

Salessa scoffs. "There must be no room for a heart in your chest when you're filled with so much self-importance. We were two children, in Evic, just trying to survive the Bravers. Now you're the Serpent Goddess?"

"I am. And you're the Falcon Goddess. What's wrong with that, Salessa? I've spent three years here learning about our fate, practicing the teachings of the O'Raha, taking on the heavy responsibilities of being a leader that people will want to follow. I am damn proud of being a Goddess and there is absolutely no reason why you shouldn't be either."

"There is a reason. They call it the One *Myth*, right? Then this could all be a lie. A tale. Myths are inherently folklore, Lexona."

The serpent shakes her head. "No. Myths are inherently legendary. That doesn't make it untrue, it makes *us* legends."

Salessa scoffs again, unable to bear the self-obsession across the table. "You will truly never change."

"But I already have, Salessa, in so many ways."

"Then prove it. Show me how you've changed. The only way that this entire journey can move forward productively is if I know you aren't the same girl who betrayed me and Naina three years ago."

"Then let's talk about what happened. Let me apologize, and persuade Naina to allow me to make amends. Whether you or your sister like it, the One Myth bonds us all and we can't create a future together on broken history." She pauses, holding firm eye contact with Salessa, as if steeling herself to deliver a difficult confession.

"Salessa," she breathes through her flicking tongue and fangs, "you know how much I care about you…how much I…" She pauses again and Salessa's heart drops.

Please don't say it.

"You know how much I lov—"

Salessa's hand shoots up, silencing the serpent. "Don't you fucking dare say that to me."

Pain evident in her gaze, Lexona leans back in her seat, just as the wide doors of the hall burst open. The leopard enters, a smile on his muzzle, and a cheerful hop in his gait. Zoya enters quietly behind him and closes the doors.

He wears a shalwar, but no shirt. Salessa's eyes traverse the anatomy of his upper body; the skin on his shoulders, chest, and the segmented muscles of his abdomen has taken on the rosette pattern of a leopard. Though he walks upright and upholds his human mannerisms, without a shirt he appears even more like a feline than when clothed.

His overwhelming musculature reminds her so much of Naina, and she feels a pang of jealousy that both the wolf and the leopard are in such peak physical fitness, while she needs to catch her breath after a walk on flat ground.

"Good morning, Salessa!" he says cheerfully to her.

Salessa smiles and nods politely. There's something inexplicable about the brightness that spreads across the room with Afzal's exuberance. Perhaps he and Naina are not so similar after all.

He takes a seat in one of the chairs halfway between Salessa and Lexona, then turns to the serpent and says, "Good morning, sister."

Lexona frowns. "Are you not going to greet your sister properly?"

Afzal freezes. His smile never falters, but he appears stunned, then shakes his head. "I'm so sorry. You're absolutely right. How rude of me!" He rises from the seat and strides over to the far end of the table where Lexona sits. She tilts her head to the side and waits as Afzal comes around and gives her an affectionate kiss on the cheek.

A smile widens on her face as she watches him return to his seat.

"How did you sleep?" he asks Salessa.

She doesn't want to seem ungrateful for the O'Raha's hospitality. "Quite well. How has your morning been?"

"Phenomenal. I got my morning exercise with a hunt, and then spent an hour writing in my favorite tree."

"Writing?" Salessa leans in, intrigued. "I didn't know you were a writer."

"He's quite the poet," Zoya chimes in.

Afzal meets her eyes and his cheeks glow. He turns back to Salessa. "She's a liar, I'm not very good. She's far better than I am."

"You're both poets?" Salessa asks.

Zoya nods. "Every now and then we have poetry nights. You're welcome to join us if you're interested."

"Oh, I'd love to as long as I'm able to listen without participating."

Afzal laughs. "We'll make a poet out of you, falcon, don't you worry."

Salessa hesitates until Zoya rolls her eyes and interjects. "Don't listen to him. You're welcome to join us in any capacity. There aren't any other poets here at Lover's Plateau, so it'll just be the three of us."

Salessa's heart races with the promise of some leisure, some entertainment. A few nights at Lover's Plateau where, perhaps, she won't be burdened by responsibility and research. Her peripheral vision catches Lexona at the other end of the table, her lips pressed into a hard line, her eyes narrow.

"What's wrong?" Salessa asks her. "Not a fan of poetry?"

"While these two are drowning in amusement and art, my head is buried in ancient texts, learning about how to resurrect the Twins. So no, not a fan."

Salessa opens her mouth to respond, but she's overcome with conflict. She dearly wants to join Zoya and Afzal for their poetry nights. But Lexona may be right; they're here to study the texts and achieve the predictions of the One Myth. The sooner she learns how to do so, the sooner she can get back home to Naina.

She doesn't have time for fun when there's work to be done.

Members of the O'Raha soon bring breakfast out to the three deities: steaming lamb stew and a stack of delicious flavorful breads, with a cup of fresh chai, and a small plate of sliced tomatoes and greens. Salessa's mouth immediately waters when the decadent aromas strike her nostrils.

Before she starts eating, she notices Afzal staring down at the bowl of stew with a frown. All brightness has eroded from his aura.

"What's wrong?" she asks him.

He looks up to meet her gaze, his smile returning. "Oh, nothing. I think I'm just so full from the hunt this morning that I'm not really hungry."

"Nonsense," Lexona comments, a thick chunk of lamb melting in her cheek, looking more like a squirrel than a serpent. "You have a second breakfast after your hunt everyday. Eat."

Afzal looks back down the bowl, frowning again, then at his paws, and Salessa realizes what's troubling him.

"Why don't you shift your paws back into human hands and eat?" she wonders.

When Afzal responds, the words fall from his furry muzzle in an inflexible, organized pattern. Almost as if he has rehearsed the response and is regurgitating it from memory.

"Sister and I have worked hard to learn how to merge and resurrect the Twins. The closer we get to the merger, the more comfort we find in our half-animal forms. It is physical proof of our divinity and if I were to shift back into a fully human form, it would be an insult to the Twins, and to all the work we've done to achieve these results."

Salessa nods slowly, taking in the bizarre cadence and mechanical intonation of his response.

Afzal looks at his paws again, then to the stew, and slowly lowers his muzzle toward it. His black lips part, hovering over the steaming surface, and he dips his tongue into the gravy, lapping it up rhythmically.

Lexona places her silverware sharply onto the table, drawing the attention of the room. "Afzal! You aren't an animal, are you?"

Afzal's spiny tongue retreats into his mouth and he slowly raises his gaze to meet her. His smile reappears but, juxtaposed with the agitation in his eyes, it appears forced.

"No, sister. I am not an animal."

"Good," Lexona responds, sternly. Picking up her spoon again. "Then don't eat like one."

Predictably, Afzal's gaze again looms over his paws.

Why won't he just shift his paws back into hands? Their progress isn't worth this much struggle.

Zoya steps forward and takes the seat next to him. "If it pleases you, Afzal, I'd be happy to help you."

Instantly, Afzal's agitation melts away. The concern in his eyes transforms into relief. "Thank you, Zoya."

Salessa's heart warms to see the affection the two shifters hold for one another, but then freezes again when she makes eye contact with Lexona. The serpent is staring at her, eyes narrowing as if a thought is occurring to her.

"Zoya!" Lexona calls.

The horse turns quickly from Afzal to his sister. "Yes, Serpent Goddess?"

Lexona's gaze pins Salessa.

What is she doing? The falcon wiggles uneasily in her seat.

The serpent takes a deep breath and utters a plea Salessa was not expecting. One that the Lexona she knew long ago would never make.

One that displays an inkling of change.

"You and all of the O'Raha can just call me by my name from now on."

CHAPTER 17:

"THE REQUEST"

***Theocracy** SunSide*
***Date** 28th Day of Month 6, Year 1629 DG*

THE FORUM NEVER CEASES TO inspire awe in Rafael. Towering windows, shimmering gems in stone tilework, the mighty rotund table in the center; the venue commands just as much authority as those who work here do.

The three humans sit together in silence, uncertain how Saila will react to their request. Will she sanction them as SunSidian emissaries to the human cities?

Ana and Kyoko lay the Sprite texts out in front of them on the table, pages open to the passages mentioning the Ancient Ones' presumed history.

Rafael pulls an envelope from his pocket, Unisa's handwriting covering it. He smiles, appreciative of her willingness to comply with the coding he developed for their correspondences. She urges him not to go to SeaBed, but he can't oblige.

Fate has carved a path for him to save his mother. Sofia's little salmon will risk everything to do so. Or to utter a final farewell.

Saila enters the bright chamber in a hurry, Kruga following closely behind. Rafael stands as the crimson nymph walks directly to the mari and embraces him, warm affection flowing between mentor and student.

The three humans put four fingers to their foreheads to greet the Chief Member, who bows her head apologetically. "I know our meeting was supposed to start half an hour ago. I've been dealing with the arrest of Tund-Ra and much of the Bravers United forces. Cells are overflowing, interrogations have been unfruitful. He won't speak; he barely eats."

"Ovida told us about the ambush," Kyoko mentions.

Saila sighs. "The SunSidian Guard took significant losses. If he cooperates, all of the bloodshed won't be in vain."

"You're doing the best you can," Rafael says. There are clear signs of stress painted across Saila's face and demeanor; dark circles under her eyes, a slumped posture, dramatic weight loss. Responsibility burdens her.

"Thank you, Rafa," Saila acknowledges, though she doesn't appear to believe it. "I have another interrogation with him after this meeting. Nothing will change until he starts speaking." She notices the texts on the table. "What's this?"

A soft smile appears on Ana's face and she sweeps her arms over the ancient books. "This is my evidence."

"Evidence?" Saila's eyebrows scale her forehead. "You have good news for me?"

Ana pushes the open text forward on the table until it rests in front of Saila. "How's your Nysabaani?"

Saila shakes her head. "Not like yours."

"Let me show you." The mari woman walks around the table and explains her discoveries: the tribal leaders who she theorizes to be the Sprites, their sacrifices to the demon plane, their desire to reopen it now, and the sacred locations from where the Three Deaths would emerge.

"The Three Deaths are coming to the human cities," Saila repeats what she's learned. "This is a strong lead. Excellent work, Ana."

Ana and Kyoko turn to one another and smile, but Rafael notices the worry lines etched across Saila's face.

"Why do you seem concerned?" he asks her.

Saila's gaze bounces between the three humans. "When did you figure this out?"

"A week ago," Kyoko responds.

The color in the pixie's cheeks drains. "Why did you wait so long to bring it to me?"

"I needed additional support," Ana explains. "To be sure."

Saila places her elbows on the table in front of her and runs her hands through her hair. She whispers something, her voice strained.

"We didn't hear you, Saila," Rafael tells her.

When she raises her gaze again, terror streaks across her face. "I've made a terrible mistake."

Rafael's heart drops. "What mistake?"

"Naina. She requested I send her consciousness into Red-Lo's, to try and extract information from him."

Rafael rises to his feet. "And you did it?"

She nods sheepishly.

"Bring her back out," Kyoko demands. "We have the answers now, she doesn't need to be there."

"It's not that simple. I can send her in, but only she can find her way out."

"How long has she been in there?" Ana asks.

"A week."

Rafael breathes deeply, settling his heart rate, injecting optimism into his tone. "She'll find her way out soon. Naina's stronger than any of us."

Saila shakes her head. "This isn't about strength. Mental planes are temporally anomalous, unstable. She could exit at any second, or…"

"Or?!" Rafael demands.

"Or her physical body could age to bone and she'll still be in there. Forever."

Rafael drops back into his seat, the weight of her words crashing down on him.

"We should have come to you with our request as soon as we found this a week ago," Ana says.

"Request?" Saila asks.

Ana and Kyoko remain silent, their eyes locked on Rafael. It's his turn.

"We think you should send the three of us as your emissaries to EverEmber and SeaBed, for us to warn them of the oncoming threat. We'll need an angi to go to PeakHaven and I'm not comfortable asking Unisa to go while she's at Ora's bedside. So, we were hoping you would ask Aissa, since she's the only other angi who knows the truth."

Saila's gaze darts between the three humans. "I have no concerns about sending Aissa to PeakHaven as an emissary of SunSide. Nor with the three of you going to EverEmber." Her eyes narrow on Rafael. "There is *no* chance I will authorize your return to SeaBed. Frankly, I'm a little offended that you think I would."

Rafael turns to his human companions. Kyoko presses her lips into a hard line and leans backward, crossing her arms.

Thanks, Kyoko. I could use some help here.

Ana steps in. "I know it's not ideal, but—"

"Not ideal?" Saila's volume rises. "An exile's return is punishable by death in SeaBed. It's out of the question. Certainly not on behalf of SunSide, they'll think we condone the breaking of their laws."

A hint of a smile appears on Kyoko's face, but Rafael ignores her.

"Then I won't say I'm there on behalf of SunSide."

Saila shakes her head. "Rafael, no. This isn't worth the risk. I already..." She hesitates. "I already may have sentenced Naina to death by obliging her request. Clearly that was a mistake. I won't make it twice."

"Naina knew the risks when she made her request," Rafael attempts to reason with her. "And I know the risks that come with mine." With every word he utters, his mother's face grows clearer and clearer in his mind.

She has to know that she isn't alone. Her son will protect her.

Saila holds his eye contact firmly before she speaks. "Aissa travels to PeakHaven tonight. You'll all head to EverEmber, when you're ready. But if you want to go to SeaBed, you go as civilians. I won't have your execution hanging over my head for the rest of my life."

Rafael nods. "I understand."

"For the record, I don't approve, Rafa. I don't know why you're pushing so hard for this, but it isn't a good idea."

Saila wouldn't understand. Kyoko wouldn't understand. They have the option to visit their mothers whenever they please. Somehow, fate has opened the door for Rafael, guiding Sofia's little salmon home. She is the only family he has left.

"I appreciate your concern, Saila, but this is where my journey is headed. To SeaBed."

Kyoko's smile is entirely erased. She speaks in a disappointed groan. "To SeaBed."

Ana closes the texts in front of her. "To Seabed."

CHAPTER 18

"THE LEADERS"

Theocracy *SunSide*
Date *28th Day of Month 6, Year 1629 DG*

IT'S A LONG JOURNEY DOWN to the dungeons. Slippery stone steps surrounded by intimidating walls that give way to shadows and the echoing moans of decrepit prisoners. Those who've resisted rehabilitation long enough that they've gone gray. And those who've just arrived and started their hunger strike.

Tund-Ra is amongst them, the strikers, yet he hasn't moaned once. His lips haven't parted in the five days since his arrival. He's chosen a single brick on which his gaze remains locked. But today, he'll speak. Saila refuses to leave the cell until she gets him to say something.

Anything.

She pushes the anxious buzz of her friends' welfare to the back of her mind, so she can focus on the interrogation.

Naina and Rafael will be fine. They will return, and all will be well.

Perhaps if she repeats it enough, the Four will take mercy on her and make it true. If anything were to happen to either of them, she'd never forgive herself. She lost Sonali, and Alba a few days later. That's already two close friends too many.

She follows the maze of grimy tunnels and tiny cells to Tund-Ra's current residence, her eyes tearing from the stench of sweat, fungus, and fear. Ovida waits for her outside the iron door.

"You don't have to stay here," Saila says to her.

"I'm not leaving you alone," Ovida replies.

"I can take care of myself against one malnourished, unarmed faerie, I promise. I even gave Kruga leave for the rest of the day."

Ovida faces her, worry lines spreading from the corners of her eyes like fingers. "I know you can. It's not your physical safety I'm worried about."

Saila's eyebrows scrunch together. "What do you mean?"

"I know how important these interrogations are, and"—she pauses—"how unsuccessful they've been. I know it's wearing down your mental well-being. I'm here to support you."

Saila appreciates Ovida's empathy, but her thoughts turn back to the meeting in the Forum where Rafael offered her some pitiful words of encouragement. The same worry lines appeared on him, as well.

Is everyone concerned for my mental well-being? Am I not exuding the aura of stoic leadership I think I am?

She props a smile up onto her lips. "You can stay if you'd like, but—"

"I would like to, yes." She turns back to face forward, chin raised, hand gripping the hilt of her sword tightly. Saila nods and walks around her to access the door through which she enters Tund-Ra's cell.

As expected, he sits on the bed, back against brick, legs crossed, hands folded in his lap, staring at a single brick on the opposite wall. He's been in this position for five days and has noticeably lost weight. His gray eyes have sunken deeper into his skull, and the dim light of the torches around the room casts gloomy shadows across his violet skin. Though his shoulder-length hair and bushy beard had streaks of gray when he arrived, Saila can't help but think his age now outweighs his resilience.

The latest meal left by the SunSidian Guard sits on a small wooden table in the corner by the entrance. Saila picks it up and carries it over to him, placing it on the bed next to him.

"Eat," she commands.

No response. Not even a blink.

Saila sighs and takes a seat on a small chair she placed in the cell on the day of his arrest. She faces him and stares back, but his eyes do not leave the brick.

"Five days, Tund-Ra. You have to eat eventually. I could've tortured you and forced them to feed you by now, and I haven't. Take it as a measure of good faith, as a show of mercy. Or don't take it as anything more than me not wanting more death on SunSidian soil; just eat something."

Silence fills the air between them.

Saila leans back in the seat and crosses one leg over the other, folding her hands, interlocking her fingers, and placing them in her lap, mimicking the prisoner.

Reflecting his resolve.

"I'm not going anywhere until you speak to me. I'm sure you've memorized all of my questions now, but I'll repeat them."

Silence.

"What's the ultimate goal? How did you get the Bravers United into and out of the attack sites so quickly? Why didn't you use the former Revolutionary Forces' abandoned resources? Do you have underground tunnels of your own? Are there any more Bravers United warriors we haven't already arrested or killed? Will you accept the deal offered by the theocracy's counselor? Your testimony will save you from execution."

Focus unbroken.

There must be something she can do differently in this session that she hasn't done in the last five days to get him talking. There must be some way to break his devotion to silence. Outside of torture, what *forces* an individual to talk? There are only two things Saila can think of that answer this question.

Contention or connection.

Their mutual anger, their hatred hasn't gotten him to respond. The only other option she has is to connect with him. Perhaps they have something in common.

"We've spent five long days and nights together, Tund-Ra, and we still know so very little about one another. Do you want to tell me anything about yourself?"

Silence.

Saila smiles. "Alright, how about I go first? I was born in a very small village on the northern coast of SunSide called Eloa. Have you ever heard of it?"

Silence.

"I didn't think you had. Surprisingly few Mega have. They teach geography in schools; any ten-year-old in Larso can find MoonSide, the Library, EverEmber, PeakHaven, or the Dissolved Nations on a map. They can find their CereCenter within SunSide, but ask them where Eloa is and they'd be entirely lost. Why do you think that is?"

Silence.

"I don't like to generalize, but it's something I've noted about city folk. There's so much activity, so many residents, so much self-contained gratification that it almost feels like the city is the entire world, and nothing beyond that world is worth learning about."

Silence.

"I didn't move to the city until I was a teenager. I lived with my mother through my early education, but when I was ready for more advanced coursework and academic programs, Eloa didn't have the resources to support my learning. Around that time, my mother started growing quite ill. She's been deteriorating slowly ever since and that was twenty-one years ago."

Her thoughts drift to her mother and a dagger of sorrow stabs at her heart. "I'll be honest, I don't think she has much time left. A good friend, Unisa, is currently going through something similar. In some ways, I envy her situation, and in other ways I don't. She had so much more time with her mother in a state of fitness and good health than I did. By the time I was twenty-five, my mother's illness had taken over much of her ability to speak."

Saila rises to her feet and begins to pace in front of Tund-Ra's bed. "But I don't envy the speed at which the Four are taking Unisa's mother from her. My mother's illness took decades to take her from me, so I had time to come to terms with it. That doesn't make it easier, and it certainly doesn't extinguish my grief, but I can't imagine how it feels to go from having normal conversations, to her having no idea who you are, in a matter of a few months."

Silence.

Saila takes her seat again, hands folded in her lap. "My mother is the only parent I've had for a very long time. I don't know if your parents have returned to the Radiance yet, but grieving a parent must be excruciating. I don't know how it feels yet, even though I've lost my biological father."

She looks down at her hands and a sad chuckle escapes her. "I *killed* my biological father. He was dangerous. I lost all respect for him a long time ago, and all love for him even before that. I didn't grieve after he died. Can you imagine what kind of father you would have to be for your own child not to grieve your death?"

"You'd have to be a father whose child doesn't understand what he's sacrificed," a gravelly voice that isn't Saila's echoes through the room.

Saila lifts her eyes and finds that Tund-Ra's gaze has shifted. He no longer stares at the one brick.

He stares at her.

"Sacrificed?" Saila asks, narrowing her eyes in disbelief. "Did you say 'what he sacrificed'? He sacrificed his own daughter. He abandoned me at home while he went to defend the MegaFather, and lost his arm in the process. If Sonali and her family hadn't taken me in, protected me, I'd be rotting in the soil now."

The prisoner breathes deeply and shifts his gaze back to the brick as he speaks. "Perhaps his actions weren't *about* you. They were about the greater good."

Saila shakes her head, heat rising to her cheeks. "No. They were about the MegaFather. They were about the faeries. They were about a promotion. His actions were *never* about his daughter."

"The daughter who murdered him?"

Saila's tone hardens. "Yes. The daughter who brought justice to the pixie who gave the orders that killed her friend."

"Are you certain he was guilty of that?"

"I am."

Again, his gaze shifts, this time back to Saila. "In which trial was he convicted?"

Saila's jaw falls slack. She pauses, gathering an answer for the unexpected line of questions. "The MegaFather confessed to the plot and detailed the Facilitator's involvement."

"After your father had already been executed," Tund-Ra challenges. "If you're wondering why I've been sitting here silently for five days, refusing to eat, you've just stumbled upon the answer. I'd rather sit here and starve in silence than expect any kind of justice from you, or from the theocracy."

"We've offered you a deal multiple times, Tund-Ra."

"I will not turn my back on my followers to save myself from execution. What kind of coward do you think I am?"

"The kind who attacks innocents in broad daylight."

"We did not attack innocents. Our rioting and disturbances were merely intended to get the SunSidian Guard to the scene, where we could inflict damage on them. Sadly, civilian casualties are part of war and some could not be avoided."

"This wasn't a war. You openly germinated violence in the streets of a city populated with innocent men, women, and children. This was reckless savagery."

"Savagery is what you'll get when you treat our kind the way we've been treated."

"Your kind? The faeries, who ruled the kingdom for the last eight hundred years?"

"Not the faeries. The Bravers, the ministers of the monarchy, the followers of the MegaFather. Anyone who has ever aligned themselves with our ideology is now being oppressed in the name of equity, as we were during Picana's reign."

"Her dynasty attempted to equalize a society that was skewed in its constructs and institutions."

"Bullshit!" His grunt bounces off every wall in the small cell. "There was already equity in SunSide before the pixies began making these claims."

"Equity? The Doruh were enslaved."

He rolls his eyes. "I meant amongst the Mega clans. What happened to the Doruh was socially acceptable at the time."

It takes every fiber of Saila's being not to breathe fire at him. "You sound like my father. The pixie whose actions you tried to justify a few minutes ago. But I was his daughter and I know exactly what he was. He was just as hateful as you are and I hope one day when you have a daughter—"

"I have a daughter!" His volume rises. "And I pray that someday, she grows up to understand that what her father did was for her own good. He did the best with what he had."

Saila nods as the truth dawns on her. "That's why you finally spoke to me. I struck a nerve talking ill of my father. The absent pixie who wouldn't know a paternal instinct if it called itself MegaFather and gave him a pat on the head."

She leans forward, her nose an inch from the prisoner's. "Tell me, Tund-Ra. What about *your* paternal instincts? Are they there, or have you chosen to be absent from your daughter's life, as well?"

Somehow, she can see the blood warming under his violet cheeks.

"My daughter will understand. She will grow up knowing the meaning of sacrifice and how important this cause is for us."

"She will hate you as much as I hated my father. Children don't care for your politics. They care for your presence. Where is your daughter now? Do you even know?"

"Of course, I know!" he barks. "Do not make assumptions about our relationship."

A sly smirk stretches over Saila's lips and she straightens her back. "I lived this relationship. For years, I wondered when my father was coming home from his crusade to kiss me goodnight."

"I am not your father."

"You're worse than my father. At least my father had status, influence, power. What do you have to show for all the nights your daughter is home wondering why you don't want to be around her? You've bartered your freedom for—"

His volume reaches a new height. "With the ore gone, I'm *finally* free! You'll see!"

The implication of the threat isn't processed immediately. It takes Saila a moment to realize what he meant. Confusion blooms first and she wonders, *why would a faerie find freedom in the absence of ore?*

Tund-Ra's eyes widen as he realizes what he blurted out. When she sees his reaction, Saila knows he's said something he didn't mean to… but what?

And then she sees it. The surge of Radiant energy. It moves up through his violet neck, glowing through his jaw and his cheeks, shifting into his eyes, causing them to glow. He harnesses the Radiance and before the beams can burst forth and burn Saila, she understands.

He isn't a faerie.

Her arm moves instinctively before the thought is even complete, rising in front of her and projecting an invisible wall between her and Tund-Ra's beams of Radiant energy. He's powerful; she can feel the heat of the blasts raising the temperature around the tiny cell.

Tund-Ra increases the energy in the blasts and Saila's entire body is pushed until her back slams hard against the door. Her heart races and a sweat breaks out on her brow, as she uses all of her energy to strengthen the invisible wall. She won't be able to hold it for very long, and Tund-Ra steps closer to her.

Thinking quickly, she steps hard with her leading foot, causing the stone tiles on the ground to form a wave moving toward the approaching prisoner. He uses the Radiance to lift up off the ground, hovering until the wave passes, then lowers back to the cold tiles.

Saila's skin burns as if he's holding her face to flames. If he makes it any hotter, her hair will catch fire. She begins to lose her hold on the invisible wall and Tund-Ra is near arm's length now. In a desperate attempt to gain control of the situation, she attempts a challenging Radiance technique she's only seen one Mega perform successfully.

Her father.

Those who've performed it unsuccessfully get their heads blown off instantly. She takes a deep breath, drops the invincible wall, and opens her mouth, creating a web of Radiant energy in the back of her throat. The beams of Tund-Ra's eyes bound toward her and enter her mouth, hitting the web, which absorbs the energy from the beams.

It refuels her.

When Tund-Ra realizes what's happening, he blinks quickly and ends the blasts, then raises a glowing fist to swing at Saila's face. Before it makes contact, Saila places her fingertips on the prisoner's forehead and says, "Sleep."

Radiant energy bursts from her fingertips into his skull and generates delta brain wave activity. His eyes close instantly and his arm, along with the rest of his body, drops to the ground in a heap.

Saila falls back against the wall behind her, beside the door, and she takes a few deep breaths to steady her heart rate. She's exhausted.

Tund-Ra had been lying to them the whole time, and his mask eventually slipped. He is far more powerful than anyone knew or realized.

Ovida bursts through the door, sword raised. She looks to Tund-Ra's snoring body, then to Saila. "What happened?"

"We need…stronger shackles…and more Radiance," she says through ragged breaths, beads of sweat racing down her temple. "He's not a faerie."

"The leader of the Bravers United is not a faerie?" Ovida asks. "That must be why we couldn't find a record of a 'Tund-Ra' or his family anywhere. It's a fake name."

Saila nods. "I finally got him to talk."

"I'll get the Assembly together," she says, turning to exit.

"Wait!" Saila calls to her. Ovida turns back around. "After you do that, I have another assignment for you." Saila's gaze falls on the sleeping prisoner. The leader of the Bravers United. The absent father.

She turns back to Ovida. "Find his daughter."

CHAPTER 19

"THE INNER CATACOMB"

Sovereign City-State *The Library*
Date *30th Day of Month 6, Year 1629 DG*

PRIME PALACE SENDS A SHIVER down Unisa's spine.

She'd been wrong to think it was a misnomer from what she'd seen in images. The estate of the Prime Librarian is palatial in its magnificent architecture and grand views. The domicile and its gardens, teeming with stunning fountains and vibrant flora, rest atop a hill that overlooks the busiest intersections of the Library. The images don't offer it justice.

Not only does the design of the estate remind Unisa of the MegaFather's tower within the Castrum, but its position above the citizens, rising like a guard tower from which the Prime can survey and scrutinize the population, does, as well. Like most of the citizens who worship the ground on which the Prime treads, Unisa once remained oblivious of the fact that the Prime is aware of every breath taken with the Library's walls.

He knows who took the breath. He knows how long they spent exhaling. And he knows what it smells like. His estate's position atop this hill, his citizens' idolization of him, and his undercover faction of Librarians make certain of this.

Knowledge empowers.

But this is what Unisa wants. It's what she needs in order to enact Alba's plan. Alba wanted the entire institution to burn, to be demolished. Unisa can't accomplish this until she gets deeper into the fold. Until she's one with the Inner Catacomb.

It's been a long day at work, but she's here now, at sunsdown, as promised, staring at the glass doors with the gold trim that lead into the Prime's home. Beyond these transparent panes are the opaque enigmas that make the Prime so elusive.

And so dangerous.

The mission's success awaits within the Inner Catacomb, in the liberation of the young women and girls allegedly held captive inside. Kanako's assured her of their existence. She lived here once, doing what she could to survive the Prime. And she says many more are still here, doing the same.

What will Unisa have to do? She'll have to be ready for anything. She'll have to be ready to uncover every skeleton in every closet.

How convenient, she thinks when the glass doors swing open and the Prime walks out toward her, *the skeleton himself approaches.*

"Unisa," the Prime addresses her as he closes the gap between them. He leans forward and, as expected, presses his lips to hers. "Welcome to Prime Palace. I'm so grateful you've chosen to come."

What choice did you leave me?

"I'm honored to be here, Great Prime. The estate is lovely."

The Prime's lips stretch into his wicked smile. "You've only seen a small portion of it. There's so much more inside and in the back." The enigma in his tone grows heavy. "You're going to see things you can't even imagine."

Unisa swallows hard. Every ounce of idolization she once held for this man has evolved into some mixture of mistrust and disdain.

"I'm not sure you know what I can imagine," Unisa counters.

The Prime leans in, so close to her face that she nearly takes a step back from him. "I'm not sure it matters."

Unisa's cheeks flare and she breathes deeply to steady the intimidation in her veins.

"Come now, Unisa. Let me take you inside."

He turns and begins the journey back to the glass doors. Unisa's feet refuse to move, but she forces them to follow. He opens the doors and steps to the side, allowing her to pass him and enter first.

She finds herself in a wide atrium, not dissimilar to the one in the lobby of the Center. The only real difference is in the material used to design the interior of the chamber; while the atrium in the Center is made up of stone tiles and brightly painted walls, the room in which Unisa currently stands is covered in gold.

Not only the walls and ceiling, but the floors, the furnishings, and the staircases on either side that lead up to the second and third stories. When the waning light of the descending suns strikes the massive crystal chandelier overhead, Unisa is forced to squint from the mighty reflections pounding her vision.

The Prime steps forward and passes the golden table under the chandelier. Unisa watches as he treks through the long chamber and reaches another set of glass doors at the other end, leading into the gardens behind the home.

The leader turns and beckons Unisa forth. "Come."

"Aren't you going to give me a tour of the house?" Unisa wonders, approaching the rear glass doors.

The Prime shakes his head. "There's nothing in the house for you to see. Not yet. Everything important is out here in the gardens."

A step past the threshold of the rear doors and the shock of the sight before her freezes the Librarian in her tracks. The Inner Catacomb is exactly as Kanako described.

Ten, maybe twelve, young women and girls roam about the gardens. Broken into groups, some pick flowers and berries from bushes, while others sit and read together. Two girls, who appear to be younger than Unisa, stand on soft mats in their undergarments, stretching and posing during an ancient Doruh exercise routine. They move slowly, intentionally, allowing their bodies to settle into each pose before moving on to the next.

Unisa can't shake her gaze from any of them. At twenty-four, she appears to be amongst the eldest women here, living in a home with a man who'd lived over thirty years before any of them were born.

What are they doing here?

"Get to know them," the Prime's voice breaks Unisa from her thoughts.

"I'm sorry?" she says, her gaze still locked on the women in the gardens.

"Your expression is displaying some"—he pauses—"judgment."

You think?

"I apologize."

"Don't." He turns to her. "Don't apologize. Just open your mind. I'm going to go upstairs for a little while and take care of some important business. I'd like you to spend some time here in the gardens with the members of the Inner Catacomb. Get to know them and your judgment will dissolve. When I return, I hope to find your perspective more"—he pauses—"empathetic."

It's not them I'm judging.

She nods and he returns through the rear doors to the main chamber, leaving her uncomfortably alone as ten or twelve pairs of eyes turn to face her. She smiles awkwardly, unsure of what to say or whom to approach, but, mercifully, one of the Doruh women breaks from her exercise to approach Unisa.

She introduces herself and the other follows, inviting Unisa to join their physical activities. The last thing Unisa would want to do is disrobe to her undergarments on the Prime's estate. She thanks them for including her but denies the offer, allowing them to return to their exercise as she meets a different set of young women, one mari and two faeries.

They're all eighteen, friends from the Academy who were assigned a special history project that they presented before the Prime when he visited their classroom. Evidently, he took a liking to them and started inviting them to visit Prime Palace. A great honor in the girls' eyes, they've now been spending most of their time here for close to two years.

They discuss ambitions and dreams, excitement pouring from them as they vomit words of praise and admiration for the Prime, who has promised to help them achieve the futures they've envisioned.

When Unisa breaks from the three eighteen-year-olds, she's greeted by five young women in their early twenties of varying species and clans. As they regurgitate similar stories to the mari's and the faeries', a startling realization strikes the angi.

He's lured them all the same way.

The Prime takes a liking to them, and invites them to the Palace. He insists they start slowly, with quick visits in which they meet the other members, who welcome them graciously. Their ears are filled with promises of dreams and ambitions realized, and then they return for longer periods until they're spending most of their time with him.

Many have their own homes, with their own families. But if the leader of the city provides a place to eat, sleep, relax, and spend time, in his own home, with a vow of professional and political advancement, financial and social elevation, and spiritual enlightenment at a young age, what need do they have for a home?

If he insists that keeping in touch with family too often would come in the way of progress, would slay all chances of being a chosen loved one of the Great Prime who bestowed these gifts, who would speak to family again? He sells them fantasies so they forget who they were before they became part of the Inner Catacomb, and all they remember is the Prime and his promises.

It won't happen to Unisa. She won't let it. Her feet itch to carry her out of the godforsaken gardens and away from this place.

The Palace where the Prime imprisons his prey. The jail where injustice is bejeweled to give it the same shimmer as the chandelier inside. How can Unisa explain what the Prime has planned for them? How can she warn them of the danger to come? The destination they know nothing about. If only there were an example of where this life of devotion to the Prime will lead.

The example steps through the rear glass doors and out onto the stone patio where the gardens begin. She appears to be a teenager, a thin, girlish pixie with skin the color of cherry blossoms. The two Doruh have to aid her to a seat because her swollen stomach throws her off-balance.

The child is with child.

Unisa stares in shock for so long, one of the other members of the Inner Catacomb places a hand on the angi's shoulder and asks, "Are you alright?"

Unisa nods and speaks in a whisper, her voice refusing to appear any louder. "Who is that?"

"Lyla? She's one of us. Part of the Inner Catacomb."

"How—" Unisa struggles to even allow the question to enter the air. "How old is she?"

"Sixteen."

A thick knot forms in Unisa's stomach. "How long has she been here?"

"Just over a year."

The knot grows thicker. She was a fifteen-year-old child when she was brought here, to live with a man of nearly sixty. Where are her parents? How could they allow her to be here in this condition? With *this* man?

The cherry blossom-skinned teenager takes a seat on a bench by a rosebush, flattening her flowing white dress with her hands until she resembles a pristine portrait. She turns and her solid gray eyes make contact with Unisa's brown pupils. The pixie smiles and, as if they're long-time friends, she gestures for the angi to step forward and join her on the bench.

Unisa's feet finally find the fortitude to fly forth.

"My name is Lyla," the pixie says when Unisa takes a seat beside her. "You must be Unisa. Alvaro mentioned you'd be coming to visit us today."

Unisa's jaw falls slack at Lyla's use of the Prime's name, but she throws it to the back of her mind. "He mentioned my visit to you?"

Lyla nods. "Whenever he considers a new member to the Inner Catacomb, he asks me to come down and greet them."

"Come down from where?" Unisa asks.

"My bedroom. The salvers have asked me not to move much these days, as it could cause"—she runs gentle fingers over her stomach—"complications."

"Then why did you come down?" Unisa asks.

Lyla looks up at her with scrunched eyebrows. "I told you; I was asked to come down."

"Then you should have refused if it isn't safe for your child."

Lyla takes a long pause before she responds. "I don't think the child is the one at risk." She keeps a smile up, but when these words escape her lips, Unisa sees some of the light behind her grays dim.

"How much time is left? Until you have the baby?"

Lyla looks down at her stomach. "Only a few weeks, I think. That's what the salvers say."

"And you wanted this?"

Lyla's gaze rises to meet Unisa's and, for a fraction of a moment, the mask drops. Fear trembles in her eyes, but the pixie washes it away quickly.

"That's enough about me. Tell me, are you excited for the opportunity to join us?"

Unisa nods slowly, subduing the urge to grab the teenager by the hand and lead her away from the Palace. "This is where I'm meant to be."

"It certainly is where we all are meant to be. Alvaro has been so gracious and affectionate to us all."

"Why haven't I seen you before?" Unisa blurts out. "At any of his speaking events. In his office. Around the Library. Do you just remain here at the Palace?"

Slowly, the pixie nods.

"What about your family?"

"We are her family," the Prime's voice thunders over Unisa's shoulder, causing her to jump back in the seat. "I think that's enough introductions for the first visit. Lyla, why don't you return to your bedroom?"

Lyla nods and the Doruh girls return to help her up. Before she walks away, she turns back and takes Unisa's hand. Her expression dims and she swallows before she speaks.

"You'll come see me again, won't you?"

Unisa knows the answer before the question is even completely uttered. "Of course. I'll come back to see you."

Her response ignites some of the brightness behind the pixie's eyes again, before the Doruh help usher her through the gardens and back to the home. The Prime takes Lyla's seat next to Unisa on the bench.

"I'm certain you have some questions for me," he says.

Unisa purses her lips tightly, unsure of how much civility will bathe her response.

"You can ask about Lyla. There are no secrets in the Inner Catacomb. Ask whatever it is you'd like and I'll answ—"

"How could you?" The words tear away from Unisa's tongue. "She's a child."

The Prime sighs, as if the question exhausts him. "Unisa, there is so much you don't understand about my relationship with Lyla. There is complexity and nuance in—"

"She's sixteen and you're nearly sixty. What is complex about that?"

"If you're going to continue to cut off my sentences, I'll never be able to explain."

Unisa takes a deep breath and gestures for him to continue, though she doesn't believe for a moment he deserves the grace of completing his sentences.

"Lyla and I have, as I have with all members of the Inner Catacomb, a mutually beneficial relationship. She was brought here to achieve the potential I know she's capable of. However, when two individuals spend all their time together, a certain intimacy grows between them. I denied it for months, but, evidently, Lyla could not. She initiated the acts that led to her current"—he pauses—"condition."

"The Library has laws that prevent these types of relations."

"Laws that include caveats related to parental consent," he counters. "Lyla has made her family quite wealthy."

It takes every ounce of strength in Unisa's hands not to wrap her fingers tightly around his throat. But she knows, sitting here in Prime Palace, there are more Cicada eyes on her than anywhere else in the Library.

"She's a child."

The Prime shakes his head. "She made the choice to engage in adult behaviors."

"Is that how you justified your relationship with Kanako?" Unisa spits out before she can chain her tongue. "Do you have any idea what that relationship has done to her?"

A shadow falls over the Prime's expression. His face glows red and venom drips from his tone. "*That* is the one and only time I'll allow you to speak to me that way." He rises to his feet. "Perhaps I've made a mistake in inviting you here. I thought, since you've served me so well over the past year, taking Alba's place at my side, you were worthy of membership into the Inner Catacomb. I thought you would be able to cast your judgments aside and open your mind to the possibility of being part of something greater. Clearly, I was wrong."

She hates him, and everything he stands for, and everything he's done. To Alba, to Kanako, to Lyla, and to Unisa herself. But when the angi's gaze traverses the gardens and she sees the young women roaming the estate, when she looks up at Lyla's bedroom window, the truth dawns on her: she must play along if she's going to free them.

Unisa takes a deep breath and injects an apologetic tone into her words. "I am absolutely free of judgment and ready to take on the responsibilities of the Inner Catacomb. I take back the things I've said, and hope you will still allow me the honor of being here amongst your most beloved disciples."

The Prime's wicked smile returns. His fingers wrap tightly around Unisa's chin, squeezing her cheeks together, and he leans down to press his lips against hers. It is not over quickly this time. He holds them here in this position for moments that feel like eternities.

When he pulls away, something inside of her feels broken. Tainted.

"I forgive you, Unisa," he says. "We can arrange for you to have a few more visits, so you feel comfortable here before you move in."

Unisa's eyes widen. "Move in?"

"Of course," the Prime responds with a nod. "After Ora dies."

Unisa's heart strikes the inside of her chest and her throat tightens. "Why would I move in here after—" She gathers the strength to say the words. "After Ora dies?"

The Prime sits back down and takes Unisa's hand. "Unisa, on these many visits, you'll have to start seeing me, and the members of the Inner Catacombs, as your family. Your biological parents left you when you were a small child. Alba left you when she died. Rafael and Kyoko left you when they forsook the Library. And soon…" He pauses so long, Unisa thinks he may not finish the thought, but he eventually does. "Soon, Ora will leave you."

Tears start to build in Unisa's eyes. Ora's death draws nearer. Her mounting grief is reaching a climax and there's nothing she can do to stop it.

"Soon," the Prime continues, holding her gaze so firmly it feels as though he's looking right through her, "the Inner Catacomb and I will be all you have left. Think of all I can provide for you."

CHAPTER 20

"The Breaking of the Bonded"

Sovereign City-State *The Library*
Date *30th Day of Month 6, Year 1629 DG*

SOON, THE INNER CATACOMB AND *I will be all you have left.*

Sitting in the cold of Yuki's apartment, the Prime's words strike Unisa's eardrums. A painful pounding erupts in her temples. She raises her fingertips to massage the area, though her hands can do nothing to alleviate the truth that the Prime has let loose into the air.

Once Ora is gone, Unisa will have nothing left. Nothing but her purpose: Alba's plan. Take down the Prime. End the lies of the Library. Free the women of the Inner Catacomb.

Save Lyla.

Lyla's last words ring in her ears even louder than the Prime's. *You'll come see me again, won't you?* It wasn't a simple question. A loose invitation to come visit again, if Unisa desired.

It felt like a cry for companionship, an attempt to reach out to someone from a world she was forced to abandon at only fifteen years old. The outside world where her parents enjoy luxury at her expense.

The citizens of the Library have *no* idea the kind of world in which they reside. Or the kind of individual who leads them.

Even after Juhi and Konni arrive at the apartment, Unisa's mind remains on Lyla, the Prime, and the Inner Catacomb. It's as if she's found Hay-Ro's letter all over again, opening up a damning realization. Except Hay-Ro's letter revealed unfortunate falsehoods.

The visit to Prime Palace revealed unfortunate truths.

With some force, she shoves the concerns of the day's revelations to the back of her mind and focuses on the task at hand; a task she's been preparing a year for: break Maksi's bonding.

"What's the plan?" Juhi asks, her eyes darting between Konni and Unisa.

"We talk to him," Unisa replies, matter-of-factly.

"You've *been* talking to him for a year and he's still Fully Bonded."

Unisa sighs, frustrated with the hawk's demanding tone. "I've been employing a soft approach. My worldview, my bonding was broken quickly, and it was painful. I'm trying to prevent—"

"Pain?" Juhi scoffs. "This is a war, there's going to be pain and shattering of worldviews. Maksi breaks tonight, or this mission is over. Alba's plan fails."

There's a knock at the door and both Juhi and Konni turn to Unisa. The angi strides past her associates and her heart pounds harder with every step.

I'm sorry, Maksi.

She opens the door and the carrot-skinned Mega stands in the doorway with a familiar, cheerful grin and a box of freshly-baked cookies in his hands.

"Good evening, Uni!" he chirps, pushing the baked goods forward into her hands.

"What are these for?" Unisa asks him.

"I've never been to your friend's apartment before. It's good manners to bring a dessert the first time you come for dinner."

Unisa's heart shatters for the polite Mega that's standing in Yuki's doorway. He won't be leaving the same person.

"What's wrong, Uni?" Maksi asks, leaning forward, his smile dimming.

The angi forces her own, realizing she'd been frowning. "Nothing at all. Please, come in." She moves aside for Maksi to enter and speaks as they step through the apartment. "Yuki actually isn't here at the moment. She's upstairs with Ora, but we do have some other friends joining us for dinner."

"Juhi!" Maksi says excitedly, reaching his hand forth to shake the Vice Ambassador's hand.

"Good to see you, Maksi," the hawk greets him. "How're things in *Witness*?"

"Never better. Though Unisa's replacement hasn't been as fun to work with."

Juhi raises an eyebrow. "Oh? Why is that?"

"She doesn't bring me stew and corn bowls like Uni used to," he quips, before turning to Konni. "I'm not sure we've met."

Konni stretches her hand out to him. "We haven't. I'm Konni. I'm an Educator, though I'll be retiring *very* soon. Paperwork's been submitted and everything."

"Congratulations! Any plans for after? Travel the world perhaps?"

Konni turns to lock her gray eyes with Unisa, then meets Maksi's gaze again. "Actually, I think I'll remain here in the city for a while. There's never a shortage of adventure within the walls."

Maksi laughs. "That's certainly true." He tilts his head back and sniffs loudly. "Dinner smells delicious."

Unisa prepares the dining table with the dishes she's prepared: two racks of lamb, seasoned rice, grilled vegetables, creamed spinach, and slices of lemon. Every item on the table is one that Ora taught her how to cook. Before she announces that dinner is served, a vision forms in her mind. Unisa sees the celadon-skinned pixie standing across the dining table from her, smiling and nodding with approval.

The angi cannot articulate her gratitude that Yuki volunteers to stay by Ora's side each night that Unisa meets with the team. But that gratitude is outweighed by guilt. Ora dedicated so much of her life to Unisa's upbringing and care, and yet, since the onset of the disease, Unisa's barely spent a few days at her mother's side.

"You know how important you are to me, right?" Unisa asks the translucent vision of her mother, her throat tightening.

The vision nods.

"But this mission is also important. I'm sorry I haven't been at your side, but I need to—"

The vision smiles and raises a hand, interrupting her. "It's alright, Uni."

Unisa swallows, holding eye contact until she can muster her voice again. "Did I make you proud?"

"Since the moment you entered my life," the vision responds before she fades away.

Unisa takes a deep breath before calling Juhi, Konni, and Maksi to the table. The four Librarians are either famished or too focused on the meal to speak. Few words are exchanged throughout the dinner and it soon ends without any discussion.

There's urgency in both Juhi's and Konni's expressions. They glare at her to begin but she doesn't know how, or what to say, so she allows her gaze to fall to her plate.

And then her meal nourishes her with an idea.

A year earlier, when Unisa and Maksi were colleagues, he would allow her to take confidential texts out of *Witness* without the authority to do so. If anyone else would have even suggested they wanted to commit such a crime, he would have reported them immediately. But because Unisa had built rapport with him, because he had some kind of connection with her, because she brought him his favorite stew, he was willing to listen.

She doesn't have time to forge any sort of meaningful bond between Maksi and her companions, but they can at least get to know one another enough that perhaps the connection between them will act as a sip of water with the pill they want him to swallow.

"You know what this lamb reminds me of, Juhi?" Unisa asks, turning to the hawk.

Juhi looks up from her plate, eyes wide. She exchanges a bewildered glance with Konni, who shrugs.

"No, Uni," Juhi responds, her tone nowhere near as loose or casual as Unisa would like. "I don't know what the lamb reminds you of."

"Lamb samosas. I mean the more common potato samosas are delicious, don't get me wrong. But a rich, flavorful lamb samosa is to die for."

A cloud of awkward silence descends to envelop the table. Juhi doesn't respond, her expression fraught with confusion. Unisa has never before desired telepathy more than she does at this moment. She attempts to gesture with her eyes to Maksi, indicating that Juhi should play along.

It works. Juhi's expression melts and she nods. "Yes, you're right. Nothing like a big mouthful of minced lamb in a pastry."

"Did you have a lot of them growing up in MoonSide before you came to the Library?"

Juhi shakes her head. "Not often."

"I didn't know you lived in MoonSide before you came to the Library," Maksi jumps in from across the table.

YES. It's working.

"My family moved here when I was ten," Juhi adds. "My parents, my aunt and uncle, and my two younger cousins. We all came together."

"I can't imagine traveling with three young children was easy for the adults."

Juhi laughs. "Hawk children can be"—she pauses—"rambunctious."

Maksi smiles, then turns to Konni. "Have you also lived elsewhere?"

Konni shakes her head. "Oh, no. My family moved to the Library generations ago. My great-grandmother was first-generation. Though I'm the first Librarian. Everyone else has run the family business."

Maksi leans in. "Oh? What business is that?"

"Civil engineering. My family's company was instrumental in the design of the Stream Network."

Maksi's eyes widen. "Fascinating!"

"You think that's fascinating?" Juhi interjects. "She's actually known the Prime since they were young." She leans in and lowers her volume. "And they used to fu—"

"Fun memories should be shared in the sitting room," Unisa jumps in loudly. "Konni, perhaps you can tell Maksi more about your *friendship*"—she shoots Juhi an admonishing glance—"with the Prime, in the other room, while I clear the table and then bring out some of Maksi's cookies with a cup of chai for each of us."

"*You* know how to make chai?" Juhi asks, an eyebrow raised.

A wide smile spreads across the angi's face, as fond memories of Salessa inundate her mind. She nods. "A dear friend taught me."

As she boils water, Unisa listens to the laughter and conversation in the next room. The plan is working. People rarely remain open to the truth when it comes from strangers, as if there's a closed window between them. But when the window is opened by a genuine connection, by common ground, by shared beliefs, then they'll sit on the sill all day and learn a new perspective. They'll listen, they'll understand.

Sometimes they'll even agree.

Unisa brings out a plate of cookies and the first round of chai. She hopes that the stronger Maksi's bonds with Juhi and Konni grow, the weaker his bonds with the indoctrination of the Library will be.

With every few degrees the moons travel along their nightly arc, Unisa brings out another round of chai, and more cookies. All four Librarians lose themselves in the bites and beverages, until they no longer keep track of the moons' positions. They simply want to continue learning more and more about one another.

"My goodness, look at the time," Maksi exclaims, hours into the night. "I have to get home, I've far overstayed my welcome."

Unisa rises to her feet. "No, no, please, Maksi. Stay for a little longer."

"It's long past midnight. The suns will rise soon."

Unisa can feel Juhi's and Konni's gazes piercing through the back of her head, demanding she begin the hardest parts of the conversation. Unisa takes a deep breath and obliges.

"Maksi, if you could take a seat, there were actually some things that Juhi, Konni, and I wanted to talk with you about."

Maksi's smile starts to fade slightly. His eyebrow raises in confusion, but he sits nonetheless.

Unisa continues. "I know you've learned a lot about Juhi, and Konni, tonight. And you already know so much about me. But there are things about all of our lives that we wanted to discuss with you."

"With me?" Maksi asks, his expression drowning further in confusion.

Unisa nods. "Yes, and I think I should begin. Maksi, last year, I didn't take an exam that allowed me to jump from Gatekeeper to Ambassador. The Prime sent me on a journey to SunSide."

Maksi sits up, alert. "SunSide? But Gatekeepers can't go beyond the walls."

"That's why he promoted me, and then sent me with Alba."

"With Alba?" His eyebrows come together. "But after the Halving of SunSide, he said Alba was killed while recording the war."

Unisa turns to Juhi and Konni, who give her a nod of encouragement. "I was there with her."

Maksi's eyes widen so far that Unisa thinks his gray eyeballs may pop from his skull. "You were at the Halving of SunSide?"

Unisa nods. "I was there for the end of it. Maksi, it's a very long story, but the point of it is that the Prime sent me on the journey because I found falsehoods in the Library."

Maksi takes a long pause, his eyes darting between the three Librarians facing him. "What do you mean by 'falsehoods?' Surely, it was a misunderstanding."

Unisa tells Maksi about Hay-Ro's letter at the back of *The Everlasting Journey*, though she omits the details of Maksi's own involvement in its revelation. She tells him about her conversation with Alba and Hassan, about Rafael and Kyoko's interaction with the TreeKeeper, about Red-Lo's true identity, and the threat posed by the Sprites.

She also reveals the truth of SunSide's occupation of MoonSide; she tells him about the violence and oppression forced on the Doruh by the faeries through the Braver organization. She tells him about the settlement walls and the body parts lying amongst broken buildings.

Unisa paints a horrific picture that has been the Doruh reality for centuries, a reality that the Library has helped to hide with their false interpretation and presentation of history. A reality that the Librarians have perpetuated and safeguarded for generations.

The more she talks, the more color drains from Maksi's cheeks. His skin goes from the bright color of carrots to the pale hue of cantaloupe. He doesn't respond to the implication that the Librarians have some responsibility in what the Doruh have faced for so long. That the entire city and its leadership have a hand in the death of millions over hundreds of years, and the collective trauma of an entire nation of innocent people. But from his expression, Unisa can tell he understands.

He understands the gravity of their complicity.

After Unisa stops speaking, Maksi's head is buried in his hands for some time. When he lifts his face, his cheeks are stained with streaks of tears.

"This can't be true," he mutters. "No, I won't believe it." The next words from his mouth are spoken with the conviction of a priest vowing the existence of his lord. "There are no fabrications in the Library."

"Maksi, I'm sorry," Unisa offers. "I know how hard this is. I've been through it, too. But everything we've been told is a lie. The Doruh are innocent people who've been subjected to magnitudes of violence we can't even imagine."

"But the radicals come from there," Maksi spews. "I know there are innocent Doruh, but the radical factions of them use the innocents as living shields."

"Not once," Juhi jumps in, her tone rock solid, "has a Doruh used another as a living shield. Bravers and faeries used us though. For their practice, for their amusement, for their crimes."

"Juhi, I don't mean to question what you think, but—"

"THINK?!" Juhi's volume escalates.

Maksi nods. "I'm sure it seemed like the violence was for nothing, but you left MoonSide when you were a child. You couldn't possibly have understood that the violence was necessary because the Bravers were trying to weed out the radicals in their underground tunnels."

"Were the tunnels under schools and hospitals? Were the children they slaughtered in front of me part of the so-called 'radicals,' Maksi?"

Maski's jaw hangs open. He doesn't seem to have a response.

Juhi continues. "There were no tunnels. There were never any tunnels, any radicals. There certainly were resistance fighters who tried to defend us from the Bravers and from SunSide. But none of this started with us. We just wanted to exist peacefully on our own land."

"But it wasn't your land," Maksi asserts. "The faeries believe MoonSide is theirs because the Four—"

"The Four are not my gods, Maksi. The Doruh do not believe in the Four and so whatever declarations the Four have allegedly made about the faeries' land ownership means nothing to us. And to be completely frank, I don't think any deities that authorize the murder of children to justify property theft are worth believing in anyway."

Maksi exhales deeply and continues. "Juhi, of all the claims I've heard tonight…the MegaFather being centuries old, the Sprites who want to conquer the planet, the lies in the Library, the distortion of faerie history to glorify their actions…the gratuitous murder of children is the one I cannot accept as the truth. What kind of monsters would do such a thing? What kind of a nation would we be if we allied ourselves with them?"

Unisa rises to her feet as another vision appears next to her. A young boy who she once saw playing in Evic with his friends. A young lamb who was stabbed in the heart by a Braver, simply for behaving the way all children behave. The boy stands next to Unisa now, translucent as Ora was, his fingers clutching Unisa's tightly.

For him, she has to make Maksi believe.

The angi turns to Konni. "Can you project my thoughts with the Radiance?"

"I-I," she responds, taken aback. "I'm not sure."

Unisa grabs the pixie's wrist and raises her arm until her indigo hand is on top of Unisa's head. "Try."

"Unisa, I can't just *try* something using the Radiance and your brain. Do you have any idea what could—"

"Please, try, Konni." Unisa turns to Maksi. "You don't think the Bravers have murdered children unwarranted? Watch." Her gaze finds Konni again. "Please, Konni."

Konni takes a deep breath. An energetic buzzing erupts into the air as the Radiance races through Konni's shoulder, down her arm, and into her fingertips. It then descends into Unisa's head and a moment later, all goes dark.

Unisa regains consciousness slowly. Sounds are muffled, her limbs are numb, and she can't breathe. Light penetrates through darkness and images appear before her eyes. A gust of air fills her lungs as she gasps, coughs, then vomits on the ground next to her. The feeling returns to her arms and she lifts balled fists to wipe her eyes.

When the sounds become clear again, she can hear Konni's voice. "Never again. Never *fucking* again will I agree to do something like that. We thought you were dead, do you have any idea how terrifying that was?"

"D-Did it wo-work?" Unisa asks through gasps.

"It did, but that's not the point," Konni responds, helping Unisa back to her feet. Juhi puts the angi's arm around her shoulders to give her support. "As soon as the vision was done, you dropped to the ground and your eyes rolled to the back of your head."

"But you saw it? You saw the boy? The lamb?"

"We all saw it," comes Maksi's frail voice between sobs. He sits on the ground, knees to chest, arms wrapped around his legs. "I have to go." He rises to his feet and quickly darts to the exit. When his fingers touch the doorknob, his entire body stiffens.

Unisa finds Konni's outstretched hand.

"He's a liability," the Mega says. "If we let him leave, he'll go straight to the Prime."

"We are not holding him captive," Unisa insists. "Let him go."

"Uni, we'll all die if he runs to the Prime."

Unsia takes a deep breath. Something in her heart is telling her to trust him. "He won't! Let him go."

Reluctantly, Konni lowers her arm. Maksi reaches for the knob again, but before he can exit, Unisa makes a final plea.

"Maksi." He remains still when she calls out to him. "I know this was a lot. But this is reality and we need your help in our fight for justice. At the very least, the Library must be stopped. The lies must be stopped. The truth is out there, and it's up to us to make it known."

Maksi doesn't respond. He turns the knob and exits the apartment.

"What do you think?" Konni asks, turning to Unisa. "Did we break the Fully Bonded?"

Unisa responds with the truth. "I have no idea."

CHAPTER 21

"CONTROL"

***Theocracy** SunSide*
***Date** Unknown*

THEY SAY THAT WHEN ONE door closes, another opens.

But Naina, trapped in a journey through Red-Lo's mind, has to *find* the next door before he can open it for her. Since the start of the journey, she's had no control. Not on the doors, not on the faerie.

Entering the latest memory, Red-Lo's eyes have dried and all remnants of his father's death are wiped clean. Walking into a new memory starts the cycle of pulling his perspective closer to her own anew.

Memory after memory, he's shown slight changes. She hopes it's indicative of a bending of the iron bars that are his eight-century-old viewpoints. This newest memory finds the two travelers in a very familiar room.

The Forum, Naina says. *My current workplace.*

The seat of the theocracy, Red-Lo adds with a sigh. *And the place where I was gifted Picana's head exactly one week after this memory takes place.*

767 DG. The year you murdered the queen and robbed her throne.

Red-Lo releases a scornful chuckle with a shake of his head. *I'm starting to grow amused by your delusion, pup. At nineteen years old, I achieved my father's dream. More than most achieve in their lifetimes.*

Naina's gaze travels across the room to the sienna-skinned pixie at the far end of the wooden table, a legion of the old SunSidian Guard behind her. *MegaMother Picana was a day away from liberating the Doruh when you killed her. It would've happened seventeen years earlier than it did, and she would've continued to right so many wrongs throughout the remainder of her life.*

She turns her head up to make hard eye contact with Red-Lo. *Forgive me if I don't view your* achievement *in a positive light.*

Before Red-Lo can respond, the doors of the Forum swing open. Nineteen-year-old Red-Lo and Drof-Fa enter with a contingent of their own warriors on their heels. Every hand entering the room is tight on the hilt of a sword, and every hand already in the room flies to one. Red-Lo, Drof-Fa, and their rebels are clad in shimmering armor. They look no less like a trained military than the old SunSidian Guard do.

Ovida and the Revolutionary Forces, centuries later, wore makeshift armor, frayed leather, and filthy rags. Their swords and weapons had dulled, and they sported worn and weary expressions on their faces. Red-Lo's well-organized, pristine warriors with sharp blades would have run through Ovida's forces like a battering ram through a pillow, had the two factions of underground rebels existed in the same time period.

Red-Lo and Drof-Fa each take a seat at the opposite end of the table from MegaMother Picana. Their warriors stand behind them in neat rows, a clear battle formation.

"I thank you for coming to this summit, Red-Lo," Picana says. "I truly believe we can achieve a long-lasting peace in SunSide if we are to come to an agreement today."

"I agree, Picana," young Red-Lo responds with a smug smirk. There are grunts of disapproval from the SunSidian Guard, but Picana raises a hand to silence them.

The audacity to call the MegaMother by her name and not, 'Mother,' Naina rebukes.

She was no MegaMother to me.

"Let us begin with your most pressing concern," Picana offers.

"Very well," young Red-Lo acknowledges. "The most egregious legislation passed in SunSide's history has your fingerprints all over it. We won't allow our slaves to be freed."

"They *will* be free," Picana asserts, melting Red-Lo's smirk away. "The Doruh have long been the victims of Mega oppression. They deserve autonomy, amends, and above all, a heartfelt apology."

"They deserve to be treated as the animals that they are." His volume rises.

Naina's cheeks burn. *That's your father talking. Perhaps if you were raised differently—*

Hypotheticals are irrelevant. This is how I was raised, so it's what I believed.

Believed? Or believe?

Red-Lo's eyes remain locked on the scene ahead, his lips pressed tightly together.

"Do you have any idea," young Red-Lo continues to address Picana, "how much SunSide's workforce will change if you enact this liberation? Who will work our fields? Who will feed and raise our children? What will the animals do, sit at our tables and eat dinner alongside us?"

"Would that be such a blemish on your honor?" Picana challenges. "To sit at the table with another individual and break bread? To look another in the eye and exchange compassion with your meal?"

Young Red-Lo's tone hardens and he delivers the next words slowly and deliberately. "Picana, I'm telling you now as a courtesy, before things get out of hand, we *will not* sit idle and allow a pixie to cleanse SunSide of faerie footprints. If you liberate the Doruh, you are responsible for what comes after."

I realized after I said those words, older Red-Lo tells Naina, *that if I wait until after the Liberation to strike, the theocracy would have recognized the Doruh as free citizens.*

That's why you attacked the day before Liberation was planned.

Red-Lo nods. *That, and the surprise of the attack. No one expected it. The victory was easy.*

Naina's heart shatters as she gazes upon the MegaMother six days prior to her assassination. She has no idea what would befall her less than a week later. The wolf yearns to reach through time, through the memory, and tell her. To save her. To end the violence before it begins.

To preserve the Liberation and the power of the pixie monarchy.

"It is beyond unwise to threaten the monarch in the Castrum, Red-Lo," Picana warns him. "Aside from Doruh Liberation, on which there will be no compromise, there were other demands in your letter. I have responses to those demands."

Picana signals to one of the old SunSidian Guards, who carries sheets of paper over to the other side of the table and drops them before Red-Lo, spreading them out so he can see them all at once.

Red-Lo takes them into his fingers, compiling them again, reads the first paragraph, and then looks up at Picana, rage blazing from his grays. He turns the sheets once clockwise and tears them into small pieces.

What did it say? Naina asks older Red-Lo.

Nonsense.

Pause the memory.

Red-Lo chuckles again. *I've told you, pup. You're not in control.*

What are you afraid of, Red-Lo? Why do you keep reminding me I'm not in control? This is your mind. These are your memories. How insecure do you have to be to keep mentioning that you're the one in control? Are you reminding me, or yourself?

Naina can see young Red-Lo's rage mirrored in older Red-Lo's eyes. She repeats herself. *Pause the memory, then reverse it. I want to read the MegaMother's responses.*

With an irritated groan, Red-Lo snaps his fingers once and the memory freezes. Picana and the old SunSidian Guard sit still, staring across the table. Small squares of torn paper float in the air around young Red-Lo's raised fingers. Drof-Fa is mid-turn, ready to storm from the room.

Older Red-Lo snaps his fingers and everyone in the room moves in reverse. The floating squares of paper rejoin to form whole pages in young Red-Lo's hands. Drof-Fa and the faerie warriors turn back to face the room.

When the papers are back on the table in front of young Red-Lo, spread out so that all are visible at once, older Red-Lo snaps his fingers and the memory freezes again. Naina strides over to the table and looks down at the pages.

The analysis in Picana's responses to Red-Lo's demands is clear. *Her rebuttals are well-supported.*

We didn't come for a negotiation, older Red-Lo responds. *We came for her surrender.*

Naina reads through the information laid out by Picana on the pages. Evidence that disproved the unfounded claims of the faeries. *How can you ignore this and continue to hold the same supremacist viewpoints?*

He scoffs. *It's all lies. Intended to bury faerie concerns. They violated the will of the Four time and time again.*

I thought you didn't believe in the Four?

I don't. But the religion of the Four is the oldest in the world, and it began amongst the faeries. It is part of our legacy. Even if I don't believe in it, my forefathers did.

Legacy is irrelevant if you lose your ability to govern. The monarchy was introduced after SunSidian citizens lost faith in the idea of a sole theocracy. That's why Picana wanted to pull religion out of government.

She looks down and starts reading from the pages again. *She passed legislation removing government oversight from personal medical decisions. It saved thousands of lives over the course of a few years. Religion was interfering in the salvers' work.*

Red-Lo shakes his head. *The theocracy protected faerie children.*

By forcing Mega and Doruh women to give birth in medically unsafe situations?

The children survived, Red-Lo counters.

The women didn't. Women who had rights when those children were cells and embryos.

Rights come from life. And those childrens' lives began as soon as the Four dropped a bead of Radiant energy into the mother.

Naina scoffs. *A bead of energy can't claim more rights than the woman carrying it.*

She doesn't have the right to extinguish a gift from the Four. That bead of Radiant energy was not the mother's to snuff out.

Even though it was within her body? What if it was placed there without her choice? What if growing that energy would kill her? What if she simply wasn't ready for it?

Then she would be free to give the child to another family after its birth.

Not if it ends her life.

Red-Lo waves her words off flippantly, and turns his face away. *A rare case.*

I don't only mean that in a literal sense. There are many cases in which a young mother will survive the birth, but the life she knew will cease to exist.

When Red-Lo ignores her, Naina continues to read on to Picana's next point. *It says here you also challenged Picana's progressive taxation.*

Of course, I did. We were slave masters and land owners, so she taxed us at higher rates. It was targeted and it was—

For all of those children you claim to have saved. You challenged the higher taxation of wealthier citizens, but did you ever ask where the money raised by those taxes would've gone?

Red-Lo turns back, eyes wide.

Public child care centers. Programs to facilitate adoptions. More salver clinics to provide healthcare and support to new mothers. She meets Red-Lo's gaze and her tone hardens. *You claim to fight for faerie children to be born, but then you fought against the taxation that paid for their survival. It doesn't seem like you cared about the life given by the Four. You only cared about the birth given by the mother. As long as that took place, you didn't care what happened to either of them after, did you?*

Naina steps forward toward him. *Even if she was forced to give birth. Even if she couldn't afford it. Even if her life was in danger.*

She reaches him and holds steady eye contact. *Even if she hadn't chosen to engage in the actions that put the child in her, you fought to take her choices away from her again.*

Red-Lo growls. *It was for the children.*

You didn't give a fuck about the children, admit it. You just needed more faeries so you could turn them into another generation of land owners, slave masters, warriors. Wealthy elites who could pretend to remove physical shackles, replacing them with social, political, and financial ones.

That's enough! His voice thunders around the room. He raises his hand, the fingertips of his thumb and middle finger ready to snap the memory away, but Naina quickly pulls his wrist back down to his side.

We aren't even close to done yet. She turns quickly and heads back to the table with the pages laid out. *You challenged Picana's expansion on the definition of the word 'family' in the law?*

Red-Lo nods. *The Four do not recognize romantic, sexual, or civil partnerships that cannot biologically produce a new generation of worshippers. A single male, a single female, and any offspring they create together. That's a family.*

Naina's fingers rise to her temples, massaging them to quell a sprouting headache. *Red-Lo, we live in a world where Doruh elders were arrested and never seen again, where children were shackled and killed, where nymphs and pixies starved to death. The Four have far more to be concerned about than who individuals—like my sister—share a life with.*

She lowers her hands and continues, *You governed the most scientifically advanced kingdom on the continent for centuries, amongst a species with the ability to harness powerful magic, and you still remain so blindly focused on all the ways your religion runs perpendicular to science, and none of the ways in which the two run parallel to each other. I almost feel sorry for you.*

Red-Lo sighs, exasperated. *We'd have focused on it if Picana hadn't constantly attempted to replace faeries and our religion. She demolished an entire district in Larso devoted to monuments of faerie forefathers. She allowed the Doruh and the angi to build temples there instead. It was the most blatant erasure we'd ever seen.*

She abolished the shrines of supremacists to allow for spiritual equity. I don't see a problem.

Red-Lo steps forward slowly approaching Naina at the table. *I know you don't find validity in faerie concerns. But they were very real. Picana's aggression toward us was the reason for her assassination. She encouraged the murder of our children in the womb, supported partnerships that wouldn't further our bloodlines, stripped us of our wealth, destroyed our monuments.*

He steps within an inch of her and she tilts her head up defiantly to hold his gaze.

It's all the same argument. Naina repeats her next words slowly and deliberately. *Our. Our. Our. Faeries advocate for faerie men. For the faerie definition of family. For faerie children, but only before they're born. For faerie bank accounts and properties. For faerie supremacy.*

Red-Lo leans down until the tip of his nose grazes the tip of Naina's. The wolf's heart rate accelerates, but not from fear. From the excitement of smelling rage and uncertainty wafting from Red-Lo like steam.

And whom did Picana advocate for? His tone holds a challenge.

Naina smiles. It's the easiest question she's been asked to answer in a very long time.

I may not know a lot about history, Red-Lo. I certainly don't know as much as my sister does. But I do know who was on the right side of it.

She raises a hand and points a finger at Picana across the table. *She advocated for the Doruh. For those whose temples she built. For nymph and pixie university students. For my sister and her right to love freely. And for the ones in whose name you took her head: the faeries.*

Red-Lo's expression contorts. His rage mellows and is replaced almost entirely with wide-eyed astonishment, as if he's been ambushed.

As a champion of the rights of women, she never excluded faeries. She gave faerie women their choices back, just as she did for Doruh, human, nymph, and pixie women. She gave them autonomy and the natural rights with which they were born. The rights the Four would truly want them to have. What did you do for faerie women, Red-Lo?

His mouth opens, but nothing further comes out.

Before he can fully muster a response, Naina takes a deep breath and closes her eyes. There is a massive, palpable shift in the energy of the room, moving into a recognizable tenor that Naina is all-too familiar with. One she carried the moment she stepped into any fight in the Pit. An air of control.

Red-Lo's words, spoken after the first memory ended, echo in her ears. *Here, I am the master. And you are the slave.*

Naina's eyes pop open and she confidently snaps her fingers. The scene around them dissolves and they're in the white void again, a door to the next memory present. Energy from the mental plane surging through her veins, she no longer feels as though she has to rely on Red-Lo to find and open the doors between memories anymore.

She is now in control. Naina smiles at the slack-jawed faerie and, before she turns for the door, says, *Who is the master now, Red-Lo?*

CHAPTER 22

"SIBLING ENERGY"

Alphocracy *MoonSide*
Date *33rd Day of Month 6, Year 1629 DG*

"PUSH!" THE LEOPARD ROARS. It cracks through the air like thunder and reverberates off tree trunks.

"I-I...I can't..." Salessa spits through labored breaths, tears forming in the corners of her eyes.

"You can, Salessa. PUSH!" Another roar rattles the forest floor beneath them.

"It...it's too h-heavy." She strains, the pain moving up her shoulders, through her neck, and hammering the sides of her head.

"You almost have it up, come on!" He gently wraps his paws around her wrists, but doesn't apply any upward pressure. "I'm just holding on to support you, but this is still all you."

Battling gravity and seated upright on a wooden bench, Salessa pushes the thick bamboo culm in her hands skyward. Attached to each end of the sturdy green stem is a stone, and every time Salessa is able to successfully raise the rod over her head ten times, Afzal removes the stones and places larger ones in their stead.

Once the culm is over her head, her arms extended, she begs, "Take it! Please!"

Afzal pulls the stem of Salessa's hands and her arms drop weakly to her sides as the tears release from the corners of her eyes. She falls onto her back, drawing in long and deep breaths, taking in the sounds of birds in the forest's canopy and the smell of old roots under them.

"Why do you and Naina enjoy this so much?" Salessa demands, the muscles in her shoulders throbbing. She's been at Lover's Plateau for ten days, and on the journey for weeks. Distance from Naina hasn't gotten any easier. If anything, she misses her sister more and more each day.

Afzal places the stem and stones down onto the ground and laughs. "I think I'm *supposed* to say something like, 'the sense of accomplishment when you move up to larger stones,' but really it's just the hormones and chemicals your body releases when you exercise."

Salessa takes deep breaths and wipes her face with a towel. "You sound like my friend, Kruga. He would've also given a very scientific response."

Afzal plops down a boulder next to the wooden bench. "You should be proud of yourself. Each session you move up to a new set of stones. That's quick progress."

"Today's exercise hurt more than the previous days I've joined you," Salessa comments.

Afzal laughs. "Exercising the muscles in your shoulders is particularly painful. Just wait until the day after tomorrow. Then you'll *really* hate it."

Salessa sits up slowly. "When I asked if I could exercise with you"—she gestures to the forest around them—"this was not what I had in mind."

"Oh?" Afzal raises an eyebrow. "What did you have in mind?"

Salessa points her forefinger up to the branches of the trees. "Something in our other forms. With you leaping from tree to tree, and me following you through the air."

Afzal eyes her coyly. "Says the shifter who hates shifting."

"I don't *hate* shifting, I just..." Her smile fades as she realizes she isn't comfortable finishing the sentence in front of Afzal. *I just don't feel as confident in my body as Naina feels in hers. I don't look the way she does. The way you do.*

The way Lexona does.

The abrupt end to her sentence, and her obvious discomfort, sits awkwardly in the air between them. Her heartbeat quickens and panic develops as she loses sight of how to complete the sentence aloud.

As if he senses her fluster, Afzal changes the topic, and Salessa is grateful. "How have your studies been?"

"You mean the hours I've spent inhaling dust from old books? My lungs are taking in more than my mind is."

Afzal's hearty, infectious laugh escapes from his muzzle and brings a smile to Salessa's face. "The dust is disgusting, but I think it's important that you're reading up on all of the notes the original O'Raha took while the Twins dictated their visions. You may be asked about some of this information when you meet with the O'Raha council."

A meeting with the elders of Lover's Plateau was mentioned to Salessa in passing by Zoya the day before, but no further information was provided. "Do you know when that will be?"

Afzal shakes his head. "Sister's working on a date and time for the meeting"—he pauses—"and to hopefully find out what they'd like to talk with you about."

The concern in his expression raises the hairs on Salessa's arms. "What aren't you telling me? Why are you so concerned about my meeting with the council? I thought they'd be happy another resurrector is here at Lover's Plateau."

Afzal breathes deeply before responding. "They are, don't get me wrong. But their devotion to the scripture can make them, uh, rigid in their willingness to accept one who claims to be divine. Before Lexona and I reopened Lover's Plateau, they accused us of fabricating our siblinghood. When we had friends and members of the community explain that we were in fact brother and sister, they refused to believe we were twins. 'One of you must be older,' they would say."

He laughs softly, his gaze drifting to the ground. "It's strange. Our parents gave Lexona away at birth to separate us, afraid that if someone found out our secret, it would endanger us. That we would be treated differently, or taken from them."

"Naina and I hid our animal forms from everyone, our entire lives, for the same reasons," Salessa remarks.

Afzal nods. "But look what happened when we told them outright. They simply didn't believe us. After fifteen hundred years of waiting,

I suppose they expected some grand entrance from four all-powerful, all-knowing beings with long, white beards and glowing eyes. Instead they had two orphaned teenagers who only knew as much about the Twins as any other Doruh is taught as a child. It wasn't until we reopened Lover's Plateau that they began to take us seriously."

"And you're worried they won't take me seriously?"

There's a long pause in which Afzal's gaze takes Salessa in. A half-smile forms on his thick, black feline lips and he replies, "They trust me, and they *definitely* trust Lexona. When we vouch for you, they'll accept you."

A warmth ignites in Salessa's chest, grateful for his support. "Thank you."

He waves a hand flippantly. "Don't thank me. It's selfish, really. The sooner we get them to accept you, the quicker we can distribute divine duties to you."

"Divine duties?" Salessa asks.

"We don't just sit around and study all day, Salessa. The council is responsible for the O'Raha's government, but they no longer govern without the input of the Leopard God and the Serpent Goddess. As if they need us to make political decisions for them. I'm twenty-one, I have neither political experience, nor the desire to govern anyone. It's been nerve-wracking."

Salessa laughs. "Lucky for you, I have both."

"Great, so we can make a deal. After the council meeting, you can take over all of my political duties, and I'll continue to let you join my exercise sessions." He puts his paw forward waiting for Salessa to shake it.

Salessa takes his paw into her hand and moves it up and down. "This doesn't feel like much of a deal for me. I'm taking on the government, but I was going to join you in your exercise sessions anyway."

Afzal leans back on the boulder and winks at her. "Maybe I'm better at politics than I thought."

She's struck by the ease with which their conversations blossom.

"You're easy to talk to," she blurts. "I lose track of time in conversations with you. That's how my conversations go with Naina, too. We haven't known one another very long, but it feels like I'm speaking with an old friend. Why is that?"

Afzal is quiet again, seemingly taken aback by the compliments. "You and Naina have known about the One Myth your whole lives, haven't you? You didn't know it by that name, but you knew about the resurrection prophecy and your role in it?"

Salessa nods.

"I'd heard about the prophecy, but I thought I was an only child my whole life, so it didn't mean anything more than an interesting story to me. And then, one day"—his gaze drifts to the forest floor as if there's something slithering beneath the leaves—"a serpent showed up at my doorstep. And when she spoke, she didn't move her lips. I just heard her voice in my head. She *gave me* her thoughts. And that's when I realized..."

His voice trails off and his lips shut tightly. Salessa leans in. "Realized what, Afzal?"

He raises his eyes to meet hers. "That my parents had lied to me my entire life. They'd died by the time Lexona found me, so they couldn't even explain or defend themselves. I had to—" he pauses to exhale deeply. "I had to just forgive them without any answers."

He wipes the corner of his eye with the back of his hand. "Maybe I'm easy to talk to because I hold space for your thoughts. I spent most of my life in the dark. And three years ago, this world stopped making sense to me. If I could be so ignorant about something so integral to my existence, who am I to judge the thoughts of others?"

Salessa's spent so many years angry about the prophecy, about the One Myth, and the way it shaped Naina's and her life. But she never stopped to think of the blessing that comes with knowing who you are, what you are, from a young age. She always thought the other set of twins named in the One Myth were out there hiding somewhere, as well.

She never considered that they might not even know who they are, and how they might struggle when they find out the truth had been hidden from them.

The falcon reaches forward and places a hand over Afzal's paw. "I have to admit, it's been difficult here. Ten days in a new environment with strangers. But you and Zoya, our exercise sessions and poetry nights, they've made things easier for me. I just want you to know that."

"We've appreciated your being here. After three years of reading old texts, and engaging in merging rituals with Lexona, I think I needed a change."

Salessa pulls her hand back. "I can imagine. Have the merging rituals helped to break up the monotony?"

Afzal fidgets on the boulder and rubs his paws together. "Um, yes. They have."

"What are they like?" Salessa wonders. "The merging rituals? You said they've been successful, right? And that's why you're so in touch with your animal half? Have you—"

"Salessa," Afzal jumps in, his volume low and tone steady. "I'd rather not talk about the merging rituals."

Confused, but not wanting to pry, she offers him a smile and a change of subject. "I read about an energy transfer practice that could help with the resurrection of the Twins." She looks up at the positions of the suns. "Zoya mentioned she would help me with mastering it and I'm going to be late if I don't head out now."

At the mention of Zoya's name, the leopard's cheeks around his muzzle burn red. "Do you mind stopping by your chambers first?"

Salessa raises an eyebrow at the odd request. "I can. Why?"

"Because you're going to need a bath, unless you want Zoya's energy to transfer all the way out of her body when she smells you."

Salessa pounces from the wooden bench and shoves the laughing leopard playfully. As they head back out of the forest toward the main complex of the city, she can't help but feel a growing closeness to her new friend. While no bond she forges here can replace the one waiting for her in SunSide, Afzal's sibling energy burns the sense of absence away, little-by-little.

His glowing spirit, his infectious smile, form an anchor of familiarity, of reason, in a world that stopped making sense to her ten days ago.

CHAPTER 23

"THE GARDEN"

Alphocracy *MoonSide*
Date *33rd Day of Month 6, Year 1629 DG*

A BOULDER OF GUILT SITS in Salessa's chest, for the many times she's poked fun at Naina. The wolf has never been particularly familiar with the more sophisticated shades of the visible color spectrum. Salessa remembers one instance in which she asked Naina to grab a lavender skirt from her trunk and Naina responded, "The only skirt in here is this light purple one."

But as the falcon now sits in the gardens of Lover's Plateau with Zoya, looking around at flower petals bursting with colors she cannot name, she's humbled.

The two Doruh sit cross-legged on a wide pink blanket, facing one another, their knees touching. Behind Zoya on the blanket is a sack she brought with her and some personal items she pulled from it, scattered around her.

Every flower, every bud, even every thorn sprinkles aromas into the air. Expected scents climb delicately into Salessa's nose—rose, lavender, jasmine, cherry blossoms—but some unexpected ones conquer her nasal passages as well—cinnamon, coconut, chai, pastries, freshly-printed books, the ocean.

"Where are all of these scents coming from?" Salessa asks, her head swiveling to absorb as many of the sights and smells as she can. Square fields of flowers spread like a sea out between waves of green. Paths of small white and gray pebbles form interconnected walkways for the O'Raha to travel, holding hands and giggling, from flowerbed to flowerbed. Fountains and streams bring a dewy moisture to the air, and a pleasant hum to the ears, bathing onlookers with refreshing mists.

Salessa's eyes rise above and if she squints past the manufactured lighting systems, she can make out the stone inner walls of the mountain around them. Lover's Plateau is truly a technological marvel for its ability to render residents ignorant to the fact that they aren't actually outside.

"Despite their beauty," Zoya responds, "not all of the flowers here are naturally occurring."

"I would think none of the flowers in the garden occur naturally inside a mountain."

A soft giggle escapes Zoya's lips. "What I mean is, they aren't naturally occurring *anywhere*."

Salessa's jaw falls slack. "The O'Raha have created synthetic plants? Without the Radiance?"

The horse nods. "We aren't only religious fanatics, Salessa. We have salvers here, and teachers, and messengers, and actors and actresses… and scientists. We've truly done our very best to build and maintain a self-contained community that needs nothing from the outside world."

"Why?" Salessa questions. "You believe in a prophecy that outlines the resurrection of divine twins who will face an end-of-times threat. Will they not save everyone? Or will they save only those who reside within the mountain?"

"You would know the answer to that better than I would. I'm not one of those who will resurrect them. I'm not a goddess. But you are." Salessa winces, and a soft smile curves the sides of Zoya's lips up. "Still doesn't feel right?"

"Will it ever feel right to be"—she pauses, steeling herself to speak the words—"worshiped and served and venerated as a goddess?"

"At some point, it certainly should. You've asked the O'Raha not to kneel. But that doesn't curb your divinity. When the Wolf Goddess joins us, we will serve her, too."

A vision of an O'Raha member dropping to their knees before Naina pops into Salessa's head, followed by another of the wolf biting their head off, in more ways than one.

"Perhaps we should begin the ritual," Salessa offers, hoping to change the subject.

Zoya nods enthusiastically. "Yes, of course. Please, take my hands." She places her hands, palms up, on her knees. Salessa reaches forth and places one hand in each of Zoya's, allowing the warmth to travel between them. "Now, close your eyes."

Salessa follows the instructions as Zoya dictates, hoping her diligent obedience permits the flow of energy between them like the stream bubbling through the flowerbeds. When Zoya asks her too, she breathes deeply, inhaling and exhaling to the same rhythm as her partner.

After some time of holding hands and breathing together with eyes closed, Salessa speaks up. "Are you feeling anything?"

"Not yet," Zoya responds. "I think, perhaps, it takes some time."

Salessa opens one eye. "Has anyone ever done this successfully?"

"Afzal and Lexona have."

Salessa's other eye pops open, as well, and she pulls her hands back from Zoya's. "Of course, they have. Merging ceremonies, energy transfer, half-human forms. These are all such complex forms of spirituality, the God will be resurrected far before Naina and I resurrect the Goddess."

Zoya tilts her head and smiles. "You can't compare a journey just begun to that of those who've been traveling for years. You entered Lover's Plateau ten days ago. Give yourself some grace."

"I think you give me enough grace for the both of us. I feel a little"—she pauses—"disadvantaged without Naina here. Afzal and Lexona have each other; they have someone here who can understand what they're going through. Someone to share ideas and thoughts with. Someone who can help them make decisions. I have no one."

"I will try my best not to take that personally." The horse winks.

"You know what I mean. This is a journey Naina and I should take together. Somehow, I started it alone and I don't know what to do now. It doesn't feel right working towards the resurrection without her. But

I can't go back to SunSide without having accomplished something or she'll never come back with me. Especially not if I tell her Lexona's here."

Zoya narrows her eyes, as if recalling some long-forgotten fact. "Lexona's mentioned that the Wolf Goddess isn't fond of her."

"Naina has *very* good reasons to not be fond of her."

Zoya nods. "I don't doubt it. And I'm sure you have your reasons for intentionally avoiding her since you arrived."

Salessa's eyes widen. She hadn't realized how obvious her distancing from Lexona has been to those around them. "You noticed."

"It is not my place to pry or to ask questions that—"

"You can ask questions if you'd like," Salessa permits her.

Zoya shakes her head. "I don't think it would be appropriate." She takes a long pause before continuing. "Though, if I may speak freely…"

Salessa rolls her eyes. "Zoya, since I arrived, this is about the fourth time you've asked me to speak freely, and I've never once chained your tongue. Consider this blanket permission to speak freely."

Zoya smiles and continues, "Perhaps it would be helpful for you to consider setting your history with Lexona to the side and continuing on your journey here with some formality. Professionalism. Respect."

"If you knew what—"

"I'm not invalidating your experiences, Salessa. But your past is not your ally right now. You talk about feeling alone, about not having someone who understands what you're going through because you don't have the Wolf Goddess. But you do have that. Both Afzal *and* Lexona can give that to you. After your goals with them are complete, you never have to speak to either of them again. The past can resume in the future. But in the present"—she picks a rose from a bush next to them and hands it to Salessa—"it's nothing but a thorn."

Salessa rotates the thorn-ridden stem in her hands, eyeing the prickly protuberances beneath the perfectly red petals. Zoya's words seep deeply into her heart and she considers how Naina would feel about the idea that Salessa would grant temporary forgiveness to Lexona in order to work with her through this process.

Don't open your heart to her again, Lessi, Salessa imagines the wolf would say.

"Thank you," Salessa says to the horse. "For your poetic wisdom, as always. You've given me some things to think about."

Zoya bows her head respectfully. "Anything to serve you."

Salessa frowns. This entire time, she had considered them to be new friends chatting, not one devotee performing a service for a master. "Zoya, if you weren't O'Raha, if I weren't the Falcon Goddess...if we were just Zoya and Salessa sitting in a garden, do you think we would be friends?"

For the first time since she arrived at Lover's Plateau, Salessa sees Zoya's smile slip. In a fraction of a second, the horse reveals so much more than she intended to. The truth of their relationship becomes plain before them, and it stings far more than Salessa expects it to.

If Salessa weren't who she is, she would be nothing to these people.

"It's certainly getting quite late," she says, saving Zoya from having to answer the question. The horse's expression melts into relief. "I'm sorry I've kept you here for so long and we didn't even achieve anything."

"Please, don't apologize," Zoya responds. "We can have another one of these sessions soon, and maybe a longer one next time, when I don't have to run off to prepare for a Devotion Ceremony." She shifts onto her knees and begins to pack her belongings back into her sack.

"What's a Devotion Ceremony?"

"One of the O'Raha's main tenets is to leave Lover's Plateau and spread the message of the One Myth. When an O'Raha has recruited a certain number to the community, they are said to have the greatest devotion to the Twins and are honored by a ceremony."

"What happens at the ceremony?" Salessa wonders.

"I'm not sure. I've never actually been to one, I only assist Lexona in preparing the room for it. All I know is that she and Afzal perform their merging ceremony there for some select members of the O'Raha, and that the one who is being honored typically leaves Lover's Plateau to lead their own temple or shrine for the Twins in the outside world. We don't see them again after the Devotion Ceremony."

"Will you be having a Devotion Ceremony?"

Zoya hoists the sack over her shoulder and rises to her feet. "My duties are to serve you, the four resurrectors, directly. And it is a great honor, I am blessed for the opportunity. But because of these duties, I don't have time to venture outside of the Plateau and recruit others to the community. I'll likely never have one."

There's something unfair, Salessa feels, about devotion being measured by one's mastery of persuasion and not by their spiritual labor. There is no one more devoted than Zoya.

After the horse departs, Salessa remains seated in the gardens, pondering on the revelation of her relationship with those around her; missing Naina now more than ever. After some time, she closes her eyes and continues her breathing, hoping to make some headway in her practice of the energy transfer ritual.

She loses track of time entirely and, after what feels like hours, she enters into a state of tranquility she isn't expecting. She's somehow wide awake, but also feels as if she's sleeping. She's sitting, but she's soaring. She's here in the gardens, but she's also standing in a desolate white void.

Where am I? Her lips remain still and the words project from her mind. *Hello? Can anyone hear me?*

Shapes take form around her. Slowly, the white void fades as figures and objects become discernible around her. She's in a jarringly familiar location: the Forum. Though, to her surprise, she appears to be in the past.

Sitting in a seat next to where she stands is Picana, a MegaMother who lived centuries earlier, and was assassinated by Red-Lo's command. Salessa turns and her heart sinks powerfully into her stomach. Standing only a few yards from her at the other end of the table is Red-Lo himself. She recognizes that it must be him because he resembles both Zar-Lo, and the younger, teenage version of himself that sits at the table across from Picana.

The MegaMother, teenage Red-Lo, and all of the guards and warriors sit completely still, frozen. There are only two figures moving in the room: the older Red-Lo…

And Naina.

CHAPTER 24

"ATONEMENT"

Alphocracy *MoonSide*
Date *33rd Day of Month 6, Year 1629 DG*

SALESSA BITES HER LIP TO hold back her tears of excitement.

Where are they? Is this real? Is Naina in the past with Red-Lo? Or is this a dream Salessa is having in the garden?

It must be. It must be a dream. Why would Naina be in the past with Red-Lo?

Salessa steps forward to get a better look at her sister. She craves a hug.

I miss you, she thinks, as the wolf angrily points to a piece of paper she's holding up and displaying to Red-Lo. She's saying something, but no sounds come from her. From anywhere. The dream is silent.

Salessa can't contain her laughter. Even in this odd, nonsensical dream, Naina's personality doesn't change. *I love you, and I'm going to come back home as soon as I can.*

Salessa reaches a hand forward to attempt to touch Naina. The moment her fingers make contact with the wolf's skin, the falcon soars again. The flight is nowhere near as calm or delicate as it was previously; it's as if she's been tied to the back of a flying horse and is being dragged furiously through scorching hot air. Her lungs are depleted entirely and she gasps for breath, but nothing comes.

The torturous journey out of the vision lasts for so long she thinks she may die, until her consciousness is finally dropped forcefully back into her body. She springs up from the blanket, where she was laying on her back, into a seated position and gasps deeply for air. Her heart pounds so hard she thinks it may burst through her chest. She shivers as if she's buried in snow, and the entire garden twirls around her.

Her eyes start to roll upward as weakness sets in. Two delightfully warm hands wrap their soothing fingers onto her cheeks, soft thumbs caressing the skin of her face. A familiar, comforting voice enters her ears and relaxes her.

"Breathe, Salessa," it says. "You're alright, just breathe. I'm here."

Salessa shuts her eyelids tight and follows the instruction, breathing deeply to fill her lungs back up. When her eyes close, the owner of the voice moves closer and wraps her arms around the falcon and holds her tightly. Salessa reciprocates and buries her face in the individual's chest, feeling the warmth and comfort radiate through her.

After what she experienced, Salessa feels at home here. The way she once did long ago. She immediately sinks into a comfort she hasn't felt in three years, and when she realizes whose arms are around her, whose voice saved her, whose chest gives her warmth, her eyes pop open violently and she pushes away from her.

"No! Get away from me, Lexona! Don't touch me." She crawls backward a few feet.

As if Salessa had withdrawn a sword and stabbed it through her, the serpent's beady eyes fill with tears. "Salessa, I just wanted to help."

"I don't want your help," Salessa says, still shaken from her exit from the vision, but standing her ground against Lexona. She continues to breathe as she holds the distance between them. Night blankets the empty gardens. The only light falling between them is the artificial starlight manufactured within the mountain.

They sit in silence for so long, staring, Salessa recovers almost entirely before either of them speaks again.

Lexona speaks first, a tear loosening down her cheek, her voice strained and feeble. "You will always see me as a serpent, and nothing more. You see my fangs, you see my tongue flicking, and you see the patches of scales on my skin. All you see are the parts of me that are animal. You reject the parts of me that are still human."

Salessa's throat tightens from the sting of Lexona's words. Never would she have thought she would make another Doruh feel this way. "That is not fair, Lexona. I have a right to see the part of you that you showed me three years ago."

"But that is all you will see unless you let me apologize. Until you let me atone. You've been avoiding me for ten days and I haven't had a single moment alone with you to talk about what happened and to prove that I've changed. *That* is not fair to me."

A battle rages in Salessa's heart. On one side, she hears Naina telling her not to give the serpent a second chance. But how long can Salessa keep this imagined voice of Naina's alive? Salessa could be here, at Lover's Plateau, for weeks, months, or years. Can she keep pretending to hear Naina for *years* because she's afraid to let someone back in? Because she's afraid to get hurt again?

On the other side, Zoya's wisdom gallops through her mind: *The past can resume in the future. But in the present, it's nothing but a thorn.*

The battle between these two sides rages until Salessa breaks into sobs. *I don't know what to do,* she thinks.

You forgave me, comes a voice from over Lexona's shoulder. Salessa looks past her to see a familiar face stepping through the gardens and taking a seat next to her.

Ray-Mi, Salessa addresses him.

I've missed you, love, he responds, his cornflower-blue cheeks popping up with his smile. *I was a Braver and you forgave me. Why doesn't Lexona deserve the same?*

Because… Salessa pauses to think, and then the answer comes to her. *A broken heart is the hardest thing to repair.*

But some people deserve the chance to try and repair it.

Salessa takes a deep breath. *Does she deserve that chance?*

Ray-Mi laughs. *That's for you to decide. All I can say is, I never met anyone, while I was alive, who embodied hope, optimism, and love the way you did. That's the Salessa I knew. What would that Salessa do?*

Before she can respond, Ray-Mi fades back into non-existence, leaving Salessa alone again to decide. She turns to Lexona and, for the first time since the serpent knocked on her door at the inn, Salessa looks past the tongue, the fangs, and the patches of scales.

And she sees the human she once fell madly in love with as a teenager.

"Let's talk about what happened," Salessa says with a deep breath. She sits cross-legged again, moving closer to Lexona. The serpent mimics her.

"I am so sorry, Salessa," she begins, a sob escaping her. "Every day I wake up disgusted with myself for trying to take the stones from your fund."

"It was so much more than some stones, Lexona. Naina and I had saved them to escape. You tried stealing our only chance of survival." Her words catch in her throat as tears break free from her eyes, as well. "How could you? I loved you."

"I lo-loved you, too," Lexona breathes out raggedly. "I was just too immature to think of anyone but myself. I wish—I wish so much that I weren't part of the One Myth, so that Naina's assault would've killed me."

Salessa shakes her head. "Despite what happened between us, you're here for a reason. We may not have the same love, but we both found our way here for a purpose. For something greater than us."

Lexona wipes the streaks of wetness from her cheeks, takes a deep breath and speaks again. "I failed your love, Salessa. Every part of yourself that you ever gave me was pure and beautiful, and I broke it because I never deserved it. I never deserved you. And that's something I have to live with for the rest of my life."

Salessa's heart shatters again for the love that they could've had, but never will. What's happened, what's gone from this world, must be buried in the past with what could've been.

"It's all in the past now," Salessa assures her. "The longer we hold onto this, the more we will both suffer. Atonement takes time." She takes a deep breath. "But this is the first step."

Lexona's mouth falls agape. "Thank you. I don't know what changed your mind, but I'm grateful."

I had a vision of my dead friend, she thinks, before realizing the environment around them may have more to do with her feelings than the visions. Salessa's gaze travels from flowerbed to flowerbed, from stream to fountain, from grass to path. "Perhaps it's the garden that inspires the idea of rebirth. Of healing."

She runs her fingers along the soil in the bed next to them. "Flowers can't grow in poisoned soil, Lexona. It has to be replaced fresh or you'll end up with nothing but wasted seeds and unusable dirt."

A soft chuckle escapes Lexona. "I think you've become far wiser over the years. What were you doing here in the gardens anyway?"

"I had read about this energy transfer ritual in one of the O'Raha texts. I had asked Zoya to come out here and attempt it with me."

"Zoya won't be able to do it," Lexona says.

"I understand that now."

"But I can." She places her hands, palms up on her knees, waiting for Salessa to place hers on top of them.

Salessa hesitates, mistrust still lingering in the air between them. It'll take time before the hatred she's held in her heart for three years dissipates, but the sun will never shine through if the darkest clouds aren't moved away. The falcon's committed to allowing Lexona in again, and she refuses to take any steps backward now.

Cautiously, she places her hands on the serpent's palm, feeling leathery scales. The two Doruh women close their eyes and breathe deeply.

The energy shifts instantaneously. It isn't at all as it was with Zoya. A warm glow shoots through her body and blankets her like the embrace of an old friend. She feels as much at home as she did with her face pressed against Lexona's chest.

For the first time in three years, Salessa feels the energy of the serpent slither its way back into her heart.

CHAPTER 25

"MISTAKES"

Sub-Oceanic Stratocracy *SeaBed*
Date *33rd Day of Month 6, Year 1629 DG*

WAVES CRASH WITH INTENTION. Currents travel in familiar directions. Sharks eat exactly the meal that catches their eyes.

The certainty of the ocean is one of the greatest blessings of the mari culture. There is no doubt, no hesitancy, when your civilization is built upon the activity of natural forces beyond control. Beyond might. Beyond mistakes.

One is forced to just go with the flow.

The muscles in Rafael's back ripple, tense, and soften rhythmically as he rows the boat along with ease. It isn't physically painful, but the lack of speed kills him. Drifting so slowly violates mari nature.

Luxury and magnificence don't bleed from the vessel. Small, wooden. Carrying two passengers and three travel bags, it's modest enough that one angry wave could condemn it to the ocean floor.

And here it is, carrying a message so heavy, it could sink the entire SunSidian fleet. A message that may save the world, if the Generals of SeaBed heed the warning.

There's no guarantee they will react favorably to Rafael's plea. As his gaze finds his wrists, the only certainty is that in a short while, they'll be shackled.

His eyes shift to the other passenger in the boat. Kyoko sits across from him with her head buried in one of the tattered Sprite texts, Ana's clothes folded neatly beside her as the mari woman swims in the waters beneath them.

Rafael swallows, trying not to think of the inevitable anger that will engulf Kyoko when she's escorted out of the city. The son of a General knows the protocols: the exile will be arrested and prepared for execution, while his companions are denied entry.

It's for the best. When they put him in chains and lock him in a cell, Kyoko won't bear witness. When they drag him before the Generals to be berated and admonished, she won't bear witness.

If they laugh at his warning, she won't bear witness. If his plan fails, and he's brought to his knees before an executioner, she won't bear witness. The last selfless act Rafael can commit for her is making sure she isn't there to see.

Kyoko's eyes slowly rise from the text and meet Rafael's. She smiles and Rafael's heart drops into his gut.

This was a mistake, he thinks. After all the time they've spent together over the past year—the late-night laughs, the lingering looks in the morning, the soft touches, the healing and vulnerability—how could he move forward with a plan that could end his life? That could end what began the day the Prime forced them to journey together.

But when his gaze falls to his sister's bracelet, he realizes it wasn't a mistake. Long before he was a man who would crawl from one end of the planet to the other to see Kyoko's smile, he was Sofia's little salmon.

Salmon always come home, Mother. Regardless of how far they go, how long they travel the ocean, they always come back home. One day, I will know it's time to come home.

He has one family member left in this world. And he will protect her at all costs.

"Where are you?" Kyoko asks, breaking Rafael from his thoughts.

The mari turns to his right, and then his left. "On a boat?"

Kyoko chuckles. "Where are your thoughts? You've been staring at me for a few minutes with a blank expression."

"My apologies." He bows his head, playfully. "Maybe I was lost in the glamour of your shimmering exoskeleton."

"Oh? Why, today, is it suddenly glamorous to you?"

The mari's cheeks ignite as he contemplates leading with candor. *You were glamorous to me even before I knew what love was.*

"Must be the light reflecting off of the ocean's surface. It's like I'm seeing parts of you for the first time."

Kyoko laughs. "I don't think there's any part of either of us we haven't seen before."

She winks coyly, and Rafael's heart hammers the inside of his chest, as his mind floods with the memory of Kyoko walking in on him showering on the roof of the Headwoman's home in Adera. The times she's seen him disrobe before a swim.

He realizes, however, Kyoko's never seen how the mari anatomy changes when fully submerged. There are still parts of him she's never seen before.

"You've never seen my gills," Rafael informs her.

Kyoko's eyes widen and her brows rise to her hairline. "Gills? I've seen you swimming before, Rafa. I've seen Ana and Alba swim. I've never seen any gills."

"You've seen us all get into the water, and you've seen us emerging from it," he explains. "But you've never put your head below the surface to see what happens when we *breathe* water."

"Alright, then," Kyoko says. "Show me your gills."

The air shifts between them. He's bared himself before her in the past, but it's different now. With the igni sitting a foot away, eyes wide, expecting to examine him.

He releases the oars and rises to his feet, swiftly pulling his top off. His fingers deftly undo the knot at his waistline and allow his pants to fall around his ankles. The igni takes in her breath sharply.

"The gills activate once we take a few breaths underwater," he explains. "Obviously, if I jump into the ocean, you won't see them. Hold on."

The mari steps to the edge of the rowboat and leans over to the surface, reaching down with cupped hands. He brings the gathered water up to his face and breathes every drop of the ocean into his piscine nares.

His gills appear above his knees. They spiral around and around, like two long serpents wrapping his thighs, up to the back of his legs, under his buttocks. The organs then swirl around his inner thighs to the front of his body, where they travel up to his hips and curve at the top to form semi-circles that meet below the navel.

Mari gills form a heart shape on the front of the body.

Kyoko's jaw falls agape, her entire face ablaze, her eyes locked on the gills. "You're right. This isn't something I've seen before."

The intimacy heightens. Baring himself physically was a different experience a year prior, before they had bared themselves emotionally to one another.

Almost too quickly, he reaches down and pulls his pants back up to his waist. "And now you've seen mari gills."

Kyoko nods, finally closing her mouth. "And now I've seen it all."

Ana assumes rowing duties when she returns from her swim, allowing Rafael the chance to plunge into the ocean. Breathing air is passive, he typically doesn't realize he's doing it. Not that breathing water is onerous, but when he can *feel* the substance from which his gills tear oxygen, he knows he is...

Alive.

He and Ana switch places a number of times over the next few hours, as the three humans make their way over ocean waves, under the roving suns. Swimming, rowing, swimming, rowing.

"I'm sorry," Kyoko apologizes to Rafael, when he has the oars again. She gestures to her injured shoulder. "I would row if I could."

"We all have duties on this mission," Rafael responds. "Rowing is not the only contribution."

Kyoko nods. "Perhaps the most important contribution I can make is reminding you of your promises."

"I remember. We walk into SeaBed together. We leave SeaBed together."

She eyes him suspiciously. "I haven't been able to reconcile how you can make a promise reliant on laws that you have no control over."

"I have no control over the laws. But I do have control over how well the warning is expressed. SeaBed's Generals are obstinate, but they aren't foolish. Even they can see that a global catastrophe is more important than one returned exile." He offers her a smile. One she doesn't reciprocate. "Conveying the danger that threatens us all is how I reconcile that promise."

There's a long pause in which Kyoko glares at Rafael. He thinks she may be able to see past his confident facade.

"I'll try to put some faith in your plan," she says slowly, hesitantly.

Rafael nods. "I appreciate that." He changes the subject. "How's the translation going?"

She looks down at the Sprite text in her lap. "I don't know how Ana does this. Nysabaani is a difficult language. Most of what I've read is either too advanced for me to decipher or too mundane to matter. There are…" Her voice trails off.

"'There are' what?"

"There are three words that seem to occur together with most of the mentions of the Ancient Ones. And these three words are placed close together, as if they refer to one person. Like a title."

"What are these words?"

"I think they're 'desert,' 'witch,' and 'meeting place.' If it is a title, it would be the Witch of the Meeting Place in the Desert? That's as far as my translation goes."

"We can ask Ana about it when she's done with her swim."

But by the time Ana returns, both Rafael and Kyoko have forgotten about the Witch of the Meeting Place in the Desert. The travelers reach the point where the two oceans meet. Directly below them, on the ocean floor, is SeaBed.

"We're here," Rafael says, gesturing for both women to look off the side of the boat. Their eyes widen instantly at the sight. Circular pools of water, distinct from both oceans, settle along the waves on the surface. They glitter and shine, reflecting many different colors from the surface of the water. There are hundreds of them.

It's as if someone has melted rainbows and poured them onto the surface.

"What are they?" Kyoko asks.

"Assimilation pools. Those who aren't mari enter the pool here at the surface, then come out a few thousand feet underwater at the ocean floor, with their bodies equipped to handle the pressure, temperature, and darkness at depth."

"And what if you are mari," Ana inquires.

Rafael smiles. "Then it saves some swim time."

She gets to her feet, then disrobes and packs her clothes into her bag, which she hoists onto her shoulder. Without waiting for a cue from Rafael, she leaps off of the side of the boat and into the glittering rainbow pool, disappearing below the surface.

"Are you nervous?" Rafael asks, noticing the strained expression on Kyoko's face. The igni nods. "Here, I have an idea."

He straps both his and Kyoko's bags to his back, and lifts Kyoko into his arms. She wraps her uninjured arm around his neck. Before they drop into the pool, he uses the Radiance to form a bubble of air around Kyoko's head. It's invisible above the surface, but underwater, she'll be able to breathe.

"Remember your promise," she reminds him again.

"We leave together," he repeats. "Hold on tight."

She tightens her grip around his neck and he counts down from three, pushing off of the side of the boat at zero, and diving head first through the glittering rainbow pool. They zoom through the water, as if launched from a cannon. The pressure is immense, but lasts fewer than a handful of seconds.

At the bottom, Rafael can see the massive lighting systems on the ocean floor, illuminating the city. Total darkness blankets them overhead.

Kyoko is still clutching his neck tightly, the bubble of air holding strong around her head. Rafael pulls her in closer, snuggling her close, making sure she feels safe in his arms, and that her injured shoulder is protected from too much erratic movement.

"How do you feel?" he asks.

"Nauseous." She burps. "And creeped out by how dark it is."

Rafael laughs. "Ready to see my home?"

A soft smile stretches across her face and she nods. He gestures below them and she turns her head. From her expression, he gathers the sight is unlike anything she's seen before.

There are hundreds of transparent domes littering the ocean floor, all surrounding the largest in the center, connected by tubes and tunnels weaving like tentacles through the water and finding their way back to the center. It resembles one massive, living, breathing organism; a cephalopod made of glass.

"Each dome is a neighborhood," he explains as Kyoko listens intently. "The largest of them, in the center, is home to commercial districts, government buildings, the homes of the wealthiest residents."

"What is it called?"

"Corazón Azul. My home neighborhood is further on the outskirts of SeaBed, clustered together with all of the other olive groves."

He carries Kyoko down to a narrow tube on the ocean floor, extruding directly from Corazón Azul. A door breaks in half vertically and slides open, allowing them to enter a chamber where Ana waits for them.

The water in the tube drains out and is expelled back into the ocean, leaving them in a holding area filled with air. Rafael puts Kyoko down onto her feet, not letting go of her until she feels balanced. The two mari take a moment to get dressed again, as Kyoko laments having kept her clothes through the journey.

"I'm going to change into dry clothes as soon as we get into the city," she huffs.

Another door opens ahead of them to reveal an entryway into the neighborhood. There's a long line of individuals waiting to enter, mostly mari. In fact, Kyoko is the only one who isn't. He turns to her and realizes she's made the same observation. Her eyebrows scrunch together and she seems to almost step behind Rafael.

"Now I know how you felt last year in EverEmber."

He takes her hand to gather her attention and she looks up at him. "You're safe. I won't let anything happen to you."

She nods and opens her mouth to respond, but before she can get a word out, Ana shakes Rafael by the elbow.

"Rafa, we have a problem."

Rafael follows her gaze to the very front of the tube, where individuals are being admitted into SeaBed. There's a legion of mari soldiers, in their seashell and turtle bone armor, staring at them. The warriors whisper to each other until one of them breaks rank and begins walking toward Rafael, Ana, and Kyoko.

Rafael's heart is void of anxiety. There's no apprehension. Exactly as he'd planned, as certain as the waves above him and the sharks around him, the soldiers will arrest him and then turn Ana and Kyoko away to return to the surface.

He turns to Ana. "Take Kyoko home."

"What?" Ana's expression contorts.

The soldier reaches them and stops so close to Rafael, their noses would have been touching, had they had them. When he speaks, he whispers so softly even Ana and Kyoko have to lean in to hear him.

"Please leave," the soldier says, his expression pained.

Rafael wasn't expecting such compassion. "I've come with good reason."

"They won't care. Please, Rafael."

"Do you know each other?" Kyoko asks.

"Everyone knows him," the soldier responds. "He looks just like his mother."

"His mother?" Ana reacts. "Who is his mother?"

"I have to see her," Rafael insists.

"Rafael, please," the soldier begs. "Your sister, your father, they're war heroes as far as I'm concerned. Don't make me drag you to your execution. Just go and we'll forget we saw you."

Rafael looks to Ana, then to Kyoko. He mouths "Trust me" then turns around completely and places his wrists together behind his back, holding his mother's face steadily in his mind.

All according to plan. Your little salmon has come home to save you, mother.

He can hear the soldier sigh as he withdraws his handcuffs and takes Rafael into custody.

Rafael turns back around and his knees nearly buckle from the shock of the sight before him. Two additional soldiers appear at the first's sides. They also withdraw handcuffs and place them on Ana and Kyoko.

"What are you doing?" Rafael demands. "Release them. I'm the exile." He steps toward them, but the soldier behind him grabs the cuffs and holds Rafael steady.

"They brought an exile to our city," the soldier taking Kyoko into custody remarks. "They will appear before the Generals alongside you."

No, no, no. This isn't the plan.

Rafael thrashes against the hold of the soldier behind him, trying to break free, but it's far too late. "Let them go! No, no, no!"

He was certain of what would happen. The son of a General knows the protocols. Or at least, what the protocols were a decade earlier.

Kyoko winces as they push on her cuffs to move her. Rafael tugs harder to try and free himself. His volume grows as his actions become wilder. "Watch her shoulder! Be gentle with her shoul—"

The soldier behind him places a rag with a foul-smelling substance over Rafael's nares and mouth. His knees become weak and darkness starts to take over, as Ana and Kyoko are led away from him, disappearing into the crowd lining the entryway.

He comes to a crushing realization while the light fades around him: the waves, the currents, the sharks are all predictable. They don't make mistakes.

But he has.

CHAPTER 26

"The Little Salmon"

Sub-Oceanic Stratocracy *SeaBed*
Date *33rd Day of Month 6, Year 1629 DG*

DARKNESS FADES SLOWLY. MUFFLED SOUNDS take eons to clear. The weight of a steel mallet strikes his temple. Disorientation; doesn't remember his name, where he is, why he's here.

The man pushes up onto his knees and drool leaks from his open mouth. Locked jaw, numb limbs. Images start to form, memories with them. Sounds impart force on his eardrums. His hands fly to his ears and he covers them. The pounding in his head is excruciating.

He blinks hard ten, twenty times and his jaw unlocks. His vision clears a little more and someone sits in front of him, facing him. She has similar features as him; long, dark hair, piscine nares in the center of her face. Her name eludes him for long moments until he finds it again.

Ana.

Slowly, he pulls his hands down from his ears. Her soft voice comes through.

"Are you alright, Rafa?" she asks. His memories return when she names him. All of them. Who he is. Where they are. Why they're here.

Everything.

He dries his mouth on the back of his sleeve and swivels his head to take in the surroundings. They're in a cell in the dungeons. The last place he sat and wept with his mother before they carried him away from SeaBed nine years earlier.

And it's the first place they brought him back.

"I'm alright," he lies, a strained voice escaping a dry throat. "I just need a minute. Where is Kyoko?"

Ana gestures with her eyes to a small bench in the corner of the cell. Kyoko sits there, wrapped in a blanket. Rafael realizes he doesn't feel as cold as he did the last time he was here. The horrific smells are gone, as well. It's clean.

With Ana's help, he slowly rises to his feet and hobbles to where Kyoko sits, still weary from the substance that was forced into his lungs. He sits down next to the igni and leans in close to her.

"Kyoko? Are you alright?" Her gaze remains fixed at the bars ahead. She doesn't look at him; she doesn't even turn her head. Rafael meets Ana's gaze but the mari woman is sitting in a corner herself, staring down at the ground.

He tries again. "Did they hurt you?"

Her voice erupts as strained as his. "Of course, they did."

Rafael's heart drops. "Where? What did they do? Tell me." Rage builds in his chest.

"They saw my exoskeleton, Rafael"—her gaze remains fixed—"and all the leniency, the mercy, the humanity, disappeared from them. They were violent when they escorted me away, brutal when they tossed me into the back of a carriage, uncivil when they forced me into a cell. And they laughed." She cradles her injured shoulder. "A year's worth of work to regain my range of motion and I'll likely have to start again."

"Kyoko, listen to me," Rafael says, hot anger burning his skin. "They will suffer for it. I prom—"

"Don't say it!" She turns so quickly, finger raised to his face, she nearly knocks Rafael off of the bench. When their eyes meet, he understands the rage he felt moments earlier was a drop compared to the ocean in Kyoko. "Don't you fucking dare say that word."

"Kyoko," the mari breathes, rising to his feet and stepping backward away from her. He's never seen her in a state like this. "I'm sorry,

Kyoko. They were supposed to bar you from entering the city. They were supposed to send you back home. They acted against protocol."

"You think I'm angry about getting arrested? Rafa, I walked into the mari homeland with an exile. Being taken into their custody was assumed."

"Then," he hesitates, trying to piece her rage together, "why…"

Her expression mutates instantly and betrays her exact emotions. Her rage melts away and all that's left is pain. Pure agony.

"You lied to me." Her eyes dart to Ana and then back to Rafael. "To us. For the past year, I heard you mumbling in your sleep, and I thought it was endearing. But not this time. Whatever they gave you, it loosed your tongue on the way down to your lungs. You told us all about your mother, the General. And about the promise you don't expect to be able to keep."

Rafael's blood runs cold.

Kyoko continues. "Then they went through our belongings. Mine, Ana's, yours." She pulls her hand out from under the blanket and brandishes Sofia's letter to her son. "You have no intention of walking out of SeaBed with us, do you? That was all a lie to get me to agree to bring you here. To what is certainly your execution."

"Kyoko, I…I…" He doesn't even know where to begin. He hadn't expected her to be here, to be this hurt. "I have to save her, Kyoko. No matter the cost."

"Even if that cost is your life? And you didn't think for a second what that cost meant to me?"

"I didn't think you would understand."

Kyoko's mouth falls open slightly and an agonized whimper escapes her. "Of all people, you didn't think *I* could understand? I've never been exiled. I haven't been kept away from my parents. But I stood there, feet from you, as you convened with Joaquina's spirit. I held you as you wept, I…" Her voice trails off. "You think I wouldn't understand how much your family means to you?"

Rafael is stunned beyond words. She's right. About all of it. She gave him support when he needed it. When it came time to give her honesty in return, to deliver a difficult truth to the person he loves most, he failed. He opens his mouth to say something—an apology, anything—but not a single sound is produced.

He's too ashamed.

Kyoko continues. "For twelve days, all you've done is ask me to trust you. You've made promises to me that we're all going to walk away from this, safe and sound. You made it seem like you had a plan to survive, when you didn't." Her tone hardens and as quickly as it left, the rage returns. "Where is the trust in *me*, Rafa? You couldn't trust me with your true intentions? Even after I trusted you against my own instincts?"

She rises to her feet. "You're a fucking hypocrite."

Her words, her tone, her expression, strikes him with such force, execution would've hurt less. He'd rather be hanged, or dried out, or beheaded a thousand times over, than hear Kyoko speak to him with such venom.

He's lost her.

The clang of the lock on the cell bars echoes around the small chamber. Ana rises to her feet as the guard announces, "It's time. The emergency evening council has convened. The Generals await you all for trial."

Rafael doesn't move. He needs more time to beg for Kyoko's mercy; to plead for her forgiveness. But prisoners cannot decide when their time is up. The guards pull him back toward the cell doors and place his arms behind his back, cuffing him again.

"I'll comply," Kyoko says to the guard that approaches her. "There's no need to cuff me." The guard turns to another of higher rank, who nods. Rafael is escorted up to the Hall of Generals in handcuffs, while Ana and Kyoko are unbound, flanked by guards.

Rafael's only been in the massive chamber twice before in his life. Once when he was a child, his father brought him and Joaquina here to show them where their mother's new workplace was after she'd been elected to the Council. The second time was when he was exiled.

And now he stands, for a third time, in this room of decision.

It hasn't changed much. Rows upon rows of wooden pews, on either side of the entry aisle, filled with civilian onlookers. A podium for plaintiffs and their counsel, another for defendants and theirs. Towering windows line the outskirts of the room, letting in illumination from the lighting systems beyond the dome. It's much dimmer than when they swam in, indicating night has fallen outside of the ocean.

On the far end of the room is a massive marble structure, a bench from where the Generals call out sentences, from where lives are fortified or shattered. Rafael, Kyoko, and Ana are guided to the defendants' podium and, only moments later, the doors beside the Generals' bench open up.

Rafael doesn't recognize the first three to step through; they must be newly elected. He isn't surprised, the three they replaced were disliked by much of SeaBed.

The fourth to enter is the leader of the Generals, the one who holds the highest position in the city, and a man who Rafael recognizes: Captain General Francisco. Rafael never liked him, particularly not the way the man spoke to his mother. General Sofia is a mightier warrior than he is, a more beloved and benevolent leader, and a more honest and merciful public servant.

Francisco is arrogant and blunt. He possesses all of the qualities that allowed him to achieve the highest title in the city; the very same that are deemed "leadership" qualities in him, and "unlikable" in Sofia. It's disheartening to see the badge of the Captain General on his chest, when the one who deserves it is…

Sofia.

She steps into the room behind Francisco. Rafael's heart stops beating for a moment as time stands still. Every single soul in the room disappears and for an instant, it's just him and his mother. He wants so badly to call out to her. To tell her he came back to save her, and that he loves her. To tear Joaquina's bracelet off and present it to her.

To let her know that he meant what he said nine years earlier: no matter where he goes, one day, he will come home.

Her once entirely dark tresses now have streaks of gray in them. Lines crawl out from the corner of her red, swollen eyes. They look exactly as they did the night he was exiled. She cried then. She's been crying now.

The five Generals each take their places at the bench. Before anyone speaks, Sofia raises her gaze and, for the first time in nine years, she makes eye contact with Rafael. The icy blues hold no smile, no surprise, no love.

With their eyes, mother and son exchange the conversation they had the night of his exile.

One day, I will know it's time to come home.

My sweet little salmon. Not this time. You must never come back. Promise.

Maybe they'll let me come home if it's for something important.

They will not show mercy twice, Rafa. Promise me, you'll never come home.

I promise.

It isn't until this very moment that Rafael realizes Kyoko is not the only person in the room to whom he's made a promise he didn't keep.

CHAPTER 27

"The Son of General Sofia"

***Sub-Oceanic Stratocracy** SeaBed*
***Date** 33rd Day of Month 6, Year 1629 DG*

IN THE SORROW OF HIS mother's gaze, Rafael finds the answers to so many questions. Why wasn't he honest with Kyoko about his intentions? Why didn't he tell her he couldn't guarantee his safety, but he had to come home anyway?

Why didn't he trust that, after all they've been through together, she would understand?

He turns to Kyoko, cradling her injured shoulder beside him, flanked by guards, and the realization dawns. The same society that expects women like General Sofia to swallow their emotions demands that men don't experience them at all. He can't blame his actions on societal expectations. They didn't tell him to lie. But they did stand over his shoulder and put bricks on his tongue.

He turns back to his mother, a woman still shackled by those same expectations. Rafael is seeing her after nine years, but for the first time in his life, he's *seeing* her.

The four lower-ranking Generals take their seats whilst Captain General Francisco remains standing. The onlookers in the wooden pews lean forward to the edge of their seats, waiting for the leader of the city to speak; awaiting the admonishment he's surely going to unleash on the wretched exile and his associates.

The exile whose actions disgraced his father's memory and killed his sister.

Francisco draws a deep breath and begins. "Rafael. Oh, how I wish I could say it's wonderful to see you again. When you left our city, you were a boy of fifteen, and now you're a man. Look at you. Strong, handsome. The Library has been good for you."

Rafael's lips press tightly together. He's unsure of how the Captain General would like him to respond.

"It's truly baffling that you would return here," he continues. "Was it not explained before you left, that there would be dire consequences to your return?"

The question is rhetorical and pompous. It's a turning of the dagger already lodged between the prisoner's ribs.

Rafael clears his throat, projecting his voice loudly for all to hear. "I'm aware of the consequences, Captain General. I've come—" he pauses when he catches Ana and Kyoko in his peripheral vision. "*We've* come to deliver a message to the esteemed Generals of the Council."

"A message so important you'd risk execution to bring it to us?" Francisco's smug grin widens on his face. He's relishing the fact that Rafael's life is in his hands.

"To save SeaBed, yes."

The Captain General raises an eyebrow. "But why wouldn't you send your two comrades alone? Why come with them when you know what's at stake?"

Rafael nods to Kyoko. "Would you have entertained an audience at the request of an igni?" Then to Ana. "Or that of a citizen of the Library who hasn't stepped foot in SeaBed since she was an infant?"

Francisco nods slowly, realization dawning on his face. "So that's why you've come. You needed our attention and you felt this would be the only way to get it."

Again, Rafael stands silent.

"Alright, then. You have our attention. What is this important message that will save SeaBed?"

Rafael's gaze travels from Francisco to the other Generals. They're wide-eyed, clearly curious about what he's about to say. All but his mother, whose hands are folded in front of her, eyes on her interlocked fingers.

The exile turns to Kyoko for support, but the wall she's put up between them remains firmly in place. She keeps her head tilted down toward the floor by her feet. Ana offers the encouraging smile he seeks.

He fills his lungs and speaks. "SeaBed is in immeasurable danger."

The Captain General's grin vanishes and his eyes narrow. "What sort of danger?"

"Catastrophic. This city is amongst three epicenters of a grave threat."

Francisco's fist lands on the table and rattles the marble. "Out with it, boy! Stop heralding vague prophecies."

Rafael forces the truth out as directly as he can. "There are two powerful, ancient beings that have been unleashed onto this world. Their magic is linked to a demonic plane from which they intend to bring forth fierce creatures called the Three Deaths. Each of these 'Deaths' will be released into our realm using one of the human cities as a portal, a gateway, potentially wiping our home from the planet."

He steadies his eye contact with Francisco, holding it firmly to convey his seriousness. "And yes, I'm willing to risk execution before I let that happen. We must defend this city."

The room falls so silent that the beating wings of a fly can be heard. The onlookers in the pews exchange uncomfortable glances. The guards posted around the room whisper to each other in bewilderment. And every General, including Sofia, turns to Francisco, awaiting his reaction.

There are so many ways in which Francisco can respond, and Rafael could've predicted any of them, except for the one response that actually transpires. After a long pause, too long for Rafael's comfort, Francisco giggles.

It's soft at first, just a series of chuckles. Then it grows into a guffaw, and continues growing until the Captain General is red in the face and wiping tears from the corners of his eyes.

The onlookers laugh from their pews. The guards around the room point and hoot. The Generals slap their knees. Only four people, in a room of over fifty, aren't laughing: Rafael, Ana, Kyoko, and Sofia.

Once Francisco's laughing fit has been conquered, he breathes deeply and meets Rafael's eyes again. "A joke, surely."

Rafael swallows and shakes his head.

"Ah"—the Captain General raises a finger into the air as if he's figured out some difficult puzzle—"then you've come to die by suicide. You've grown tired of life in exile, but you don't want to admit it, so you've concocted some deranged story of ancient beings and demonic planes. But the truth is you've just come to die at home."

"The truth is exactly what I told you," Rafael responds. "It's not a story. This message is going to save SeaBed. The Ancient Ones are prepared to raze this world, and they have the power to do so. This is so much bigger than me, or you, or SeaBed, or politics."

The Captain General rises to his feet. "Messages are sent *by* someone, Rafael, and carried by messengers. You're just the messenger, so tell me: who sent it? The Prime Librarian? Chief Member Saila?"

Saila's words from the Forum ring in Rafael's ears. *If you want to go to SeaBed, you go as civilians.*

Rafael loses his words and doesn't know how to respond. He can't drag Saila into something to which she explicitly expressed opposition. And the Prime would never authorize a mission rooted in so much mythology and magic.

But as Rafael gathers a response, he realizes this message *is* being sent by someone or something far greater than any one nation or kingdom on the planet.

"Whatever forces beyond our control that govern the wheels of fate, that is who sends this message."

Again, Francisco is lost for a few seconds in laughter. "Ah, deities! So you're a very pious man now? The boy has grown into a believer."

Joaquina's instructions from his childhood archery lessons emerge onto his tongue. "I believe only in one thing, Captain General: protecting the ones I love. My mother sits there"—he gestures to General Sofia—"beside you. My father and my sister are buried here beneath the city. The innocent citizens of my home deserve to survive the inevitable brutality that threatens them. I even care for your safety, and the safety of the other Generals, and the officers in this room."

The guards stop whispering amongst themselves and pay attention to the exile's words.

"I know I've sealed my fate by returning to SeaBed. But I am not afraid to die knowing I've saved the city. Please, heed the warning.

Accept the message for exactly what it is: fate's intervention. Something greater than all of us is giving you the chance to save your people from catastrophe. Don't turn your back on it."

Again, the room falls into a dense silence, as all eyes focus on the Captain General, who speaks skeptically still. "What an emotional plea. You certainly have grown into quite the orator, haven't you, boy? But we are Generals and politicians and public servants. We cannot make decisions based on emotions." He turns his head and locks his slippery gaze on Rafael's mother. "Isn't that right, Sofia?"

General Sofia raises her swollen eyes to Rafael and slowly nods, then brings her gaze back down to her hands.

"And there you have it," the Captain General announces as his smug grin relapses. "Normally, the Council of Generals would vote on whether or not we want to take action on this plea. But I think it's fair for me to assume that we won't be entertaining this story of yours."

Rafael's stomach tightens when he sees the three Generals to Francisco's right nod in agreement. He grows nauseous, staring in disbelief as the leaders of SeaBed turn his warning away. Death is so much closer now than it was a moment ago.

And not just for Rafael.

"With that being said," he continues, "we will convene once again tomorrow morning to set the date for the exile's execution. Until then, he will be held in the dungeons." The Captain General raises a heavy gavel and slams it down, the echoing bang reverberating throughout the room.

Rafael knew his execution was likely. But he wasn't expecting the outright denial of an impending event that could wipe the city off the map. He was expecting to, at the very least, save SeaBed before he dies. Save his home.

Save his mother.

"Any final words, Rafael?" The Captain General asks.

Rafael turns back toward Kyoko and Ana, his stomach in knots, his heart bursting from his chest, then raises his chin to face Francisco.

"Despite the outcome of this meeting, I know you are capable of justice. The travelers who joined me are innocent. They've committed no crime and deserve to be set free."

Francisco strokes his chin, before finally nodding. "Alright. These women are free. We'll honor your final request." He snaps his fingers and gestures for the guards to take Ana and Kyoko from the Hall of Generals.

"No!" Kyoko shouts, moving toward Rafael and clinging to his waist with her uninjured arm. "You promised me we were leaving together."

Rafael is stunned again. In an instant, the wall she'd put up melts away. He sees it in her eyes. The realization that she's never going to see him again. And it's breaking her.

It breaks him, too. Droplets of light tenderly reflect off the glistening stone of Kyoko's exoskeleton. Her cheeks, her eyes, her voice, the flow of her hair, the sway of her hips.

The courage in her heart, the brilliance in her mind, the goodness in her soul; everything about Kyoko, inside and out, has captivated him from the moment he tossed his prejudices away and peeled back the layers of his admiration for her. The depth of everything they've built between them over the past year hits him harder than he ever thought it would, in this moment when it becomes abundantly clear...

These are the final moments he will ever see Kyoko. She has to leave SeaBed, for her own safety, and she must continue the mission for the world's. And once she steps out of the doors of the Hall of Generals, and he is returned to the dungeons, she'll be gone.

Forever.

He wants to lean forward and press his lips to hers. To whisper "I love you" to her. He desperately wants these to be the last words she hears in his voice. But he knows that if this happens, she'll never accept his fate. A fate neither of them have control over, and this goodbye will become far more violent for all of them than it needs to be.

He leans in close to her and hardens his tone. "Kyoko, let go of me. You have to leave, it's not safe for you here."

"I'm not leaving you, Rafa," she insists. A guard places his hands on her shoulders and begins to tug at her, so she clutches Rafael tighter, wincing from the pain of the guard pulling on her injury.

"Kyoko, I can't protect you when I'm chained. Please, leave SeaBed."

A layer of moisture forms in her eyes. "No. You can't do this. Fight." Her voice wavers and becomes strained.

He places his forehead gently against hers. "I can't, Kyoko. It's over."

Her free hand rises, through the agony in her shoulder, just enough to touch his cheek. "You promised me."

"I failed," Rafael blurts out. "I failed in keeping all of my promises. I overestimated their sense of justice." His sensibility dies and his heart takes control of his tongue. "Kyoko, I lo—"

The guards pull harder and Kyoko is tugged away from Rafael, interrupting his confession. She screams in brutal pain as she's dragged by two large guards toward the exit where Ana awaits her.

"Ahh! Let go of me! Rafa, I'll get you out! I'll get you out of this! NO! Rafa!"

His name is the last thing he hears before the doors slam shut and she's taken away from him, still shrieking in agony. The room goes blurry behind the tears congregating in his eyes.

Goodbye, Kyoko.

It becomes clear in this moment, more than any other moment before it, how much he wanted to spend more time with her. How much he feels cheated out of the years they would've had together. He wasted twenty-three years of life existing without knowing her. The gods, the universe, whatever forces are at play…they owe him twenty-three years *with* her.

Rafael turns around to find the Generals, all of them standing, ready to turn and exit the Hall. The wooden pews have emptied, all but two of the guards have taken leave, and the Generals will soon depart.

He finds his mother's gaze. She bites her lower lip, tears threatening her eyes, as well. Rafael shakes his head and raises his chin as two beads of moisture break free and travel down his cheeks.

More of their conversation from nine years earlier travels between them.

Keep your head raised every second that you breathe. Conquer every challenge. Never forget who you are. You are the son of General Sofia.

Until his final moment, Rafael will never forget who he is: the son of General Sofia.

CHAPTER 28

"PIXIE, BRAVER, FATHER"

Theocracy *SunSide*
Date *33rd Day of Month 6, Year 1629 DG*

SAILA HOLDS A HEAVY BREATH in her lungs, before slowly allowing it to exit her mouth, taking her trepidation with it. Her fingers surround the cold metal of a doorknob that will lead her back into Tund-Ra's cell. Back into the small chamber where he nearly bested her with a surprise attack five days earlier.

A surprise for him, as well, it seemed. Saila recalls the wide-eyed expression on the prisoner's face when he blurted out the truth of his clanship. The truth that returning to an ore-free Larso was a blessing, a release from his cage. A return to the Radiance. Something that wouldn't have mattered had he been what Saila, Ovida, Kruga, the theocrats, and every SunSidian citizen had assumed he was.

A faerie.

Saila survived his attack because she has more control over the Radiant energy in her body than he has over the words on his tongue.

Trepidation is not a becoming emotion on a leader. Concern is not a suitable expression on a ruler's face. None of those who held this station before her exuded these feelings for the citizens to see, let alone the prisoners.

She'll swallow it all until there's nothing left but courage and conviction. A soft smile spreads across her mouth as she etches confidence into her heart, hoping it will keep her chin raised throughout the conversation she's about to have.

She turns the knob and opens the iron door.

Ovida and a lavender-skinned SunSidian Guard hover over the prisoner. Tund-Ra sits on his bed, back against the wall, his hands folded in his lap and his eyes closed. The Guard has her hands stretched out in front of her, clearly using the Radiance to restrain him.

Ovida hears Saila enter and turns to face her. "We're just preparing for a shift change. The next Guard should be in shortly to take over."

"Tell them not to come," Saila instructs.

Ovida narrows her eyes and leans in closer. "What do you mean?"

"Leave me with him. Alone. Dismiss the next Guard when they arrive."

Ovida's gaze jogs the floor, as if she's trying to find a response at her feet. "Saila, I-I have to advise against it. Keeping a pixie in a faerie cell is a massive risk, and until we can free up a chamber that has Radiant restraints on it—"

"This isn't going to go the way our last meeting did." Saila leans slightly to her left to peer over the General's shoulder and address the prisoner. "Isn't that right, Tund-Ra?"

Tund-Ra's eyelids break apart slowly, and he turns his head to Saila and nods.

Ovida leans in. "Saila, please. This is unwise. He's dangerous."

Saila smiles and raises her chin, hoping to display the confidence she's sewn into her veins. "So am I." The pixie steps aside, freeing a path between the General and the exit.

The orange-skinned Mega and her subordinate begrudgingly step through the doorway, leaving Saila alone with Tund-Ra. The pixie ruler takes a seat beside Tund-Ra's bed, from where he eyes her like a vulture eyes a carcass.

"After our last interaction," he says with a voice as soft as silk, "I wouldn't expect you to be alone with me so easily."

"I put you to sleep in our last interaction," Saila counters. "I have no qualms about doing it again."

The prisoner nods, lowering his gaze. "I'm disappointed in myself. It's atypical of me to lose control of my tongue that way. There are things that were said, that shouldn't have been. Things were done, that shouldn't have been."

Though she keeps her confident shell unbroken, genuine surprise bubbles into her chest. Of all the emotions he's exhibited since being taken into custody, remorse hasn't been one.

"I disagree, Tund-Ra. There were so many things that I'm grateful you said. Grateful you did. Had our last interaction gone differently, had you remained as silent as you had the five days prior, I never would've found out that you're a pixie. I never would've found Pina."

Tund-Ra's eyes rise to meet hers. His expression mirrors the shock she felt moments earlier. "You've spoken with my daughter?"

"I have. It took me three days to find her, and another two to convince her to speak with me. We just met this morning."

Tund-Ra remains quiet for some time, his eyes narrowed, as if assessing Saila's intent. "What is this, Saila? Are you threatening my daughter to elicit my cooperation?"

Saila shakes her head, bewildered that he would think so little of her. "I'm not you. Pina has nothing to do with this."

"Then why did you speak with her?"

"Because you were silent for five days, Tund-Ra. I needed answers. Your motives, the organization. There are so many unanswered questions and I thought, if you wouldn't give me the responses I needed, perhaps Pina would."

She holds steady eye contact to deliver the most pressing question of all. "I needed to know: why would a pixie lead a faerie organization like the Bravers United?"

"Did Pina answer that question for you?"

Saila shakes her head. "She told me some things about your life, but not much. I don't think she trusted me."

"That's my daughter." He beams with pride.

"Since she didn't answer my questions, it's up to you now. Will you finally speak to me, Tund-Ra?"

He purses his lips and sits silently, staring at Saila for so long that she starts to think he won't respond. Then, unpredictably, he lies down on his back with his hands behind his head and his ankles crossed. It's the most relaxed she's ever seen him, as if he's lounging in a hammock on a beach somewhere, with the rays of the suns massaging him.

"How old are you, Saila?"

The sudden, loose posture confuses Saila, but she keeps herself composed, focused on the prisoner's question, hoping her cooperation will inspire his own.

"Thirty-Six," she answers him.

"Pina's your age."

Saila nods. "It's one of the things we spoke about."

"Have you ever been in love?"

Another question that pulls the rug from under her. *Where is he going with this?*

"I'm not sure. There have been times in my life where I thought I was, but"—she pauses—"hindsight and experience change perspectives, rot memories. Have you?"

A sad smile melts his expression and he nods slowly. "Once, when I was twenty. We met at work."

"What did you do for work?" Saila probes him.

"Construction. He and I were a good team. We were often assigned projects together, just the two of us. We built entire homes, sturdy homes, faster than crews of ten."

"Was your love reciprocated?" she wonders.

A soft chuckle escapes his lips as he continues to stare up at the ceiling. "Oh, yes. He loved me as much as I loved him, if not more. So I brought him home one day to meet my family."

The smile on his lips fades, but the sadness accompanying it deepens. Saila's hardened shell starts to crack as Tund-Ra's expression darkens the room. She remains quiet to allow him space to continue.

His voice flows considerably softer than before. "My parents had"—he takes a long pause—"concerns. That our bloodline would be lost to my inability to conceive a child with another man. And that..."

He blinks his anguish away and shifts to the edge of the bed, letting his feet rest gently on the prison floor. He clears his throat and continues, "And that our clan, pixies, would never accept a relationship between myself and a faerie. And they were right."

"You were twenty years old. An adult. Free to love whomever you desired."

Tund-Ra folds his hands together and rubs the knuckles of one hand anxiously. "I loved my parents more than anything or anyone else."

He pauses before correcting himself. "Except for Loro. He launched me into depths of love I had never known. Intelligent, selfless, empathetic, honest, creative, kind. But when you're twenty years old, and serving your parents and your community is all you know, their disappointment hurts more than love heals. So when my *pixie* parents, and my *pixie* community turned their back on me, I didn't think I had a choice. I let him go."

Saila begins to understand. Tund-Ra's leadership of the Bravers United isn't out of a love for faeries. It's born out of a hatred of his own clan.

The prisoner continues, "Shortly thereafter, my parents forced me to marry a young pixie woman. She was lovely, I held no anger in my heart toward her. I fathered Pina with her, but she realized quite quickly after our daughter was born that my heart remained elsewhere. I begged her to stay, and promised her I would try, but she knew it wasn't going to work. I don't blame her. She deserved better than the damage I brought to the table."

Saila feels a pang of compassion for the pixie. "You were heartbroken, not damaged."

"Two words for the same affliction. Now I had a mouth to feed, a baby to house, a child to raise. And I was doing it alone. So I started my own construction company. My parents, the community, they all rallied behind to show their support. But..."

"But what?" She encourages him to continue.

"But then Loro walked into my workshop, and it all came back. The emotions, the memories...the heartbreak. We talked for days, which became weeks, and then months." Another sad smile stretches across his lips. "Before I knew it, he moved his belongings into my home and was helping me raise Pina. There was no conversation about what was between us, we just naturally slipped into these roles."

Saila leans in, hopefully. "And you were finally happy together?"

"For a short time, yes. But neither my parents, nor the pixies had progressed in their views. Their construction projects were keeping my business running, so when they withdrew their support, after learning about Loro returning to my life, my business failed."

"I'm sorry," Saila offers.

"I'm not," Tund-Ra responds honestly. "The failure of that business gave us the push we needed; the signal that it was time to leave this small-minded community and move to Larso, where we would have more freedom to love openly. The only problem was that there were no construction jobs available for me, and Loro's work was barely enough to feed Pina, let alone all three of us. I had a friend who was settled in the city. I asked him to help me find some work and he did."

Realization dawns on Saila. "Your friend was a Braver."

The prisoner nods. "I know what you've thought about me ever since finding out that I'm a pixie who's a Braver. You think I'm a monster, like your father. A traitor who joined the organization that oppressed his own clan, to serve his own sense of selfish ambition."

Saila presses her lips tightly together. That's exactly what she thought.

"None of that was the case. I didn't join the Bravers because I was ambitious, or because I didn't care about my own clan. To me, I wasn't a pixie who was a Braver. I was just a father trying to feed his daughter."

His expression hardens, and his tone drips with venomous hatred as he speaks. "Do you know who *didn't* see me as a father? Who *only* saw me as a pixie Braver and nothing more?"

Saila keeps her lips pressed. She knows the answer but doesn't want to say it.

"Say it," he commands.

She takes a deep breath and exhales a single word. "Pixies."

Tund-Ra nods slowly. "I've heard your speeches, Saila. A decade of them. You parade yourself, so proudly and vividly, as a champion of clan solidarity. But where the *fuck* was that solidarity when I fell in love? When he moved in to help me raise a child that wasn't his? When I needed work to feed that child? Where were the pixies? They only showed up when it was time to admonish me. To chastise me for joining an organization that oppressed us throughout history."

He rises to his feet and, for a moment, Saila thinks she may need to defend herself, but instead, he begins to pace back and forth from one end of the cell to the other as he speaks.

"Oppression. We've spent so much time focused on how others oppressed us that we've become negligent to the persecution within our own clan. Do you know what it's like to constantly be told to have clan solidarity with a group who ostracizes you?"

He stops pacing in front of Saila and meets her gaze again. "Do you have any idea how fragile your clan solidarity is? When it's pixies against faeries, it's so easy to have solidarity. But what about the moments that aren't about the oppressor? Shouldn't the solidarity be strong enough to bring us together at all times? Shouldn't the bridge remain even when no one is standing on it?"

He sits back down, but his gaze lingers, holding Saila hostage with his grays. "There are many forms of solidarity, and we should all stand in the spaces where they intersect. But the pixies don't."

Saila's mouth falls slack, but she's unable to offer a response. His questions stun her into silence, challenging everything she's believed about the socio-political framework that's held her life's mission together.

That mission is falling apart before her eyes.

It was simple. It was easy. There were oppressors, and there were pixies. There were the bad, and there were the good. But Tund-Ra's experiences don't align with such categorical perceptions of history and society. He didn't choose the oppressors over his own clan.

For him, the oppressors have *been* his own clan.

"There is no easy answer to any of this," he mercifully continues. "Everyone has a unique combination of experiences. Where they live, who they love, who stares back at them in the mirror, what they're capable of, what clan they were born into; all of these are different legs on the same spider. And the arachnid cannot be whole if some of the legs are cut off."

Saila nods and slowly begins to form words, despite the cyclone of thoughts and emotions tearing through her mind and heart. "The pixies ostracized you, and the faeries accepted you. Every part of you."

"They did more than accept me, Saila. They empowered me. When Loro fell ill, and the pixie salver couldn't save him, the faeries were his pallbearers. My faerie mentor helped me move up the Braver ranks and eventually, I shed my pixie name. The name my parents gave me is dead to me. My Braver brothers named me Tund-Ra. It's the only name that means anything to me."

Saila and the prisoner sit quietly for some time, as she absorbs his story and tries to reconcile what she believed with what he experienced. When her curiosity piques, she asks, "Who was your mentor?"

A suggestive smile dances onto Tund-Ra's face. "Do you remember why you came to speak with me in the first place?"

Saila heals the crack in her confident exterior, shielding her confusion from her expression. "I wanted to know the purpose of the violence you engendered throughout the city. The mission of the Braver's United."

"Retribution. We would not let Braver memories be swallowed by the night. Especially not the memory of my mentor, who fought the rebels at the Halving of SunSide one year ago. You should know his name."

Like a tsunami decimating a goldfish, the realization crashes down on Saila. It nearly pushes her down to the ground. When she speaks the name of Tund-Ra's mentor, it's released in a shocked whisper.

"Vy-Ro."

Tund-Ra nods. "Vy-Ro gave me a job when I needed it. He taught me everything. He raised me up in rank and skill. He gave me the name Tund-Ra. And a year ago, the pixies took him from me."

"Vy-Ro tried to kill me," Saila says, finding her voice. "And when I wasn't home, he killed one of the two people in this world I considered sisters. I can't say Vy-Ro's death was a worthy reason for all of the danger you caused in the streets. Citizens have been injured. Many may not recover. For what?"

"For justice," he snarls. "Too many Bravers burned their uniforms, and too many more traded them in for the armor of the New SunSidian Guard. Those of us who remained loyal wanted to make sure the city didn't rest until the theocracy proved their worth as leaders."

His eyes lock on hers and his smile widens again. "Tell me, Saila. Do you think you've proven yourself as a worthy leader?"

Chip. Chip. Chip.

The question starts to chip away at the confident shell surrounding Saila. *Don't listen to him. You are a good leader.*

He continues to prod, chipping away further at her conviction. "What happens to me now? You've arrested me and most of the Braver's United. The threat is gone. I've given you the answers you wanted. What happens next?"

Saila takes a deep breath to steady herself. "You put a lot of citizens in danger, Tund-Ra. Your crimes have sealed your fate under theocratic law. The punishment is execution."

Tund-Ra's smile remains on his face as he leans back against the wall behind him. "I accept. No match burns hotter than a martyr. You can light me up, but it will ignite a fire, Saila."

Chip. Chip. Chip.

Saila exhales deeply. "Then I will snuff out the flames."

"Tell me something." He learns forward again, eyeing her quizzically. "Is that what you think a good leader does? Execution after execution after execution. You want, so badly, to distance your leadership from the MegaFather, and the Bravers, and the faerie supremacy. But here you are ready to execute me like your predecessors executed both Alba and Sonali."

Her confidence no longer chips away. It shatters entirely.

She's been so concerned with being a good leader, she's never defined what that actually means. She's been leading within the same status quo she spent so long fighting. A norm of leadership that was challenged for centuries.

"I know what you're doing, Tund-Ra."

"And what is that?"

"You're trying to get out of the execution."

Tund-Ra shakes his head. "I most certainly am not. You see, I've waited a long time to make my Radiance-Return. For Pina's sake, I've stayed here in this world. But now, I'm ready to see Loro again. I'm excited for it."

"Then why question me and my leadership. What do you get out of it?"

"Nothing. But *you* get something out of it, Saila. You are my daughter's age, and if the last thing I do in this world is impart some small wisdom on you, I'll consider my end worthwhile. Here's the wisdom: Rule on your own terms, guided by your own convictions. SunSide is in your hands now, and you can rule it however you see fit. Just don't become the thing you hate."

"Is that what happened to you?" She challenges him. "You became the thing you hate?"

Tund-Ra looks down at his violet hands. A tear loosens from his face and lands on his pixie palms. "No. I was born the thing I hate."

CHAPTER 29

"THE PARAGON AND THE PUPIL"

Sovereign City-State *The Library*
Date *40th Day of Month 6, Year 1629 DG*

THE HUSTLE OF THE TOP floor of the Center becomes a simmering hum when the workday ends. The desks fall empty, the lights start to dim, and Unisa, still reviewing paperwork Juhi submitted the night before, is amongst the few remaining souls.

Despite her attempts to focus on work, memories of what transpired ten days earlier occupy her mind.

Scientists taught the world that every day is the same length of time. That days can be counted. Measured. Eighty-six-thousand-four-hundred seconds. Fourteen-hundred-forty minutes. Twenty-four hours.

They want everyone to believe that days can be so easily quantified and that, no matter what unpredictability happens, the one thing that can always be relied on, is the fact that the length of a day will never change. It'll always be the same number of seconds, and minutes, and hours. It'll always be fifty days to each month, and ten months to a year.

The suns will never race across the sky any faster than they have since the birth of time itself. The moons will never speed up or slow down.

Well scientists are liars. They must be. Because Unisa has lived through many, *many* days in her twenty-four years, but the past ten have been so much longer than those that came before them.

It's been ten days since Juhi, Konni, and Unisa came together in Yuki's apartment to attempt to break the Fully Bonded. To attempt to pull Maksi from his indoctrination. It ended with tears and Unisa's thoughts being projected for everyone to see. It ended with Maksi fleeing into the night, giving no indication of where his loyalties lied.

It ended with a single question from Konni. A question Unisa didn't have the answer to then, and still doesn't have an answer to now.

Did we break the Fully Bonded?

They may not have succeeded. Maksi may not be joining their group. The number of warriors in their army may still be four.

But, at the very least, Maksi hasn't betrayed them to the Prime. That much is blatant from the fact that they're still alive.

Unisa stacks the papers she's reading and stuffs them into the drawer of her desk. There's no point in forcing herself to read when she's not retaining anything. Her mind is exhausted, there's an anxious percussion in her heart, and she's getting late to visit Lyla.

Lyla. The teenager's cherry-blossom cheeks appear in Unisa's mind, surrounded by rosy hair in two braids down her shoulders. They fall on a stained nightgown that the Mega wears when she's in bed; a stark contrast to the pristine white dresses the Prime makes her wear to entertain guests against her salver's orders. Her pregnancy comes with risks, but the mari leader doesn't seem to care. The risks are to Lyla, not to his future child.

So to him, it's no risk at all.

You'll come see me again, won't you? Lyla asked when Unisa visited Prime Palace for the first time.

Of course. I'll come back to see you.

Unisa's kept her promise. Despite her anxiety that Maksi will tell the Prime everything about their plan, despite Juhi and Konni asking her to stop arriving late to their meetings, despite having to ask Yuki to care longer for Ora while the Librarian is away, Unisa has kept her promise. She hasn't missed a single visit to the Inner Catacomb in the past ten days.

Once her desk is cleaned, she gathers the items she's taking home and places them into her travel bag. As she's about to depart, a heavy hand falls onto her shoulder and startles her. She jumps back into the desk and slams her knee into the metal.

"AH!" she screams, rubbing her injured leg. "What the fuck?!"

The Prime's Gatekeeper stands beside her, eyes wide. "Uni! I've never heard you swear before."

Unisa continues to massage the sore spot. "Why would you sneak up on me like that, Andres?"

"I'm really very sorry, Uni, but the Prime asked me to come get you and—"

Instantly, the pain in her knee evaporates. "The Prime wants to speak with me?"

Andres nods. "Yes, in his office. I'm on my way out for the day"—he gestures to his own bag—"so I thought I would just mention it to you on my way to the exit. I'm sorry again." He continues to apologize before leaving Unisa alone to her fate.

The angi takes a deep breath and tries to rationalize. *This isn't about Maksi. Or Alba. Or the plan. He doesn't know anything. Maksi wouldn't do that.*

Memories of Maksi informing superiors about legal and social transgressions flood Unisa's mind and she begins to sweat. It was not an uncommon occurrence when they worked together. Fear cuts off the passage of air to her lungs. She breathes deeply, labored.

I'm fucked.

Steeling her nerves, she marches forth to the black door at the back of the room. Through it, she enters the small waiting area with the Gatekeeper's desk. She strides past it to the next door, leading directly into the Prime's office.

The angi raises a trembling fist and knocks. She swallows hard, waiting for an answer, and moments later, the Prime is standing in the doorway, staring down at her with his eyes that are somehow hot and cold at the same time.

He's smiling.

Is this a good sign or a bad one?

"Uni," he says almost cheerfully, opening his arms wide. She knows exactly how he wants to be greeted. Her stomach protests every time, but she holds it down. The angi steps forward and the Prime places his hands on her shoulders, pulling her close enough to place a chaste peck on her lips.

She puckers them slightly to appear enthusiastic about the gesture; he hates it when the members of the Inner Catacomb don't show interest in his greetings. He steps to the side and allows her entry, so she takes a seat on one of the three chairs facing his desk. He closes the office door and returns to his own seat behind it.

"Apologies, Uni," he says, leaning forward and interlocking his fingers. "I can see you were heading out when I asked Andres to retrieve you."

Unisa nods. "Yes, I was actually going to head over to the Palace and visit Lyla."

"Oh." He raises an eyebrow curiously. "I understand you've visited Lyla every day for some time now."

Of course he knows. Despite my leaving before he even gets home.

"Yes, I've gone every day since you brought me there the first time."

His eyes widen. "Every day? That's highly irregular, Uni. When I'm considering membership into the Inner Catacomb, I typically ask the candidate to visit once or twice a month, if that, to get to know the other girls gradually. *All* of them, not just Lyla."

"I do visit all of them," Unisa lies.

"That's not what I've heard. A passing salutation isn't a visit. You won't get to know anyone that way and, to be frank, I think you may be disturbing Lyla. She needs adequate sleep and rest for her own health and the baby's."

To be frank, you couldn't care less about Lyla's health.

"I will take that into consideration, Great Prime. My apologies. If you'll allow me a visit with Lyla tonight, I'll reduce the frequency until such time that you feel it appropriate for me to come daily again."

"Daily visits will be appropriate when you move in."

The Prime's words from her first visit to the Inner Catacomb ring in her ears. *After Ora dies, the Inner Catacomb and I will be all you have left.*

Unisa doesn't voice a response; she knows that if she opens her mouth, nothing will come out but more profanity. She nods, then rises to her feet and turns, but the Prime stops her.

"Where are you going?" All cheer in his tone has been tossed from the window. It's hard, abrasive.

"Sorry, Great Prime, I thought the conversation was—"

"Sit." A tiny word, but the tone of the command is so harsh it feels as though he's swung a club covered in nails at her. "This discussion about Lyla is not why I called you here."

Once Unisa's backside is firmly planted into the chair again, the cheerfulness in the Prime's tone returns and his smile reappears.

"The reason I called you here to my office so late is because I need your help."

Curiosity brews in Unisa's chest.

"We have an application for the Youth Education program that has stalled. It's the same program to which your parents applied when you were brought here."

Unisa nods. "I'm aware of the program, Great Prime. What can I do to help with this application?"

"The birth parents attempted to rescind it. Evidently, they weren't aware of every aspect of the program, and after having learned about it in detail, they no longer wish for their daughter to become a Librarian."

Unisa's heart begins to race as she anticipates what he's going to ask her. "What would you like me to do?"

"I need you to speak with them. As someone who's successfully completed the Youth Education program, you can advocate for its virtues. You are a paragon of the program's greatest achievements."

The word "paragon" incites out-of-body delirium. Unisa grows dizzy and lightheaded. The room spins around her as a crushing realization lands on the angi's shoulders.

She's become Alba.

Physically, she's sitting in the exact same seat in which Alba sat a year prior when the Prime forced them to go on their mission to Sun-Side. Symbolically, she's taken Alba's place as the Prime's pawn. His puppet. The perfect Librarian paragon that he uses to authorize and edify his schemes.

The example he points to and says "Look what I can create" adding weight and credibility to the claims that force the innocent into his servitude, his indoctrination.

The realization knocks Unisa deeper into her seat. The Prime stands on a pedestal, high above everyone else, where he's glorified and worshipped. Alba *was* his pedestal, and after she died, he needed to replace her.

Uni is now the pedestal.

Her mouth falls agape. She tries to respond, to tell him she'll never do his dirtiest jobs for him, never condemn a child to the Youth Education program by convincing their parents of its merit.

Never be the reason a child was abandoned the way she was.

But no sounds escape her throat. She can't seem to gather a voice, as she knows there's no other option. She wants to reject him, to deny him access to her as a poster child, but she knows that within the golden gates of the Library, the Prime gets his way. Until Alba's plan is enacted, until the Prime is removed, his will is the word of a god.

Before she can form a sentence, there's a soft knock on the office door.

The Prime rises to his feet. "They're here."

"They?!" Unisa stands as well. Her heart hammers with panic. "The parents?"

The Prime nods. "They're here to discuss their daughter's application for the program. All you have to do is talk about how it changed your life for the better. Understand?"

He doesn't even wait for Unisa to respond because he knows she'll comply. The Prime heads for the door, opens it forcefully and welcomes the couple into the room.

Two angi women step cautiously into the dim office, their fingers interlocked, silver-feathered wings tight against their backs. Their outfits instantly brighten the room, displaying what Unisa recognizes as Gara designs, a traditional and ancient angi method of dyeing textiles. One woman's outfit is covered in bright greens, the other's is coated in deep purples.

This is an aspect of her own culture that Unisa read in books, instead of being taught by her family as she should have been, had she not been accepted into the Youth Education program. The program that tore her from her roots. The program into which she now has to convince these two women to release their daughter.

They seem wary until their gazes find Unisa. She can see their shoulders visibly relax and their expressions melt into smiles. Unisa does that for them. She, another angi woman and Youth Education success story, provides them a symbol of safety in an intimidating situation.

And now she has to betray them.

It's all happening too quickly for her to resist. She goes with it. When they reach the chairs facing the Prime's desk, Unisa reaches her hand out to greet them and introduces herself. They reciprocate and the three angi women occupy the seats across from the Prime.

"I'm so glad you've agreed to speak with us," he says to the couple. "I know it is a difficult decision to let your child go, but when that child shows the kind of promise and potential that your daughter does, the decision should be easy. Your daughter should be a pupil here. A protege."

"Our daughter can achieve her potential at home, in PeakHaven," the mother in green argues. "There is no truth to the argument that greatness can only be fostered in the Library."

Unisa's heart warms. She's aching to throw her arms around the women, to embrace them and thank them for defending their daughter.

Suddenly, Alba's words from the year prior appear in her mind.

Your parents rescinded your assignment to the Library when they were told they wouldn't be able to come visit you. The Prime stepped in and convinced them he could give you a better life than they could. The words of this man you revere so much are the reason you were forsaken.

Her parents were here twenty years earlier. They sat in these chairs, across from the Prime. He told them the same lies, and they believed him. And now he wants Unisa to do the same to another angi child.

"I do not doubt the educational programs in PeakHaven," the Prime responds, holding his hands up defensively, "but I must insist that the aptitude your daughter displays for history and memorization and mathematics is not something PeakHaven's academics can bloom. She needs to be a Librarian. She could be an Educator within a few years, with pupils and proteges of her own, and then, who knows? An Ambassador, a Supreme. Perhaps, one day, the Prime. Don't hinder her growth because you'll miss her."

"This isn't just about missing her," the mother in purple replies. "She's five years old. How can we put her in the hands of a Librarian we don't know, to raise her in our place? I understand we're allowed to write letters to her, but not being permitted to visit? It's too extreme."

Yes. It is too extreme. Go home, protect your daughter.

"It isn't extreme at all," the Prime counters. "We all—everyone in this room and everyone in this city—want what's best for your daughter. And what's best for her is to be pulled away from distractions. What's best for her is to be a pupil in the program. When she graduates the Academy, she is free to walk out of the gates and flap her wings back home. Unisa can attest to the success of the program."

He gestures to Unisa and her moment begins. To advocate for the separation of a child from her mothers. The two angi women turn expectantly to Unisa, friendly smiles shining from their expressions. They wait on her to say something encouraging about the program. To say something that will ease their concerns and give them a reason to send their daughter away for more than a decade with limited contact.

The Prime waits for her to lie for him.

She holds back her tears as the truth needles its way into her mind. There's no choice. If she wants to enact Alba's plot to remove the Prime, she has to lie. If she wants Ora to continue receiving care during the day, she has to lie.

If she wants to save Lyla, she has to lie.

Unisa opens her mouth, and the words that stumble off of her tongue disgust her. "Without my family distracting me, I became an Ambassador. The Prime is right, sending your daughter to the Library will change her life forever. If you want what's best for your daughter, you'll resubmit the application for the Youth Education program."

The words come from her mouth but they burn in her soul. It takes everything in her power not to drop to their feet and beg for their forgiveness. It takes everything not to burst into wails and sobs, and denounce the Library and the Prime. Not to forsake the evil that surrounds them.

But Unisa knows, in her heart, that this young angi child must be sacrificed for a plot that is bigger than her, bigger than Unisa, bigger than any one person. As the two angi women smile and turn to the Prime to discuss the re-submission of their daughter's application, Unisa knows that one day when she frees the Library of the Prime's control, when she breaks down all the lies and starts the system anew, as Alba commanded her to, she'll save this young angi, too.

And then, perhaps, the paragon and the pupil can fly back to PeakHaven together.

CHAPTER 30

"CHERRY-BLOSSOM CHEEKS"

Sovereign City-State *The Library*
Date *40th Day of Month 6, Year 1629 DG*

AS UNISA SOARS THROUGH THE Loop Network, headed from the Center to Prime Palace, she realizes she never knew before today that a taste can sit between bitter and sweet. That it can be unrecognizable, indistinguishable between the two.

She holds so much bitterness on her tongue for the words that will inevitably shackle a young angi girl to the Library. Words that shackled Unisa herself. There was logic and reasoning to it, but the guilt tears through her.

At the same time, a sweetness is left lingering. She wasn't called to the Prime's office because Maksi betrayed them. He hasn't informed the Prime of the brewing rebellion under the apartment building. They've had no contact with Maksi for the ten days since they attempted to break his Bonding, but it appears, at least for now, that all is well.

But only the universe, the gods, and fate know how long all will remain well.

She exits the Loop Network but doesn't land. With measured flaps of her polished silver wings, she remains airborne, heading in the direction of Prime Palace. Ten daily visits have given her a certain familiarity with the route. A rhythm and a pace that's become as easy as breathing. Even if the journey were difficult, even if she had to walk barefoot over scorching coal or broken glass, she'd make the trek to Prime Palace to see Lyla.

As the bright lights of the grand domicile get closer and closer in the distance, Unisa's mind juggles between reasons why her visits with Lyla have become so important to her; why she feels an obligation to protect the girl. Is it her youth? Her pregnancy and the health risks that come with it? The Prime's control over her?

Why does Unisa feel responsible for saving the teenager with the cherry-blossom cheeks?

She lands deftly in the front courtyard, enters the home, and marches up the golden steps to Lyla's bedroom, waving unceremoniously to the other young women of the Inner Catacomb as she passes them. When she reaches Lyla's bedroom door, she knocks softly, hoping not to disturb her if she's already gone to bed.

"Come in!" Lyla chirps from inside, and Unisa steps forward into the room. The teenager sits with her back against the headboard, legs under the comforter, a book in her hands. She still dons the same stained nightgown. Unisa hates it, so she makes a mental note to bring a clean one for her during the next visit.

She closes the door behind her and steps into the dimly lit bedroom, taking a seat at the foot of the bed, an inch beyond Lyla's toes.

"You're late today," Lyla mentions. It isn't said with anger or frustration, rather with curiosity.

Unisa nods. "The Prime asked me to stay back at the office to help him with something."

"Wow," Lyla responds, eyes widening. "Alvaro never asks for help. It must be something important."

Even after ten days of hearing it, Unisa hasn't gotten used to Lyla's informal use of the Prime's name. She hasn't heard anyone but Konni use it, and to see someone so young speak about an elder so informally sends a peculiar chill through her spine.

She tries to change the subject. "How are you feeling today?"

Lyla places a hand on her stomach and gently runs her fingers over it. "Better today. I had a visit with the salver and they insisted I should stop leaving the bedroom."

"They should be telling the Prime that," Unisa remarks.

The light behind Lyla's eyes dims a little, and she keeps her lips tightly pressed together. She agrees, but she isn't able to vocalize it. "It's alright, I know how important it is to Alvaro for me to entertain his guests. He's never been as adept at social interaction and etiquette as I have."

I'm shocked.

"Nonetheless, he should heed warnings from the salver. He's pulled you away from the outside world, from your family, from all the things you love, and left you in a bedroom, only letting you out when it's time to make him look good."

Unisa has made statements like these many times during her visits. Statements that reveal her true feelings toward the Prime's relationship with Lyla. They were subtle at first, but have become more blatant over the course of the visits.

Lyla's smile never wavers. "Alvaro loves me. He wouldn't ask me to do anything—"

"You have many loved ones in this world," Unisa says, placing her hand on Lyla's affectionately, cutting off the girl's rehearsed defense of her captor, "but someone who asks you to perform against a salver's wishes, when your health is at risk, isn't one of them."

Lyla swallows hard, as a thin layer of moisture forms like a shield over her eyes. Her smile never fades, but her light dims. The mask falters.

Unisa continues. "You deserve so much better, Lyla. This can't possibly be what you wanted. Stuck in this bed, kept away from everyone, paraded around to social elites like a purebred."

The moisture over Lyla's eyes thickens and the edges of her lips slowly descend.

Unisa points to the bedroom door behind them. "It's closed. Right now, in this room, it's just you and me. Talk to me, Lyla. Say everything that's been boiling in your heart for a year now." She squeezes Lyla's fingers gently, reassuring her. "You are safe with me."

The mask drops entirely. That's all Lyla needed: to know that she's safe. Quietly, almost silently, the teenager releases a sob and buries her face in her hands. Unisa bounds forward from the foot of the bed to wrap her arms around Lyla's shoulders. The young girl reciprocates the embrace and buries her face in Unisa's neck, continuing to sob as quietly as she can. They sit this way for some minutes as the girl weeps, and Unisa weeps with her.

For her.

When she speaks again, her words trickle out in whispers, and she keeps her head resting on Unisa's chest. "I didn't want this. I wanted to be a Librarian. The best Librarian, like Alba was. I never met her, but I'd heard the legends. She exuded power and wisdom. When the Prime asked me to visit him at the Palace, I was overjoyed. I thought my dreams were coming true. That I'd have the opportunity to learn from him and become a revered Librarian."

"What happened to those dreams?" Unisa asks.

Lyla pauses, then continues. "He changed them. There was a period of time in which he treated me so differently than everyone else. Special. More affectionate. I thought maybe I was imagining it, until..."

"Until what, Lyla?"

"Until he kissed me. I was fifteen, but he kissed me like we were the same age. Like we were romantic partners. I was so stupid. I kissed him back thinking it was the greatest thing that could have ever happened to me. I didn't know what would come from it."

Unisa leans back and Lyla lifts her head from the angi's chest. They make eye contact. "You are *not* stupid. You were young. What happened was not your fault. I need you to understand that."

Tears break through from Lyla's eyes again. With a quivering lip, a strained voice, she continues, "I asked him, in the early days of my pregnancy, if we could talk to the salvers and see if they could give me something to cleanse myself of it. I'm not ready for this."

"He didn't agree?"

"He did. At first. And then, somewhere along the way, he realized this was his heir in me. And he changed his mind. He decided I would keep the pregnancy throughout the term, despite the risks that came with it to my health."

Rage boils Unisa's blood. She spews her anger with venom. "Why does the Prime choose what happens to you?"

"He said he was protecting the baby."

"And what about you? You're an individual, with sentience and rational thought and logic and emotion. A living, breathing being who holds the ability to make decisions about what is best for your body. At the time you asked him, whatever was inside you, was a part of you. A small part of your body that you had a right to hold onto, or to let go of. You have a right to your future. To your dreams. Why did he get to forsake those dreams on your behalf?"

They sit huddled together this way for a long while, until Lyla's tears leave dry streaks on her cherry-blossom cheeks.

"I'm scared," she finally says. "I don't want my dreams to die." She pauses and takes a deep breath. "I don't want to die."

Unisa breaks away from her and places her hands on the sides of Lyla's face, holding strong eye contact. "Listen to me. You are not going to die. I'm going to make sure you are taken care of."

Lyla places her hand affectionately over Unisa's and a sad smile spreads across her face. They stare this way in silence as the truth is relayed on their gaze: Unisa has no control over Lyla's health and well-being. The Prime has made it so that no one does, but him.

Unisa returns to where she was sitting beyond Lyla's toes, giving the girl space to wipe her eyes and steady her breathing.

"Why are you so dedicated to taking care of me?" she asks Unisa. "Since the day we met, you've been coming over here to check on me and allow me to speak my thoughts aloud. Why?"

"I've been wondering the same thing, actually," Unisa admits, recalling her thoughts from her flight over to Prime Palace.

"Well your family is very lucky to have someone as caring and thoughtful as you to take care of them."

Though she meant it as a compliment, Lyla's words break the dam in Unisa's heart, flooding her with guilt. Ora is her family and instead of caring for her, as she should be, Unisa is either working, visiting Lyla, or plotting the demise of the Prime. Yuki now spends more time with the elderly pixie than Unisa does.

And who knows what little time Ora has left.

"I appreciate your kind words, Lyla, but I'm not as caring and thoughtful as I should be."

Lyla raises an eyebrow. "What do you mean?"

"My mother is quite ill. Her mind has deteriorated significantly from what it once was, and I haven't spent as much time with her as I should. She's a pixie, who took me in when I was brought to the Library as a child. She raised me and cared for me, and now when it's time for me to take care of her, I..."

Her eyes widen as the realization dawns on her. All questions are instantly answered, as the truth of Unisa's devotion to Lyla drops on her like a stone building. Why does Unisa feel responsible for protecting the teenager with the cherry-blossom cheeks?

"What's wrong?" Lyla asks.

"You asked me why I'm so dedicated to taking care of you. I think I know. I hadn't realized before, but it might have to do with Ora, my mother. A pixie cared for me my whole life. Protected me. Loved me. And I think caring for you, protecting you, loving you, a pixie, is my way of repaying her. Of putting into action all of the gratitude I hold in my heart for her."

Lyla's smile brightens again. "I appreciate that you feel so strongly about caring for me, but you don't have to."

"But I do. As much for me as I have to for you."

Lyla pauses, then nods. "Ora raised an incredible daughter. I'd like to meet her one day. After the baby is born, and I'm allowed to leave again, will you take me to visit her?"

With great caution, with powerful forethought, Unisa doesn't let her smile falter for a single moment. She doesn't let her expression betray her thoughts for even a second. She doesn't want to cause any alarm or distress in the young pixie.

Her thoughts are plagued with the truth. The undeniable, heartbreaking truth of Lyla's detainment in Prime Palace: he won't let her leave. Not before the baby is born, not after it. Not for many years, at least until she is mature and he can be seen in public with her. Until then, she is his prisoner, and by that time...

Ora will likely be gone.

CHAPTER 31

"ALREADY GRIEVING"

Sovereign City-State *The Library*
Date *40th Day of Month 6, Year 1629 DG*

THE PRIME'S SUSPICIONS MUST BE growing. On her journey home from Prime Palace, Unisa notices more Cicadas than she ever has before. Their unwavering gazes fondle her in ways that make her feel violated. Despite being an undercover faction, she's grown skilled at picking them out of crowds.

Or perhaps she's grown more suspicious. Perhaps not everyone who walks by and glances at her, or offers a lingering smile, or peers in her direction from a local fruit stand, is a Cicada. When one isn't aware of the Cicadas' existence, they aren't looking for a secret society of Librarians, so they won't find one. But when one *is* aware, when the secret is out, they see it in the windows and fire escapes. They smell it in the crowds. They feel it along their skin, within their bones. They taste in the food and drinks offered to them.

They hear it in the whispers.

Either way, whether the Prime has become more suspicious, or Unisa has, his command that she should visit Lyla with less frequency should ease some of the tension of the situation. Lyla won't be happy, and neither will Unisa, but the Prime will.

She takes a different route home than usual, as a precaution. Zig-zagging through alleys, soaring over fences and through neighbors' yards, she enters her building from the rear door. If she *was* followed, she had to have lost them at some point.

Up the stairs to Ora's apartment, she starts to remove the bag from her shoulder, so she can quickly drop it inside the home, greet Yuki and Ora, and then head down to the Nest to meet with Juhi and Konni. She's two hours late, so she knows they'll be unhappy with her.

Ora's apartment is dim when Unisa enters. She calls out for Yuki, but there's no response. The angi's heart sinks to the floor when she turns the lighting panels up to full brightness and realizes Yuki isn't in the apartment. She isn't here to take care of Unisa's mother as she always is when Unisa gets home. As she promised she would be.

Ora is alone.

Unisa runs to Ora's bed and looks down at her. She's asleep, seemingly unharmed, resting peacefully. There doesn't appear to be a hair out of place.

Where is Yuki?

Unisa turns quickly on her heels, exiting the apartment and locking the door behind her. She races downstairs, in flight, to the igni's apartment and bursts through the door without knocking, grateful that it was unlocked.

"Yuki!" she calls out.

One second. Five seconds. No response.

Unisa travels through the apartment, room-by-room, calling out, but there's no response. Her stomach twists into knots when she reaches the sitting room and sees the center table moved to the side, the sand brushed away, and the wooden door leading down into the underground tunnels, down to the Nest, down to their secret meeting place, wide open.

Her mind urges her to bound forward and descend into the tunnels as quickly as she can. But her feet remain planted, disobedient. An anxious hum in her heart questions what she might find in the Nest. Juhi and Konni? Yuki? Cicadas?

The Prime?

What if he's found out about their plot? What if Maksi told him while she was visiting Lyla? What if they're waiting for her to come so they can ambush her? Should she just run back up to Ora's and try to escape with the elderly pixie? Escape to where? How would she travel with her? The answer to every single one of these questions resides in one place.

The Nest.

Unisa takes a deep breath and slowly descends into the underground tunnels. The torches on the walls are lit, as she expected them to be. Someone is down here. She walks carefully, stepping slowly forth, waiting for a figure—or ten or twenty—to lurch from the shadows and attack her.

She isn't armed, not that a weapon would help her. With basic Librarian combat training she refuses to hone, holding a blade would be as meaningless against a Cicada as holding a banana.

Step-by-step, she inches forth, lighting up an atom of dark hallway at a time, until finally, a smidgen of sounds drips into her ear. The Nest is up ahead. Someone is there.

When she's a few feet away, the sounds get louder: a blade cutting through the air, blasts of Radiant energy exploding. The sounds are unmistakable, but it's far too quiet for a battle. With a deep breath, Unisa turns the corner and enters the Nest.

Juhi swings the blade through the air, with no opponent facing her. She's training. Konni does the same with her beams and balls of Radiant energy, tossed around the room at invisible opponents.

Standing closest to Unisa, near the entrance of the Nest, watching them, is Yuki. Her back is to Unisa, but when the angi calls out to her, flooded with relief, she turns around.

"I'm so glad you're alright," Unisa says, breathing easy for the first time in some very long minutes. She wraps herself around Yuki, whose arms slowly and lightly rise up to reciprocate the embrace. Unisa steps back and asks, "Why aren't you with Ora?"

Having considered the possibilities of what could've been awaiting her down in the Nest, she's just glad that Yuki and the others are alright. There isn't any anger in Unisa's tone.

But there is in Yuki's. There's an undercurrent of concern, but it's unmistakably dipped in disapproval. "Where have you been, Uni?"

Unisa is stunned. Her eyes widen and she takes a step back as if Yuki's words have pushed her. The angi's eyes dart back and forth from Yuki to Konni, and then to Juhi. The hawk sheathes her sword and begins to step forward toward Unisa. Konni does the same.

All three of their expressions are scowls.

Unisa tries to conjure a bewildered response. "I-I was at Prime Palace. You know that. All three of you know that."

Konni and Juhi break apart and start to head toward the walls of the Nest, while Yuki side-steps around Unisa. In moments, Unisa realizes that the three women are circling her, forming a perimeter like birds of prey waiting for their kill to take its final breath. A maelstrom of disappointed currents charging around the confused, swirling eye in the center.

"You went to see Lyla again?" Juhi asks, her tone mimicking Yuki's.

"I did."

"Why?"

Unisa's confusion grows. Why are they behaving this way? "She needs me."

"We need you," Konni counters. "Ora needs you. We've seen you twice in the last ten days, how many times has Lyla seen you?"

Unisa doesn't respond. She knows they won't like the answer.

"You know I love Ora, and I am committed to caring for her, Uni," Yuki says as they continue to circle her. When she speaks her next words, the scowl dissipates and the anger withers into genuine disappointment. "But it almost feels like you're intentionally staying away."

Heat rises to Unisa's cheeks. It's an accusation. A maddening one. "I'm not staying away from my mother, Yuki. I'm committed to caring for her as well."

"Are you?" The igni disagrees, her tone still soft. She stops walking and steps forward. "I know it terrifies you how little of Ora's mind is left. I know it breaks you to see her like this. But it's going to hurt even more after she's gone, and you wish you had spent more time with her."

Unisa's throat tightens. Her lungs contract as if all of the air has been squeezed out of them. Her knees begin to rattle with weakness. This confrontation, this criticism, this challenge, was the last thing she expected.

Fight, flight, freeze, fawn. They all start to set in at once, as her legs try to maintain their footing, or carry her away from the Nest. As her instincts try to appease Yuki, or respond aggressively.

Fight wins.

"Ora would understand that I'm trying to care for someone young in a suffocating situation. In fact, she'd be proud of me. But you don't have to worry about it anymore. The Prime has asked me to visit Lyla less. You're welcome to stop caring for Ora at all, I won't ask you to sacrifice your time anymore."

Yuki's eyebrows rise and a frown etches onto her lips. She looks both surprised and saddened at the same time. "That's not what I meant, Uni. You know how much I care about her. And how much I care about you."

Unisa's words continue to erupt with venom as waves of defensive fury thrash her heart. "I don't need your care. I can take care of my mother *and* save Lyla."

"How exactly are you going to do that?" Juhi challenges her. The hawk's tone softens as well. "The best way to save Lyla is following through on Alba's plan. Our plan. The one we've been working on for nearly a year. All of us here in the Nest came together because of you. You were supposed to lead us. But you haven't been here since Maksi's failed breaking. We're worried about you."

Unisa's rage continues to build into her eyes, burning as tears collect in them. "You don't have to worry. I'm fine."

Yuki's hand falls gently onto Unisa's shoulder and she makes impenetrable eye contact with the angi. "It's alright if you aren't, Uni. This is a terrifying experience." A half-smile curves the edges of her lips up and she softly whispers, "We're here for you."

The four words linger in the silence between them, causing the air to grow heavy. Unisa breathes deeply to inhale as much as she can, but her lungs won't accept it. Something deep inside her clicks and the truth of her behavior settles in. The truth she's been running from by visiting Lyla so much.

They're right. She's scared of watching her mother die.

Unisa drops to her knees, chest tight, tears raining to the ground. They blur her vision and she heaves into sobs. "Sh-she used to be so strong, so sh-sharp. I c-can't see her like this." Memories of the pixie's youthful strength and wit, from Unisa's childhood, inundate her vision. She remembers exactly what Ora was like.

While she was still Ora.

A pair of arms helps her to stand, then embraces her. A second pair of arms does the same, and then a third. The four women stand together, holding each other, as Unisa weeps for the mother whose body is just upstairs, but whose mind is long gone. She was running from this building, from Ora, from the Nest, not because she doesn't care.

She was running because she's already grieving.

They hold each other until Unisa's sobs come to a quiet end, and when they separate, a fifth voice rings out through the chamber, drawing their attentions.

"Is this a bad time?" Maksi asks, stepping into the Nest.

Juhi, Konni, Unisa, and Yuki all exchange stunned glances, as Maksi steps forward through the wide chamber and approaches them.

"I didn't know what to expect when I went to Yuki's apartment, but it certainly wasn't a wide open hole in the ground leading to an underground tunnel."

"That's my fault," Unisa says, drying her eyes and cheeks. "I rushed down here thinking they had been ambushed. I never closed it behind me."

"Where have you been?" Juhi asks him. "It's been ten days. We were waiting for the Prime to show up and arrest us with the Cicadas."

"I've been thinking. And reading. And rereading. And learning. And unlearning. I went through every text in my home, and so many in *Witness*, and it all looks different now. It's like I was reading everything in black-and-white before, and now you've shown me color."

Unisa knows exactly how he feels. To have your eyes opened to the lies that have been fed to you for your whole life. Have been fed to the world for generations. It feels like seeing through a window, and not just staring at the glass, for the first time.

The angi steps forward and places a hand on her former coworker's shoulder. "Welcome to the Nest, Maksi."

"Thank you," he responds with a smile. "I'm here to serve the Hawks."

The groups exchange more confused glances between them.

"Who are the Hawks?" Yuki asks.

"You are. We are. This group."

"We don't have a name," Unisa says.

"Shouldn't we? Juhi can shift into a hawk. And the way the rest of you cornered me the other night, I felt like I was being circled by birds of prey. And your underground meeting place is called, 'the Nest.'"

"I guess we can vote for a name and see what everyone—"

"The Hawks, it is," Juhi says with a wry smile. Everyone turns to her and she seals the decision. "Hawks eat Cicadas."

CHAPTER 32

"NAMES"

***Theocracy** SunSide*
***Date** Unknown*

NAINA CLOSES THE DOOR AND it fades into a stone wall behind her. Red-Lo, a few feet ahead, faces a brightly-lit bedroom; torches and braziers glow around them, a fireplace burns bright, starlight drips in.

A more mature Red-Lo than the one from the previous memory sits at a stout wooden desk, a writing utensil in his hand. He's leaning over a long strip of paper with his eyes darting back and forth on it with keen focus.

We jumped past MegaMother Picana's execution, Naina notes to the Red-Lo traveling with her. *You're certainly not a teenager anymore, I can count a handful of silver strands in your beard.*

I'm thirty-two here, Red-Lo informs her. *This is the year 780 DG. Thirteen years after the last memory.*

How can you tell? Naina wonders. *The last memory was the same year as a war. This one is just you sitting at a desk in the middle of the night.*

There's a long pause in which Naina wonders if Red-Lo is ignoring her, and then he finally responds in a meek, damaged voice. *This is the most meaningful memory you're going to see, pup.*

Why is that?

Red-Lo gestures for her to follow him. Behind the wooden desk, they each stand over one of Past Red-Lo's shoulders. The paper is freshly cut, white and pristine, and the writing utensil is a calligraphy quill. Past Red-Lo dips it into the inkwell deliberately, slowly, and then thinks carefully before applying any stroke to the page.

He's making a sign, with a name on it: Tha-Lo.

I hadn't realized you were so artistic, Naina mentions. *The calligraphy on this sign is quite good.*

I spent nine months learning the craft. I wanted this sign to be perfect.

Your hard work paid off. Is it a gift for someone? Someone named Tha-Lo?

Red-Lo swallows hard. *You could say that. It's a banner to hang over the entryway to a nursery. For my daughter.*

Oh, Naina responds, putting the puzzle pieces together. *Nine months learning calligraphy because you started when you found out Drof-Fa was pregnant.*

Red-Lo nods, *That's correct.*

Where is Drof-Fa? Naina's eyes scan the room.

With Hay-Ro and the other salvers. As I make this sign, she's down the hallway giving birth.

Ah, now I know why you remember this night so vividly.

Red-Lo shakes his head. *No, pup, you don't. Not yet.*

Before Naina can respond further, there's a knock on the bedroom door.

"Come in," Past Red-Lo says, looking up from the paper and deliberately placing the quill back into the inkwell.

The door creaks open and a young Doruh woman in a deep purple shalwar kameez and matching dupatta walks in. She closes the door behind her and approaches the desk, walking with a light step and a breezy gait. There's a smile on her face.

"Good evening, Father," the woman addresses Past Red-Lo with a cheery tone. "I'm so sorry to disturb you on such an auspicious night, but a message has come for you from the Library. The Prime has asked for a quick response, so I thought I'd bring it to your attention."

Past Red-Lo smiles at the servant and matches her tone when he speaks. "I appreciate your sense of urgency, Safina, but the Prime will have to wait until tomorrow."

Safina performs a short bow of respect. "Of course, Father." She turns and heads for the door, but before she exits the room she faces Past Red-Lo again and says, "One more thing…"

Past Red-Lo pulls his head up from the paper again. "Yes, Safina?"

"Congratulations."

Past Red-Lo nods in gratitude and Safina leaves the room.

Naina's mouth falls agape, struck with the stark differences between this memory and the ones that came before it. History books, oral retellings, and Naina's travels along the mental plane have imagined a vastly different master-servant relationship from the one she just observed.

This woman, Safina, appeared clean and healthy, well-dressed in her traditional attire. She smiled in the presence of the MegaFather, and approached him on floaty strides. There was no fear in her eyes. No marks on the visible parts of her body. No malice between her and the one who shackled her. She smiled when she spoke to him, using a tone that was almost cheerful.

And he used her name when he spoke to her. He never once raised his voice, nor did he address her with a slur.

She seemed, Naina pauses, *happy.*

Drof-Fa changed almost immediately after we took the throne, Red-Lo explains. *She spent a lot of time with the servants, and a lot more reading the texts that Picana left behind. I should've burned them when I took the throne. Over time, my wife removed servant uniforms and allowed them to dress in their cultural attire. She had the servant quarters razed and built large bedchambers for them. And then she asked me…*

He pauses, as if Drof-Fa's request holds so much weight, it's difficult for him to move it off of his tongue. *She asked me to start using their names.*

There's power in that, isn't there? Naina asks him.

He turns to her, an eyebrow raised. *Power in what?*

In using someone's name, and in using it properly. She meets his gaze. *Red-Lo, I don't think you can imagine what it's like to be called a slur. That lack of empathy is one of the many social and political criteria that come together in order for a crime as heinous as enslavement to occur. When you can't even understand why it's important to address someone by their given or chosen name, how can you possibly hope to see them as an equal?*

Enlighten me, pup. Why is it important to address someone by their name?

Did we watch the same memory? How can you not see it? Names hold power. They convey respect, they foster community, they identify the speaker's readiness to accept the named as an individual.

Naina turns back to the spot where Safina stood moments earlier. *This servant walked out of this room with her chin raised because the Mega-Father used her name.*

When Naina turns back to Red-Lo, she's shocked to find his eyes locked on her. His expression isn't dismissive, it isn't enraged, it isn't antagonistic in any way.

He's digesting her words in a way he never would have before the last memory.

Naina points to the nursery banner that Past Red-Lo is working hard on. *Names are valuable to you, too. You spent nine months mastering calligraphy to be able to put a name on a banner for your daughter. As someone who knows the power of a paternal bond, I can tell you didn't take naming your daughter lightly. What does Tha-Lo mean?*

The Vessel, Red-Lo responds. *She was meant to be the vessel that carries our legacy forth.*

So you chose that name with a purpose. How would you feel if someone had called her a slur instead of the name you gave her? A name that meant so much to you.

Red-Lo turns his face and takes a step away from her. She can hear him clear his throat, as if emotions are rising into his throat, and she recognizes that her words may be having some impact.

He shakes his head and turns back to Naina. *I do remember a change in the way the servants spoke and behaved after we'd implemented Drof-Fa's suggestions. Though, I still saw them as animals.*

Because you still treated them like animals, Naina replies.

Red-Lo's eyes widen.

I want to make something clear, despite what may seem like positive changes—the new bedchambers, the cultural considerations—the Doruh were still in chains. She steps around the desk and speaks as she strides toward the spot where Safina stood. *Cages or concourses, it's bondage. Covered in dirt or diamonds, it's bondage. Shackled by iron chains or frayed thread, it's bondage. I won't praise the MegaMother for making servitude easier when there shouldn't have been servitude to begin with.*

Again, Red-Lo's gaze eats up Naina's words, but there's no anger or antagonism in his posture or expression.

Before either of them can speak again, the door bursts open without a knock, startling Red-Lo, Naina, and Past Red-Lo. A faerie wearing a leather apron rushes in, blood dripping from both the apron and his puce hands. Naina immediately finds the resemblance between this faerie and the former Braver General, Vy-Ro.

"What's wrong, Hay-Ro?" Past Red-Lo asks, taking to his feet.

Hay-Ro rushes around the desk until he is face-to-face with Past Red-Lo, their gray eyes meeting an inch from one another.

"Say something! Is Drof-Fa alright?"

Hay-Ro places his bloodied hands on Past Red-Lo's shoulders and speaks in a haggard, empty voice. "Father, there are some complications."

The color drains entirely from Past Red-Lo's face. He goes from turquoise to translucent. "What do you mean?"

"I don't have a lot of time to explain, but both Drof-Fa and the child are at risk."

Past Red-Lo falls back into his chair, mouth agape, a cold disbelief in his eyes. "No."

Hay-Ro leans forward and presses his hands to Past Red-Lo's cheeks. Naina is in utter shock at the informality. "Father, you have to listen to me. The hour of decision is upon you."

The tide rises in Past Red-Lo's eyes. "What decision?"

"Drof-Fa or the child."

A tear loosens and Past Red-Lo shakes his head. "No." His voice becomes a whisper, a defeated glimmer of what was once a bright beacon. Naina's heart breaks. This isn't a decision she would wish on anyone.

Not even her enemy.

"There is a Negative Radiance Infection in her. We've stopped it from spreading, but we cannot remove it. We can only guide it into one of them and free the other of it. Decide."

"I c-can't," Past Red-Lo breaks into a heavy sob. "H-How can I make a de-decision like this?"

Hay-Ro crouches down, keeping his gaze firm. "Life waits for one of them, Drof-Fa or the child, while death races here to claim them both. Please, Father, make this inconceivable decision before it arrives and takes everything from you."

"This isn't fair, Hay—"

"Choose!"

"Save Drof-Fa!" Past Red-Lo's eyes widen as if he's surprised himself. Hay-Ro stands still in front of him for a moment until Past Red-Lo confirms the decision. "If anything happens to my wife, I'll tear this world asunder. Go! Save her!"

Hay-Ro nods and a moment later, Past Red-Lo is alone again. The world goes silent as the air becomes heavy with tense bewilderment. More tears race down Past Red-Lo's cheeks as he sits stunned, staring at the doorway from which Hay-Ro exited.

And then, he erupts. He opens his mouth wide and releases a guttural, primal roar. It's dripping with his anguish, with his suffering, with his grief. His hands fall onto the banner with the name "Tha-Lo" painted over it, and he tears it into pieces, tossing the shreds into the flames of the fireplace.

The scream continues as he releases the pain of losing all of the moments he will never have: celebrations, milestones, victories, affection. All the good that comes with having a child.

The honor of giving her a name.

Past Red-Lo places his hands under the wooden desk and in one swoop, he flips it entirely over and starts to tear it apart, continuing his anguished rampage until it's in pieces and he's lying on the floor, on his back, hands bloody, weeping for all he's lost.

Naina's blood goes cold and her vision blurs with tears. His suffering is palpable and painful. She scans the room for the Red-Lo she's been traveling with and finds him sitting, quietly, on the edge of the bed at the other end of the room. He's watching his past, centuries later, on one of the most difficult nights of his life.

Now Naina understands why he remembered the year of this memory so quickly. It's not something one can ever forget.

She joins him on the bed, sitting next to him. His eyes are dry, but his expression betrays his agony as he watches the scene.

I'm sorry, Naina says, unsure of what else she should say. *For what you've experienced.*

He breathes deeply, shakily. *Thank you, Naina.*

For the first time, Red-Lo calls her by her name.

CHAPTER 33

"Blood"

Alphocracy *MoonSide*
Date *2nd Day of Month 1, Year 1626 DG - 3 Years Earlier*

BRISK BREEZES BLOW INTO SALESSA'S blood. She braces against them, burying herself in her coat, crossing her arms over her chest. Customers of Sultana's Chai Palace pass by with a friendly nod to the young woman, wondering why she's standing out in the freezing temperatures during winter.

She would enter the establishment and lose herself in a cup of chai, had she not been banned. Sultana was once akin to a caring aunt, a warmhearted elder in the neighborhood, but all of it changed when Salessa's relationship with Lexona began.

"That girl is a troublemaker," she had admonished the falcon. "I can't understand why a good girl like you is"—she paused, as if the words were made of lead and were too heavy to come out naturally—"*spending quality time* with her, but you're no longer welcome while she's around."

Spending quality time. Salessa often wondered why the euphemisms were necessary. The time she spent with Lexona *was* quality, but Sultana's choice of words erased the romance from it.

Salessa blows on her hands, then balls them into fists and shoves them into her underarms. If Lexona doesn't show up in another ten…

"Why aren't you waiting inside?" Lexona asks when she approaches. She leans down and presses her lips softly on Salessa's, warming the falcon.

"It was too crowded inside," Salessa spits out quickly, exactly as she'd rehearsed.

Lexona narrows her eyes. "I know when you're lying. You're not good at it." She turns toward the chai house, but Salessa grabs her by the elbow.

"Lexi, no! Please don't make a scene."

"That heartless bitch can't make my girlfriend stand out in the cold."

Salessa recoils from the profanity. "I asked you to watch your language."

"We're eighteen." Lexona rolls her eyes. "Naina swears all the time. You don't tell her to stop."

"I don't want to waste my breath. Naina wouldn't listen to me anyway."

A coy smile stretches across Lexona's face. "So you think I'll listen to you?"

A fire builds in Salessa's stomach, as she returns the smile and pulls Lexona closer, their noses nearly touching. "I think I know how to get what I want with you." She pushes her face forward and kisses Lexona again. "If Sultana doesn't want us around, we'll stop meeting here, but you have to stop being so angry and reactive all the time, Lexi."

"I can't help it, I'm a serpent. There's venom inside, and it keeps me"—she pauses—"intense. Like all the time." She places a hand on Salessa's cheek and the fire in the falcon's core rages hotter. "But I think you might just be the antidote in my blood."

Salessa's cheeks burn as she starts to lose herself in Lexona's gaze.

"I brought something for you," Lexona says.

Salessa's eyes widen. "For me?"

"Call it a joint New Year and two-year anniversary gift."

"No," Salessa replies, "we'll call it a New Year gift. Our anniversary is next week and I expect something for that, too."

Lexona laughs and reaches into her pocket, withdrawing a small wooden falcon statue. Salessa's heart skips a beat. Memories of her childhood in Arlun, before the incident, flood her mind; the twins and their father sitting by a warm fire under blankets, as he shows them his latest carved statue, and their mother brings them warm cinnamon cookies.

A tear breaks loose and Lexona wipes it off of Salessa's cheek with her thumb.

"Where did you find it?" Salessa asks, taking the delicate item into her hands and cradling it. "It's just like the ones my father used to make."

"I made it. From your descriptions."

Salessa's mouth falls open. She leans in, as if she hadn't heard the serpent properly. "You...you *made* it?"

Lexona nods proudly. "I spent the past few months learning how to whittle. I wanted to surprise you. Help bring back a piece of your childhood. I hope you like—"

Before she can finish her sentence, Salessa's arms are wrapped around her neck, her lips pressing against Lexona's again.

"I love you so much, Lexi," Salessa says, pressing her forehead affectionately against her girlfriend's. "Thank you."

Lexona's finger travels along the wings of the wooden falcon. She lowers her volume so no one can hear her but Salessa. "One day, when everyone knows the truth, when you're able to shift without worrying that someone might see, you can pick me up in your talons and we can fly far away from here together. The falcon and the serpent."

Salessa nods. She doesn't ask where Lexona would want to fly to, because it doesn't matter. The falcon would fly anywhere the serpent wanted to go. She brings Salessa to life. She warms her, heart and soul, on even the coldest days.

Salessa can feel that warmth in her blood.

Alphocracy *MoonSide*
Date *40th Day of Month 6, Year 1629 DG - Present Day*

SALESSA WONDERS IF HER EYELIDS are made of brick. Every time she opens them and checks the clock on the wall, the four lit circles have inched forward, but Salessa hasn't moved much further on the page.

It's frustrating. She teaches history at the orphanages and schools in Evic. She loves history. Why is she having such difficulty focusing on the ancient tomes and texts of the O'Raha?

This library is massive, housed within one of the largest edifices in Lover's Plateau. For over seventeen days, she's buried her face in the histories and tales transcribed and stored here by generations of the Twins' followers. Rows upon rows of towering bookshelves form a maze of information, a sea of pages, a desert of history, with each grain of sand being a text.

Written accounts of the Twins' visions. Their predictions about the oncoming catastrophe. The duties of the four resurrectors, who will bring the Twins back to life, and those of the O'Raha who will be there to serve them. Salessa is used to absorbing and retaining historical information like this.

Then why does she feel so far removed from it?

Now I know how Naina feels when I try to discuss history with her, Salessa thinks.

She pulls her face away from the book and rubs her eyes, then looks over at Afzal two seats away. His thick, black leopard lips part, releasing his tongue. The feline licks the fur on the back of his hand feverishly and then rubs the moist hair against his muzzle and the top of his head.

Footsteps approach. Lexona strides toward them with a soft smile on her face, clad in an elegant fuchsia shalwar kameez. A week ago, Salessa's blood would've ignited with rage at the sight of her.

Today, she feels nothing. And that is a wide step in the right direction.

Exactly seven days since their emotional reconciliation in the Gardens. Since Lexona begged for her right to atonement. Since Salessa saw the vision of Ray-Mi that convinced her to allow Lexona back in.

The serpent hasn't taken the opportunity lightly. Even Salessa admits that Lexona has worked tirelessly over the past week to prove her devotion to forgiveness. To prove how sorry she is for her actions three years prior.

To prove that she's changed.

"Where have you been?" Lexona asks when she gets to the table. She takes the seat across from Salessa. "I've been looking for you all morning."

"We were up early to exercise this morning," Salessa explains, "then went back to our rooms to bathe. Since then, we've been here, studying." She gestures to the open text in front of her.

"Only you bathed," Afzal corrects her. "I'm bathing now." He resumes his grooming.

"Afzal"—Lexona gathers his attention—"are you an animal?" Her tone isn't harsh or sarcastic, it's a gentle nudge.

The leopard stills, his tongue still hanging out of his mouth. He pulls it back in and shakes his head, the human cheeks above his muzzle burning pink.

"Then why don't you go back to your room and bathe? In a tub, perhaps?"

Afzal nods and rises to his feet. "Of course, Sister. You're right."

He bids farewell to the women and marches off to his chamber.

Salessa's newfound comfort around Lexona empowers her to freely speak her mind. "Why do you ask him that?"

Lexona leans in, her eyebrow pulling together. "Ask him what?"

"Almost every day, since the day I arrived, at least once, I've heard you ask him if he's an animal. Why?"

Lexona sighs and her gaze falls to her hands, folded on the table. Her tone fills with concern.

"Ever since we started our merging rituals, Afzal and I have flourished in our spirituality. But, as you can see"—she gestures to the patches of snake scales on her skin, and to the thin tongue darting in and out of her mouth—"it's had some unexpected physical effects, as well. I've remained anchored to my human side"—she turns to the exit from which her brother left the library—"but I worry about Afzal. It feels like I'm losing my brother to the leopard."

She meets Salessa's gaze again. "I ask him that question to remind him to fight the urge to become more leopard than he already has. He's human first and if I, as his sister, have to remind him of that, I don't mind doing it daily."

Salessa's taken aback by the thoughtfulness of Lexona's response. She isn't trying to embarrass or belittle Afzal; she just wants to save her brother from becoming lost to the other half. Perhaps Salessa shouldn't be surprised. The serpent has shown thoughtfulness before, when they were together.

"May I ask you a question now?" Lexona wonders aloud, respectfully. Salessa nods and smiles to encourage her. "Why have you been exercising with Afzal so much?"

Her smile fades instantly.

Lexona continues. "You didn't exercise much when we were"—she hesitates—"when I knew you back in Evic. And Afzal mentioned you've been joining him nearly every day. I suppose I'm just...surprised."

Salessa nods. "You're right, I didn't focus on my fitness until I came here."

"Why is that?"

Salessa holds the serpent's gaze tightly. She's tempted to lie. *For my health. For battle. For coordination.* But something about Lexona's desire for atonement, something in her warm eyes, drives Salessa to be honest and open with her. She deserves it.

And with her sister so far away, Salessa needs someone to open up to.

"Because Naina turns heads every time she walks into a room. Anytime she flexes her bicep, or raises her shirt to display the packed muscles of her midriff, eyeballs nearly pop out of their sockets. And I've noticed the same happens to Afzal."

Lexona stares at her for some time, leaning back and drinking her in. Salessa starts to grow mildly uncomfortable until the serpent finally responds. "Salessa, your brain is able to hold onto specific dates and names and events from history, and then you recall that information to teach it to your students. Your heart has withstood all manner of grief and loss."

She reaches forward and gently places her fingers on Salessa's wrists, turning her hands over until Salessa's palms are facing up. "These hands have protected yourself and your sister for over a decade." She gestures to Salessa's abdomen. "Your body is capable of creating life, and giving birth. And even if it isn't, or you don't want to, it's capable of so much more."

She leans back in her seat again and Salessa's eyes meet hers. "There is power and divinity already in your body, Salessa. Don't tie your self-worth to something that adds so little to that power. Muscles or not, you are strong. You are intelligent, brave, caring, and you are beautiful. Stop searching for a silver coin while resting on a mountain of gold."

Salessa's breath catches in her throat and a horde of butterflies burst through her stomach. A fire ignites in her that was extinguished three years prior. The falcon had lost her flight somewhere along the way and, just like that, Lexona has made her airborne again.

If only she felt as beautiful as she knows Lexona believes she is.

The serpent continues. "If you let it, this world will make you believe that you are less worthy of love, attention, and respect, if you don't look a certain way."

Salessa clears her throat and blinks away the building moisture in her eyes. She still isn't ready to shed tears in front of Lexona.

"What did you want to talk to me about?" She changes the subject. "You mentioned you've been looking for me all morning?"

"Oh yes! Two things actually. Firstly, I wanted to remind you about the meeting with the O'Raha council this afternoon. You *cannot* be late."

Salessa nods, recalling her conversation with Afzal, in which he expressed his views on the O'Raha elders' rigidity. She shivers at the thought of stepping before them to be examined and interrogated.

"What was the other thing?" Salessa asks. A smile widens on Lexona's lips and she reaches into her pocket to remove a small wooden falcon statue.

Time suddenly stands still, but the room spins around Salessa. Her knees become weak, her mind cloudy, and her breath ragged. As if she isn't controlling it, her hand slowly moves forward and takes the statue into her hands.

Tears fill her eyes again and, this time, she doesn't hide it. So many memories flood her mind, from her childhood, as well as her teenage years, when her relationship with Lexona wasn't broken.

When *she* wasn't broken.

"Where did you…how…is this the same…" she tries to form a question, but the tightness in her throat prevents it.

"I had it when," Lexona begins but pauses. "When I had my falling out with Naina."

"I thought I had lost it," Salessa admits, her voice strained.

Lexona shakes her head. "I had taken it from you a couple days before. To paint it."

"But you attempted to steal our money instead?" Salessa spits out before her eyes widen and her hand covers her mouth. "I'm sorry. You don't deserve that."

"I do," Lexona says, sadness and shame washing over her expression.

Salessa shakes her head. "No, you don't. Truly." She reaches forward and takes Lexona's hand, holding the falcon statue in the other. "This means so much to me, thank you."

Lexona smiles and squeezes Salessa's hand affectionately. The falcon pulls it back and continues to examine the statue. It's exactly as she remembers it.

Lexona's eyes fall on the open tome. "How has your studying been going?"

Salessa forces a smile and nods. "Well. I'm learning a lot about the Sprites, the Twins' resurrection, their vision for the battle and how we're meant to defeat the ancient ones."

Lexona narrows her eyes, pausing to take in the falcon's expression. "I know when you're lying. You're not good at it."

Salessa's heart jumps. Those words were part of a rhythm of another age, long-gone. She sighs. "I'm just having some trouble focusing and it's frustrating."

"Trouble focusing? These are all first-hand transcriptions. You've always loved this."

Salessa places the delicate falcon down gently and runs her fingers through her hair. "I *have* always loved this, you're right. But I can't seem to wrap my mind around this."

"Why not? The information in this library is more relevant to us than anything else you've ever read."

"I think that's the problem." Salessa starts to realize. "They talk so much about the Twins, the God, the Goddess, the resurrection, the resurrectors, the Sprites, the enemies, the battle, the catastrophe…it's all so fantastic and mythological and legendary. It's just hard to accept that they're…" She sighs. "They're talking about me. Things I have to do, things I have to become, things I have to prevent, enemies I have to defeat. How do I whittle it down to make it feel more…"

"Relatable," Lexona offers.

Salessa nods. "Yes. Exactly."

Lexona leans forward to see which text Salessa is reading, then smiles. "If you want relatability, you picked the right one." She reaches forward and flips the book to one of the final pages. "This chapter is amongst the most pertinent."

Salessa looks down and reads the title aloud. "Blood." She looks up at Lexona again, an eyebrow raised.

"This is one of my favorite chapters. Do you have any idea how important blood is?"

Salessa shakes her head, unsure whether she should be intrigued or disgusted.

The serpent continues. "Think about it. Blood is life. It carries spiritual energy throughout our bodies. It's the only physical part of our body that transcends both space and time. You lost your telepathy with

Naina when you moved far from her. But she's still your sister. No matter where you are in this world, you'll always be linked by blood."

"What about time?" Salessa asks. "You said it transcends time as well."

"Generation after generation, blood links ancestors to descendents. There's nothing but blood linking you to some falcon from a thousand years ago who was in the same familial line. And blood also links you, and me and Naina and Afzal, to the Twins. Why do you think we're the ones who will resurrect them?"

Salessa shakes her head. She's never thought about why.

"Because their divine blood runs through us. Blood is divinity. It cleanses and purifies. It's there at birth; it's there at death. All at once, it is both a small part of who we are, and the entirety of who we are."

Salessa becomes lost in Lexona's passion. She wishes she could have Lexona summarize all of the O'Raha texts for her in this manner.

"Blood binds us to the natural, supernatural, and cosmic mosaics of the universe. Things within the planet, like the tides, have patterns. Things beyond the planet, like the moons and stars, have patterns. Similarly, your blood has a pattern of release each month. Having a pattern harmonizes your body with the spiritual energy of both the ground beneath you and the skies above you."

"You make it sound so glorious," Salessa responds.

Lexona smiles and continues. "Your feminine strength, the conquering might of your womanhood, the energy of rebirth, is empowered in your veins. Your blood is magic, it's sacred. Whole societies and civilizations have cowered from it; have stigmatized and minimized it because they know the power that being a woman holds."

Lexona gestures to the falcon statue. "Be proud of who you are. The falcon. The Goddess. Your body, your blood. Be proud of all of it."

There's a long baited breath in which Lexona seems unsure of whether or not to speak the next words on her mind. And then, between flicks of her serpentine tongue, she lets them free. "I am proud of you."

Lexona's smile, her confidence, her enthusiasm, and her thoughtfulness bring Salessa to life. The serpent warms her, heart and soul. Salessa can feel that warmth in her bones.

And in her blood.

CHAPTER 34

"The Falcon Goddess"

Alphocracy *MoonSide*
Date *40th Day of Month 6, Year 1629 DG*

"IT'S STILL NOT MY STYLE," Salessa remarks, staring down at a saffron saree laid out on the bed.

"I understand," Zoya acknowledges, beside her. "I meant what I said on your first day. You are a goddess. You can wear whatever it is you like."

"But?" Salessa sighs. "What's the 'but'? I can feel it coming."

Zoya laughs. "But a meeting with the council of elders is quite important. Lexona would like your presence to come across as divine. Regal. Elegant."

The falcon imagines herself wearing it and finds an entirely different person than woman in the mirror.

"This is about more than a saree. More than fabric and lace and outfits." She turns to the falcon and they hold steady eye contact. "What's wrong, Salessa?"

Zoya's words cut through the fog in Salessa's mind and strike the truth. Like the soft rays of morning, that truth shines now.

"I miss Naina," she says. "I'm making decisions with half a brain. Feeling things with half a heart. Existing with half a soul." She turns to the outfit again. "The Salessa who Naina knows wouldn't wear this. If she saw me in a saree, she wouldn't recognize me. And that…"

"Scares you," Zoya assists her.

Salessa nods. "I don't want to become someone else while I'm here. I don't want to move further away from Naina than I already am."

The two women stand, staring at the dress for some time before Zoya speaks. Freely. "For what it's worth, I don't think you've made any truly fundamental changes to who you are while you've been here. You were a goddess then, you're a goddess now. Embracing your divinity, your regality won't touch your core. Your essence."

Salessa smiles, genuinely. "Thank you. I've spent more time with you than I have with anyone else here, including Afzal and Lexona. I appreciate your counsel, as always."

As she takes in Zoya's gaze, the weight of her own words falls heavily on her. The horse has been by her side since the first day. Serving her, sure, but also curing her boredom at Poetry Nights, honing her spiritual energy in the Gardens, sharing wisdom in the library.

She can never take Naina's place. No one can. But she's as close a sisterly substitute as can be. She's given Salessa a comfort the falcon didn't know was possible in this place.

And the falcon trusts her.

Salessa turns back to the saree and for the first time, she smiles while looking at it. "Can you help me tie it?"

An excited grin stretches across Zoya's lips. "It would be my pleasure."

When Salessa arrives at the council meeting, she's clad in the elegant saffron, Zoya at her side. Thick, marble doors creak open and every head in the chamber turns to her. It's never happened before; there's a flutter of anxiety in Salessa's core when every eye is on her.

"Is everything alright?" Zoya leans in and whispers. "I can feel you tense up."

"They're all staring."

"A goddess just stepped into the room," Zoya responds. "Let them stare."

She takes Salessa's hand, interlocking her fingers with the falcon's. Salessa turns to her, mouth falling slightly agape. Zoya has always been respectful in her service of the divine. Touch was a barrier rarely broken. She's certainly never taken Salessa's hand without request.

It's a small gesture of encouragement, familiarity. One that Naina would've done, and one that etches a smile onto Salessa's lips.

Hand-in-hand, the women step forth on a golden carpet laid out in an aisle between two sections of wooden benches. There are at least twenty rows, and every seat is occupied with O'Raha men, women, and children. Families, friends, neighbors. An entire community has come together to bear witness to the first meeting of the council of elders in which there are three deities present and not only two.

Ahead of the benches is a wide open area with shimmering gems etched into the stone tiles. Four throne-like seats, mimicking the marble doors in their composition, rest on the gem-soaked tiles, and face a massive stone platform erected at the far end of the room.

Afzal sits on the marble throne at the far left, Lexona on the one to its right. Zoya guides Salessa to the next throne in line, and when Lexona's gaze finds the falcon in her saffron saree, her eyes widen.

"You wore it," the serpent breathes. "And you look..." She loses her words.

"Thank you," Salessa responds, her cheeks burning. Zoya releases her hand and enters the first row of wooden benches on one side of the room.

Ten elders sit upon the stone platform at the end of the room, cross-legged on wide pillows that remind Salessa of the red ones on which patrons of Sultana's Chai House sit. The elders face the deities, clad in colorful, vibrant robes, so long that they bloom out over the pillows and touch the stone platform in some spots.

Every elder is wearing a headband tied around their forehead, with the image of an animal centered on it; Salessa assumes these must be their animal forms. Their expressions are as stone as the platform on which they're hoisted.

When all eyes have turned away from Salessa, and are focused on the elders, even as the meeting begins and the council speaks, the falcon realizes that Lexona is still stealing glances. And Salessa's cheeks are still glowing.

"This is a special council meeting," begins one of the elders, seated in the center of the group, a flamingo on his headband, "scheduled and organized at the request of the Great Serpent Goddess." He raises a hand to gesture to Lexona, who performs a short bow of her head respectfully.

"It appears," another elder speaks, a brown bear on her headband, "we have a claimant in our midst, who purports to be one of the remaining two resurrectors of the Twins. By the conclusion of this meeting, the council will have made the decision whether to accept this claim or not."

Salessa swallows hard. Though she's seated on a throne, the elders on the soft pillows command the room. They're loud and intimidating. Above all, they're skeptical, and Salessa has no proof of her divinity.

"Wise elders of the council," Lexona addresses them, rising to her feet, her forest green saree glowing from the synthetic starlight pouring into the room. "I called this meeting to prove that a third resurrector is amongst us." She gestures to Salessa. "Your language betrays your skepticism. I'm surprised. You doubt the judgment of the Leopard and the Serpent?"

There's strength to Lexona's tone. An unwavering confidence. A challenging accusation. It simultaneously rouses awe in Salessa's heart and warmth in her abdomen.

"You are indeed our goddess," Flamingo confirms, "and the Leopard is our god. But until the resurrection of the Twins, your divine souls are housed in these mortal forms. Forms that are susceptible to clouded logic and foggy reasoning."

"Your prior relations with the claimant draw our skepticism," Brown Bear clarifies. "We can understand the desire to have someone familiar amongst the resurrectors. But that is not proof of the claimant's legitimacy."

"When you and the Leopard God came forth, you came together," Flamingo reminds her. "The claimant comes alone. Why?"

Salessa turns to the empty throne next to her, a longing ache tugging at her heart. Naina should be in this seat; the elders aren't wrong.

"It is my fault that the fourth resurrector hasn't come," Lexona responds. "Salessa should not be held accountable for my mistake. I called her here alone, but I should have called her twin as well."

"Indeed," Brown Bear agrees. "The identities of the four resurrectors is of vital importance. Not only to the O'Raha, but to the world. We must follow the guidance issued by the Twins and their visions." She begins to recite the One Myth. "One from the land, one from the seas. One from the skies, one from the trees. The Leopard of the trees, the Serpent of the seas. From where does the claimant come?"

Lexona turns to Salessa.

I guess it's my turn.

"The skies," Salessa utters, her voice crawling from her throat.

The elders all lean forward and Flamingo raises his voice. "Speak up, girl!"

Lexona gestures with her eyes for Salessa to stand. The falcon rises to her feet and, gathering all of the confidence she can, roars a response. "The skies. I'm a falcon."

"This is your Great Falcon Goddess and you will address her with the respect she deserves," Lexona reinforces.

"Not until she's proven her divinity," Brown Bear replies, her tone hard. "Alright then, girl, what evidence do you have to support your claim?"

Every eye in the room targets Salessa again. As if she's suddenly standing on the surface of one of the suns, a sweat breaks out onto her temple. She isn't used to the attention in casual, friendly settings, let alone in an interrogation. As her gaze travels from one elder to the next, from one grimace to its neighboring scowl, an intimidating realization dawns on her.

"You've already made up your minds," she says. "I have no proof or evidence of my claim." There are gasps from around the room, and the elders' eyes narrow. Salessa takes a deep breath, steeling her nerves, ignoring the reactions, and continuing. "You've called me here to deny my claim and disqualify my evidence. You don't *want* to accept me."

"Why wouldn't we want to accept you?" Flamingo scoffs, leaning back with incredulity. "We simply want the truth."

"The truth is staring you in the face and you still can't see it." More gasps, louder gasps. Salessa turns to Lexona, expecting an equally horrified expression, but the serpent is smiling, arms crossed over her chest. She's beaming with pride, as she winks to Salessa to continue.

Feeling empowered, Salessa goes on.

"My healing is divine, but I can't prove that here and now, unless you'd like to tear me apart and watch me come back together. My telepathy with my sister is divine, but, again I'm not able to demonstrate that when she isn't here. My claim is supported by two individuals you've already accepted as divine, but suddenly you don't trust their word. So what can I do to prove my legitimacy as your deity?"

The elders sit quietly for a moment, considering, before Brown Bear speaks. "I suppose you cannot prove it until your sister comes. We'll revisit the claim at that time. The meeting is conclu—"

"You damn us all," Salessa interrupts her from adjourning the meeting. From a kingdom away, Salessa channels the wolf's rage.

"Watch your tongue, girl!" Flamingo warns. "Or we'll have you thrown from Lover's Plateau."

"It's the truth. By denying my claim, you're setting the resurrection backward. We have work to do, and it must be done quickly, but I need the support of the O'Raha. Their insight, their experiences. *Your* wisdom. If you don't accept me as one of the resurrectors now, it'll be too late when catastrophe is at your doorstep. The Sprites will conquer after releasing the Three Deaths."

The room initially falls so silent that Salessa almost thinks it's emptied out. Slowly, murmurs and whispers start up, like the rhythmic flow of a stream. It grows louder, into the raging rumbles of a river, as confusion takes hold of the onlookers.

Flamingo raises his hands, silencing the crowd, before leaning in toward Salessa. He speaks slowly, with a tone of confusion. "What... are...the Three Deaths?"

Salessa's eyes widen and she realizes she may be able to prove her claim after all. She knows things they don't.

"The Three Deaths are demon beasts that the Sprites, the Ancient Ones, have threatened to release before the final battle. The Twins will take on the Sprites, but before then, this world must survive its first test: a beast of the sky, a beast of the soil, a beast of the sea."

More gasps, more whispers, this time from amongst the elders, as well.

"It mirrors the prophecy of the resurrectors," Brown Bear observes.

Salessa nods. "Just as the Sprite siblings are an evil reflection of the Twins, they threaten to call forth an evil reflection of the resurrectors. We don't know when or where they will enter this world but we're trying to figure that out before they get here."

"*Who* is 'we'?" Flamingo asks.

"My allies. They're working tirelessly to prepare for the arrival of the Three Deaths. If the world defends itself, if it survives the attack, it will give us all time to uncover the secrets of the resurrection and bring our God and Goddess back to life. The Sprites grow stronger every day. They have been feasting for eight centuries on the essences of a powerful Mega's bloodline. I have no doubt that they are strong enough, now, at this very moment, to call the Three Deaths forth."

The room falls, once again, into stunned silence. The Doruh in this room, and generations of their ancestors, have memorized every word of their scripture. Every letter that the original O'Raha transcribed while listening to the Twins dictate their visions.

And Salessa provides them with new information for the first time in over fifteen hundred years.

"There is no mention of the Three Deaths in any of the scriptures," Flamingo says, so astonished his voice is barely louder than a whisper. "The Twins dictated their visions comprehensively, detailing the Sprites, their resurrectors, their return to life. The One Myth outlines all. How do you know something we don't?"

Salessa hesitates, considering whether or not she should divulge the truth of Rafael and Kyoko's conversation with the TreeKeeper. Whether or not to spin the long yarn of their journey, and the revelations that came from it. But something in her chest chains her tongue. Something in her head seals her lips.

It's a voice, one she hasn't heard in weeks, though it feels like years. Naina's voice. The wolf isn't in the room; she isn't even in MoonSide. But Salessa can feel her presence as if her sister is standing right next to her.

The wolf takes control of her vocal cords. Salessa responds to the elders with all of the rage bubbling in her chest, with all of the fury they deserve for doubting her. She responds the way she knows Naina would, the way a goddess would.

The way the Salessa who came to Lover's Plateau never could have.

"Because I'm your fucking Falcon Goddess, and you will recognize me as such."

Silence fills the room again as most of the jaws in the room hit the ground. Lexona's eyes twinkle with awe, Afzal and Zoya freeze. The silence lasts for some long seconds before the elders slowly begin to rise from their pillows. The O'Raha take to their feet as well, standing at the wooden benches.

Salessa breathes deeply to maintain a confident exterior, though her heart pounds in her chest with worry. *What're they going to do to me?*

Slowly, one-by-one, the elders bow their heads before Salessa. The falcon turns and finds the O'Raha doing the same. Before long, the entire room is either bowing, kneeling, or entirely prostrating before the three deities in the room.

And for the first time since she arrived, Salessa accepts their act of worship, no longer feeling unworthy of her divinity.

The meeting is adjourned shortly thereafter. While the wooden benches empty, and the elders descend from the stone platform to exit, Zoya approaches the Falcon Goddess.

Salessa opens her arms and pulls the horse into an embrace, bathing in the feeling of sisterhood as she would if she were embracing Naina. Over the horse's shoulder, her eyes fall on the empty throne where the wolf should be seated.

For all her talk of missing Naina, of channeling her, of wishing she were here with her, Salessa has not once written to her sister. It's time, now that she's been legitimized as a resurrector, to reach out.

It's time for Naina to come to Lover's Plateau.

She breaks away from the embrace. "I need to write a letter, Zoya."

CHAPTER 35

"FIFTEEN SECONDS"

Sub-Oceanic Stratocracy *SeaBed*
Date *40th Day of Month 6, Year 1629 DG*

ONE WEEK BEFORE KYOKO AND Kanako left EverEmber for the Library, their father asked them to join him on a fishing trip. Kanako refused outright, choosing instead to spend her final days in their homeland with friends.

"Teenagers," their father scoffed at his sixteen-year-old. He turned to Kyoko and asked, "What about you, Kyo-chan?"

Kyoko loved spending time with her father, but was terrified of sharks. Her father assured her there were no sharks in the area where he fished, and he promised her that they would both be safe.

It was a sunny day, a lovely afternoon, and Kyoko still holds the memories dear to heart. Her father brought a lunch basket for them to share on his small rowboat, and they caught some fish to bring back home. Under the glowing rays, drifting on calm waters, Kyoko's smile touched each of her ears. It was one of the happiest days of her life.

Until about three hours in, when Kyoko and her father were getting ready to head back to shore. He was known in the community for his sense of humor; for distributing smiles to those who needed them most, whenever they needed them most. His humor was always good-natured, genuine. Until the day it wasn't.

While Kyoko was rowing, he widened his eyes and pointed behind her, over her shoulder, screaming, "SHARK!"

Kyoko remembers how it felt. Her heart sunk so deep into her stomach she thought it might never come back up. Instantly, she was in tears, screaming for her life and jumping into her father's lap. It wasn't until she heard him laughing that she opened her eyes and realized it was a cruel prank.

Her father couldn't contain his laughter, holding his sides, while Kyoko breathed deeply, trying not to return her lunch to the boat. Even as she wept, partially from relief, partially from embarrassment, he continued to laugh. She'd always known her father to be funny; she'd never seen him be cruel.

As he laughed, and she regained her composure, there were so many questions racing through her mind. Why would he do that? Why did he find it funny to scare her? How could he be so cruel?

Just as she was about to ask him one, or all, of these questions, the boat became unsteady. Her father's laughter had rocked the vessel, and before he was able to stop it, the momentum caught up to him.

He fell into the water.

When mari fall into the water, they swim. They swim *on* the surface, they swim *under* it, they do whatever they want because the mari are at home in the water. The igni are from an island nation and are no strangers to open ocean either.

But it's not the same thing when your skin is made of stone.

Kyoko waited five seconds for her father to come back up to the surface. Then ten seconds, and then fifteen. People don't realize how long fifteen seconds is when you're waiting for someone to survive. Or not to survive.

For all Kyoko knew, those fifteen seconds could've been fifteen days. Fifteen years. Fifteen lifetimes. Her heart beat against her chest as she waited for her father to bounce through the surface and take a long breath. To smile and joke with her again.

It's a bizarrely confusing position to be in, when you love someone with all of your heart, and they wrong you, and before you get the chance to reconcile, to forgive them, the opportunity is snatched away from you.

The loved one is snatched away from you.

Kyoko loved her father. She worried for his safety and, for fifteen seconds, she shoved the hurt he had caused to the back of her heart. She may have been angry with him for the prank, but she would be even angrier with him if he didn't keep his promise. Before they had stepped onto that boat, he had promised that they would both be safe.

Rafael had promised that they would both be safe as well. But his promise was broken. Kyoko is safe, but Rafael is not.

Today is the day that Rafael dies.

He broke his promise and now Kyoko is twelve years old again, sitting on the rowboat, waiting for Rafael to come up for air. Except he hasn't been below the surface for fifteen seconds. He's been there for a week. And one of the last things Kyoko did was call him a fucking hypocrite.

It doesn't seem possible. How can Rafael be executed? Surely, he'll walk into the room at any moment, with his bright smile, his contagious laugh, and they'll be on their way to EverEmber together. He certainly has a sense of humor like her father. Maybe it's all just a cruel prank.

Or maybe it's a nightmare and she hasn't woken up yet.

Fate is the one playing a cruel prank. It robs Rafael of his life, and his opportunity to apologize for lying, for breaking his promise. For not trusting that Kyoko would support him.

Fate robs Kyoko of her chance to dole out forgiveness. To reconcile and rebuild what Rafael's omissions have broken between them. It robs them both of all the future nightly conversations they could have, as they've had for over a year now in the Bunker. Ana always slept early, leaving Rafael and Kyoko time to exchange thoughts, share dreams and goals and ideas, and to trade emotions.

To establish an intimacy of the heart that Kyoko has grown to cherish.

Fate strips them of the opportunity to mend the shards of their shattered connection. Kyoko will have to live each and every day knowing he died while their relationship was tarnished, and she'll never have the opportunity to put the pieces back together again.

She swallows hard to break the tightness in her throat. There wasn't even an opportunity for a proper goodbye. She now lies on her back, sinking into a comfortable bed in General Sofia's palatial home, her arm and shoulder cradled to her chest in a sling. The igni's gaze rises through the window, and finds the positions of the four circular lights affixed to the dome around Corazón Azul. The lights are moved in an arc to mimic the movements of the suns in the sky above the ocean's surface, allowing residents to tell the time.

Rafael dies in an hour.

There's little time left to save him. Had her shoulder not been injured, had she her full range of motion, they would've been in Ever-Ember already. Kyoko would've slipped into the cells and released him long ago. They likely would've reconciled by now.

The battle with Vy-Ro has taken more from her than just her shoulder. It's taken her ability to save, to protect. Rafael will die because Vy-Ro stole the mechanism with which she would've stopped his execution and freed him from the prisons.

Kyoko turns her head and her gaze catches Ana sitting at a metal desk across the room, the Sprite texts laid out before her. They'd had an argument the day before; Kyoko couldn't stand watching her translate while Rafael rotted in a cell.

"How can you just sit here and—" Kyoko had started to yell.

"If I don't keep myself busy, I'm going to break down," Ana yelled back, keeping her eyes locked on the book, a tear dripping from her chin to the page below. She lowered her volume and continued, "I can't lose another person I care about. I just lost Alba."

Kyoko embraced her and they wept together, with a new understanding between them. The mari sits feverishly translating still, searching for a breakthrough to keep her mind off of the fact that the minutes wind down to the swing of the executioner's blade.

This has been one of the most agonizing weeks of Kyoko's life. She and Ana had been escorted out of the Hall of Generals by mari guards, ordered to leave SeaBed at once. Rafael had used his final request, a dying man's wish, to set them free. It was typical of the Rafael she's known for a year, not the one from these past few weeks who kept secrets from her.

While the guards were transferring her and Ana to the military wagon that would escort them out of the city, they made the mistake of turning their backs on a trained Librarian. Even without the use of her arm, Kyoko managed to take Ana by the hand and slip away, losing the guards in the crowded streets.

They spent five days sleeping in basements and alleyways, and the hay stacks of some farmer's barn. Eventually, someone caught up to them, but it wasn't a guard.

It was Rafael's mother.

Kyoko was genuinely amazed that she'd tracked them down. But she was even more astonished that she didn't give them up to the authorities. Instead, she brought them home. Kyoko never asked her why she helped them. She never questioned the salvers who were sworn to secrecy as they secured Kyoko's shoulder in a sling.

She never inquired what the consequences would be if General Sofia were discovered to be harboring fugitives.

The door creaks open and the General enters the room, clad in colorful ceremonial armor that makes her shimmer like a beacon. Ana looks up, eyes wide, and Kyoko swings her legs off the bed and onto the ground, moving into a seated position. The three women stare quietly at one another for a moment, bathing in awkward silence, before the General speaks.

"I've brought these for you," she says to her guests, gesturing to the ragged hooded cloaks in her hands. She hangs the garments on a rack behind the door, then turns back to the travelers. "The execution is in about forty minutes. I'm required to be there, but you aren't. You can dress yourselves in these cloaks, and my driver can take you to the city square. From there, you can hide in the crowds all the way to the exit of the city and find your freedom. It's a little bit of a walk, but—"

"Freedom?" Kyoko blurts out, bewildered. "We were offered freedom seven days ago, General. We aren't going anywhere without Rafael."

General Sofia visibly tenses. She swallows hard and looks down at her hands folded in front of her. Kyoko's mind is assaulted with questions. Her father was underwater for fifteen seconds and couldn't answer them. Rafael has been in chains for seven days and cannot answer them.

The General *will* answer Kyoko's questions.

"Ana," Kyoko says, gathering her friend's attention. "May I have some privacy with the General, please?"

Ana nods slowly, then rises from the seat and exits the room, closing the door behind her. When Kyoko and the General are alone, the silence grows thicker until Kyoko finally breaks it.

"Do you know why Rafael is here?"

The General raises an eyebrow. "You all came to deliver a message, didn't you? The end of the world. The ancient beings. The Three Dea—"

"He came for you."

The General's eyes widen.

Kyoko continues. "I also thought we were here on a mission. Ana and I came in service of it. But Rafael came only to see his mother."

When the General speaks, her voice trembles. "H-How do you know that?"

"Because I know you wrote him a letter. I know he's been reading that letter for weeks. I know he brought that letter with him to SeaBed, clutching it to his chest like it's his mother's heart on paper." Kyoko rises to her feet. "Rafael came to SeaBed to see the one person he loves more than anyone else on this planet." Her eyes narrow. "And you think I'm just going to put on a cloak and abandon him? The way you did?"

"Watch it," the General responds, her tone hardening. "I saved you."

"Then why won't you save your son? He's forty minutes from having a sword run through his throat. Don't you care?"

The General takes a step back, as if Kyoko's words have pushed her. "Of course, I care."

"Then stop the execution."

"It's not that simple," she murmurs, shaking her head.

Fury clouds Kyoko's vision. Her skin is hot with rage, as if she's been lit aflame. "What's complicated about it? He's your son and they want to execute him."

"He committed a crime."

"It was your letter that drove him to it."

"But he's getting executed because of you."

Silence. Kyoko is stunned. She doesn't know how to respond, except for a short whimper and, "Me?"

The General takes a deep breath. "Maybe Rafael came back to SeaBed because of my letter. Had he come alone, I could've saved him from the execution. But *you*, an igni, showed up on his arm. There's no saving him after that. The execution is in forty minutes, but you killed Rafael the moment you decided to join him. Congratulations."

Kyoko's knees grow weak and she drops back down onto the edge of the bed, burying her fingers in her hair. If Rafael dies, his blood is on her hands. The General is right.

But that is *if* Rafael dies.

After fifteen seconds, Kyoko's father returned to the surface. He took a long inhale and, with Kyoko's help, got back onto the rowboat. As soon as he caught his breath, he apologized to Kyoko for the prank, and for falling overboard. He frightened her on both accounts, but he did apologize. And he kept his promise.

Rafael hasn't come up from under the water, and Kyoko's just now realizing that she may have pushed him overboard.

"We can't just give up," Kyoko says, raising her gaze to meet the General's again. "You have to fight for your son's life."

Sofia hesitates. "I…I can't, Kyoko."

The rage returns, the frustration climaxes. "Why not?"

"Because they'll see it as weakness. I've worked so hard for decades to get to where I am. You don't understand, any sign of emotion, they'll hold it against me."

"You think *I* don't understand," Kyoko scoffs. "My entire career, I've had other Librarians tell me I'm 'too emotional.' Men who would punch a wall if they got angry. As if they didn't realize, anger is also an emotion. Despite their attempts at holding me down, I rose to a higher rank. But what is the point of rising if you can't use your power to save people you love? What is the point of anything that makes you forsake your duties as a mother? Where I come from, mothers are seen as a symbol of strength."

"My people feel the same way, but those in government don't. They'll ridicule me until all that's left is the legacy of a woman who put her motherhood before her duty."

Kyoko hardens her tone and steadies her eye contact. "That's better than the legacy of a woman who put her image before her son's life."

The long, tense silence resumes until the General clears her throat. "I'm getting late. The cloak is yours to use and to keep. Good luck." She turns to leave.

"Come with us," Kyoko blurts out before she can stop herself.

The General stops walking but keeps her back to Kyoko.

"I'm going to come to the Hall of Generals, and I'm going to try to save Rafael. If I do, you are welcome to join us."

Sofia turns back around to face Kyoko. "Join you?"

Kyoko nods. "Francisco and the other Generals will not heed our warning about the Three Deaths or the Ancient Ones. SeaBed is doomed, and few will survive. Evacuate with us."

"I'm not leaving my people. I'll evacuate, but only after I've helped as many others evacuate as I can. I swore to serve the public, and I won't leave them to die."

Kyoko nods and the General's gaze falls. She looks like she's contemplating whether or not to leave. When she looks back up at Kyoko again, her eyes have grown wet, and when she speaks, her voice trembles.

"Is he still an archer?"

Kyoko stands confused by the unrelated question. "What?"

"Rafael spent years training with his sister." A soft sad smile stretches across her lips. "Archery was a way for them to bond. It meant so much to him. Is he—she pauses, seemingly nervous about how Kyoko might answer—"still an archer?"

Memories flood Kyoko's mind of their time in the Hearthbark, when Rafael saved her life, and all the times she's seen him wield a bow since. She can't help but smile as she responds.

"The best archer I've ever known."

CHAPTER 36

"Fifteen Minutes"

Sub-Oceanic Stratocracy *SeaBed*
Date *40th Day of Month 6, Year 1629 DG*

IT'S UNFAIR, THE KIND OF expectations that are put on people facing certain death. If they're not smiling, or standing with their chin raised, they're a coward. Even if the idea of death makes them nauseous with terror, only the brave look death in the face and laugh.

But Rafael is not laughing. He's not smiling and his chin is not raised. The mari's eyes are red and swollen from weeping, his hair and beard matted with grime from the past week of not being allowed to bathe or wash, his frail body shivering from the cold. A semi-circle of bruised skin borders the bottom of his eye, and a crust of dried blood rests under one of his nares. Gifts from the guards.

Despite his lack of cleanliness, or the ache of his face, nothing can steal his thoughts from the rattle in his heart.

He's frightened.

A year earlier he stood atop a building in Larso, during the Halving of SunSide, with a Braver onslaught headed toward him. He thought he would die then, but he wasn't afraid. It was a call to war, and his time to answer. He thought he would be with Joaquina soon and he wasn't afraid of the prospect.

But this situation is different. That would've been the death of Rafael, the martyr, the warrior. Today, he will die as Rafael, the exile, the fool who came back because he missed his mother.

Joaquina's bracelet is in the pocket of his haggard prison rags. He'd removed it before they stripped him, so they wouldn't see it, and dropped it into the pocket of his new outfit as soon as he was dressed again. It's the same place his mother put it the night she said goodbye to him the first time, and sent him off to the Library and an uncertain future. Her only remaining child.

The metal locking mechanism on the cell bars clanks and Rafael turns his stiff neck to see who it is. A guard opens the door, allowing General Sofia to enter. She's wearing her ceremonial robes, exuding the same formal regality she's maintained since Rafael was a child. He's flattered she dressed up for his execution.

The guard closes the door behind the General and reminds her that the execution's scheduled time is in twenty minutes. The most he can give her is fifteen.

Fifteen minutes to say goodbye.

With the way she's dressed, the way she's carried herself all his life, the way her icy blue eyes have always implied a frozen heart that puts duty before all else, he expects her to make a formal farewell.

But today, in the final minutes of his life, General Sofia breaks all expectations.

When Rafael meets her gaze, the General's eyes are as red and swollen as his. The ice around her blues has melted, and what remains is the warmth of the blue skies on a summer day. What remains is the crystal-clear blue of the ocean water around SeaBed.

Rafael opens his mouth, but his throat is so dry, the word barely makes it out of his throat. "Mother."

She doesn't say anything. Sofia takes two long strides to her son before she collapses onto the cell bench next to him and wraps her arms around him, heaving in sobs, holding his head to her chest. He wraps himself around her, as well as he can with the metal around his wrists, reciprocating the embrace, stunned by the warmth of her body.

And her actions.

Between sobs, she breathes out, "My little salmon, you came home."

Rafael tries to hold his composure, tries to keep his tears in their ducts so as to remain brave for her in the face of what's coming next.

"I love you," Sofia says, unexpectedly.

Rafael loses himself to sobs as well, and the tears break free. The words he's been waiting twenty-four years for her to say, he hears now in his last fifteen minutes. In the final moments of his life, he isn't able to remain brave. He's a coward who weeps because he's saying goodbye to the world. To his mother. To Unisa.

To Kyoko.

They weep together, holding each other tightly for some minutes, cursing the damned fate that brought them together for such a short time, only for him to be taken forever.

Finally, the General breaks from the embrace, but takes Rafael's hand as she speaks. "You've grown into a man, Rafa. You're so handsome, you look just like your father."

Rafael speaks with a strained voice through a dry, sad throat. "I wish I were brave like him."

"Why did you come back, Rafa?" she asks. "You could've written a letter. Why did you come back here?"

Rafael reaches into his pocket and pulls out Joaquina's bracelet. Sofia gasps, as the blue gems shine twinkling light onto her olive face.

"You put this in my pocket before I left for the Library," Rafael reminds her, "and told me to take care of it. I came to return it to you, so you have something of Joaquina."

Sofia shakes her head. "Why? She gave it to you. It's yours."

He breathes deeply, hoping his next statement isn't conveyed as a dying madman's hallucination. "I spoke to her."

"What?" she breathes out, eyes wide.

"I know it sounds like nonsense, but it's true. I spoke to Joaquina. She's happy."

"How, Rafa?" Her tone is nearly begging for an answer. "How did you speak with her?"

"It's a long story," Rafael begins to explain, "but it was the Radiance. Human Radiance. It exists still, in all of us. I've rediscovered it."

Sofia's eyebrows scrunch close together. "Rafa, I-I don't understand."

Rafael closes his eyes and takes a deep breath. He channels the Radiant energy in his body and pushes it out to his wrists. When his eyelids part, the metal cuffs have moved from his wrists to Sofia's.

She looks down and realizes she's now cuffed. The General launches up to her feet and stares down at them as if they're live snakes wrapped around her wrists. Rafael channels it again and the cuffs fade, returning to him.

"Human Radiance thrives, after a millennium," Rafael says, holding up his cuffed wrists. "And in less than ten minutes, it will be snuffed out from this world again."

Slowly, Sofia descends back to the bench. "Rafa, this is…remarkable. How have you done this?" Her eyes dart to the iron-barred windows. "Why haven't you used it to escape? You could leave here, Rafa. You can save yourself."

Rafael has asked himself these questions many times in the week he's been here. Each and every time, his thoughts revolve around a single answer.

"Fate brought the Radiance back to life after a thousand years, Mother. I can think of so many reasons the universe would want human Radiance in this world again." He sighs. "Evading the consequences of my actions is not one of them. I can either die with my integrity, or I can live the rest of my life knowing I slithered out of facing the justice I deserved."

Sofia stares at him, disbelief in her warm blue eyes, before she finally says, "You truly are your sister's brother. And your father's son."

"And my mother's, as well," Rafael adds.

A soft, sad smile stretches across her lips.

Rafael places his hand on Sofia's chest, over her heart. "Joaquina told me she is here. With us, always. And after today, I will be here, too. With you, always."

Sofia's lip quivers as she sobs again. Rafael places the bracelet into her palm.

"Take care of the bracelet." He places his hand on her cheek. "And please evacuate SeaBed before the Three Deaths come. Even if no one else leaves, I need you to get to safety."

"I can't leave my people, Rafa, you know that." She takes Rafael's hand from her cheek and holds it. "I took an oath to serve them."

"But you'll die if you don't run."

Sofia nods. "I can either die with my integrity, or I can live the rest of my life knowing I slithered out of my vows."

Rafael's mouth falls agape, hearing his own words echoed back at him. It is more apparent now, than ever, that he is his mother's son.

"You know why I can't stop the execution, right?" she asks him, holding his gaze. "I want to, but I can't."

Rafael nods. "I understand."

"Tell me you forgive me, Rafa," she begs.

"Mother, there's nothing to forg—"

"Tell me!"

Rafael breathes deeply and nods again. "I forgive you."

Her shoulders relax and her expression melts, as if a boulder of guilt has been lifted off of her. "There isn't much I can do for you now."

Rafael and his family have never been spiritual, never believed much in higher powers. The next words out of his mouth surprise him.

"Can you pray for me, Mother?"

His mother seems as surprised as he is, but she nods and kisses his forehead anyway. "I'll pray for your friends' safe return today, as well."

Rafael raises an eyebrow. "My friends? Today? What do you mean?"

"They're still here."

Rafael's heart sinks. "I told them to leave."

"I know, but they didn't listen. They escaped the Generals' escort, and spent a few days on the run. I tracked them down to the old Ortiz farm before the soldiers could, and let them stay at my home. They should be leaving today."

Rafael silently prays that they leave before his execution.

"I failed you. But I wanted to, at the very least, save those close to you."

"You didn't fail me," Rafael says. "But thank you for watching over Kyoko and Ana. They have been there for me through so much that has happened over the past year. Kyoko…" His voice trails off as words fail him.

"I know," she says, allowing him the grace to not explain further. "I saw how she reacted when they separated you two. I think that's why I went looking for them. I knew she was special to you."

"She is," Rafael admits, for the first time aloud. "Kyoko's done so much for me. Personally, spiritually. I'm just disappointed I wasn't able to share parts of myself and my life with her that she got to share with me."

"What do you mean?" Sofia asks, leaning forward in interest.

"Last year, I went to EverEmber with her. I wore a yukata, dipped my feet into an ashiyu, ate with chopsticks, and walked the streets with her through a hot spring village. There was magic in being able to visit her homeland with her."

His eyes travel to the window. "I'll never get to share that magic with her again. To explore the winding streets of ancient towns, and stand in the awe of our architecture. To have a late-night paseo, or a heartfelt sobremesa. To bathe in the serenity of a walk through our family's olive groves as the suns rise over the horizons, and then sit to enjoy churros. All she's seen of my home is the same thing she's seen everywhere else: hard-hearted politicians who, perhaps, once represented their people, but no longer do."

He can't speak further, as his throat closes. It's as if his body is refusing to speak aloud the tortured truth of his inability to experience the purest love, after coming so close, and remaining so far.

Sofia embraces him one more time. One final time.

"I told you never to come back, Rafa. We sat here in this cell, nine years ago, and you promised you wouldn't come back."

Rafael clears his throat. "And I told *you*, salmon always come back home. I'm home, Mother. This is where I should die. At home."

She holds him for a few moments and then finally speaks a question she seemed to be holding in. She blurts it out as if she is dying to know the answer. "How are you feeling?"

Frightened.

"Fortunate."

"Fortunate?"

Rafael nods, his head still against her chest, his arms around her, melting into the embrace he longed for as a child.

"I'm fortunate to have existed in a time where I could be born as your son, regardless of how short a time it was. I'm fortunate to have had a brave father, and a loving sister. I'm fortunate for my second sister, Unisa, and that fate brought Kyoko to me."

He breathes deeply, allowing the warmth of his mother to melt his suffering and his fears away, "Mother, I only lived for a short time, but for every moment of it, I was fortunate."

CHAPTER 37

"THE PRISONER AND THE EXECUTIONER 1"

Sub-Oceanic Stratocracy *SeaBed*
Date *40th Day of Month 6, Year 1629 DG*

KYOKO CAN'T REMEMBER THE LAST time her foot involuntarily tapped so hard. Ana, seated to her right on the wooden benches in the Hall of Generals, gently places her palm on Kyoko's knee, calming the igni's bouncing leg. To her left is the barricade preventing civilians from entering the aisle where they'll be escorting the prisoner to his execution.

Kyoko notices things now that she hadn't the first time she was in the room: the onlookers' shimmering jewelry, pristine outfits, impeccable posture, posh accents. The civilian audience isn't a random sampling of mari; it's a group of exclusive invitees from the upper crust. An audience of noblemen and noblewomen from the farthest financial reaches of SeaBed's society, here for a show, a riveting performance.

This is likely the first execution-after-exile SeaBed has had in generations, and will likely have for many years or decades to come, and they want to be able to say they were there for the historic moment.

Kyoko and Ana keep the hoods of the cloaks Sofia gave them pulled over their heads and on the sides of their cheeks. Kyoko may not have been able to break Rafael out of his cell, but stealth is still in her repertoire. She can sit in an audience, or slip into a crowd, without being noticed.

And she can teach Ana to do the same.

The five Generals are already seated at the massive marble bench at the far end of the room. Like a madman waiting for blood to be drawn, Captain General Francisco sits at the center, a smug grin across his face. Sofia sits directly to his left, lines of despair and desperation etched across her face. Kyoko wonders if she's had a chance to say goodbye.

The deafening creak of the doors draws every eye in the room. They swing open and it takes everything in Kyoko's bones not to gasp loudly at the sight. Rafael is led into the room by an entourage of guards surrounding him.

He's barefoot, clad in prisoner rags. Dried blood cakes his clothes, and his face under his nares. The uniform is too small for him; it neither reaches his ankles, nor does it traverse his forearm fins, which are cracked from dehydration.

He sports a bruised cheek, a black eye. His beard and hair are matted with the grime of the dungeons, and he's lost a noticeable amount of weight, as his swollen eyes sink into their sockets. The young man of only twenty-four seems to have been treated so poorly, he could easily pass for sixty-four.

The mari's wrists are held closely together in front of him by metal cuffs, and the jangle of ankle chains scraping the floor echoes throughout the Hall. They're treating him as if he's dangerous. As if they caught him in the act of mass murder, when his only crime was coming home. Was delivering a message to save them all.

Kyoko clenches a fist and breathes deeply, gathering every ounce of strength in her body to resist from hopping over the barricade, drawing one of the guards' swords, and paying them all back for what they did to him.

As Rafael passes her by in the aisle, just a few inches beyond the barricade, she battles the urge to reach out and take his hand, to offer him some comfort. To tell him it'll be alright and, though he's minutes from his execution, she'll think of something to release him.

Or, at the very least, she'll be here with him in his final moments. Her throat tenses at the thought.

What am I going to tell Unisa? She'll never forgive me for allowing this to happen.

This could've been avoided had he told them about the letter from his mother. Had he not hidden his true intention when coming back to SeaBed. Kyoko would've asked him to write a letter of his own. She would've delivered the bracelet to General Sofia and he could've stayed in SunSide.

Kyoko's eyes widen as she realizes: he was right. Not for hiding things from them. Not for lying when he promised they would all walk out of SeaBed safely together.

But he was right in his assessment that the General would never have entertained an audience with an igni and a mari who was taken to the Library as an infant. These noblemen and noblewomen would never have come to hear Kyoko and Ana speak.

They are only sitting here in the Hall of Generals, and they only got to address the leaders of the city, because Rafael grasped their attention and hasn't let go in a week. And he knew that would be the case. He was well aware that they would never entertain Kyoko or Ana, but that his arrival would require their involvement. He forced them to listen to the message. Forced them to hear the warning.

As Rafael reaches the execution platform set up at the center of the Hall, between the two podiums and directly in front of the Generals, the truth dawns on Kyoko: This was never a preaching mission for Rafael. It was a sacrifice. He willingly gave his life to get their attention. To beg them to save SeaBed. Knowing he would have their ear as soon as he walked in, he sacrificed his life in the hopes that it would save his home and, in the process, he'd be allowed to see his mother one last time.

Kyoko is twelve years old again, waiting for Rafael to come back up to the surface of the water within fifteen seconds, but after a week she's realized he had no intention of coming back up. He threw himself off of the boat fully intending to drown, but hoping to save an entire city in the process.

There's only room for two individuals on the execution platform: a prisoner and an executioner. A guard steps up next to Rafael. He's the stockiest of them. Kyoko wonders why they would need someone so large to swing a blade; they should all be skilled enough to do it.

Her question is answered when the guard removes the typical mari warrior armor from his arm, and is fitted instead with a gauntlet that goes up to his elbow. It's metal, similar to the armor he just removed, but over his forearm fins are a series of curved blades. It resembles four daggers shooting out of his forearm, as if his natural forearm fins have been lengthened and sharpened.

Kyoko realizes the method of execution when she sees the executioner swinging his arm in front of him with swift, rounding punches. The forearm blades will journey through Rafael's throat, front to back, severing his head from his shoulders with a single punch.

It's a beheading, and a rather violent one.

Captain General Francisco rises to his feet and the room's attention shifts from the guard, still practicing his execution punch, to the leaders of the city. He knows his name is about to be etched into SeaBed's history books, as the Captain General who executed the exile.

The guard standing beside Rafael is as much an executioner as the blade is. A weapon. A tool. He's nothing more. Francisco is the true executioner here.

"Rafael," Francisco calls out to him. Rafael raises his head weakly, meeting Francisco's gaze. "At the time of your arrest, you were magnanimously offered a final request by the Council of Generals, and you used it to free your accomplices."

Rafael nods, keeping his lips tightly together.

"Though they've slipped from our grasp, they will likely be apprehended soon, and then their fate may resemble yours."

Ana sinks deeper into her seat on the bench, but Kyoko shakes her head and gestures for her to resume her position upright. They have to blend in. She turns back to Rafael and realizes he has no reaction to the information that Kyoko and Ana escaped.

Does he know?

"Regardless," Francisco continues, "we, the Generals of SeaBed, have voted in favor of offering you a final statement as well. You may speak now, if you so desire."

Rafael's gaze travels from one General to the next, until he finds Sofia's. He offers her a smile and then speaks.

"I'm grateful for the opportunity to speak before the Generals." His voice is hoarse, damaged. It's difficult to hear, from where Kyoko sits, so she leans forward slightly. "I know I violated my exile by returning to SeaBed but I had good reason. I'm not lying, I'm not playing a game. The catastrophe that comes for this world will attempt to destroy all of SeaBed in the process. I beg of you, prepare for it."

Francisco scoffs. "*You* want us to prepare? The man who was exiled for sending his sister to war in his place?"

Kyoko's blood boils as the civilians seated around her laugh.

Rafael nods. "You're right, I didn't go to war when I was called to it. And it cost my sister her life. That is something I live with every day. But I love this city. I love the people in it, including you, Captain General."

Francisco's smile is wiped clean.

"I want you to be safe. The oncoming threat is greater than our politics, our disagreements, our squabbles. Innocent people, an entire city, will be decimated if this world doesn't put their egos aside to come together and fight the Sprites as one. Please, as a dying man, I ask you to believe me. For the safety of your citizens."

Rafael stops speaking, seemingly awaiting some response or reassurance from the Generals. But Francisco simply leans forward and asks, "Are you finished?"

Rafael turns to Sofia and says, "I love you."

Sofia's expression cracks as her lip quivers and tears break from the corners of her eyes. It's the most emotion Kyoko has seen her display.

"Alright, then," Francisco says, "let's get on with it." He signals to the executioner, who turns to Rafael.

Time slows to a near standstill, as Kyoko's heart sinks into her stomach. Terror breaks free from her own eyes, as she begs fate, the universe, every god and every goddess from every religion, to come forth and stop this execution. Rafael let Joaquina go to war for him, he once held prejudices against Kyoko and her people, he lied to her because he knew she'd never let him sacrifice himself, he violated the laws of his exile, and there may be so much more Kyoko isn't even aware of.

But not a single flaw warrants an execution. After every single one of these mistakes, Rafael has grown. He's shown that, given the opportunity, those who make mistakes can always make them right as well.

Unless they've been executed.

As the executioner winds up, ready to swing the blades at Rafael's throat, Kyoko feels a hand grab hers. Ana's hand. Kyoko squeezes the mari's fingers, as Ana releases a soft, quiet sob. The two women hold each other, waiting for the man they've gotten to know so well over the past year, to die. The avalanche of truth drops on her: she's about to exist in a world without Rafael. A world where there could have been so much more to what they had.

She's done it before. For twenty-eight years, she existed without knowing Rafael. But it occurs to her now that it only took a single year of knowing him to erase what it was like to live without him. As if she's returning to a homeland in which she no longer knows how to live, because she spent a year somewhere else.

She doesn't want to go back. She doesn't want to relearn how to live in a world where Rafael doesn't exist.

They watch as the executioner's swing begins and the blades start traveling toward Rafael's neck. Nausea bubbles in Kyoko's throat and the room around her starts to spin. A vision pops into her head of her future, sitting as an old woman next to an old man, whose face is obscured. Suddenly, the man fades away, and older Kyoko is alone.

The igni's heart shatters and she releases a heavy sob. Devastating grief overcomes her, tightening her throat until she can't breathe, forcing bile up, as only one thought swirls in her mind. *How can I just sit here and watch Rafael die? Someone, anyone, please, make the executioner—*

"STOP!"

The cry is so loud, so powerful, Kyoko thinks the very domes protecting the city might shatter from it. Her sobs cease and her jaw drops as she realizes, it came from neither her nor Ana. It came from no one in the audience, nor any guards. It certainly didn't come from Francisco.

Sofia is on her feet, her arm outstretched, reaching toward her son, her mouth open still from the cry. Her eyes are so wide, it seems as if she's even surprised herself from the outburst. Blood drips from one of the executioner's forearm blades, and Rafael stands with his hand over a small wound on the side of his neck, applying pressure to stop the bleeding where a bit of the first blade had entered before the executioner pulled his arm back.

Nearly every jaw in the Hall is on the floor. All except one. Captain General Francisco leans back in his seat, grinning.

"I knew it," he says, shaking his head, staring up at the woman, the General, the mother, next to him. "I knew you'd let your emotions get the best of you. I've been waiting for this day, Sofia. Sitting here with tears, whimpering. The moment you were appointed, I knew it was a mistake."

Sofia turns to him, her volume striking the towering ceiling. "Let. Him. Go."

"What?" Francisco scoffs. He turns to the other Generals. "Are we truly going to allow this?"

Sofia's face burns red as she continues. "Let my son go, NOW."

"He's a criminal, Sofia," Francisco sighs. "He must pay for his crimes."

"He came to save us. Willing to sacrifice himself to save an entire city. This is obviously a unique circumstance."

"You want to bend the laws for your goddamned *maternal instincts*." The last words he speaks drip with venom. "I will not have it."

Sofia shakes her head. "No, I just want to initiate a vote for his release, pending a demonstration."

"Demonstration?" Francisco scoffs. "This is absurd. What are you talking about?"

She turns to Rafael. "Show them."

Rafael silently shakes his head.

Sofia's fist rattles the desk. "Goddamn your integrity, Rafael, show them!"

Again, Rafael stands still and silent.

She does it so quickly, no one in the room has a chance to react. Sofia reaches down and pulls a dagger from a small sheath on Francisco's hip. As his eyes widen in surprise, she turns it on herself and plunges the dagger toward her own chest.

It vanishes. Fades away as if it were never there to begin with. There's a deafening clang that echoes throughout the room. All eyes turn to the execution platform, where the dagger has fallen from Rafael's hand onto the floor.

The executioner tries to grab him but quickly realizes the wrist cuffs and ankle chains now bind him and not Rafael. Other guards collapse forward hoping to restrain Rafael, but they can't move forward, as the stone tiles melt quickly, and then harden again, holding every guard in the room in place. The blood on Rafael's neck remains, but the mari has healed the wound from which it flowed. His skilled use of the Radiance leaves the entire room, including Kyoko and Ana, in bewildered astonishment.

Rafael holds his hands out and the dagger rises quickly back into his palm. He teleports onto the desk in front of Francisco, who yelps like a frightened child, and places the dagger down in front of him, then teleports back to the platform.

After a tense moment of silence, the audience erupts in cheers and hoots, chanting for Rafael's release. That's all it took to turn a villain into a hero: a demonstration beyond their wildest imaginations.

Francisco rises to his feet, raises his arms, and shouts, "Enough!" The room goes silent again. "Explain yourself!"

"I have unlocked the secrets of human Radiance. After a millennium, it has returned."

"And if you execute him," Sofia adds, "a significant moment in human history, in human evolution, is wiped out for possibly another millennium, or forever. This is about so much more than Rafael or my maternal instincts, Francisco. Ignore the warning if you wish, but you *cannot* ignore that my son was chosen by fate to bring humanity into its next evolutionary stage." She locks eyes with the other Generals. "A stage that is now in all of your hands."

One of them, a man around Sofia's age, meets Rafael's gaze. "Why didn't you show us this before?"

Rafael breathes deeply and says, "I didn't find it honorable to use this gift for personal benefit."

The General shakes his head. "But your survival is a benefit to us all. I would've found it dishonorable, for you to allow a gift for our species to die with you, without having shared it with the rest of us. You understand that, right?"

Rafael's eyes widen with realization. "I do now, sir."

Francisco proclaims, "A vote, then. All in favor of carrying on with the execution, hand-to-heart." He places his hand over his chest, and is the only one to do so.

"All in favor of releasing Rafael back into exile," Sofia says, "hand-to-heart." Each of the remaining four Generals, place their hands on their chests.

Rafael is free to go.

Kyoko feels, for the first time in a week, as if she's able to breathe again. Ana is squeezing her hand so tightly, Kyoko thinks the mari may have broken through her exoskeleton. But now, she isn't sobbing.

She's smiling.

Rafael closes his eyes and the stone tiles melt again, releasing the guards from their hold. They step forward to take him into custody, but he shakes his head and raises his hands. "That won't be necessary. I can see myself out." He disappears from the platform and reappears at the door.

More cheers and gasps of awe come from the crowd. They applaud him and rise to their feet. Kyoko and Ana do the same. From over the heads of the audience members, Kyoko can see Rafael holding steady eye contact with his mother and, having gotten to know him as well as she has, she knows exactly what is happening.

He's taking a final look at his mother. This will truly be the last time he ever sees her in his life. Rafael says his final goodbye to her.

Tears stream from Sofia's face, as she quietly mouths the words "I love you." Rafael nods and raises his palm to his lips, sending her a kiss from where he stands. He mouths back over the audience's applause "Goodbye, Mother."

And then he turns to exit the Hall of Generals, an exile once again, but alive.

CHAPTER 38

"GOVERNANCE AND LEADERSHIP"

Theocracy *SunSide*
Date *4th Day of Month 7, Year 1629 DG*

SAILA DESPISES DISHONESTY. IT ISN'T something she's comfortable with, and she certainly had made every effort throughout her life to avoid it. But she's learning now that, sometimes, it can save someone's heart.

The pixie sits in her chambers at a small, wooden desk in the corner of the room. It's quite late at night, but she hasn't dimmed the lighting panels in the room yet. The paper in her hands keeps her awake.

It's a letter, dated the 50th of Month 6, the last day of the prior month. Four days in transit with a messenger.

She hasn't eaten, slept, or thought of much else since it came. She doesn't know what to do with it. Does she respond?

No, she couldn't possibly, could she? Why would she respond to a letter that isn't addressed to her. Why did she even *open* a letter that isn't addressed to her?

Because the person to whom it's addressed is currently stuck, indefinitely, in Red-Lo's mind. Saila's gaze drifts down to the signature portion of the letter at the bottom. Salessa signed it before she sent it off for Naina. The messenger couldn't find Naina, obviously, so she brought it to Saila, asking her to hold onto it.

Saila instructed the messenger to tell people it was delivered to Naina, directly, if anyone asks. The messenger was confused, but agreed nonetheless. This was Saila's first dishonest action in a very long time. She feels guilty, but there's not much else she can do. If word got out that Naina is nowhere to be found, people will start to ask questions.

"Where is my sister?"

"I sent her into an eight-hundred-year-old's mind, where there's no concept of time, with no protection and no way out."

If Salessa came home from her journey to find Naina on such a dangerous quest, she'd never forgive Saila. The pixie wouldn't even be able to explain why she thought it was a good idea at the time. She simply honored Naina's wishes, despite her own reservations.

Saila puts the letter down and slides it to the side, then pulls out a blank page with a quill and inkwell. As much as it pains her, she'll have to be dishonest again.

"Dearest Salessa," she begins to write, before she scoffs, crosses the salutation out and crumples the paper up. *Naina would never use the word "Dearest." And she calls Salessa "Lessi."*

She pulls out another fresh page, but before she starts writing again, she reviews the contents of Salessa's letter first. The falcon apologizes for taking so long to write, then assures Naina that she is healthy and well. She talks a little about finding the author of the note, and going with them to Lover's Plateau, but doesn't give any further information, though she does ask if Naina is willing to make the journey to join her, as it's important for them to be together for the resurrection of the Twins. She ends the letter asking Naina to let her know how things are going in SunSide, and whether or not she's willing to join her at Lover's Plateau.

The final words of the letter, before Salessa's signature, are, "I love you, and I miss you."

Guilt washes over the pixie. Naina will not see this letter if she isn't able to find her way back out of Red-Lo's mind. Fortunately, whatever Salessa's busy doing, it doesn't appear she'll be home anytime soon. Saila just has to buy some time.

Before she starts writing, she raises her hands to the sky and begs the Four for their forgiveness and mercy for the dishonesty. She's about to commit a grave sin.

Then she finally puts ink to paper:

Lessi,

Glad to hear from you. It's relieving to know that your journey has been fruitful, and that you've found the author of the note. I hope it's been an interesting quest for you, and I can't wait to hear the stories when you get home. Unfortunately, I'm not able to join you on Lover's Plateau at this time, but as soon as I become available, I'll write another letter requesting directions.

Everything is well here! Saila and the other Members have renamed the theocracy "the New SunSidian Assembly" to match the military's New SunSidian Guard. We've also managed to stop the Bravers United from their campaign of unrest, and their leader is in custody. Tomorrow, at our Assembly meeting, we'll set the date for his execution.

No further updates on the situation with Red-Lo. Saila continues her interrogations but they don't seem to be going anywhere. The latest information we have is that the Three Deaths can strike anywhere in the next three months. Hopefully some new information will come about soon.

Don't worry, take your time on your journey. Keep doing what you're doing, and we'll all see you when you get home. Everything is perfectly fine. I love you and I miss you, too.

Naina

Saila stares down at the page, waiting for the ink to dry. The word "fruitful" shoots daggers at her. She would gamble a lot of stones on the fact that Naina has never once in her life used the word. But here she is, sending a letter, pretending to be the wolf, with the word in the first sentence.

This is going to be a disaster.

She feels a drop of relief that, while the letter is covered with a fabricated facade, there are grains of truth in it. Saila *does* hope Salessa's journey has been interesting, and she truly can't wait to hear the stories that'll come from it. The Assembly *did* get renamed, the leader of the Bravers United *is* in custody, and the theocracy *will* be setting a date for his execution tomorrow.

She takes a deep breath, folds the page, and places it into an envelope, planning to hand it off to a messenger first thing in the morning. Just as she yawns, stretches, and starts to change into her nightgown, there's a knock at the door.

Starlight drips into the room, reminding her how late it is. An odd hour for visitors. Cautiously, she steps to the door and opens it. Standing on the other side is Member Rayga, the pink pixie from Ward's Fall who was the first elected Member of the New Assembly.

"Member Rayga," Saila says, her tone betraying her surprise. "Is everything alright? It's so late."

"I'm so sorry for disturbing you so late, Chief Member," Rayga apologizes with a respectful bow, "but there's something I wanted to speak with you about and—" She pauses. "I don't think it should wait until morning."

A sinking feeling nags at Saila's stomach, but she nods and steps aside to allow Rayga entry into her chambers. After closing the door, she turns to find the pink pixie standing sheepishly at the foot of the bed.

"What's wrong?" Saila encourages her. "Please, speak freely."

"At our last Assembly meeting, I mentioned that some residential complexes have been completed in the first new city you wish to build, to house the faeries returning to SunSide from the MoonSidian settlements."

Saila nods, recalling Rayga's statements from the meeting a little over thirty days prior. "Yes, I remember. You had mentioned that the expected completion of City One would be in two to three years."

"I said two to three years, *at best*. But I've recently learned that due to some unforeseen circumstances, it'll likely be closer to five, maybe six, years."

Saila sighs, her heart sinking further. "Rayga, our temporary shelters are already overflowing. More and more faeries pour in from MoonSide each day as we continue to dismantle the settlements. I need at least one of these cities done by the end of the year."

"It's just not possible with the workforce I have, Chief Member. I already have my laborers working to the bone. I need more."

Saila narrows her eyes. "Tell me the truth. Why are you in my bedroom in the middle of the night telling me this?"

Rayga hesitates. "I know how harsh and judgmental some of the new Members can be. I felt that if I brought this up at the meeting tomorrow, it would make you seem..."

"Incompetent?" Saila finishes her sentence, realizing that Rayga is here in the middle of the night as an act of mercy.

Saila sits down on the bed, elbows to knees, hands folded. If she had started to feel somewhat confident in her leadership skills, she doesn't anymore. She's lost, trying to figure out exactly what kind of leader she aims to be. Tund-Ra's words, from his last conversation with her three weeks prior, echo in her ears.

Rule on your own terms, guided by your own convictions. SunSide is in your hands now, and you can rule it however you see fit. Just don't become the thing you hate.

Was she becoming the thing she hated? Red-Lo and the many monarchs before him made constant promises to their subjects that they never upheld. Saila has promised new housing by the end of the year. A place for everyone to live, abolishing houselessness. And now, Rayga stands in her bedroom, telling her it won't be possible.

The pink pixie takes a seat on the bed next to Saila. "I'm sorry, Chief Member."

Saila shakes her head. "No, I'm actually quite grateful. You could've brought this up at the meeting tomorrow and you're right, I would've looked incompetent. I think there was a time when I dreamed of being Chief Member. Of leading the theocracy and serving the public. But there's so much about governance and leadership I just...didn't know."

"It's a difficult situation," Rayga consoles her. "I understand how taxing leadership is, particularly in a predicament like this one. You need homes built by the end of the year, but you don't have the workforce to complete it. It's not like you can just plant seeds into the soil and have workers pop up from underground."

Rayga chuckles at her own attempt at humor, but Saila isn't laughing. Her eyes widen as the brilliance of Rayga's comment strikes her. Another echo of Tund-Ra's words, from their last interaction, rings through her ears.

Construction. We made such a good team that they would assign us projects together, just the two of us. We built entire homes, sturdy homes, faster than crews of ten.

These were the words Tund-Ra used when describing how he met his husband.

Saila turns to Rayga with a wide smile. "You're a genius, Rayga."

Rayga raises an eyebrow. "I am?"

"You are. I may just be able to pop some workers up from underground. The seeds are already planted."

CHAPTER 39

"The Prisoner and the Executioner 2"

Theocracy *SunSide*
Date *4th Day of Month 7, Year 1629 DG*

SAILA STANDS OUTSIDE THE IRON door that leads into Tund-Ra's cell. There's a guard beside it, a young one who asked Saila if he should go get Ovida, but the Chief Member told him it wouldn't be necessary. Despite his uncertainty, the young soldier stepped aside to allow Saila entry into the prisoner's enclosure.

She had started to prepare a pixie cell for him, with protections against the Radiance, but after their previous conversation, in which he admitted his discomfort with using it, she cancelled his relocation.

Ovida disapproved, but Tund-Ra's sincerity in his personal history, his grief in losing his husband, and his rage at the pixie clan were all palpable. Saila trusted him not to use the Radiance to escape when he said he wouldn't.

Perhaps she was an incompetent leader after all.

When she turns the doorknob and enters the cell, she finds him lying on his bed, as she expected him to be, reading a book. He has access to the Radiance and could've escaped at any point in the past three weeks. Or at any point since his arrest. But he hasn't.

She closes the door behind her and Tund-Ra realizes she's there. He puts the book down and smiles. The Chief Member takes note of his condition. Clean clothes, combed hair, bathed, well-fed. It's a stark contrast to how many other nations and cities and kingdoms treat their prisoners, particularly those who are awaiting execution.

How those who led SunSide before her treated their prisoners.

"Well, well," Tund-Ra says, rising to a seated position, "the executioner herself. It's been a while since you've come to check on me. I was expecting to see you next on the day my execution is set. Is that why you've come?"

Saila strides through the cell and, for the first time, she doesn't sit on the seat across from Tund-Ra's bed. This time, she sits next to him.

His eyes widen. They've never physically been this close before.

"That's not why I've come," Saila admits. "The Assembly is meeting tomorrow to set the date of your execution."

"Then what brings the Chief Member to my cell so late at night? Your guards served me dinner hours ago. It must be well past midnight."

"It is."

Tund-Ra keeps his gaze locked with Saila's, but she doesn't say anything, hesitating. He leans forward and raises his eyebrows. "Saila, if you wait too long, I'll be executed before I get to hear what you have to say."

Saila takes a deep breath, trying to keep a stoic expression and not to smile at the prisoner's humor. "Do you remember the things we talked about that last time I was here?"

Tund-Ra goes silent this time. He considers the question for some long seconds before responding. "I do remember. You sat over there"—he points to the small chair across the cell—"and listened to me blather on about my daughter, and my dead husband, and how I became a Braver and why I started the Braver's United and how I feel about the pixies—"

"Yes!" Saila interrupts him. "How you feel about the pixies. That's why I'm here."

Tund-Ra sighs and leans in toward her. "You'll have to start using your words. I'm an old man, your father's age, and I certainly cannot read your mind. What are you talking about?"

"Tund-Ra, last time I was here, you asked me if I have any idea how fragile the pixies' clan solidarity is. You told me that pixies only showed up to admonish you, to chastise you, to ostracize you. They were never there when you truly needed them to empower and uplift you."

Tund-Ra nods. "I still stand by every one of those statements."

"Well, it's hurtful to me. Because you're right. Those haven't been my experiences with my pixie brothers and sisters, so I have no idea how fragile clan solidarity is. I preach solidarity because I believe in it, because the pixies have never failed me. But they have failed you, and you don't deserve that. You deserve better from your clan."

Tund-Ra's eyebrows scrunch together. "Saila, where are you going with this?"

"I'm cancelling your execution."

Tund-Ra's mouth drops open. "What?"

"Tomorrow, when I meet with the Assembly, I'm going to cancel your execution. You were right, I don't know how fragile clan solidarity can be. But *you* don't know how powerful it can be."

"But—" Tund-Ra's expression contorts as he tries to make sense of what he's hearing. "But last time we spoke, you said my crimes warrant execution. That's written in theocratic law, and historically, it's always been that way."

"Execution after execution after execution. That's what *you* said. And you were right. There was a specific way in which the theocracy and the monarchy governed SunSide for centuries. Millennia. It's time for change. I have to forge my own way as a leader. This is my way. You and the other Bravers United will no longer be executed."

Tund-Ra leans back, staring at Saila, seemingly trying to process what he's hearing. Finally, he responds, "Then, what will happen to us? We'll rot in these cells?"

"You could. Or, you can make a deal with me that will allow you all some sunshine and minor freedoms."

Tund-Ra raises an eyebrow. "I'm listening."

"I can't let you free, after the crimes you've committed. So any warrior of the Bravers United who wishes to live out their days in a tiny cell is welcome to. Or, you can allow me to transport you all, in chains, to Ward's Fall."

"Ward's Fall? What would we do there?"

A smile crosses Saila's lips. "Construction. You told me that's how you and Loro met before you got married. You built sturdy homes faster than a crew of ten. Can you still do that?"

Tund-Ra's expression betrays his suspicion. "So you're not going to execute me, but you'll send me to Ward's Fall, along with my followers, to do something I enjoy? What's the ploy, Saila?"

Saila holds up her hands defensively. "No ploy. I need to get a lot of homes built by the end of the year. The current projection of completing these homes, with the workforce I've allocated to it, is five to six years. Can you lead your warriors to complete this project in four months?"

Tund-Ra pauses, contemplating, stroking his chin. "I don't know. I'll need to convince most of my warriors to follow me there."

Saila shrugs. "You are their leader, after all. If anyone can persuade them to join my cause, as opposed to rotting in a cell for the remainder of their lives, it's you." She puts her hand out toward him. "Do we have a deal?"

Slowly, still suspiciously, Tund-Ra reaches forward and shakes Saila's hand.

"You truly are something different than those who came before you," Tund-Ra says.

Saila smiles. "I hope so." Tund-Ra's gaze shifts to the floor. He falls silent and pulls away from the conversation, as if something is troubling him. "What's wrong?"

Tund-Ra releases a soft chuckle. "I knew the punishment for my crimes was death. Since the day of my arrest, I had started looking forward to my execution. Now, I'm left with a question that, I think, only a pious theocrat, someone devoted to the Four like you, can answer."

Saila nods. "I'll answer if I'm able to. What is it?"

"If the Four are all-powerful…if they are loving and fair and just, why are they stopping my execution? I don't deserve mercy."

Saila is taken aback by the question. It's the kind of candid sincerity with which Tund-Ra has always spoken to her, and yet she can't help but be surprised. She thinks deeply for some long seconds before replying.

"I don't know. I've devoted my life to serving the Four, but I can't tell you what they think. Perhaps, one day, you'll find the answer to your questions on your own. Perhaps they'll lead you to the answer."

Tund-Ra scoffs. "Almighty powers and they can't just give me a straightforward response?"

Saila stands, smiling. This is a question she's heard before. Every devotee has asked this question at some point in their lives. "There is a test of discipline and willpower and devotion in staying on a path that leads to answers. There's a journey involved in finding those answers."

She turns and steps toward the iron door. "And journeys are an act of worship."

CHAPTER 40

"THE HAWKS"

Sovereign City-State *The Library*
Date *4th Day of Month 7, Year 1629 DG*

HOW OFTEN DO PEOPLE THINK about the ways in which the course of their lives is altered by singular events or decisions? On a day-to-day basis, few often consider the molding of their lives as a result of one occurrence.

Unisa is one of the few. She sits now, in the Nest, thinking about how much her life has changed since the Prime decided to curtail her daily visits with Lyla. Their blossoming friendship, their flourishing sisterhood had triggered his suspicions. Sharpened the surveillance of the Cicadas.

Events, and decisions like the Prime's, shape lives the way forks in the riverbed change the direction in which a current travels. Forged through millennia of mighty erosion, rivers are set on their paths, until they reach a fork that splits them into distinct branches. One branch continues in the same direction, allowing the current to carry on without interruption. But another, affected by an event or decision, rages forth on a new path, eroding the landscape for a new reality.

Had the Prime not made this decision, Unisa would've continued seeing Lyla, and the Prime would've lost his grasp on her. He'd lose his ability to monitor and surveil and wrap his wicked fingers around a vulnerable teenager. He'd never allow that to happen. It's been two weeks and she's only seen Lyla three times.

The Prime is back in control of both Lyla's and Unisa's lives.

It was on that same night that Yuki, Juhi, and Konni had confronted her about her absence from the mission, from the Nest.

From Ora.

They were right. Spending less time with Lyla these past two weeks has afforded her more time recruiting new members to the Hawks. And she's spending more time with her mother. The team appears more satisfied now. Alba entrusted this mission to Unisa, not to them. Her duty is to lead and guide. She belongs in the Nest.

At Ora's side.

And yet, anxiety burdens one shoulder while guilt encumbers the other. She still feels responsible for Lyla's protection, and it concerns her to abandon the teenager with the cherry-blossom cheeks.

Mercifully, during the three visits she's had in the past two weeks, Lyla has appeared healthy and in good spirits, particularly while asking Unisa for stories from her childhood. Lyla can't get enough of them; stories of a, relatively, healthy childhood in Ora's care. She's asked, on nearly every occasion, to visit the elderly pixie once Lyla's had the baby. Unisa continues to smile and nod cautiously, unsure how that'll be possible considering Ora's rapid deterioration and the Prime's control over Lyla's movements.

Life is unpredictable. Unisa spent so long fearing Ora's decline, weeping over it with a tight chest. And now, there are times when it doesn't even register in her mind that she's speaking to the same individual. The pixie who raised her, who protected her, who loved her. The patient appears to be someone unable to speak or eat on her own, and yet could very well understand everything that's being said to her without being able to respond back.

Sometimes Unisa feels grief that she's losing Ora, sometimes relief that the pixie's suffering will end, and sometimes she feels nothing at all, except the guilt that comes with feeling nothing at all.

"Where are you, Uni?" Konni asks, taking a seat next to her at the table.

Unisa looks around the Nest, confused by the question. "I'm right here?"

Konni chuckles. "No, I mean mentally. We've been training"—she gestures to Juhi, leading a group of their newest recruits in combat training—"but you seem to be...lost."

"I am, a little," Unisa agrees, apologetically.

Konni leans in and lowers her volume. "Anything you want to talk about?"

"No, I'm alright." She shakes her head and turns to the training session.

Juhi leads a pack of twelve new recruits. With the five existing members of the Hawks, there are seventeen of them total. It certainly isn't an army, but it's more Fully Broken warriors than Unisa thought they would ever have a few weeks prior.

"Something's changed," she remarks to Konni.

"What do you mean?"

"Generations of indoctrinated citizens have come and gone without the empowerment to speak openly against the Prime, or the Library's allies. It took me months to recruit you, Juhi, and Yuki because I didn't think I could raise my voice safely. And it was nearly impossible to break Maksi, the Fully Bonded. Yet, in the past two weeks, we've gained twelve new recruits. How is that possible?"

"Maybe we're aiming for the right demographic now." Konni gestures widely at the group. "What do they all have in common?"

Unisa takes a hard look at the group. There's no commonality in their species or clans; there are nymphs, faeries, pixies, Doruh, and humans. She stares for a few long seconds before she realizes what binds them. "Their age."

"Exactly," Konni nods. "I'm the oldest one here. Everyone else here is under the age of thirty."

"What does that mean?" Unisa wonders.

"It's the youth. It's always the youth who want to change the world. They won't let the injustices of their forefathers be passed down. It'll end in their lifetimes."

There's something both soothing and chilling about Konni's thoughts. It's optimistic to think that the youngest of a society are willing to change that society in ways their elders aren't. It fosters hope that the world will continue to progress, from one generation to the next.

But why does it take youth for people to recognize injustice? Why is it so easy for the oldest of a population to walk past a garden without planting a flower, only because they know they won't be around to watch it bloom?

Unisa and Konni continue to observe the new recruits until it's time for the angi to retire back to Ora's apartment. As she heads towards the exit of the Nest, a distant sound blooms in the air, stopping Unisa in her tracks. She looks around, twirls, trying to locate the source. Juhi hushes her students and then does the same. Konni's indigo palms light up with Radiant energy, seemingly recognizing the noise as it amplifies. As it moves closer.

"What is it?" Unisa asks.

Konni raises a glowing finger to her lips before closing her eyes. She allows the sound to flow into her ears before her eyelids pop apart and she whispers, "It's a battle."

The sounds become instantly clearer. Grunts. Growls. A struggle. A blade striking something. Wounds opening. Blasts of Radiant energy. Menacing laughter.

The hallway leading into the Nest bursts alight, so brightly that Unisa's forearm rises to shield her eyes. When she lowers it again, Maksi appears, soaring through the air in tattered clothes that reveal gaping, dripping wounds along his carrot-colored skin. His arms are locked around an angi man, in a similarly injured condition. The winged attacker, clad in civilian attire, wields a blade, laughing as his strikes cut through the Mega's flesh.

It all happens in a blink. Juhi shifts into her hawk form and, matching speed with the chaotic battle slamming against the ceiling, digs her talons into the angi's arm. The man cries out and the sword drops from his hands. With pinpoint precision, Konni raises her palm and a blast of blue Radiant energy passes both Maski and Juhi, punching a hole through one of the angi's wings.

The path of the chaotic battle grows even more unpredictable, as the man's injured wing guides them left, then right, back and forth, uncontrolled. Juhi is tossed into a wall, hitting her head and shifting back into her human form, barely moving when she hits the ground. Maksi is released from the angi's grip, slamming hard into the stone floor, lying still in an expanding pool of his own blood.

Unisa rushes to the Mega's side and attempts to employ first aid to stop the bleeding and keep Maksi breathing. Konni joins her, using the Radiance to begin healing some of Maksi's more extensive wounds, inundating his body with energy so the healing remains even when she walks away.

"Come on, Maksi," Unisa begs. "Wake up." She turns to Konni. "How bad is it?"

Konni's expression hardens gravely. "He's alive. For now. But it's going to take a while to recover."

Maksi's eyelids flutter slightly. There's a word hovering on the tip of his tongue, but in his weakness, he can't release it.

Unisa attempts to catch it. She leans down and places her ear as close to his lips as she can. "Louder, Maksi. I can't hear you. What are you trying to say?"

When the word becomes clear enough for Unisa to hear, her heart instantly strikes the floor and her eyes widen. She turns to Konni and repeats the word that Maksi utters just before he loses consciousness.

"Cicada."

There's a guttural battle cry released into the air. By some stroke of incredible misfortune, or remarkable training, the angi Cicada has found his sword, and is surrounded by the Hawks' newest recruits. The twelve lightly-skilled warriors are disarmed so quickly by the Prime's disciple, he resembles a farmer cutting through thin strands of wheat in a field.

Before any of them can retreat, two of the young recruits meet bloody ends at the tip of the man's blade, who smiles as they bleed out at his feet.

When he turns to a third recruit, Konni launches onto her feet and uses the Radiance to attempt to subdue him. The man avoids her attacks masterfully, a dancer on a stage, a cheetah in chase, but his injured wing eventually fails him, and Konni is able to retrain him. She brings him to his knees and Juhi, clothed again in her human form, physically drags him to a chair behind the table.

"I can't hold him forever," Konni says through gritted teeth. Though the energy of the Radiance binds him, the man slowly moves his arms from behind his back and rises from the chair. It's a testament to the Prime's training of his warriors. "He's breaking through my hold. Get some rope or shackles, something."

Juhi's prepared. She pulls a box out from under the table and withdraws two pairs of metal cuffs, stepping behind the Cicada and placing them on his wrists and his ankles. Konni finally releases her hold with a sigh of relief, then rushes back to Maksi, assisting Unisa in laying him onto a cot while the Radiant energy works on healing him.

Unisa and Konni join Juhi and the remaining recruits next to the table, where the bodies of the two fallen Hawks lie.

"We should give them proper burials. They gave their lives for a cause we haven't even truly begun to fight yet."

"The fight has begun," Juhi says, her eyes locked on the Cicada seated behind the table. She balls her fist and with all her strength, she punches the man across the face. Two small, white teeth soar from his mouth and land on the ground. He turns back to Juhi and smiles wide, his mouth entirely crimson with blood.

"You'll pay for that, animal bitch," he grunts.

Juhi winds her fist back to hit him again, but Unisa catches her wrist and holds it back. Recognizing the opportunity they have before them, she shakes her head.

"What are you doing?" Juhi asks.

Unisa pulls her away from the Cicada again. "You've asked me so many times, since this mission began, if I'm willing to do *anything* for it. And I told you I don't want to engage in any violence. That I can fulfill other roles."

"What are you talking about, Uni?" Konni asks.

"Interrogation. We have a Cicada now, thanks to Maksi. I don't have to draw blood if I can draw information instead."

Juhi and Konni exchange cautious glances, before Juhi agrees. "Alright, Uni. You're our interrogator. You want to keep your hands clean? Get him to talk. But if you can't get anything useful from him, I'll put a sword in your hand myself."

Unisa nods. "Deal."

Konni and the recruits break away to take the bodies of the fallen to a burial site. Once they're gone, Unisa and Juhi are left alone with the Cicada.

"What do we do now, interrogator?" Juhi questions her.

"Search him," Unisa instructs, buying time to think of what questions to ask.

Juhi steps forward and examines the stranger. Where his clothes have become tattered from battle, she sees a dark tattoo on his side, near his hip and above his right buttock. It seems almost intentionally placed, hidden.

She calls Unisa over and they squint, looking closely at it and trying to make out the image. They realize the design of the tattoo: a circle with a scroll in it.

"What do you think it means?" Unisa asks Juhi, who shrugs.

"Take my pants off entirely and I'll show you something far more eye-catching than a tattoo," the vile man spits before Juhi hits him across the jaw again.

The man laughs and more blood drips from his mouth onto the floor. "I can't wait to pluck you clean, birdie, one feather at a fucking time."

Juhi takes a deep breath, then turns to Unisa and whispers through gritted teeth, "Start questioning before I kill him."

Unisa steels her nerves, before addressing the Cicada. "What's your name?" Silence. The Cicada stares at her blankly. "How old are you? Where do you live?"

Juhi grabs Unisa by the elbow and drags her away from the prisoner.

"Are you looking for information, or a boyfriend? What kinds of questions are you asking?" She turns quickly and hits the Cicada in the face again, blood spraying all over the floor and his clothes. She leans down close to his face and bellows, "What does the Prime know about our operation? Did he send you?"

The Cicada leans his head back, gathers all of the bloody spit in his mouth, and launches it into Juhi's face. "Do you like that, baby?"

She stumbles backward, then regains her footing and raises her fist again, but Unisa grabs her and pulls her back.

"Stop letting him goad you. If you knock his head off, we're going to lose our asset."

"We're not getting anywhere with your questions," Juhi protests, wiping the blood and spit off of her face.

"I'll ask better questions but, please, you have to control yourself."

Juhi takes a deep breath and cracks her knuckles. "Fine. But if your next few questions aren't better than, 'What do you do for fun?' I'm taking over."

She walks back to the table and takes a seat, as Unisa thinks, *I never asked him that.*

The angi steps in front of the Cicada and thinks, long and hard, about what information they need. Unisa and the prisoner hold steady eye contact with each other for so long, it almost does start to feel a bit too intimate, even for Unisa, but she doesn't want to rush a question that isn't going to satisfy Juhi, or that isn't going to get an answer from the Cicada.

Finally, she thinks of a question to which the Hawks truly need an answer.

"How does he recruit you?"

Juhi sits up in her seat, alert.

The prisoner doesn't respond, so Unisa elaborates. "The Prime is a craven, wicked man. But he's also a master of upholding his righteous facade. That's how he, and so many Primes before him, swindled the city for generations, into striving for their indoctrinating ideology: the Fully Bonded."

Unisa starts walking, circling the man in the chair as she speaks, hoping to rattle his confidence with her presence. "But…you. You and the other Cicadas aren't indoctrinated into this foolishness of being Fully Bonded or Fully Broken. You know all about the facade, and the truth of who, and what, the Prime is. You know his secrets. You know about the young girls he keeps hidden away from their families in his home."

She steps in front of him again and puts her face close to the prisoner's. "And yet, he's still recruited you to do his dirty work. How? Did your ethical compass fail at some point and you thought he could put it back together and show you the way? Did he tell you *why* you're surveilling us?"

The Cicada remains silent, but he's no longer smiling. His eyes are focused on Unisa's.

"How did you get into a fight with Maksi? I've seen your"—she pauses—"colleagues around the city, watching me. You're not as stealthy as you think you are."

"I can assure you, we are," the Cicada responds, fighting back against Unisa's attempt to bruise his ego. "Whomever you *think* you saw, it wasn't us."

"So you are following us? Why? Does the Prime know about us? And what we're doing here?"

Silence again.

"He doesn't. I know he doesn't, because there would've been a hundred, or a thousand Cicadas down here already after you."

The Cicada scoffs. "You think he cares enough about me to send others here to protect me?"

Unisa laughs. "No. He doesn't. That's the point. He doesn't care about anyone but himself. If he knew we had you, he would've sent other Cicadas down here to kill you. To protect whatever information is in your head. To protect himself, not you."

The Cicada shuts his lips tightly, nervousness bubbling up in his expression. Unisa is making progress.

"That answers one question, at least," Unisa continues. "The Prime doesn't know where we are. He doesn't know what we're doing. Which means we still have a chance to win the war."

"No one will win a war against the Oath Master," the Cicada professes in a low, menacing growl.

"Is that what you call him? The Oath Master? Did he make you take an oath?"

The Cicada's eyes widen. He realizes he's said more than he should have. He closes his eyes and turns his head away from her.

The interrogation is over.

Unisa walks around the table to where Juhi sits. "I'm sorry, I don't think I'll be able to get—"

"No, I'm sorry," Juhi says. "I suppose you don't have to get your hands bloody to lead us. That was enough information for a first interrogation. There's still a lot we need to know, but you got him talking and that's enough. For now."

Unisa shakes her head. "It's not enough. I have two more questions to ask." She approaches the Cicada. He sees her coming and defiantly presses his lips together.

Unisa leans downs, taps the man's hip, and asks, "What does the tattoo mean? Did the Oath Master give it to you?"

CHAPTER 41

"The Incest Doesn't Last Long"

Theocracy SunSide
Date Unknown

LEAVING THE MOST PAINFUL MEMORY of Red-Lo's life is jarring. Naina no longer feels the desire to rush him through, as she has for every prior one. She gives him time to experience the worst night of his life, again. Not because he suffers, but because the suffering appears to bring him peace.

Closure.

They sit on the bed together as past Red-Lo weeps over the decision he was forced to make, choosing between his wife and daughter. Even after Hay-Ro returns to tell him that Drof-Fa survived, he continues to sob. Loudly.

Eventually Naina turns to present-day Red-Lo and asks, *How are you feeling?*

Calm, he responds, still watching quietly. *Thank you for asking, Naina.*

Hearing him use her name, instead of referring to her as "pup," is alarming.

I'm sorry, he continues. *I don't mean to delay us.*

Naina chuckles. *Delay? I don't think we have a time limit. Saila said I wouldn't be able to tell the real-world time in here anyway, but I couldn't have been in here for longer than an hour, maybe two. Hopefully it's only been an hour or two out there, as well.*

Are you afraid? Red-Lo asks.

Of what?

The fact that you could return to your body and it could be eighty or ninety years old. The fact that your sister could've lived out her life without you, while you were in here with me.

Naina doesn't respond immediately. She allows the question to settle into her heart, finding an answer within herself before she releases it from her tongue.

No, I'm not. Whatever happens, I came in here for a purpose. I did it for the good of others. All others. The world. Whatever happens to me, I did the right thing. That's all that matters.

Red-Lo pauses, seemingly pondering on her statements the way she did on his. *I've been wrong about a great many things, Naina.*

Naina's eyes widen, her ears protesting in disbelief.

He continues. *Watching so many of my memories back, conversing with you about the injustices we perpetuated against so many, seeing the difference that was made by the smallest gesture of using someone's name, and reliving the most painful suffering of my life has brought to light so much of the truth that I had thrust into the darkest part of my mind for so long.*

And what truth is that? Naina asks.

Pain. Suffering. Selfishness. Joy. Empowerment. Love. Respect. Family. Faith. Siblinghood. He turns his head to her. *Empathy. These are all commonalities in the individual experience. Whether that individual is a faerie, a pixie, a nymph, human, or Doruh. We all feel the same. And that's what makes us equals. No one supreme to the next.*

Naina's breath catches in her throat. She's never experienced another's epiphany before. *What makes you, finally, see that? After an eight-hundred-year life?*

Red-Lo smiles. *In eight-hundred years, I've never had someone walk me through my experiences before. The agonies that I endured through centuries, but never addressed. Never before did I discuss the roots of my views, and realize I didn't get anywhere with faerie supremacy. It's a road with no end, and it started before I was even able to read.*

He turns back to the scene around them. *All I wanted since the day I lost my daughter was immortality. Was the promise that I could hold onto my wife, my clan, and my kingdom for all time. But look what's happened. I lost my wife only three years after that night. I lost my kingdom eight hundred years later. And my clan is no better off now than they were when this all started. I don't even remember, Naina.*

Naina leans in. *Remember what?*

The point. The goal. What were we trying to accomplish by enslaving others? By talking down to them and stripping them of rights? What good comes from holding my father's supremacist views in a life we all experience the same way?

He stands and holds his hand out to her. Naina hesitantly stares up at it. His realizations and disillusionments, all of the unlearning and reframing it took to get him there, it's all valuable and has a place in a society that is able to forgive.

But Naina struggles to assess if *she* is in a place to forgive, especially when she hasn't received any genuine display of remorse, apology, or atonement. Nevertheless, her journey must continue until she gets the information on the Sprites that she needs. The wolf takes a deep breath and places her hand in his, rising to her feet to join him.

Red-Lo snaps his fingers. The void surrounds them and the next door appears within it. *Come, Naina, let's move on to the next memory.*

Naina releases his hand and steps to the door. A frigid breeze chills her to her core and she wraps her arms around herself to keep warm. Red-Lo appears unfazed.

They stand at the bottom of a canyon, towering stone walls standing at attention around them like soldiers guarding the valley. A few yards ahead, a warming fire provides respite for two Mega: one turquoise, another magenta.

You and Drof-Fa, Naina observes. Red-Lo nods. *When is this?*

Three years after the last memory. 783 DG.

Naina puts her hands out, allowing heat from the flames to lick her palms, and then rubs her warmed hands against her arms. *Around the time of the Everlasting Journey?*

Red-Lo pauses before he responds. His gaze is locked on Drof-Fa, and he stands so still, Naina thinks he may have been turned into a statue. Finally, he responds. *This is the Everlasting Journey. You're about to watch me lose my wife.*

He steps forward and takes a seat next to the memory of Drof-Fa, who stares at the flickering flames, unaware of the consciousness next to her. He lifts his turquoise fingers and gently caresses her cheek.

And she turns to look at him.

His eyes widen, and Naina can see the genuine terror in his gray eyes. They aren't supposed to be able to interact. A small lizard creeps about behind Red-Lo, and both he and Naina realize together it's what caught Drof-Fa's attention. She turns back to the flames and Red-Lo continues to nostalgically watch her.

This is my first time seeing my wife in eight-hundred-and-forty-six years. She is just as beautiful as I remember.

Past Red-Lo holds out a fist toward the fire and the flames roar outward, illuminating much of the canyon, including a portion of the stone wall that was previously hidden by the darkness. It sits behind a bed of boulders, and hosts the mouth of a cave with the symbol of knife carved over it.

Past Red-Lo and Drof-Fa leave their campfire behind as they enter the cave, Drof-Fa leading the way, her palms illuminated with Radiant energy. Naina and Red-Lo follow behind them.

I had found a riddle, Red-Lo explains as they continue to follow his past self and his wife through the cavern, *that spoke of immortality as a prize to anyone who frees two entities from their prison within this cave.*

Where did you find this riddle? Naina wonders.

In a text that once belonged to the Sprites. It must have been one of their followers who wrote the poem after they'd been imprisoned, hoping to lead a reader to this cavern on Panaerth to free their masters.

And you and Drof-Fa were those readers who freed them.

Red-Lo sighs. *Sadly, yes. I got the immortality that I had started craving after we lost our daughter. But it came at a price.*

The cave opens steadily the deeper they go, and the wet walls give way to a wide, egg-shaped space with torches along the walls.

Lit torches. As if someone has been here recently.

"It's warm here," Drof-Fa whispers.

"Not warm," Past Red-Lo replies. "Hot. Too hot." He ventures further into the egg-shaped room, and the time-travelers follow him.

Past Red-Lo's gaze is glued to the far end of the room. In the shadows between the torches, a column of rock stands four feet tall, unnaturally carved and placed with purpose. On top of the stone pedestal is a small clay pot with a lid.

"It's a shrine, I believe," Past Red-Lo remarks.

I made such astute observations, Red-Lo mocks his younger self.

Drof-Fa flanks him and bends forward to get a better look at the container. There's a design etched into the outer rim.

"Flames," she says.

"Find the water in the flames," Past Red-Lo repeats a verse of the riddle. "A continent away, in the cavern below the knife. If this pot has water in it, we'll have found the water in the flames."

Red-Lo, standing next to Naina, shudders. *Opening that little clay pot is the greatest mistake I've ever made.*

Past Red-Lo reaches forth and pulls off the lid and a vibrating beam of light erupts from the pot. Naina and Red-Lo cover their eyes, but the beam blasts Drof-Fa off her feet. Past Red-Lo shrieks, covering his eyes, and stumbles backward.

Drof-Fa manages to gain her footing and helps Past Red-Lo stand. She unsheathes her sword, and her husband steps behind her.

Then, the light disappears back into the pot.

What was that? Naina questions in synchronization with Past Red-Lo.

It was the liberation of your enemies, Red-Lo explains. *Those with whom the Twins are destined to engage in battle. The ones you have to defeat to save the planet.* He gestures to the far end of the room. *The Sprites. The Ancient Ones.*

Two figures, one male and one female, stand in the hot room with them. When she sees them, Naina shrieks *What the fuck?!* and drops to her knees to vomit onto the floor of the cavern. They are grotesque.

The two creatures stand wet and naked. Water drips off their bodies, but they are also drenched in a number of other fluids, including blood, mucus, pus, and feces. Their faces, torsos, genitals, arms, and legs are covered in blisters, burns, and scarring, as if they've been through an intense battle.

Entirely hairless, they each have two pairs of arms: one pair at the shoulders, the other extruding from their ribs. Their eyes are small and crimson, their skin too decrepit to ascertain a color. There is an odor coming off of them that is so horrific, it changes the entire texture of the air, a mixture of years of decomposition and warm excrement.

They're so thin and skeletal that their arms, legs, and hips look as angular and raw as avian talons.

Their most unusual features, Naina notes, are what seem to be remnants of wings. Not light, feathery wings like Unisa's, rather, they seem to have once resembled those of butterflies, but are now little more than interconnected loops of bone.

The two creatures are hunched over at first, grasping the top of the stone pedestal and breathing laboriously. Then, they turn to look at one another and when their eyes meet, they smile. Inside their mouths, Naina sees brown, degraded teeth and a long serpentine tongue.

"Brother," says the female, "we've been freed." Her voice is grimy.

"We have indeed, Sister," the Brother responds with a voice of similar quality. "Our imprisonment has ended."

The Brother and the Sister move their faces closer until their mangled mouths are mashed together. They slither their serpentine tongues into each other and moan loudly.

I'm begging you, Naina says to Red-Lo, rising to her feet again and wiping her mouth, *is there any way you can move us quickly through this part.*

They're almost done, he assures her, *the incest doesn't last long.*

"Look, Sister," the male Sprite says. "The ones who freed us from our bondage." The two creatures walk around the stone pedestal and stand in front of it.

Drof-Fa asks them who they are.

"We go by many names, Mega. The Drowned Sprites. The Burning Succubi. The Ancient Ones."

"Sprites?" Past Red-Lo raises an eyebrow. "It's been over three thousand years since the Sprites' extinction."

"Three thousand years." The female Sprite sighs. "We've been confined for millennia, Brother."

"I cannot believe it, Sister. We are finally free again. We will find Vala's progeny and they will pay."

Vala? Naina asks. *Who is Vala?*

Red-Lo shakes his head. *I haven't the slightest idea, Naina. They never mentioned her after this night, in all the centuries I served them.*

He turns to meet Naina's gaze. *I wasn't lying during Saila's interrogations. I served the Sprites, that's true, but all I did was offer them essences to feed on. They didn't sit around and have conversations with me. They didn't tell me who Vala is, or their plans, their goals, their timeline. Nothing.*

Naina sighs. *Then, I guess, it was a good idea for me to come into your mind. We can keep going until we find the information I'm looking for.*

The wolf continues to watch the memory as the Sprites enter into Past Red-Lo and Drof-Fa's minds and forge a mental connection to them. They then offer Red-Lo immortality in exchange for the essences of his offspring. Every generation in which Red-Lo brings them an essence to feed on, they will place his essence in the body of his descendant, and he will continue on in younger bodies, generation-after-generation.

It's exactly as Kyoko and Rafael explained after their conversation with Drof-Fa, the TreeKeeper.

Finally, the Sprites make the threat of the Three Deaths. "There will be consequences if the agreement is unfulfilled. We will unleash the Three Deaths upon this world. A beast of the sky, a beast of the sea, and a beast of the soil. They will raze this world to the ground, and we will rise up to create our kingdom upon the ashes."

Everything I already knew from Rafael and Kyoko, Naina says with a sigh. *This memory was interesting, but unhelpful. Maybe we should just continue on to the next one now.*

Red-Lo snaps his fingers and the memory pauses. The male Sprite is standing with all four of his palms facing Drof-Fa, who is paralyzed before him. Red-Lo stands next to her and Naina sees a twinkle of light on his cheeks. When she steps closer, she realizes it's tears.

He's weeping.

This is it, isn't it?

Red-Lo nods. *This is the last time I saw her. I thought they killed her. For eight centuries, I thought she was gone. Until last year when Unisa told me she's still alive. Since then, Saila has held that over my head. She knows how badly I want to see my wife again.*

He reaches his hand forward and caresses Drof-Fa's cheek again. *I'm trying my best to help you with the Sprites, but I truly don't know anything. You may find something as we continue to travel through my memories, but I promise you, I'm not hiding anything intentionally.*

Why are you telling me this, Red-Lo?

Because I miss my wife, Naina. And I'm begging you to uphold your friends' promises. Unisa promised to take me to my wife. Then Saila did. I'm here, withdrawing my consciousness into my own mind to help you. All I ask in return is that you deliver the promise on which no one else has been willing to deliver.

He turns to her, his gaze burning through hers with sincerity. *Promise me you'll take me to Drof-Fa.*

CHAPTER 42:

"THE SIX"

***Alphocracy** MoonSide*
***Date** 10th Day of Month 7, Year 1629 DG*

"COME IN," SALESSA CALLS AFTER a soft knock at her chamber doors. She sits on the edge of her bed in a silk lilac saree, embellished with glittering gold thread work.

Her fingertips delicately grasp a sheet of paper, the torn envelope in which it arrived next to her. She hasn't stopped analyzing the letter in over twenty-four hours.

Zoya enters the room clad in a plain sapphire shalwar kameez with a white dupatta. "Are you ready for your escort, Salessa?"

"Mm-hm," Salessa responds, her gaze and thoughts focused on the paper.

"Salessa?" Zoya attempts to get the falcon's attention. She softly places a hand on Salessa's shoulder.

Salessa's eyes pop up. "Oh! Zoya, sorry. I didn't even realize you'd come in."

"You asked me to come in." The horse raises an eyebrow.

"Yes, sorry, I'm ready."

Zoya points down to the letter. "What is this?"

Salessa hesitates. "It's a letter. From Naina. She responded to the one we sent."

"Wow, that was quick. What did she say? Is she coming to Lover's Plateau?"

Salessa shakes her head. "I don't think so."

"Oh," Zoya frowns. "I'm sorry to hear that."

"I mean, she might, in the future. But she seems busy at the moment."

Zoya pauses, then asks, "Is there something else?"

There is, but Salessa isn't sure how to articulate it. "Maybe. Maybe not. Forget it."

"No, talk to me." The horse sits down on the bed next to Salessa. "What's wrong?"

Salessa hands the note to Zoya for her to examine. "I don't mean to sound paranoid, but Naina didn't write this."

"Who do you think wrote it?"

"I'm not sure. This definitely isn't Naina's handwriting, and it isn't her voice. The letter ends with 'I love you,' and 'I miss you, too.' I can count on one hand the number of times Naina has told me she loves me. And I don't need any hands to count how many times she's said she misses me. Well, I guess that one doesn't count because we've never been apart from each other, but the rest of it is definitely strange."

Zoya raises her finger to stroke her chin. "If you're truly suspicious of it, we can always write another letter, and you can put something in it that only Naina will be able to respond to. A joke between the two of you, or a reference to something only you two will understand. And see what comes back from it."

"You don't think I'm being too suspicious?" Salessa asks, surprised.

Zoya laughs, "Of course not. You know your sister better than anyone."

Her validation warms Salessa's chest. The falcon smiles, feeling a sororal love that was missing the moment she stepped out of SunSide and away from Naina.

"We should start heading to the Devotion Ceremony chamber," Salessa suggests. "I don't want to be late. We can think more about this later."

The journey brings Salessa across an entire city of O'Raha. Men, women, children, elders. They all smile at her, stopping to bow, show their respects, wish her a good day, or thank her for the blessings she's brought into their lives.

The atmosphere has evolved since the Flamingo, the Brown Bear, and the other elders recognized her officially as the Falcon Goddess twenty days earlier. Prior to that meeting, the O'Raha had already recognized her as their goddess. But something greater has taken form since the elders stamped their approval on Salessa.

It's as if the O'Raha were following a suspicion before, and now have confirmation that they've been worshipping the right person. Their smiles are wider, their acts of worship more meaningful, their gratitude more heartfelt.

Something has changed for Salessa as well. She isn't sure what it was about that meeting that carried her over the bridge of divinity, but a comfort now exists in accepting the kneeling and prostration, the respect and gratitude. She is proud to be someone they can worship.

And she's appreciative of Lexona's gifts, that help her dress for the part.

They climb an ungodly number of stairs before they reach the top floor of the stone tower where the Devotion Ceremony chamber resides. Outside the towering doors, Zoya turns to Salessa and says, "Have a good time. I'll return soon to escort you back to your room."

"Wait," the falcon responds, taking hold of Zoya's elbow to stop her departure. A nervousness drums in her chest. "You're not coming in with me?"

Zoya shakes her head. "I'm only allowed to enter when I'm asked to prepare the room for a Devotion Ceremony. I have no place in your meeting. And I have other tasks to tend to. I'll be back in an hour to escort you back to your room."

Salessa releases Zoya's elbow and watches her walk down the hallway, feeling suddenly lonely again. She takes a deep breath, pushes the mighty doors open and enters the Devotion Ceremony chamber.

The room is larger than Salessa expected it to be. Directly in front of her, a few yards forward from the entrance of the room is a massive stone platform raised three feet up from the ground with steps to ascend. Around the platform are impressive marble columns with a thick dome on top, connecting them all.

It's an altar.

To the left of the altar is, what appears to be, an area for entertaining guests. A carpet has been rolled out, with tables scattered across the room, and a few pillows around each table for seating. On the back wall, beyond the entertainment area, are some double doors that appear to lead to a kitchen.

To the right of the altar are four marble thrones, identical to the ones that sat facing the elders in the council meeting. They're so similar, in fact, that Salessa wonders if they might be the same ones and have been moved here.

"Welcome to the Devotion Ceremony chamber, Salessa!" Lexona calls out to her from the altar platform, opening her arms wide and presenting the room. "Isn't it grand?" Afzal stands behind her in a mantis green shalwar kameez. The tightness of it around his muscular chest, shoulders, and arms makes Salessa think it may not have been fitted properly.

"It's—" Salessa pauses searching for the word. "Certainly a surprise."

"Come join us on the altar."

Salessa obliges and ascends the stairs to the massive marble structure. Somehow, it feels even wider, and more open, when she stands at the center of it.

"Is this where the honored guests of the Devotion Ceremonies are celebrated?"

Lexona nods. "Oh, yes. They stand right here at the center of the altar while we praise them and shower them with gifts. Then we move to the seating area"—Lexona gestures to the carpeted region beyond the altar—"for dinner, chai, and desserts."

"Sounds like fun," Salessa remarks. "Maybe I can join the next one. To observe."

Lexona nods. "Observe, participate, whatever you'd like."

"Why did you want to meet here? Zoya mentioned there's no Devotion Ceremony today."

"We have work to do," Lexona responds, "You and I have been practicing our energy transfer rituals now for nearly thirty days. Afzal and I have mastered them. These rituals are a big part of the resurrection, and all four of us will need to perform them, together, if we're going to rebirth the Twins."

"And you want to do it"—Salessa gestures to the altar—"here?"

Lexona nods. "This chamber is a spiritual place. What better location for us to attempt a ritual with three of us here for the first time? We can come here again when Naina joins us."

Salessa's gaze moves from Lexona, smiling confidently, to Afzal, who seems withdrawn in this space. There is something indescribable, something awry about the energy in the room, particularly with the way Afzal is reacting to it.

"Is everything alright, Afzal?" Salessa asks. The leopard raises his gaze, alarmed. His eyes dart from Salessa to Lexona, and then back to Salessa again. A smile stretches across his muzzle, though with the steady anxiety flowing in his eyes, Salessa can tell it's forced.

"Never better," the leopard lies.

She doesn't want to put a spotlight on him, so she nods. "Alright, then. Let's perform the ritual together. All three of us."

Lexona sits on the floor, cross-legged, in a sari, as easily as Salessa imagined she would. She makes something that can be challenging look so simple. The saris, the elegance, the dexterity, it all comes so naturally to her.

Salessa attempts it, but quite quickly, she realizes it'll be easier for her to sit in a different position, with her knees bent and legs tucked under her. Afzal sits, also cross-legged, facing them. The three Doruh form a circle, Afzal to Salessa's right, Lexona to his.

Salessa reaches out, palms up, waiting for Lexona and Afzal to place their hands in hers as the serpent taught her. There's a pause in which she notices Afzal's gaze travel to Lexona hesitantly.

"I want to try something a little different today," Lexona explains. She's smiling, but Afzal's perturbed energy is distractingly unnerving.

"Alright," Salessa responds, tentatively. "What did you have in mind?"

Lexona nods to Afzal, who reaches into a sheath in his waistband that Salessa hadn't realized was there, and withdraws a small dagger. Salessa's blood runs cold and the color drains from her face. The serpent reaches forth and takes her hand to soothe her.

"Relax, Salessa," she says with a laugh.

The falcon exhales, her eyes locked on the short blade.

Afzal hands the dagger to Lexona, who pokes her fingertip with the point, releasing a few droplets of blood onto her finger.

"Do you remember the conversation we had," the serpent asks, "the afternoon before the council meeting in the library? About the importance of blood?"

Salessa nods, recalling the conversation, trying to keep her ears on Lexona's words and her eyes off the bleeding finger.

"It's important for you to trust me, Salessa," Lexona continues. "You do trust me, right?"

Salessa isn't sure how to answer. She turns to Afzal, whose gaze is lowered again, and then back to Lexona. "Of course."

"Excellent. Because I meant every word I said that day. We carry the blood of the Twins in our veins, and I think it'll be a monumental factor in the resurrection. With that being said"—she turns the dagger around and puts the hilt into Salessa's open palm, who wraps her fingers around it—"I think an exchange of that blood will bind us all together in ways we previously have been lacking. I think it'll propel us much farther into the resurrection than we currently are."

Her fingers tightly wrapped around the dagger, Salessa's heart pounds against her chest. Naina's voice has been absent for so many weeks, but Salessa knows exactly what the wolf would be telling her.

Put the fucking dagger down and run, Lessi.

But Naina isn't here. Salessa has to make her own decisions. She offered Naina the opportunity to join her and Naina refused. She wants to stay in SunSide and doesn't want to participate in these rituals.

If Naina even wrote the letter at all.

Lexona is here, and Afzal is here. They've been here with her for nearly forty days now. Living and breathing these rituals, exercising with her, spending time with her, sharing their poetry and vulnerabilities with her, defending, empowering, and uplifting her.

Celebrating her.

Salessa takes a deep breath, ignores the words she knows the wolf would say, and makes a decision for herself. The falcon places the tip of the dagger to her fingertip and pokes it open. She then hands the dagger to Afzal, who does the same, poking one of the leathery pads under his paw, and placing the dagger back into the sheath.

Afzal and Lexona perform the exchange first. She holds her fingertip out toward him and his massive tongue breaks out from his black leopard lips and licks it. Then, Lexona leans forward and puts her lips over the small cut in his thick paw pad. It only lasts a few seconds before she pulls back and her serpentine tongue flicks out of her mouth rapidly, colored red with blood.

The leopard turns to Salessa and her heart sinks. Hesitantly, she mimics what she saw the siblings doing and puts her fingertip near Afzal's feline muzzle. His tongue reaches out for her finger and if the situation weren't so disconcerting already, she would've commented on how rough his barbed feline tongue is. He then holds his own furry paw toward her. She finds the cut on his pad and places her mouth over it, sucking some of the metallic blood out and trying not to gag.

Finally, Lexona turns to her. The serpent lifts her finger into the air, in front of Salessa's mouth, and the falcon thanks the Twins that none of the scaly serpentine skin on Lexona's body is on her fingers. Salessa opens her mouth and Lexona places her finger into it. Their eyes lock on each other and, in a moment Salessa cannot explain, a warmth rises in her core as she sucks the blood from Lexona's finger.

There's an enigmatic intimacy exchange between them with the blood and it's like nothing Salessa has ever felt before.

After Lexona pulls her finger back, Salessa raises hers and Lexona takes it into her mouth. At first, Salessa holds back giggles from the ticklish nature of the serpentine tongue in Lexona's mouth. But the humor of the situation quickly dies as Lexona holds Salessa's finger in her mouth far longer than she needs to.

Salessa pulls her finger back. "I think I'm ready to move on to the ritual."

Lexona nods, still smiling. "Of course. From here on out, it'll be exactly as we practiced."

Once again, Salessa places her hands out, palms up. This time, both Afzal and Lexona place their paw and hand in hers and they all close their eyes. As they've practiced many times before, Salessa allows the serpent's energy to slither into her, and passes her own falcon energy into Lexona. It's a warmth that fills the veins of her arms and travels throughout her body, giving her a sense of calm and completion. As if she is a portion of a person who is now whole.

She does the same with her other hand, sending out her energy to Afzal, and receiving the leopard's energy in return. The calm grows, and the completion intensifies. Soon, she feels as if she's simply floating through the air, a being made purely of energy.

She hovers and floats and flies around in this energy form, until something changes. The blue, clear skies transform into dark reds and oranges, like gaping wounds in the sky. She can smell burning flesh and pungent brimstone. She can hear the harrowing final breaths of those surrendering to death's embrace.

Salessa lands. She's on a battlefield. Heat wraps her, nearly burning her flesh off. They're surrounded by mountains with hundreds of thousands, maybe millions of bodies. Soldiers strewn about the area of battle. On the opposing side, Salessa sees two silhouettes.

The Sprites, she thinks.

She turns around to the nearer side of the battlefield, expecting to see the Twins, but she sees so much more. There are additional warriors beside them. The Twins' silhouettes aren't alone in the final battle against the Sprites. Salessa counts their companions and finds four more. The Sprites battle against six warriors.

As if she is a puppet being pulled back with a string, Salessa's energy is dragged off of the battlefield and harshly tossed back into her body. She nearly falls backward as her eyes dart open and she takes in a long breath. She's disoriented for a moment, breathing deeply to catch her lost breath, until she realizes she's still in the altar.

"Did…you…see it?" Lexona asks them through similar labored breaths.

Afzal nods. "How many did you count?"

"Six," Lexona says. She turns to Salessa.

When her heart stops drumming, she responds. "I saw six as well. Who are they?"

Lexona shakes her head. "I have no idea. I've read almost every text in that library. I know every vision of the battle the Twins have ever had. They never mentioned four additional warriors facing the Sprites alongside them."

"What if it was the wrong side of the battle?" Afzal asks.

Lexona and Salessa exchange glances.

Afzal continues. "What if the Twins have to face six enemies, and the Sprites have four allies?"

Lexona shakes her head. "Why would we have landed on the side of the battlefield with the six on it then? I don't think the Sprites need, or want, any allies, from what I know of them. There must be four others on our side."

"Who are they?" Salessa asks.

"I'm not sure. Maybe we'll have to do more of these to find out."

Salessa is already exhausted from one, but she knows Lexona is right. In the coming days, there must be more of these rituals in order to have more visions.

"I've never had a vision so"—she pauses, searching for the right word to describe what she felt—"visceral before."

Lexona nods. "Neither have I." She smiles, holding up the small cut on her finger. "I think my theory about the blood was right. We've opened ourselves to new possibilities."

Salessa acknowledges the wisdom and cleverness of Lexona's theory. Naina can feel however she may about the serpent, but her aptitude for creative, cunning, and ingenious solutions is unmatched.

"That's the goal, then," Afzal says. "Find out who the six are. The Twins and four allies."

Lexona nods. "Find the six."

CHAPTER 43

"WOMAN OF STONE, WALL OF ICE"

Court Democracy *EverEmber*
Date *10th Day of Month 7, Year 1629 DG*

KYOKO DESCENDS GINGERLY, NEARLY ON tiptoe. Light from the morning suns pours in through the staircase window and strikes her stone exoskeleton, casting speckled diamonds and spectacular rainbows, illuminating the staircase walls. On the bottom step, she peers around to the family room, finding Kanako alone, knitting.

"You don't have to walk so quietly," Kyoko's older sister advises her. "Natsumi isn't here."

Kyoko releases a breath of relief. For the twenty days they've been staying with Kanako and Natsumi, her steps, her cooking, even her speaking has occasionally woken the three-year-old up from her naps. *This is the lightest-sleeping baby on the planet,* she thought a few days in.

"Where is she?" Kyoko asks, joining Ana at the far end of the room on a long table with the Sprite texts laid out.

"With Rafael," Kanako responds. "She was getting restless, so he volunteered to take her out."

The child hasn't let Rafael out of her sight since they arrived. Kanako theorized she may remember him from the year before, when he and Kyoko were in EverEmber on the Prime's mission to find the TreeKeeper. In return, Rafael's care has been diligent; he's put Natsumi down for naps, fed her, taken her to playgrounds and other outdoor activities.

"At least he's busy with something other than getting tossed out on his ass," Ana mumbles.

Kyoko gently places a hand on the mari's shoulder, inundating her tone with a confidence that doesn't truly exist, hoping to provide Ana with some reassurance. "We'll get in. The Court can't keep us out forever."

Ana pulls her face out of the Sprite text she's translating to meet Kyoko's gaze. "Of course they can. You and Rafael are no longer Librarian diplomats. I'm mari. Why would they meet with us?"

"We have the letter. Saila refused involvement with SeaBed, but we have an official statement from SunSide's leadership this time. We will be heard here." She gestures to the Sprite texts, hoping a change of subject will help. "Any success with translating?"

Ana shakes her head. "I'm starting to lose hope again. If only I could find the Sprites' location. Or what they want. Or *anything* valuable."

A distant memory jogs into Kyoko's mind. Something in Ana's lamentation brings it forth. "The Witch of the Meeting Place in the Desert."

Ana raises an eyebrow.

Kyoko rises to her feet and walks around the table to Ana's side. She flips through the text until she finds the page with the information. "Before we entered SeaBed, I had attempted some translating to help you, but I forgot to tell you what I found."

She places her finger at the title of the chapter. "I think it says, 'The Great,' uh, 'Look Back'?"

"'The Great Betrayal,'" Ana corrects her. "In Nysabaani, when those two characters are together, it literally means 'to look behind,' but figuratively it means 'to be betrayed.' So you found a chapter on someone who was betrayed?"

"Not just anyone. Someone betrayed the Sprites."

Ana leans in, intrigued. "Who?"

"The Witch of the Meeting Place in the Desert." Kyoko stands proudly by her translation until Ana rolls her eyes and turns back to the page.

"Can you show me where you found that?"

Kyoko searches the page until she finds the characters that represent 'Witch,' 'Meeting Place,' and 'Desert.' Ana's eyes widen until she drops the book and says, "The Oasis Mage."

"The who?" Kyoko asks, raising an eyebrow.

"These two together don't mean 'Meeting Place in the Desert,' they mean 'Oasis.' And you were right about this third word translating to 'Witch' in most contexts. But this chapter talks heavily about this individual's power, which makes me think it means 'Mage' here."

She turns up to meet Kyoko's gaze. "An elite witch, wizard, warlock, or other magical person was exalted by the Sprites with the title of 'Mage.' That was a major aspect of their culture. I'll read on to confirm, but from the looks of it, you've found someone called the Oasis Mage, and I think she's important."

"Who's important?" Rafael asks, entering the home with Natsumi sleeping in his arms. He passes the toddler off to her mother, as the girl inevitably and irritably wakes, then joins Kyoko and Ana at the table.

"The Oasis Mage," Ana repeats. "I'm not sure who she is, but this chapter seems to imply that she's already defeated the Sprites once before."

"A strong lead," Rafael says, sitting up in his seat.

"Kyoko found it," Ana replies, gesturing up to the igni.

Rafael's gaze meets Kyoko's. "Great job."

The compliment may as well come from a stranger. Someone Kyoko doesn't recognize. Certainly not from someone she had grown to care deeply about over the past year.

Weeks earlier, Ana and Kyoko howled with joy as they reunited with Rafael outside the Hall of Generals. He was a free man. Kyoko wept as she held him, knowing he was safe. But as soon as they were out of SeaBed, away from the danger, a wall of ice rose between them.

No matter how much she goes over the events leading up to SeaBed in her mind, Kyoko struggles to pinpoint Rafael's offending actions. But she does know that the answer lies in a nightmare she's had every night for the past twenty nights.

She and Rafael stand at the edge of a cliff, ready to jump, to escape a monstrous beast chasing them. Rafael assures her that he has a plan to save them. Trusting him, she leaps. As they descend from the cliff, the mari snaps his fingers and, magically, a parachute appears to save Kyoko.

To save only Kyoko.

Rafael knew there was no parachute for him. When he promised safety for both of them, he knew it wasn't true. He played with his life when he knew how much that life meant to her. How much she cherished that life. How much it would hurt her to lose him.

He didn't trust her enough to be honest about *why* he was willing to jump despite not having a parachute. Because leaping from the cliff distracted the oncoming monster from his mother. Despite the consequences, his actions could've saved her life. And he was willing to leap if it meant he could protect her.

This is something he thought Kyoko couldn't understand? After she stood by his side the year prior when he convened with his sister's spirit? After *he* stood by *her* when she reunited with Kanako. He thought she couldn't understand how much family meant to him?

Did he ever know her at all?

She won't give him the opportunity to be dishonest again. When he speaks, she turns away. When he addresses her directly, asks her a question, the responses are seldom more than a single word. He no longer gets to speak to the woman of stone. Now all he gets is a wall of ice.

What breaks Kyoko's heart most is that, though Rafael escaped execution in SeaBed, though he miraculously survived, something between them died that day.

"How was your walk with Natsumi?" Ana asks him, after Kyoko ignores his compliment.

"Significant," Rafael responds. "I spoke to a tavernkeep who says one of the Courtmen comes in for a drink, and a little more, a few nights a week."

"A little more?" Ana asks.

Rafael clears his throat. "He doesn't want to get caught at a local brothel, so he pays for the brothel to come to him."

Ana's cheeks bloom like roses. "Got it."

Kyoko deciphers Rafael's plan, but keeps her gaze on Ana when she speaks. "We should meet with him in the tavern." Her companions agree and a plan is set. A good plan. At the very least, the best one they've had in twenty days.

They arrive at the tavern shortly after dinner, dressed in casual evening wear. The smell of ale enriches the air, musical offerings coat their eardrums, and the taste of tomorrow morning's regret lingers on the tips of seventy tongues.

As they enter, Ana asks Rafael if he has the letter from Saila.

"Right here," he replies, tapping his pocket.

They find an empty table near the stage where a short bard with long sideburns, clad in a loose, purple linen shirt, animatedly regales the locals with music and tales of his travels. Behind them, a gargantuan, bald, burly igni man and a thin raven-haired Mega woman with tattoos compete in a drinking competition as their friends cheer them on.

A waitress brings some wine, cheese, and bread. It goes untouched initially, but as the night wears on, Kyoko loses herself in the music and ale, while Rafael fills his belly with cheese and bread. Eventually, the burly igni man comes over to their table and Ana shares some wine with him. They seem to get along quite well, and he asks her to join him at a local inn not far from where Kanako lives, but she declines the offer and he steps away disappointed.

"We'll come back tomorrow when we're not on a mission," Kyoko says. "You've had your head buried in those texts for a year. You deserve a little fun."

"Spending the night with him is not what I consider fun," Ana remarks. "The mission is not why I declined his offer."

Kyoko nods, understanding. She points to the raven-haired Mega who defeated the man in the drinking competition. "What about her then?"

"Not her either."

Confusion blankets the igni. "Not him. Not her. Who then?"

"No one," Ana responds quickly and coyly, taking another sip of her wine.

The ale must be getting to me, Kyoko thinks, having difficulty deciphering what Ana means. "So you...you've never—"

"No, I've never," Ana responds with a laugh.

"Because you haven't found the right person?" Kyoko probes. "Or you're celibate?"

Ana shakes her head. "Celibacy is behavior. I'm talking about attraction. I'm not drawn toward other individuals the way you are."

The ale loosens the igni's tongue far more than it ever is sober. "What about love and romance?"

"Neither of those things have to do with my desire not to share my bed. I experience love and romance, both, just fine, without having to engage in acts that repulse me."

"*Repulse* you?" Kyoko's eyes widen. "Have you met anyone else who's felt this way? I've never heard that before."

"I have. Not all are repulsed. Others don't desire romance, whereas I do. You can't assume you know what every cat looks like because you saw one with an all-black coat. Some are white, some are orange, some are gray, and some have spots."

Kyoko's next follow-up question drops from her mind when Rafael taps her on the shoulder to get her attention. Driven by the liquid slaughtering her inhibition, she meets his gaze and heartache bubbles up into her vocal cords. "Don't touch me!"

Rafael's eyes widen and he jerks his head back as if she's physically tried to bite it off.

Ana's jaw drops open.

Patrons nearby search for the source of the violent bark.

Kyoko's own hand nearly rises to her lips, but she maintains enough composure to keep her fingers tightly on the mug of ale. Something in Rafael's expression surprises her. Obviously, he's deeply hurt. But having spent as much time with him as she has over the past year, she recognizes something else, as well.

Relief.

For twenty days, he's been conversing with a wall of ice. Now, Kyoko has shown him fire. A small portion of the ice melts away to reveal a glimmer of passion. Of provocation. Of emotion.

Fire burns. But it also inherently provides warmth.

"I just wanted to..." Rafael begins meekly, his voice nearly trembling, before he trails off and gestures behind her, guiding her gaze to the entrance of the tavern. Kyoko turns to where he's pointing and the sight provokes enough anger in her to immediately sober her up.

She identifies a well-dressed man entering the tavern as Courtman Takeru. He's a senior member of the Court. Well respected around Ever-Ember's religious upper crust for launching a campaign against brothels.

Fucking hypocrite.

Two igni warriors flank him as he strides to a door in a poorly-lit corner of the back wall. Once Takeru closes it behind him, the warriors stand directly outside at attention, hands on hilts.

"Ready?" Rafael asks the two women.

"Change of plans," Kyoko says, recognizing one of the guards standing outside the door. "Ana and I have as much of a chance of distracting that guard as we do beating the raven-haired Mega in a drinking contest." She holds her hand out to Rafael, her gaze still on the door in the back wall. "Give me Saila's letter. I'll speak to Takeru. *You* have to distract the guard."

Throwing on their most flirtatious smiles, the two mari sit at a table near the guards and lightly begin conversations. It takes longer than expected, but after about an hour, the two warriors are so enraptured by the conversations with the mari, their eyes have left the door completely. Two brothel workers have come and left together in the time that Rafael and Ana have been distracting the guards.

Slipping along the back wall, Kyoko breathes coolly and enters the room. There is no more revealing and vulnerable situation in which she could've found the Courtman, than the one she walks into.

He smiles when he sees her, lying with his hands behind his head on a heart-shaped bed, nothing covering him but sweat and hypocrisy. A low grunt exits his throat. "Ah, I wasn't expecting a third, but I think I have a little juice left to squeeze from the lemons." The bald, wrinkly man with yellow, crooked teeth steps off the bed toward her, but she covers her eyes with one hand and holds out the letter in the other.

"Put your clothes on and read this."

The man's expression falls. "What is it?" He sniffs the air and scowls. "Ugh, you reek of cheap ale."

"You do *not* want me to comment on what *you* smell like right now, Courtman."

He narrows his eyes and rips the letter from her hands, opening it violently. Steam rises from his ears. "It's you. You and your friends have been incessantly trying to meet with the Court every day for weeks. How did you get in here? Guards!"

"They won't hear you," Kyoko tells him.

"Get out!"

"Courtman, this is important. All of EverEmber is in danger."

"If we wanted to hear your doomsday fantasies, we would've listened at the Court. Now, step aside." He charges forth, heading straight for the door.

She thinks quickly. "If you don't arrange a meeting with us at the Court tomorrow, I will tell people in the upper districts about what you were doing. They may not care down here, but they definitely will up there. You'll lose your seat on the Court, your image, everything."

The nude igni man takes a step back, his jaw hitting the floor. "You wouldn't."

"Try me."

The Courtman growls. "You don't understand. The Ore Monger tried to commit genocide against our people to make the ore. He—"

"Is rotting in a cell. Chief Member Saila is not the Ore Monger."

"The Court will not see it that way. They will only see gray eyes. Pointed ears."

"One meeting and I'll forget I was ever here."

The Courtman sighs, folds the paper back up, and hands it to Kyoko. With shoulders slumped, he says, "First thing in the morning. Don't be late."

CHAPTER 44

"THE MOTHER'S COURT"

Court Democracy *EverEmber*
Date *11th Day of Month 7, Year 1629 DG*

EVERYTHING IN EVEREMBER LEADS BACK to Mount Mother. Historically, spiritually, socially, politically. The volcano is, in every way, the center of the city. Kyoko already had a strong understanding of its influence on her people and homeland. But it becomes far more apparent as she, Rafael, and Ana walk up to the Mother's Court.

The gates, fences, and guard towers are built of dark, volcanic stone, towering intimidatingly over visitors and passersby. The armor and weapons of the igni soldiers guarding the court are designed from the same. The walkways and fountains and decor are all constructed of it.

And the sixty-foot Court, boasting four-hundred rooms, including the chambers and living spaces of the seven Courtmen and Courtwomen, and their staff and families, is made of volcanic stone. The edifice is architecturally designed to hide the base of the building within stout volcanic boulders, giving it the look of erupting from the ground, as Mount Mother herself does.

Weeks of denied entry have left the three travelers frustrated, but today, Kyoko marches up to the gates and guards with renewed confidence. Courtman Takeru will allow them entry, he has to. For his benefit more than theirs. When they arrive, the guards' gazes travel from Kyoko's toes to her hairline, scowls forming on their expressions. Today, refusing her would be disobeying a direct order.

As a guard escorts them through the complex to the Court, Ana leans toward Kyoko's ear and whispers, "Why do I get the feeling that all politicians are the same? They only want to hear from you when addressing concerns helps them hold power?"

After a long trek through the complex, and an even longer one through the maze of a building, the guard leads them through double-doors into a wide open chamber not unlike the Hall of Generals in SeaBed. As Rafael, Kyoko, and Ana stand silently before the seven members of EverEmber's Court, the leaders of the city gaze down upon them, not a smile in sight.

Ana is right, Kyoko thinks, *EverEmber or SeaBed, the Library or SunSide, it all feels the same when you stand before politicians.*

Finally, an elderly Courtwoman sitting in the center of the seven speaks. "We have refused you entry for weeks now, and for good reason. Your fanciful claims are a waste of the Court's time." She turns to the familiar politician to her right. "Nevertheless, Courtman Takeru has insisted that we entertain the letter you've brought us from SunSide. We shall read it and render a final verdict. If we decide not to move forward with your plea, you will be banned from the complex's grounds, and any violation of that ban will result in your arrest. Do I make myself clear?"

Kyoko, standing between Rafael and Ana, nods. The two mari do the same. It was her idea to center herself, the igni, before the Court, hoping that interacting with her will make the information more palatable for them.

"Very well then," the Courtwoman continues. "Bring the letter from SunSide forth." Kyoko steps forward and rises onto the tips of her toes to hand the letter to the Courtwoman, then marches back to the spot where she was standing.

Awkward silence consumes the room as each of the seven members of the Court pass the letter back and forth to read, while the three travelers wait patiently for a response. Finally, the elderly Courtwoman folds it again and hands it to a guard who delivers it to Kyoko.

"I'll allow my colleagues to speak for themselves," she proclaims, "but I'm not convinced, even after reading the letter, that this isn't some ploy for SunSide to get their military onto our shores. It will leave us supremely vulnerable to an attack."

Kyoko's heart sinks as the other members of the Court nod. She clears her throat. "The SunSidian official who wrote that letter, who pleads for you to host her military, is the one who put shackles on the Ore Monger, and is working to return the ore. So that the igni who died to make it can be put to rest with digni—"

"So she can prevent a war," the Courtwoman interrupts. "Make no mistake, the pixie isn't blessed with some powerful sense of altruism. She knows that if we don't get that ore, if we can't mourn our dead, EverEmber will sail to SunSide. Armed and ready."

Kyoko swallows, her throat going dry. "Courtwoman, I've spoken with the Chief Member myself, at length. She feels heavy remorse for what the Ore Monger and SunSide did to the igni on Lily Beach. She has no ulterior motives to send her soldiers here. This is about so much more than politics. The citizens' lives are in danger. The city itself is in danger. Mount Mother is in danger."

"Mount Mother has stood, exactly as she is, for thousands of years. The Sprites came into existence, and the Sprites went extinct, all within Mount Mother's lifespan. If what Chief Member Saila has written in this letter is even true, let the Sprites and their beasts come. Mount Mother will protect us all."

"Not if you aren't prepared," Kyoko counters. "Your military must be mobilized for this effort. One of the Three Deaths will come into our plane, our realm, our reality through EverEmber. And if it's not stopped as soon as it springs to life, this city, including Mount Mother, will be razed. I beg of you, heed Saila's warnings."

The elderly Courtwoman opens her mouth to respond, but she's cut off by another, younger Courtwoman at the far end of the bench.

"I know you," she says. "You were a Librarian, weren't you?"

Kyoko nods. "I was, for over a decade."

"Yes, I remember some of your visits here, accompanying Ambassador Alba."

Courtman Takeru raises a finger to stroke his chin. "Curious. How does a former Librarian come to find herself as a diplomat for SunSide?"

Kyoko shakes her head. "We are not diplomats or any kind of formal officials in SunSide. Rafael and I are both former Librarians. Ana is a trained Nysabaani translator and Alba's sister."

The younger Courtwoman frowns, turning and speaking directly to Ana. "I'm so sorry for your loss. We all held Ambassador Alba in high esteem."

Ana nods with gratitude.

"If you're not diplomats," Courtman Takeru continues, "why are you here?"

A soft smile washes over Kyoko's face. She answers with all the sincerity in her heart. "We are three civilian messengers, trying to save as many people as we can before the inevitable catastrophe comes. Our expert translator has been poring over ancient Sprite texts for a year now. You don't have to believe myself or Rafael when we explain what we've heard from the TreeKeeper. You don't have to accept the pleas of SunSide's highest ranking politician."

She points to Ana. "But listen to what *she* has to say. As a Nysabaani expert, as Alba's sister, as the one with the most knowledge about the situation in this room, don't ignore the warning. You'll regret it."

The fourteen eyes of the Court turn to Ana at once and the mari's skin goes pale. This wasn't planned or prepared. Kyoko had volunteered to be their voice, but she understood, as soon as Alba was mentioned, that neither she nor Rafael would have as much credibility with the Court as Ana would.

She gestures with her eyes for Ana to speak up. The mari inhales a deep breath, then slowly exhales it out, bringing the color back into her face and clearly steeling her nerves. The former Librarians have experience with public speaking; it's part of their training.

Ana does not.

"Everything in Chief Member Saila's letter is corroborated by information gathered from the ancient texts of the Sprites. Across many different tomes and guidebooks, I've found numerous mentions of the Three Deaths, including information about their arrival in our world that wasn't given to Kyoko and Rafael during their journey. The use of the three human cities as their entry point into our plane, from their demonic home, was drawn strictly from contextual evidence within a Sprite text."

Her gaze travels from one Courtman and Courtwoman to the next. "I know that my being mari is not a benefit to me in this situation. I've walked into EverEmber for the first time in my life, and am now addressing the very Court that once declared war with SeaBed."

She reaches into her bag, pulls out an ancient text, and holds it up for them to see. "But my only allegiance is to knowledge. The more I learn, the more I hold love for all living beings. I may be mari, but I don't want to see anyone harmed by these monsters."

She puts the text back into her bag. "And let me be absolutely clear. They are coming. Whether you believe us or not, sometime in the next three months, a demonic beast will be at your doorstep. How much damage it does, how many lives it takes, how much of your Mother it destroys"—she holds her hands up to gesture to the members of the Court—"that is entirely, directly, and strictly up to you."

I should've given her the podium to start with, Kyoko thinks, pride bursting in her chest.

The seven members lean in close together and whisper to one another for, what likely is, a few minutes, but feels to Kyoko like a few lifetimes. They separate again and the elderly Courtwoman speaks directly to the group of three travelers.

"I don't know what makes it so difficult for us, humans, to admit mistakes. I suppose the ego is a mightier beast than the one you're predicting will grace our shores."

Get on with it.

"We were wrong. There must be some veracity to your claims, if they have brought SunSidian officials, former Librarians, mari, and igni together. And if this wise young woman"—she gestures to Ana—"shares her sister's integrity, we can put our faith behind her."

Kyoko's jaw drops. She had thought it would be an affront to the Court to have mari addressing them instead of an igni. Never in a millennium would she have guessed that the power of Alba's integrity, a year after her death, would outweigh any prejudices, any enmity leftover from the war between EverEmber and SeaBed.

"Chief Member Saila writes in her letter," Courtman Takeru mentions, "that she is willing to pledge a third of the New SunSidian Guard, as well as General Ovida, to join the efforts of training and preparation here. As our militaries are of a similar size, we find it appropriate to pledge the same: one-third of EverEmber's warriors will be mobilized for the protection of the city from this threat."

Kyoko keeps her lips tightly pressed together, despite her tongue's pleas to inform them that one-third is not nearly enough. A third of the New SunSidian Guard was meant to join the *entire* igni military.

"However," the Courtman continues, alerting Kyoko, "we do have a specific condition, on which this alliance hinges."

Of course they do.

"No generals or military leadership from EverEmber will be reassigned to this mission. And General Ovida of SunSide will not lead our igni warriors."

Kyoko wonders if the effects of the ale from the tavern haven't yet worn off. "Apologies, Courtman, I don't quite understand. If you're not willing to offer up a general to lead your warriors into battle, and don't want SunSide's to do so, who will be leading the igni?"

A knowing smile stretches across half the Courtman's face. "You will."

Kyoko is stunned into silence again. "I-I'm sorry, I don't understand. I'm neither a general, nor am I part of the EverEmber military."

"You're not a general, but you *were* a Librarian. I'll assume you're trained in combat, weapons skills, and military strategy?"

Tentatively, Kyoko nods.

"Ambassador Alba was known throughout the continent for her abilities, and she mentored you. You're also igni, one of us, which General Ovida is not."

Kyoko's heart sinks, and her gaze drops to her injured arm. "You don't understand, I'm not—"

"She accepts," comes Rafael's voice. Kyoko turns quickly to him, surprised by the interjection. He keeps his eyes on the Courtman and continues. "You've made the right decision by selecting Kyoko. There is no one more capable."

What are you doing? Kyoko transmits to him with her mind. *I...I can't do this.*

As if he hears her thoughts, as if the wall between them has melted away and the Rafael she once knew stands before her, he meets her gaze and replies, *Of course you can.*

Kyoko turns back to the Court members. "Is there no other way?"

Courtman Takeru shakes his head. "If our warriors are going to be forced to prepare for a threat like this, we need someone leading them who truly *believes* in this mission. We need someone leading them who they relate to, and is igni, and knows combat strategy. We need someone who is well-acquainted with General Ovida, who can receive her and the SunSidian warriors upon their arrival and manage duties with her. Frankly, I don't think there's anyone on the All-Sphere who meets those qualifications quite like you do."

It all sounds like compliments, but Kyoko can't help but wonder if he's punishing her for the way she entered his special lounge in the tavern the night before.

With an anxious drum in her heart, and an uncertain air around her, Kyoko nods. "I accept your condition."

CHAPTER 45

"WOMAN OF STONE, WARRIOR OF FIRE"

***Court Democracy** EverEmber*
***Date** 11th Day of Month 7, Year 1629 DG*

"ANGI? MEGA? ANYONE WHO CAN fly?" Kyoko questions, nearly begging.

The igni Messenger Captain raises his palms defensively, backing away from Kanako's doorstep. "I'm sorry. Truly, I am. But every flyer I have on staff is out on assignment. It'll have to be by ship or not at all."

Kyoko grunts in frustration, reaches into her pocket, and pulls out a pouch filled with stones. She grabs the messenger's wrist and pulls his hand down, dropping the pouch onto his palm.

"This is far more—"

"Sail through the night," Kyoko instructs. "This is the most urgent message you'll carry in your entire life. It needs to be in Chief Member Saila's hands, and no one else's, as soon as possible."

The Captain bounces the pouch in his hand, smiling broadly, then pockets it and meets Kyoko's gaze. "Yes, ma'am. I'll deliver it myself."

"You better." Kyoko shuts the door and heads back to the dining room, where Rafael and Ana are almost done clearing the dinner table.

"How'd it go?" Ana asks.

"No flyers," Kyoko says with a disappointed shrug. "I paid for them to sail it through the night. She should have it by tomorrow evening, which means Ovida and the SunSidian warriors should arrive within a week."

"You must be excited for your leadership duties, General," Ana says.

Kyoko swallows, her fingers rising to her injured shoulder. *I'm not.*

"No one can lead this mission better than you can," Rafael encourages her. The momentary lapse of the ice wall in the tavern, and then again in the Court, is over. Rafael the Stranger has returned, as have Kyoko's chilled responses.

"I'm going for a walk," she says, turning to exit. She needs distance to clear her mind. From Rafael. From Ana and her reminders of the impending task. But when she reaches the front door, footsteps approach from behind.

"Kyoko," comes Rafael's voice. "Can I join you?"

She turns sharply to meet his gaze. "No."

"Please, Kyoko. I know I'm the last person you want to walk with but..."

He's right, he is the last person she wants to walk with.

"I need to be alone," Kyoko insists.

Rafael sighs. "Alright. I'm sorry, I just...they were nights like these, and..."

Nights like these. She repeats the words, juggling them in her mind. Kyoko knows what he means but she wants to hear him elaborate. He's talking about the nights that meant so much to both of them.

"What do you mean? *What* were nights like these?"

More relief floods his expression, the way it did in the tavern. A small glimmer of fire through the ice. "Warm nights with a cool breeze, right after dinner, with the starlight bathing your exoskeleton, that I felt most comfortable just...just being myself in front of you."

Kyoko swallows to break open her tightening throat. These were the nights of emotional connection that built her affection for a man who now feels long gone, despite standing right in front of her. Nights she yearns to experience again.

Battling the urge to turn him away, seeking a droplet of what they once had, Kyoko nods and says, "Join me."

He's quiet as they walk. If he wasn't going to say anything, why did he even come?

They reach a sandy shoreline with glittering waves lapping up the beach. Rafael removes his shoes and rolls up the sleeves of his pants to his knees, then gestures for Kyoko to do the same. She obliges and the two sit, side-by-side, water rushing up to their ankles, starlight dancing along the surface of the water.

"Can I ask you something, Kyoko?" Rafael says after some time.

Tentatively, she nods, burying her toes in the cold sand.

"What can I do to atone? Other than apologizing, which I've already done. What more can I say to bring us back to where we were?"

Her throat tightens again, as the answer to his question becomes clear in her mind. "Can you bring someone back from the dead, Rafa?"

The mari hangs his head. He knows what she means, and he knows the answer is "No."

Kyoko continues. "Do you remember our journey last year? We went through something in a few short days that I think most people don't experience together in their entire lifetimes. And then it was over, and I thought we'd end up as friendlier acquaintances than we were before that day Unisa dragged you into the Prime's office."

"I remember." His voice is strained.

She exhales deeply, as she thinks about all that happened after the journey. "But for the next year, we were together each morning. Together each night. You were the first person I saw when I woke up. The first person I *wanted* to see. We had all of those talks after dinner."

She turns to him, memories bringing a warmth to her skin. "Nights like these. Where I saw a different side of you, and I was able to share a different side of myself with you. I cherished those nights, Rafa."

"So did I," he says. "Kyoko, none of that has to change."

Kyoko's voice hitches in her tightening throat. "Everything's changed."

"How, Kyoko?" He leans in, his face contorting with confusion.

"Because the Rafael I spoke to on all of those nights would never do what you did. *That* Rafael trusted me with his thoughts, his dreams, his entire heart. But the one who looked into my eyes and made promises of safety he knew he couldn't keep, that Rafael murdered the one I knew. The one I waited all day, each day, to spend the night talking with…he's dead."

"Kyoko, I—"

"Why didn't you tell me about the letter from your mother? About why you truly wanted to go to SeaBed?"

He hesitates. "It was a mistake to think you wouldn't understand. I know that. If I've learned anything over the past year, it's that I can be myself around you, bare my heart and mind in a way I can't with anyone else. This is all so new to me, and it's in that unfamiliarity that my mistake was made. I never should have hidden things from you. I should have trusted you."

She nods. "Yes, you should have. All I wanted was your safety."

"I'm here. I'm alive, I'm safe."

Kyoko's vision blurs with tears, as her chest fills with the powdered debris that was once a whole heart. "Then why am I grieving?"

Even in the limited starlight, Kyoko can see how astonished he is.

"I never meant to hurt you."

Kyoko takes a deep breath and wipes her cheek dry. "The Rafael I knew would have known his death would've hurt me. He would never have put his life on the line knowing what his death would do to me."

Rafael hesitates, then asks, "What would it do to you?"

Kyoko turns her head away from him to gaze out at the water. "You don't get to ask me that anymore, Rafa."

Rafael sighs. "Kyoko, I don't know what else to say or do. I'm trying to show you that, despite my mistakes, I'm still the same person."

"Is that why you've been so supportive of me?" She meets his gaze again. "Telling the Court they made the right choice. Trying to encourage me. Is it all part of a scheme to prove something to me?"

He pauses before he responds, his expression contorting with genuine agony. "Of course not, Kyoko. I believe in you. I wish I were half the warrior you are."

Kyoko scoffs and gestures to her injured arm, her suffering mounting. "*I'm* not even half the warrior I used to be. Thanks to fucking Vy-Ro."

Rafael shakes his head and leans in, his tone hardening. "You really don't see it, do you?"

"See what?"

"He may have taken your mobility, but he could never take your heart. Your shoulder didn't make you a warrior, your fiery spirit did." He leans back again. "You can believe what you want to believe about my intentions, but I'm not saying these things to get you to forgive me. You can hate me for the rest of your life, if you want. But please, promise me you'll never forget who you are."

Kyoko's eyes fill to the brim again, and she sobs softly after seeing a glimmer of the Rafael she can't seem to find anymore. Her arms beg her to reach forth and embrace him, but her broken heart continues to hold her back.

Her tongue begs to thank him for believing that this woman of stone is still a warrior of fire.

CHAPTER 46:

"WARD'S FALL"

***Theocracy** SunSide*
***Date** 14th Day of Month 7, Year 1629 DG*

THE AIR IS DIFFERENT AWAY from the city. An admission Saila can only make in the countryside, or in her mind. Had she said it aloud anywhere near Larso, the city folk would've rebelled.

And she just finished quelling the last one.

But sitting on the outskirts of Ward's Fall, a small village at the base of the PeakHaven mountain range, Saila can't deny the ease with which air passes through her lungs. She inhales deeply, holds her breath, then lets it out.

Perhaps she should leave the city and come out to the countryside more often.

A SunSidian Guard peeks his helmet-clad head through the entry way of her tent, disrupting her thoughts. "Chief Member, your visitor is here."

"Allow him in," she commands.

The soldier nods and Tund-Ra enters the tent. His silver hair has been cut and styled neatly, and he dons new clothes, replacing the rags he wore while he was in his cell.

"Please sit," she invites him, holding her hand out toward the chair on the opposite side of her desk. "What is your assessment?"

Tund-Ra takes the seat and sighs. "End of the year is going to be tough. *But,* with so many of the Bravers United"—he pauses and winces, as if the words are covered in thorns and stinging him on the way out—"*former* Bravers United warriors agreeing to work on your construction project, it's possible."

"I'm lucky you agreed to lead them. I don't think they would've joined without your buy-in. Thank you."

Tund-Ra's eyes narrow and he nods slowly.

Saila recognizes the suspicion. "Why are you giving me that look?"

"I'm just trying to figure you out. Haircuts. New clothes." He holds up his unbound wrists. "Many of us aren't even shackled. You have guards surrounding us, but the cells we're staying in are more like apartments than dungeons."

She grabs two chalices and a bottle of wine sitting at the end of the desk. "I'm not hearing the complaint, Tund-Ra."

"Why are you treating us this way?" His eyes follow her hands as she pours wine into the first chalice.

"What way?" She starts pouring wine into the second chalice.

"Like we don't have blood on our hands. Like we're free men and women, and not criminals in your custody."

Saila puts the bottle of wine down and slides one of the chalices across the table to Tund-Ra. She picks up the other and begins to sip from it as she speaks. "How should I treat you?"

Tund-Ra reaches forward, takes the chalice delicately into his fingers and takes a long sip. "Don't play games with me, Saila. Why are you being so lenient with us? Because you need us to work on your project?"

"I have good reason to treat you and the other prisoners with respect." She points in the direction of the small village nearby. "Do you know why they named this area Ward's Fall?"

Tund-Ra shakes his head.

"Long ago, in the Era of the Nysabaan, around"—she closes her eyes and performs the calculation in her head as quickly as she can—"fifty-one or fifty-two-hundred years ago, the three Mega clans were in their evolutionary infancy. Wars had broken them apart, forcing each clan to inhabit a different area of the land we now call SunSide."

"I'm going to need more wine." He takes another, much longer sip.

Saila laughs. "Alright, I'll summarize. The faeries occupied the forest to the south. The nymphs inhabited the entire northern corridor above Ona's River. And the pixies came and settled here, in what we now call Ward's Fall. In a war between the nymphs and the pixies, a young nymph named Nytra was orphaned."

Tund-Ra sits up in his seat and leans forward. "The pixies killed her parents."

"They did. She was two, maybe three years old at the time. The soldier who found her after the battle couldn't bear the thought of taking the life of a child, so he brought her home and raised her. She wasn't treated as a nymph, or as an enemy, or as an outsider. She was a beloved ward of the family. Eventually a time came when the war was at their doorstep."

"What happened?"

"Nytra fought. Alongside her adoptive clan, the pixies. By all accounts, they were her family and the ward sacrificed everything to protect them. Everything. The nymphs lost that battle and were driven back, but only because the pixies rallied together after Nytra gave her life defending the community. The very next day, they named the village Ward's Fall."

"To honor her." He finishes the wine and places the empty chalice back on the table.

Saila nods. "Nytra's name was sadly lost to history, but her legacy lives on every time the village's name is taken. This is the oldest extant community in SunSide. Eloa, Larso, Small Beauty, Anairda Village, they were all founded after Ward's Fall."

"So how does the history lesson answer my question?"

Saila smiles. "A young nymph gave her life, and saved so many pixies, solely because of how she was treated. She wasn't bonded to them by blood or lineage. She was bonded to them by compassion. The compassion of a young soldier who had to choose between taking her life, or giving her a new one."

Tund-Ra nods, seemingly understanding.

"I won't dismiss or overlook the blood on your hands, Tund-Ra. But I think the role that compassion plays in our communities can have a direct effect on the number of prisoners in our custody. Perhaps, had some of these prisoners been shown compassion earlier in life, had society provided them with resources, these crimes never would've happened. And maybe, if they're shown compassion now, we can get them to a place—socially, physically, spiritually—where they can enter society again and not be a danger to anyone. Where they can atone for their crimes."

"Is that the goal?" thunders Ovida's voice as she enters the tent. "Rehabilitation?"

Tund-Ra turns to find her glaring at him, and then meets Saila's gaze again. "Thank you for the talk, Saila. It's been eye-opening, truly."

"If the prisoners need anything, extra blankets, longer meal times, a place to rest, just let me know."

Tund-Ra nods gratefully, then turns and exits the tent, leaving Saila alone with Ovida's scowl.

"You let him call you by your name?" she growls.

"How can I help you, General?" Saila asks, gesturing to the seat Tund-Ra just vacated.

Ovida takes heavy steps forward and takes the seat.

"Innocent civilians died from their actions. I've spoken with the families of their victims, Saila. I promised them that the Braver's United would end up without their heads." She points a heavy finger at the entrance of the tent. "Why does he still have his?"

Saila inhales, pausing to gather her thoughts, relating deeply to the emotions of the victims' families. "I know how they feel, Ovida. Just last year, I was in Eloa visiting my mother when Unisa told me my father was amongst those responsible for Alba's death. I immediately craved retribution, and I came back to Larso to get it."

"Then why don't these families deserve the same?"

"They do. I'm not disagreeing with you. I simply believe that a society, and the leaders of that society, have to continue to be better than those who came before. I wasn't wrong to want Saith dead. But I was wrong in believing that the answer to violence is just more violence. Did it heal me? Did it bring Alba back?" She shakes her head.

"And who are we to decide whether executions will heal these families or not? Simply because they didn't heal you. I understand that they won't bring the victims back, but there is healing in justice. And it is our duty, as a government, to promote justice for the good of all."

"And what about justice for those who are victims of the court's failure? Those who are executed and later, when it's far too late, exonerated. Those who are convicted of a crime not based on evidence, but based on their pointed ears, or their fins, or their ability to shift? I wish I could believe that our system is perfect, but we both know it isn't. It makes mistakes and executions are irreversible."

Ovida scoffs. "None of what you just said applies to the Bravers United. We know they're all guilty; we arrested them in the middle of an open rebellion that caused the death of dozens of citizens." She leans forward and hardens her tone. "Not everyone can be rehabilitated, Saila. Some are born violent. Remorseless. They *need* to face the violence they find in the mirror."

Saila shakes her head. "Those are exactly the kind of people who need societal compassion, Ovida. Long before they commit a crime, long before they take a life, they need salvers. Social services. A proper evaluation. Diagnosis. Treatment." She softens her tone. "I long for a day when there won't *be* any victim's families, because there won't be any victims. A day when society has learned to care for its citizens in ways that reduce crime and violence to non-existence."

Ovida leans back in her seat, crossing her arms over her chest. "Until we achieve your fictional society, we have real citizens searching for justice."

"And I hope they can one day understand why the Bravers United weren't executed. Why I worked to help them atone for the crimes they committed while they were imprisoned. I'm not infallible, Ovida. And I'm not so naive as to think that this is a discussion with an easy right or wrong answer. Every argument you've made, and I think the ones I've made as well, have merit."

The Guard at the entrance of the tent pokes his head in again. "Chief Member, there's a messenger here—"

"Can you not see we're busy?" Ovida barks at him.

"I'm so sorry, General, but the messenger says this is urgent."

"Let him in," Saila calls out to the Guard over Ovida's irritated grunts. The messenger is a lanky, maroon-skinned pixie in a green uniform. Saila recognizes him as one of Larso's confidential messengers. They deliver often to the Castrum, as many of the correspondences she receives are politically-sensitive.

The messenger bounds forward and speaks at the speed of a galloping stallion. "This message arrived two nights ago at the Castrum. An igni messenger delivered it with urgency. They sailed through the night to make sure it arrived in Larso as quickly as possible, and then when they realized you weren't there, I was asked to fly it here. It was sent by someone named Kyoko and—"

Saila rips the envelope from his fingers. "Thank you very much, that'll be all."

The messenger places four fingers over his forehead to salute the Chief Member, then exits. Saila tears the envelope open and reads through Kyoko's message.

"What does it say?" Ovida asks.

Saila raises her eyes, wide from the surprise that the travelers were able to get the EverEmber Court to agree to hosting her military, despite the political tensions the Ore Monger created.

"Pack your things," Saila instructs her. "You and a third of the Guard are headed for EverEmber."

CHAPTER 47

"THE PRISONER AND THE EXECUTIONER 3"

Sovereign City-State *The Library*
Date *18th Day of Month 7, Year 1629 DG*

THE CICADA PRISONER'S NAME IS Brimah. In the two weeks since his capture, the Hawks' numbers have doubled from fifteen to thirty. The existing warriors invited friends and like-minded acquaintances from their social circles. Konni's hypothesis proved accurate.

The youth will change the world.

She's over the moon anytime a new recruit walks through the door. The more young people that join, the wider she smiles. Although she is nearly sixty years old herself, the Prime's age, she sees the inherent value in passing a revolution to those who can carry it forth for decades to come.

Juhi doesn't. Despite being under thirty-five herself, she thinks the youth who've joined lack the discipline required to monitor when and where they discuss the Hawks. She doesn't trust that someone so young can control their tongue long enough to make certain a Cicada isn't around before speaking.

But it depends on the individual, doesn't it? That's how Unisa feels. She, Maksi, and Yuki are all in their early twenties, but none of them are irresponsible with their words and surroundings. Particularly not Maksi, who is still recovering from his battle with Brimah, and is more alert now than ever about who is hovering nearby.

Since the night of the confrontation, Unisa has learned how it all happened. Maksi had come to the Nest after work, but made the mistake of not checking to make certain there were no Cicadas around. Out of the corner of his eye, he identified Brimah as someone who was watching him earlier in the night when he left *Witness*, and realized he had been followed.

Maksi chased after him and the confrontation ensued.

Unisa has interrogated the prisoner every night since, with Juhi at her side. She hasn't visited Lyla once. A knot of guilt forms in her stomach every time she thinks about the abandonment that the pixie must be feeling, the agony of not knowing why Unisa stopped coming to visit her. But the Hawks are right. Unisa's priorities should lie with them.

Lyla will be fine, she thinks. *I can free her once we get the information we need.*

Brimah's tattoo is one that all Cicadas have, typically around the same area of the body, near the hip and above the buttock, hidden by clothing. Cicadas start as standard Librarians, and are chosen by the Prime—whom they call the Oath Master—to join the Cicadas when they show proficiency in specific skill sets: combat, espionage, impersonation, physical strength, endurance, and agility.

Once inducted, they're asked to turn in their tunics, take an oath of fealty and secrecy, and are provided a fictional personal history and occupation. And then their work as the Oath Master's silent assassins and steady eyes begins.

According to Brimah, the total number of Cicadas is fewer than Unisa had imagined it would be. When she learned this fact, her heart seemed to fill with a bit of optimism, but then Brimah reminded her that the Oath Master still has the standard Librarians, who can be militarized at a moment's notice. This would make them, by far, the largest military in the world. Cicadas or no Cicadas, the Prime has tens of thousands of Librarians.

The Hawks have thirty.

Unisa enters the Nest after work and greets the recruits, who are in the middle of a training session with Konni, as Maksi looks on from his cot.

"How are you feeling today?" Unisa asks him.

"Better than yesterday," Maksi says with a smile that illuminates his scarred face.

"Those scars are going to make you the Library's most eligible bachelor," Unisa remarks with a wink.

Maksi laughs. "I guess the pain was worth it then, if it makes me seem like a warrior."

Unisa affectionately places a hand on his shoulder. "Maksi, you *are* a warrior."

The Mega's gray eyes brighten further. He gestures to the door at the back of the chamber. "Juhi's waiting for you."

Unisa rolls her eyes. "I'm sure she is. I think she enjoys these interrogations more than I do."

"Do you enjoy the interrogations at all? I never really took you for someone who finds comfort in tense situations."

"I find purpose in them. I appreciate that there's a role I can fulfill that precludes me from combat. As long as I'm useful, Juhi hasn't pressed me about taking up arms, thankfully."

"Combat or no combat, you're the most important part of the Hawks, Uni. Never forget that."

Unisa smiles, her cheeks warming. As he's recovered, as Unisa's sat by his bedside, Maksi appears to have grown far more candid than he's ever been with his thoughts.

She leaves him to rest and strides across the room to the heavy wooden door against the back wall. Prior to Brimah's capture, they had been using it as storage, but all of the weapons, restraints, maps, compasses, and other items Juhi secured for the Hawks have now been piled together outside the door, emptying the small room for their interrogations.

Unisa can hear some conversation from within as she approaches the door. Maksi was right; it appears Juhi has eagerly started without her.

"Good evening, Juhi," Unisa greets her upon entrance.

"Welcome back," she responds, holding a spoon of rice and shredded chicken up to Brimah's mouth. "I was just feeding our pet."

"I see. How is the dinner, Brimah?"

Brimah nods as he chews. "Exceptional."

"Are you both ready to get started?" Unisa asks, putting her work bag down in the corner of the room and leaning against a table with her arms crossed over her chest.

"I definitely am," Juhi says, pulling the dinner plate away from the angi prisoner. She places it on the table behind Unisa, withdraws a medical wrap from her pocket, and covers her knuckles with it.

"Am I going to lose any more teeth tonight?" Brimah asks, matter-of-factly.

"Maybe," Juhi responds with a shrug. "I had a large dinner, so I'm feeling extra strong." She bashes her right fist into the palm of her left hand.

"Lucky me." Brimah keeps his gaze cool.

"Alright, so where did we last leave off?" Unisa asks.

"We were in the middle of asking Brimah about the Fully Broken and where the Cicadas take them for—" she pauses, inching the word out sarcastically, as if it'll break if she releases it too quickly—"re-ha-bili-ta-tion."

"Ah, yes," Unisa remembers. "And then we had to stop because your last right hook nearly knocked him unconscious."

Juhi holds up her hands defensively. "Sorry, I'll hit softer."

"Start from the beginning, Brimah," Unisa begins. "Where do you take the Fully Broken? Are they killed right away? How are they determined to be Fully Broken?"

As he always does toward the start of the interrogation, Brimah keeps his lips tightly sealed at every question.

"You have ten seconds," Juhi says, starting to count down. The prisoner remains quiet as Juhi hits "Zero" so she cracks her knuckles, then her neck, and steps up to where he's shackled. Unisa turns away as Juhi swings once and makes contact with his jaw.

"Where do you take the Fully Broken?" Juhi repeats Unisa's question. No response. Another punch.

Unisa tries again. "Where do they go, Brimah?"

No response. Another punch, this time with blood spattered across the wall next to him.

Unisa sighs. "Last chance, Brimah. What happens to the Fully Broken?"

Silence.

Juhi raises her fist again, but Unisa grabs her wrist. "Alright, break time."

Juhi nods and takes a few steps back, leaning on the table again.

Unisa withdraws a handkerchief and starts to wipe the blood from Brimah's face. "It's a very simple question, Brimah. We need to know where the Fully Broken are taken. The physical location. And what happens to them there? Is there a process by which they can be rehabilitated or is that some fictional story to hide the fact that they're killed right away?"

Brimah's silence is deafening. Unisa crouches down so that she is closer to his eye level.

"Brimah, the man you're protecting doesn't care about you. Your Oath Master would have you killed the second he realizes we have you. You gain nothing from being loyal to him, but helping us could save a great number of people."

"You can't save them," the prisoner finally responds.

"Why not?" Unisa questions, but Brimah's silence fills the air. Juhi steps up again and unleashes another round of fists.

"Is it because they're all dead, Brimah?" Unisa questions further. "Why can't we save them?"

Silence. Fists.

The interrogation continues this way for another hour. Silence and fists, alternating back and forth until Brimah spits out more teeth and can no longer see through the swelling in one of his eyes.

He finally murmurs a response, but his volume is so low, and his mouth so full of blood, Unisa can't understand him. She moves her ear closer to his mouth. "What was that, Brimah? Say it again."

There's no response. Juhi steps forward, her fist dripping with his blood, but Unisa raises her arm to block her from the prisoner.

"He's not responding," Juhi remarks.

"Because you've turned his jaw into porridge. Slow down for a second, you're not an executioner."

Juhi grunts and backs up again. Unisa puts her hands on Brimah's hanging head to lift it up, and brings her ear to his lips.

"One more time, Brimah, please. Say it one more time."

The prisoner breathes and then releases the words to the best of his current state. "The Fully Broken aren't dead. They're in cells."

"Where?" Unisa demands.

"Not in the Library."

"How many?"

Brimah shrugs. "Hundreds? Thousands?"

"Where are they?"

He doesn't respond. Not because he doesn't want to, but because he's no longer able to. His head falls limply to the side as he loses consciousness.

"Get Konni in here," Unisa instructs Juhi. "Now!"

Konni is brought in to administer healing treatments with the Radiance, as she has each night for the past two weeks. Unisa and Juhi step out of the room, as the interrogation ends for the night.

"You have to stop hitting him so hard," Unisa tells her.

"It's not the force, it's the frequency. But I'm not going to decrease the number of times he gets hit. He keeps his lips closed, I'm going to open them."

"Did you hear what he said at the end?"

Juhi shakes her head. "He was whispering."

"The Fully Broken aren't dead. They're being held outside of the Library in some kind of prison. He said it could be hundreds"—she pauses—"or thousands."

Juhi's eyes widened. "That's our army. We have to find out where they are."

Unisa turns to the wooden door behind which the prisoner is being held. "Only he can tell us."

As Juhi and the others depart for the night, and Unisa heads up to Ora's apartment to relieve Yuki of her duties, she remembers Alba's words from a year prior, after they had entered MoonSide and Unisa had witnessed the truth.

History is not all that's buried under the city, Uni. You'll find equal parts books and bones.

Was this hyperbole? Or was Alba simply unaware of this off-site detention center? She appeared to be certain that the Fully Broken are immediately dispatched and buried. Unisa considers how old this detention center might be. The ideals of the Fully Bonded and the Fully Broken have been used to control the citizens for ages. Centuries.

Since the time of the corruption that turned the moral and wise founding Primes, who wanted nothing more than to catalogue the history of the world, from social, spiritual, and political leaders to…

Oath Masters.

CHAPTER 48

"The Answers You Seek"

***Theocracy** SunSide*
***Date** Unknown*

NAINA TEARS HER EYES FROM the grotesque memory of her enemies, the Sprites, shortly after their release from imprisonment, to hear Red-Lo's plea.

This is the last time I saw her. For eight centuries, I thought she was gone. Until last year when Unisa told me she's still alive. Saila has held that over my head. She knows how badly I want to see my wife again.

He reaches his hand forward and caresses Drof-Fa's cheek again. *I'm trying my best to help you with the Sprites, but I truly don't know anything. You may find something as we continue to travel through my memories, but I promise you, I'm not hiding anything intentionally.*

Why are you telling me this, Red-Lo?

Because I miss my wife, Naina. And I'm begging you to uphold your friends' promises. Unisa promised to take me to my wife. Then Saila did. I'm here, withdrawing my consciousness into my own mind to help you. All I ask in return is that you deliver the promise on which no one else has been willing to deliver.

He turns to her, his gaze burning through hers with sincerity. *Promise me you'll take me to Drof-Fa.*

Feathers and Saila have kept the truth of Drof-Fa's second life as the TreeKeeper hidden from Red-Lo. He believes her to be alive somewhere in the world. In a place where he can visit her. The faerie has no idea that his beloved has been sentenced to live out the immortal existence he himself desired.

As a servant of the World Beyond. A final ferry to carry essences from this world to their eternal resting place.

Naina considers whether she should be the one to tell him, to explain. Feathers and Saila want to use Drof-Fa as a bargaining chip for whatever information he can provide about the Sprites. But this journey has proven that Red-Lo has no information to volunteer. If there is anything here, she'll have to find it on her own, which means there is no reason—other than spite, animosity, or enmity—to keep Red-Lo from Drof-Fa.

For the first time in a very long time, Naina abandons what *she* would normally do, and wonders: what would Lessi do?

Red-Lo, there's something you should know.

The faerie turns from his wife's paralyzed memory to face the wolf.

When they told you Drof-Fa was alive, they weren't lying. But they also weren't being entirely truthful.

Red-Lo's eyes narrow. *What do you mean?*

Naina takes a deep breath. *Drof-Fa exists. But not in a form you can readily visit.*

Red-Lo steps toward her, leaning forward as if moving his ear closer to her will help him to understand. *Naina, if there is any moment to forsake obscurity and murry clarity, it is this one.*

Naina's finger rises and she points to the scene in front of them, of the Sprites paralyzing Drof-Fa moments before blasting her with flames. *I know this is the last time you saw your wife, being burned alive, but she didn't die. The Sprites transported her to a place called the Bridge Tree. It's a resting place for essences between this world and the World Beyond. Drof-Fa was reborn as the TreeKeeper, bound to the Bridge Tree, tasked with ushering essences to the Sprites the same way that you were.*

Red-Lo's eyes widen. *You've seen her yourself?*

Naina shakes her head. *My friends, Rafael and Kyoko. They met with her and then relayed all of this to me. Drof-Fa, the TreeKeeper, has since severed the Sprites's connection to her.*

But she maintained a connection to me, Red-Lo adds. *Unisa told me she's been watching all of my actions since…* His gaze travels to the scene around them. *Since this night.*

Yes. She's still connected to you.

Why are you telling me this now? Red-Lo asks, turning back to the wolf.

Naina pauses, juggling her words before presenting them. *I believe you. When you tell me that you're not intentionally hiding information from me. I'll find the information I need on my own, while I'm here in your mind. But there's no longer any need for me to hide this truth from you. I know you want to see her, but the only way is when your essence reaches the Bridge Tree. Upon your death.*

Kill me, he begs.

Naina steps back. *What?*

You heard me. Kill me and send my essence to my wife. His finger rises to the scene around them. *This night I fell for the Sprites' trickery. I thought they were blessing me with immortality, but it's a fucking curse. It's kept me away from my wife for over eight centuries. I don't want it anymore; I just want to see my Drof-Fa again.*

He drops down onto his knees before Naina. She takes a step back in stunned silence.

I beg of you. He clasps his hand together before the wolf. *Please, promise me, Naina. As soon as we're back, you will kill me and send my essence to my wife. Promise me.*

Red-Lo, get up, Naina demands, discomfort swelling in her chest. For so long, she'd thought she'd jump at the chance to kill the faerie conqueror. But something about his feeble, pathetic sniveling is ruining the moment for her. It feels dirty.

Red-Lo shakes his head. *No, I won't. Not until you agree to kill me.* He drops his forehead to the ground and completely prostrates himself before the wolf. Sobs rattle the ground as the Ore Monger weeps at her feet.

Red-Lo, get up! She commands him.

His sobbing stops abruptly and she thinks he may finally be calming down and coming to his senses. She waits for him to rise and wipe his cheeks so they can move on to the next memory.

Red-Lo remains completely still, his forehead to the ground.

How long are you going to stay down there?

There's no response. He remains utterly silent.

Too silent, in fact.

Naina reaches down and places her hand on his back. She recoils quickly when she feels the texture of stone. She tries again, and the sensation is the same. His skin has taken on the grayish hue of rock.

The Ore Monger has become a statue.

She backs up, her breath hitching her throat. As if it's made of snow on a sunny, summer day, the memory, the scene around her, melts away. All that's left is Naina, Red-Lo, the grotesque Sprites released from their prison, and the white void.

Naina looks down at her hands. She never snapped her fingers to move onto the next memory. Red-Lo, still frozen in stone, certainly didn't either. Then why is she in the white void and where is the door to the next memory?

"There are no more memories to view, Naina," comes a male voice echoing throughout the void, as if the white space itself were addressing her.

Naina circles around quickly, a growl erupting in her chest. *Who is that?*

"You can use your voice now, Naina. We'll allow it. You don't have to think aloud anymore."

Naina clears her throat. She's been speaking her thoughts aloud for the past few hours she's been here in Red-Lo's mind. Red-Lo had told her it was the only way to communicate in this realm. She opens her mouth and hears her voice again.

"Who are you? What's going on?"

A female voice. "We are the answers you seek, Naina."

A wooden door finally appears behind her. She reaches for the doorknob but pulls her hand back when she sees it turning on its own. The door opens inward, away from her, so she backs up.

When she sees them, every muscle in her body tenses. Down to her core, to her breathing, to her very cellular activity, everything stops and enters into a state of sheer panic. She recognizes them immediately.

They're clad in colorful, lush robes, long enough to drag along the floor and hide their feet. Nearly every color Naina has ever seen is represented in them. Their skin is so clean and fresh, she perceives it as glowing.

One of them, a female, has stunning dark hair that travels all the way down to her lower back, with silken lavender skin. The male's is a velvety blue that resembles the sky on the brightest days, with short hair slicked backward and a beard that reaches slightly past his chin.

Their eyes are identical: the most tranquil, deep blue pupils Naina's ever seen. Though their skin and pointed ears would suggest that they are Mega, their eyes tell a different story, as do the extra set of arms extruding from their ribs, and the striking, magnificent butterfly wings shooting from their backs.

They each have crowns on their heads, made of a sparkling silver metal that appears so pure it almost looks clear, with dazzling gems that project the rainbow into the void that envelops them. Naina's never seen anything like it. All royalty, all regality of the outside world pales in comparison to the elite majesty of the two beings before her.

"It's nice to finally meet you," the female says to her. "We've been waiting. Watching your journey through Red-Lo's mind."

"I know who you are," Naina says, her voice entering the air with little volume.

"Oh?" the male says with a coy raise of his eyebrow. "And who are we?"

Naina swallows, wishing she were wrong, knowing she is right. "The Ancient Ones. The Sprites."

The female smiles and claps slowly, hauntingly. "Well done. Now—" she gestures widely and three stout, shimmering crystalline thrones appear in the void—"take a seat, Naina."

Her blue gaze zeroes in on the wolf's. "There is *so much* we'd like to talk to you about."

CHAPTER 49

"POETRY NIGHT"

Alphocracy *MoonSide*
Date *18th Day of Month 7, Year 1629 DG*

THE ELEGANT SILK SAREES SALESSA'S been wearing, the beautiful and bountiful gifts Lexona has presented to her, cover more than just her skin and muscle and bone. They shield the world from the Salessa that she's always been.

As she sits on her bed, clad in a plain cotton shalwar kameez, light blue with a white dupatta, she wonders how much she's changed since she's arrived at Lover's Plateau. If she walks back into SunSide with an elegant silk saree, Naina wouldn't recognize her. But how much of the change is irreparable?

Salessa shakes her head, realizing she's being unfair to Lexona. The serpent has been nothing but devoted to making Salessa feel at home. She's helped her with understanding and connecting to the contents of the O'Raha texts. She's defended Salessa before the elders.

She's empowered her in more ways than Salessa thought were possible.

Perhaps a change of clothes has changed her at the core. And perhaps that is for the best. Change isn't inherently undesirable because it was encouraged by Lexona. Naina may think that's the case, but...

Naina will have to accept that Lexona is going to be part of their lives moving forward.

Salessa holds the letter written by someone pretending to be her sister. Or, perhaps the falcon's changed so much that she doesn't recognize her own twin anymore.

Will it feel unfamiliar when their telepathic connection resumes? They've never been apart before, and now they've been apart for months. It felt so debilitating at first, to be so far from Naina that her voice couldn't reach Salessa's mind.

She hated it. Hated not having a sibling, a second half, to encourage her, make decisions with her, be part of her journey.

But she has that now, without Naina. Afzal and Zoya can never fill the telepathic void in Salessa's mind, but they have somehow healed an emptiness in her heart. Perhaps this will allow the twins to be more independent of one another even after her return to SunSide.

After all, she wears plain cotton shalwar kameez when she's with Afzal and Zoya.

Salessa puts the letter down, rises to her feet, and smoothes out her outfit with her hands, then reaches into the drawer of her nightstand and withdraws a small notebook. She takes a deep breath and exits her chambers, marching to Zoya's. For most of her time here, she hadn't realized how close their rooms were. She reaches the horse's door and gives it a knock.

After a moment of silence, she hears, "Come in!"

Salessa turns the knob and enters the home, closing the door behind her. The layout of Zoya's chambers is nearly identical to her own and, though she hasn't been in many others, Salessa assumes they all must have been designed the same way.

She enters the main chamber and her feet immediately freeze in place. Zoya sits on the edge of her bed with Afzal's head in her lap. She rubs the top of his head with one hand, and under his furry muzzle with the other.

Afzal lies on his back, paws bent at the wrists and a wide smile on his face. His deep purrs burst out from his chest and throat, rattling the entire room.

"What's wrong?" Zoya asks, catching Salessa frozen at the entrance of the room.

"Would you…like me to…come back later?" the falcon asks.

Zoya's forehead creases with genuine confusion. "Not at all. It's poetry night. You just got here."

Salessa nods and forces a smile through the discomfort of watching a grown man…grown leopard-man being pet.

Zoya pulls her hands back. "Afzal, time for poetry night."

Afzal lifts his head, yawns, then hops onto the floor on all fours and stretches his legs and back. "Thank you, Zoya, that was fantastic." He moves to a chair on the other end of the room and plops down.

"Always a pleasure," she says to him with a respectful bow, then turns to Salessa. "Shall we get poetry night started?"

Salessa, sitting in her usual seat near the window, with her notebook of poems resting in her lap, nods enthusiastically.

"Whose turn is it?" Afzal asks.

Salessa raises her hand. "I had the last turn. So I think that means it's Zoya's turn to start tonight."

"Wonderful," Zoya says. She reaches under her bed and pulls out her own notebook, this one slightly thicker than Salessa's, and flips to a page toward the end. "I wrote this one last night, actually. Inspiration came to me during the day and I couldn't resist getting some thoughts down. I just want to warn you ahead of time, it isn't very good. Not polished or anything, it's just kind of straight from the—"

"Would you read it, already?!" Salessa demands. "Title and rhyme scheme."

Zoya's face contorts as if she's attempting to figure out a complex mathematical equation. "I, uh, haven't really thought of a title. Just a Spiritual Ode to the Divine, I suppose. Something like that. The rhyme scheme is 1-1-2-1 for all stanzas throughout."

Salessa nods, encouraging her forth. Zoya takes a deep breath and begins to recite:

Breaker of Darkness, Herald of Light

Answer my plea as I pray through the night
Give me the strength to rise off my knees
Take me in your service, but don't take my fight

Riches to rags, you have it all
Handsome and fierce, good and tall
I'd give you my heart as a token of devotion
If it weren't a gift, unworthy and small

Bent at the knee, the world finds me odd
But what good is this life, if not for my god
Take me by soul, and mind, and body
Bare me, oh Lord, so I can drop the facade

As soon as the recitation ends, Zoya's gaze rises from the page and meets Afzal's. The entire human half of his face is flushed, his eyes wider than Salessa has ever seen them. Some kind of silent energy passes between them.

I guess I wasn't imagining it, she thinks, realizing the poem appears to be written about one divine spirit in particular.

"Zoya, that was"—Salessa pauses—"stunning. You have a gift, truly."

Zoya smiles and turns to the falcon. "Thank you. I was nervous to read it but, I think, sometimes"—she meets Afzal's gaze again—"there are things better said, than left unsaid."

"Very true," Afzal agrees with a nod. He closes the notebook on his lap and places it down on the floor next to his chair. "I believe it's my turn next."

"Are you not going to read from what you've written?" Salessa asks, gesturing to the closed book.

"No, I think I'll just speak from the heart this time. The title of the poem is, 'A Silent Tale,' and the rhyme scheme is 1-1-2-2-1, throughout." He clears his throat and recites:

Her voice is a force
Full of power, of course
But even unspoken, it regales
The romantic tale
Of a leopard and a horse

Silences drown lies
Remove all surprise
All that I've heard
Every single word
She's said it with her eyes

Play a tune, oh, my heart's fife
Your love is music, oh, future wife
I hold you so dear
As you're the only thing here
That still gives me life

His eyes don't shift from Zoya, whose cheeks now glow like two red apples. No poetry night has been so daring and so candid before. Something's changed now, as the two Doruh have become emboldened to share their feelings for one another plainly. It's a beautiful sight to witness, but Salessa shudders with uneasiness, as if she's intruding on an intimate moment.

"You know, I actually haven't written anything this time"—she feigns a yawn—"and it is quite late. I think I'm going to head back to my chambers."

A frown instantly breaks out on both Zoya and Afzal's faces.

"Already?" Zoya asks. "Salessa the night's just begun."

The falcon rises to her feet. "I know, but I'm just so tired."

"Salessa, please stay," Afzal asks her. "I know the poetry has been a bit heavy so far, but I have written some lighter ones that I wanted to share and—"

"Oh, it's not that," Salessa lies, shaking her head. "Truly, I loved the poetry."

It's the longing looks and petting that weren't doing it for me.

"Then, please, stay for just a little longer," Zoya asks.

Salessa takes in their pleading looks and nods, accepting the request. She sits on her chair by the window and, as it's her turn, she recites something she recently wrote. The energy of the room, and the night, shifts.

Afzal was right; the remaining poetry is lighter, or more thought-provoking. It is everything but the blatant displays of intimate declarations that she's previously sat through.

To some degree, Salessa admits, having spent weeks here with the new Lexona, their emotions resonate with her.

The mood shift allows Salessa to shed her discomfort and become part of the night again. She loses herself, and the time, in their laughs, their discussions, and the love they all share for written expression. Before she knows it, the night passes and it's the early hours of the morning.

"I really have to go back to my chambers and get some sleep now," Salessa says with a far more sincere yawn. "This was truly one of the best poetry nights we've had, thank you."

She rises, but before she leaves, Zoya stops her.

"I was wondering if you might be interested in attending the upcoming poetry festival with us. It happens each year in the Northern Hills, so it's a little bit of a journey out of Lover's Plateau and down to the base of the mountain."

"But it's well worth it," Afzal adds. "There are hundreds of poets there, both professional and amateur, along with a parade and fireworks, lots of food." He taps his belly with a smile.

"It sounds fantastic," Salessa replies, her heart racing with excitement. "I'd love to go."

She's grateful she stayed. Had she left earlier, she wouldn't have been invited to the festival, and she wouldn't have regained the sense of comfortable kinship she feels to the two Doruh standing beside her.

I'm so lucky to have found them, she thinks and, abruptly, she feels something in her mind that she hasn't felt in weeks. It's almost a foreign feeling, as if she's feeling it for the first time. It isn't painful, like a needle, but it's perplexing, like a puzzle.

It's another voice in her head.

Lucky to have found who?

Naina? She wonders. No, it couldn't be Naina's, the voice was too deep.

Naina? Is this Lexona?

Lexona? It's Salessa, who is…

Salessa's gaze meets Afzal's and their eyes widen. Simultaneously, they utter the same statement telepathically.

WHAT THE FUCK?!

CHAPTER 50

"EVERYTHING"

Court Democracy EverEmber
***Date** 22nd Day of Month 7, Year 1629 DG*

HAD SOMEONE TOLD RAFAEL A year earlier that he'd find himself striding through an igni military garrison, wearing their armor, training their archers, he would've asked them how much ale they'd had to drink.

But life is enigmatic. It can change so much in a short time. In only a year, long-held prejudices, deeper than the ocean, have evaporated, revealing citizens who never supported the war with his people. Revealing soldiers who never wanted to step onto the battlefield.

In only a year, he went from hating the igni, to loving one. And in that same year, he lost her.

General Kyoko's leadership began ten days earlier, when this encampment was set up on one of EverEmber's longest coastlines. Rafael and Ana have been here with her to assist, but she hasn't needed them. Kyoko is a warrior.

Always has been, and nothing can change that.

An igni soldier, bow in hand, quiver behind, approaches Rafael when the mari reaches the training grounds. Targets sit, lined up along the shore, with igni warriors forming long lines to take turns shooting.

The young soldier can't seem to hit his mark, so he begs Rafael for guidance. A year of teaching students in SunSide, and a year before that in the Library, have given Rafael a strong understanding on the ways in which people learn. Any class of two or more students could hold two or more learning styles; two or more forms of intelligence.

There's only one way to hit a bullseye: the way that's best for the individual archer.

The soldier nearly weeps when, after a few educated pointers from the mari, he hits the bullseye for the first time. Rafael accepts his grateful bow and then continues on through the garrison, ensuring it's set up according to Kyoko's plans.

Tents and housing furthest inland. Salvers and food halls further out, where the sand meets the boardwalks outlining the shore. Weapons storage and military training out on the coast. If one of the Three Deaths rises from the water, the warriors will be ready to force it back down.

Ovida patrols nearby as the SunSidian Guard eat, sleep, drink, and train alongside EverEmber's military. Flashes of light burst through the air as many of the nymphs and pixies train with the Radiance. The faeries take up arms and stand toe-to-toe with the igni soldiers.

The fusing of militaries hasn't been easy. The igni and the SunSidians have been locked in six days of pissing competitions and Kyoko, Rafael, and Ovida haven't been able to stay dry. When one skirmish is resolved, two more pop up in its place.

Kyoko remains frustrated. Logistics, training, all else has transpired smoothly. The one thing that she can't seem to get a hold of is the egos. She has to get them to work together, or they'll kill each other before a single one gets the chance to defend the island.

As nightfall nears, another conflict breaks out; an igni and a SunSidian cross paths and, inevitably, one must have looked at the other in a way they didn't appreciate. Before Rafael can get there, Kyoko's broken it up. He can see the rage in her eyes. She's exhausted.

To her right is a table where dinner is being served. She steps up onto it, her igni armor glinting in the fading purple light of the setting suns, her hair wrapped in a tight bun atop her head, her shimmering exoskeleton giving her a radiant glow.

She captures every eye nearby. Igni warriors and SunSidian Guard alike find her perched and stop what they're doing to pay attention. Her gaze, drowning in rage and frustration, admonishes them before her lips even part.

"Igni! We gathered here ten days ago on the promise that when a threat comes for Mount Mother, we will defend her. Are we still interested in that goal?"

The igni in the crowd raise the swords and grunt in the affirmative.

"SunSidians! Six days ago, you arrived on *these* shores to slaughter any adversary that would one day wind up on *yours*. Are we still focused on that objective?"

The SunSidian Guard raise their weapons, as well, bellowing in agreement.

"We are all on the same side. Here to defend these islands, this home, because today it's EverEmber, and tomorrow it'll be SunSide. The only thing that stands between this world and utter destruction"—she sweeps her arm, gesturing widely at the soldiers standing around her—"is *us*. You can stand around and continue these juvenile spats, like little boys and girls who don't know how to play nicely. Or"—she uses her uninjured hand to withdraw the tanto on her hip, a weapon she wields for the first time in a year—"you can pick up your sword and aim at the enemy, like a *real* warrior."

The crowd erupts into cheers. Many of those who were seated at the table rise to their feet.

"You are not enemies. You're here for a common goal. Men, women, human, Mega, SunSidian, I don't give a fuck, frankly. We're not here to fight each other, we're here to fall or succeed together." She points the tip of the tanto toward Mount Mother. "We're here to defend *her*. As long as you stand on these shores, ready to give your life for something greater than politics or species, you are a warrior of EverEmber."

She leans in, inhaling deeply, as the crowd around waits with bated breath on her final words. "Today, we are *all* igni!!"

The crowd erupts so loudly it rattles the shore. Warriors of all species embrace, slamming the breastplates of their armor together. Those who were fighting amongst themselves deliver heartfelt apologies, as brothers and sisters of the same battlefield.

Rafael watches, admiring the shift in energy that Kyoko created. A hand on his shoulder draws his attention from the scene. He turns to find Ana behind him, standing at the entrance of his tent, a grave expression hardening the lines around her nare slits.

"What's wrong?" he asks her.

"Come with me," she responds, nodding toward his tent. "We have to talk."

Rafael's heart sinks. She leads him to an open book on a small wooden table at the center of the tent, and says, "Vala."

He waits for her to elaborate. "Is that supposed to mean something to me?''

"That's the Oasis Mage's name. She was a Sprite who knew the Ancient Ones. Not only did she betray them"—her finger falls and lands on the open page—"she's the one who imprisoned them."

"Alright," Rafael says, digesting, "does it say how she did it?"

Ana shakes her head. "It doesn't."

"Then it doesn't help us. We need to know how to imprison them."

"Then we should ask her."

Rafael's forehead creases. "Ask her? You said she knew the Ancient Ones. She lived in their time, three thousand years ago. How can we ask her?'

Ana lifts the book into her arms and reads from it, then translates for Rafael. "The Sprites practiced wizardry, witchcraft, warlockery, and sorcery. It was all similar to the Radiance, but it required verbal incantations to bind the energy to the user, the same way in which physical movements allow users to access the Radiance."

Rafael nods.

"When Vala was nearing her death, the Sprite Empire built her a shrine. The Temple of the Oasis Mage. In an effort to keep her consciousness accessible, in case the Ancient Ones were ever released from their prison, Vala imbued her essence into a statue within the Temple of the Oasis Mage."

"The Sprite Empire is dead, Ana. Long gone. This temple likely with them."

"You know how powerful the Ancient Ones are. If there's a chance this temple still exists, and it holds the key to our victory, wouldn't you want to take it?"

Rafael's eyes widen. She's right. It doesn't matter if the oasis or the temple are likely gone with the Sprite Empire. If there's a chance to save the continent, they have to take it. "Someone will have to go to the oasis and convene with Vala's consciousness. Find out how to defeat the Sprites."

"Someone? Who?" Ana utters the golden question. "You and I are mari and the oasis is in a desert. It has to be Kyoko."

Rafael shakes his head. "We vowed to the Court that she would remain here. And I don't think it should be you, no offense."

Ana holds up her hands in acceptance. "No offense taken. I've been chugging water all day and somehow my forearm fins are still cracking from dehydration. I wouldn't last ten seconds in a desert."

"Then it's me," Rafael says softly, allowing the danger of the mission to settle in. Once again, he's walking into a situation he has a very small chance of walking safely back out of.

Ana clears her throat, lowers her volume, and sheepishly leans closer to Rafael. "May I offer a suggestion?"

Rafael nods.

"Don't tell Kyoko where you're going. I've lived with both of you for a year now. I know there's something between you two."

There was, he thinks, remembering what she said on the beach.

Can you bring someone back from the dead, Rafa?

Ana continues. "She'll never let you go. She won't be able to put her feelings aside to let you walk into a desert, no matter how much water you take with you." Her gaze remains steady on his as the gravity of her words sink into his mind. "Just don't tell her where you're actually going. It'll be easier for you."

Rafael doesn't hesitate for a moment to respond. He doesn't consider Ana's suggestion for even a fraction of a second. The answer, the choice, is clear to him.

"No."

"No?" Ana's eyebrows jump to her hairline.

"I won't do it. I won't hide anything from her again. Kyoko understands me better than anyone, and she'll understand the importance of this journey. I misjudged her before, and it cost me *everything,* Ana. She was everything, and I lost her."

"And you found her again." A woman's voice. It echoes from behind him. Rafael turns around to find Kyoko standing at the entrance of the tent, still clad in her igni armor, still with her hair in a bun, still with the tanto on her hip, still the most divine person he's ever seen.

She storms toward him, eyes locked with his. He panics, confused, unsure of what she's about to do. Her eyes are glazed with some emotion but he can't identify it. Rage? Agony?

"Kyoko?" he calls out to her, trying to gauge a reaction, but there is none. There's only the sparkle in the corners of her eyes, as light reflects off of the tears breaking through.

He's still confused when she stands before him, reaches up to grasp the armor on his neckline, and tugs on it harshly. He's bent quickly forward and before he can react, Kyoko presses her lips to his with the fervor of a forge, with the intimacy of a vulnerable late-night conversation.

Rafael's confusion melts away as his arms wrap around her waist, as naturally as his breathing, and pulls her tighter toward him. He kisses her back as if it's her love itself being passed through their lips, into his chest, to mend what's broken within. He kisses her back as if separating from her will cause the world to collapse on itself.

He kisses her back as the man who lost everything, finds everything once again.

When they separate, tears stream from her eyes. "I guess you *can* bring someone back from the dead." She presses her forehead against his and they close their eyes, feeling the warmth of one another envelop them like the rays of the suns on a blooming flower.

"I have to go," he says. "To the oasis on Panaerth. Ana found something that may be"—he pauses—"the most important thing we've ever found."

"It has to be you?" Kyoko asks, pulling her head back.

He nods. "It has to be one of the three of us. You have to stay. So I have to go."

"Can you promise me you'll come back to me?"

Rafael's heart races as he does the hardest thing he's ever done: he delivers a difficult truth to the person he loves most. "No. I can't promise. But I hope you know I will fight anything, from this realm or any other, to come home."

Kyoko nods. "That's all I want. Just come back home." Her gaze travels the tent and she chuckles. "Even though this isn't your home."

Rafael finds her gaze and pours all of the sincerity in his heart onto his tongue. "*You* are my home. I'll come back wherever you are."

Her kisses bring with them an understanding that Rafael never previously had. He'd understood the duties of loving his sister as a brother, or his parents as a son. But the love of a romantic partner, the chosen love, requires a constant, moment-to-moment devotion to honesty, trust, and communication.

Rafael finally understands the power of intimate devotion to another. Long after she's left the tent, after she's walked away, after he's left EverEmber heading for Panaerth, Kyoko's devotion lingers on his lips.

CHAPTER 51

"DEATH AND CONDOLENCES"

Sovereign City-State *The Library*
Date *25th Day of Month 7, Year 1629 DG*

PEOPLE THINK YOU'RE CALLOUS, HEARTLESS, cruel when your mother dies and you don't shed tears right away. Especially when that mother stayed up late at night, cradling you in her arms to rock you to sleep when you were four years old. When she would remember to bring your favorite chocolates on the way home from work, just because she was thinking about you. When, after you moved out on your own, she would look forward to your next visit before you'd even left the last one.

When she would remind you daily that you were loved unconditionally by someone who sacrificed so much to see you smile.

Unisa is required to shed tears. If she doesn't, there must be something wrong with her. But the tears don't come immediately. They don't come when the salver declares the time of death. They don't come when the staff of the Radiance-Return service come to take Ora away, and prepare her body. They don't come as Yuki, Juhi, Konni, Maski, the Prime, and so many others extend their condolences.

But they do come eventually. Once Ora's service is over, once everyone walks away from the gravesite leaving Unisa alone, once the duty of completing the final rites of her Radiance-Return is satisfied, Unisa releases the breath she started holding when Ora took her last one.

And with it, the tears flow. She doesn't sob, or heave, or yell. The tears just quietly blur her vision and then break free from her eyes, traveling down her cheeks and dripping off of her chin. It's not intentional. She has every right to scream. But Unisa started grieving this loss months ago and now, she's only saying goodbye.

And that's okay.

One of the more jarring aspects of a funeral service, at least of a Radiance-Return burial, is the small, temporary name plate placed on the grave site until the permanent one is designed and set down. It just says "Ora" written in someone's handwriting on a piece of paper, with the years of her birth and death underneath the name.

Unisa knows they mean well to do this, but *that* feels more callous than anything else. This was the pixie who signed up to take Unisa in when she was four years old. The pixie who stressed strong oral hygiene practices right before bed and immediately after waking up. The pixie who told Unisa that she would conquer anything she set her mind to, as long as she never forgot the core of who she was and what mattered in life.

But now? She was a name written in ink on a piece of paper, as if her entire life, all of these moments, all of the things she said and did, could be summed up by two dates and three letters. She was more than that. Though it feels as if she was here and gone in the blink of an eye, as if she were just someone in a different boat floating along the same lazy river of life as Unisa, and now she's just drifted away, she was more than what's on this piece of paper.

She was the truest definition of a loving mother. And Unisa will never forget. Despite how many times she reminded Ora, in her last few days, of who she was.

"It's me. Unisa."

"Ora? It's me."

"It's Unisa."

"My name is Unisa."

"It's me, Unisa."

"Hope you're feeling alright today. It's me, Unisa."

"Thank you for everything, Ora. For everything you did for me. It's me, Unisa."

And then in her final moments, as she choked out her breaths. "I love you, Ora. It's me. Unisa."

Ora died on the morning of the Twenty-Third of Month Seven, and by the evening of the Twenty-Fourth, Unisa had completed all of the Radiance-Return rituals that Ora wanted, as a pixie. By that time, she'd heard from everyone close to her, offering their heartfelt love and support.

Except for Rafael, though she didn't blame him. He was on his mission to save the world. He didn't even know that Ora had died, and Unisa didn't want to tell him in writing. She wanted to tell him in person so she could embrace her adopted brother; the one person who loved Ora almost as much as she did.

Who loved Ora as much as he loved his own mother.

The last letter she'd received from the group was from Ana, a few days earlier, expressing some relief that they'd finally had a little success in EverEmber. After some "small hiccups" in SeaBed—as Rafael had described in a previous letter—they'd convinced the Mother's Court to devote a share of the igni military to preparing for the coming of one of the Three Deaths.

Unisa had even heard from the Prime after Ora's death. It was flippant, and alluded to Unisa's future residence in Prime Palace with the other members of the Inner Catacomb, but he'd said *something* to her. Death and condolences tend to bring out the best in people.

Even when their best is still pretty awful.

By the evening of the Twenty-Fifth, Unisa hadn't heard from Lyla either and, just as she didn't blame Rafael, Unisa didn't blame the pixie either. For one thing, she was nearly full-term pregnant and could give birth at any moment. For another, in Ora's final weeks, at the Prime's request, Unisa had barely visited Lyla. She'd spent more time caring for her mother and acting as a leader for the Hawks, but had to sacrifice the time she had with the pixie. The young girl with the cherry-blossom cheeks must've felt so abandoned and wasn't ready to offer condolences for Unisa's loss.

Unisa feels terrible for having left the pixie alone with the Prime for so long. But now that Ora had made her Radiance-Return, perhaps she could devote time to Lyla again. Especially since she may have to move into Prime Palace. She'll be there, day-in and day-out, to care for Lyla and the baby when it's born.

She decides to visit Lyla, hoping to apologize for her absence over the past few weeks and mend whatever may be broken between them. As she soars through the Loops, heading to Prime Palace, she prays silently that Lyla will be able to find it in her heart to forgive her.

Unisa's familiarity with the route hasn't waned. She exits the Loop network and, instead of landing, remains airborne all the way to the front courtyard of the towering domicile. When her feet finally touch the ground again, her heart sinks. Not because she sees or hears anything amiss, but because she *feels* something. The air itself has a mucky texture. Breathing it leaves a bitterness on her tongue. It's dragged through her nose like barbed wire over soil.

Something's wrong.

Unisa steps slowly up the stairs to the front entrance and through the foyer, up the golden steps to the second floor. Every step she takes past the front doors, her heart sinks deeper into her stomach, her blood runs colder. A house that usually hosts a number of residents, who are typically loudly chirping about the grounds at this time with all of the lights on, is now dark and quiet. It's eerie and terrifying.

Where is everyone?

At the top of the golden stairs, immediately upon entrance to the second floor, is a wide circular chamber with hallways that lead to each of the various bedrooms for the members of the Inner Catacomb. Before she can even reach the hallway that leads to Lyla's bedroom, Unisa's feet freeze at the sight of the Prime standing in the center of the circular room, cradling something delicately in his arms, clad in his nightgown.

Next to him stands a salver wearing a surgical outfit, which is typically light blue in color, but is now so soaked crimson that no blue is visible at all. He looks down, over the Prime's shoulder, smiling at whatever the leader of the Library is holding so carefully in his arms. Unisa narrows her eyes and, through the darkness, she finally makes out what it is. A half-pixie, half-mari infant. The Prime's baby.

Lyla's baby.

Unisa marches forth taking quick but mighty steps toward the two men. She catches the Prime's attention, who turns to her and smiles.

"Unisa! What a pleasant surprise! Look, you've come just in time. I'm a father." He tilts the infant in his arms slightly to show Unsia the face, but she doesn't even glance at the child, as she sprints down the hallway to Lyla's bedroom.

She opens the door so fast and so hard, she thinks she may have torn it off the hinges. Her entire body stiffens and bile rises up into her throat. The sight is so horrific, Unisa thinks she's stepped into a nightmare.

The stench of a number of bodily fluids and substances strikes her. Her knees shake as she steps forward to find Lyla on the bed. Every inch of the bedsheets has absorbed blood. There are towels and buckets of warm water everywhere, all red and dripping. It appears as if there had been, at one time, many people in this room, aiding in the delivery of the infant. But now that the baby is born, Lyla is alone.

She isn't wearing her nightgown. She isn't wearing anything. Her legs aren't bent in a birthing position any longer, they're stretched out, as if she's relaxing, but she isn't. Her expression is contorted in pain. Every bit of her cherry-blossom skin is now a translucent, sickly yellow-green.

Unisa rushes to the young girl and places her hands on the pixie's cheeks. Having *very* recently seen a dead body, the angi thinks for a moment that she might be too late, but Lyla's cheeks are still warm. When Unisa's fingers clutch the sides of the girl's face, she opens her eyes and they make eye contact.

"Unisa?"

It's the weakest voice the angi has ever heard. Lyla breaks into quiet sobs.

"I'm going to get help," Unisa says quickly, turning to race back to the salver, but Lyla's pleas stop her.

"No, don't leave me." Her voice is still strained, but her tone is unmistakable. She's terrified.

Unisa hardens her gaze and her tone. "Lyla, the salver is right down the hall. *Please.* I have to go get him. I'll be *right back.*"

With whatever little strength she has, the girl wraps her cold fingers around Unisa's wrists and sobs out, weaker than before, "Pl-please don't leave me."

Unisa bends forward and kisses the girl's forehead. "I won't leave you. I'm here, Lyla, please, I'm begging you, stay with me."

There are no tears in Unisa's eyes. There's nothing in her chest but sheer panic. Tunnel vision has set in like it never has before and her mind is empty of all thoughts but one.

Save Lyla.

Projecting as hard as she can, she screams at the top of her lungs. "SOMEBODY HELP!!!!!" She waits for a moment, still clutching Lyla's hand tightly, and screams again, "SOMEBODY!!! GET THE SALVER!!!"

She turns back to Lyla, whose eyes start to close, "Lyla, please, wake up. Please." She taps the girl's cheek and her eyes open again slightly. Unisa wishes she herself were a salver, but she has no idea what to do in a situation like this. "Lyla? Lyla, wake up!!"

There are footsteps behind her at the door and Unisa turns with a shred of hope in her heart. The young women and girls of the Inner Catacomb step into the room, lining up at the door and closing it behind them.

Unisa's jaw drops when she sees them standing there, calm, their expressions emotionless. "Don't just stand there! Go get the salver!"

Not a single one of them moves. Unisa wants to question them, but there's little time. She can ask them for an explanation later. If the salver won't come, and no one will help her, Unisa will have to take Lyla to the salver herself.

She quickly releases Lyla's hand, and wraps the pixie in the bedsheets, covering her still-bleeding body. The entire time she's whispering, begging. "Please, Lyla. Stay with me. We're going to get you help, okay? I just need you to stay with me, Lyla. *Please, please, please.*"

With all of the strength Unisa didn't even know she had, the angi lifts the bedsheet-wrapped pixie into her arms. She makes it three or four steps past the foot of the bed before she collapses from the weight.

Finally, as she sits on the floor on her knees, with Lyla dying in her arms, and the members of the Inner Catacomb watching expressionless, the tears start to come. There is no greater feeling of defeat in the world.

In a last ditch effort to save the pixie, the angi screams again through sobs. "PLEASE!!! ANYBODY!!!! I'M BEGGING YOU, PLEASE HELP HER!!! SOMEBODY SAVE HER!!!" She releases every ounce of rage and despair in her chest through her throat and into the air, as Lyla begins to gasp. It's the same gasps that Ora took a few days earlier.

Final breaths.

The bedroom door opens up and a small glimmer of hope reignites in Unisa's chest. Behind the line of young women and girls blocking the doorway, the Prime's face appears, still holding the infant. Unisa thinks he may have brought the salver to save Lyla.

But when she sees his irritated expression, she understands he isn't here to help.

"Please," Unisa begs. "Please, Great Prime. I'll do anything you ask. Please, just bring the salver."

The Prime's words are released with the coldness of an icy wind on a mountaintop. "If the salver could've saved her, he would have. He's tried everything, Unisa. Lyla is just not going to make it." He offers condolences. "I'm sorry."

Unisa's jaw drops. "Sh-she's still alive."

"Not for long." The three words linger in the air between them as Unisa loses herself in disbelief and sobs harder than before, her heart shattering. After a few moments, the Prime says his final words before closing the door. "Now keep it down or you'll wake the baby."

After he leaves, it isn't long before the women and girls of the Inner Catacomb follow. Unisa wraps Lyla tighter in the bedsheet to keep her warm, but it isn't much use. She can see the young pixie with the cherry-blossom cheeks slipping away.

"Lyla," she whispers, unsure what else to say. "I love you."

Miraculously, a soft, sad, scared smile curves the edges of Lyla's lips up slightly, and she says "Thank you" before her expression goes blank and her breaths become ragged. She chokes out the last ones in Unisa's arms, as a final tear breaks free from the corner of her eye.

Unisa sits with her for a long time, holding her as tightly as she can, imbuing as much love into her as she can. The girl's words from thirty-five days earlier echo in Unisa's ears like a broken record.

I didn't want this. I wanted to be a Librarian. He decided I would keep the pregnancy throughout the term, despite the risks that came with it to my health. I'm scared. I don't want my dreams to die. I don't want to die.

When Lyla's final breath escapes her lips, from a choice that was made for her, her dreams die, she dies, and something inside Unisa dies as well.

CHAPTER 52

"Hate and Anger"

Sovereign City-State *The Library*
Date *28th Day of Month 7, Year 1629 DG*

LYLA'S FUNERAL IS ALMOST AS tragic as her death. It's a spoonful of salt on an open wound, the greatest affront to Lyla's memory Unisa could've imagined.

The pixie's parents hadn't a clue how she would've wanted to make her Radiance-Return, how she'd want her funeral to go. Evidently, when they sold her into the Prime's custody, they hadn't planned for the possibility their teenage daughter may end up dying in childbirth. It was that very limited foresight that allowed them to sign her over to the Inner Catacomb in the first place.

Initially, Unisa feels terrible for having such thoughts. For holding such venom in her heart for parents who are likely grieving the young pixie as much as Unisa is. But she tosses the guilt aside the moment she sees them arrive at the funeral in the most expensive carriage she's ever seen, with two drivers, a doorman, and the finest attire stones can buy.

All funded by the Prime.

It takes everything in Unisa's power not to flap her wings over to them and wring their necks. But she resists.

Because they didn't know how Lyla would've wanted her Radiance-Return to go, and because Unisa had just buried a pixie four days earlier, they contacted the angi, requesting she organize the burial. Unisa was in utter shock to find them standing at her doorstep. They mentioned they got her address from the Prime.

By some miracle, the Prime approved additional time off for Unisa's bereavement, beyond what she had already requested for Ora. The same rituals and final rites she performed for her mother, four days later, Unisa performs them for Lyla.

Old wealth is often accompanied by grand cemeteries and mausoleums in which ancestors and descendants are buried together. However, because Lyla's family is newly endowed, they don't have a specific cemetery in which the tombs of their family are kept. So Unisa requested that Lyla be buried next to Ora.

They accepted.

A small fraction of Unisa's obliterated heart is mended knowing that these two pixies whom she loved so much will be here together, and she'll be here with them one day, as well. Lyla always wanted to meet Ora, but never got the chance. Ora wasn't in a state of mind to understand who Lyla was, but Unisa knows that, had they met while Ora's mind was healthy, she would've loved the pixie with the cherry-blossom cheeks as much as Unisa did.

And now Unisa can come and visit them here together.

The Prime and a couple of the young women from the Inner Catacomb attended the funeral as well; the two oldest women of the group, for whom it's socially acceptable to be seen with the Prime. The world never truly saw the Prime and Lyla together, so they didn't know about their relationship. They don't know about Lyla's child, whom the Prime is now caring for. But they know that the Prime had worked with the pixie as a mentor, and as a spiritual and academic guide.

As he makes a speech that, a year earlier, Unisa would've fawned over as everyone in attendance does, the angi clenches a fist and starts to flap her wings, ready to launch over to where he's standing, and punch his brains out.

But that would be a decision that lacks foresight. It would annihilate the entire plan and the Hawks would be for nothing. Juhi has foresight, so when Unisa's wings stretch out and flap once, she wraps her fingers around Unisa's wrist tightly. The angi turns to meet her gaze, and Juhi simply, slowly, shakes her head. Unisa retracts her wings tight against her back again.

After all of the funeral rites for Lyla's Radiance-Return have been completed, he and the two Inner Catacomb members depart. Then Lyla's parents do. Then everyone else does. Finally, Unisa and Juhi are the last two remaining at the grave.

Unisa stares down at the ink and paper name plate they placed over her. "Lyla." Somehow, it seems even more disrespectful than Ora's.

"You should take some time," Juhi says to her softly. "Away from the Hawks, away from work…maybe away from the Library."

For a moment, Unisa agrees with her, but then she thinks: *Where would I go?*

Rafael, Kyoko, and Ana are preparing for the Three Deaths. Should she go to war?

Saila and Naina are busy with their leadership duties in SunSide, and the country reminds her so much of the Library, it wouldn't be much of a vacation anyway.

And Unisa tries not to think about Salessa too often because she remembers no one's heard from the falcon in months and it terrifies her.

Unisa shakes her head. "Do you remember what you told me? What you've been telling me for months now?"

Juhi turns to meet her gaze.

"You wanted assurance that the people by your side are willing to kill for this cause. That, if you give your life for it, you'll be avenged."

"I still want that."

"You have it." The angi turns and begins the trek back to the Nest, growling over her shoulder, "Give me a fucking sword."

When they arrive at the Nest, Unisa marches straight to the box of weapons under the wooden table, ignoring the bewildered glances of Maksi, Konni, and the recruits, and arms herself with a blade.

As she bursts through the door separating her and the Cicada prisoner, she can hear Juhi grab a sword behind her as well. Brimah sees the sword in Unisa's hand, and the agonized fury in her expression, and his eyes widen. For the first time since his capture, he looks petrified.

Unisa steps quickly behind him and places the sword against his throat. He's already told them about the detention center where the Fully Broken are being held; where her future army is awaiting her. But he's only mentioned its existence, not its location.

"Tell me, Brimah," she demands. "Where are the Fully Broken being kept?"

"U-unisa, just w-wait." He stumbles over his words in panic. Juhi arrives and closes the door behind her so the two Hawks have privacy with the prisoner.

Unisa presses the blade harder against his skin, breaking through and drawing blood. "I will slit your fucking throat. Where are the Fully Broken?"

"Fuck!" Brimah groans. "I don't know, Unisa."

"You have five seconds," Unisa announces, before starting the countdown. "Five…four…three…two…"

"It's in the Prime's office!"

The room falls silent.

Unisa leans in. "What?"

"I don't know the location, but it's written on a document in a safe that's under the Prime's desk. In his office."

Unisa's gaze meets Juhi's and they nod. It isn't the exact information they needed, but it's enough.

The events that follow occur in such rapid succession, Unisa doesn't even realize what's happened until it's too late. Once again, Brimah displays the unparalleled training of the Cicadas. The angi man throws his head backward into Unisa's nose, knocking the sword out of her hand. It drops and he deftly catches it despite his wrists still being bound. With a quick flick, he slices through the ropes and frees himself.

In a fraction of a second, the Cicada goes from bound and bleeding at the throat, to lunging at Unisa, sword in hand. Juhi acts quickly, charging Brimah from behind. Unisa sees the end of her blade break through Brimah's chest, as she stabs him from the rear, and he falls limp. Unisa moves quickly to the side as blood explodes from Brimah's mouth and his body drops.

The angi sits down on the ground, bringing her knees to her chest. After a moment of silence, she breaks into sobs. Juhi is at her side, looking over her face and body.

"Are you hurt? Are you alright?" The hawk continues to search for injuries all over Unisa's body until the angi speaks.

"W-why can't I do this?" she asks. "Even when I hold so much hate and anger in my heart for the Prime, and the Cicadas, and for everything we oppose. I still can't hold my own in a real battle. What's wrong with me?"

Juhi places her hand on Unisa's cheek and guides the angi's gaze to her own. She speaks in a steady, but empathetic tone.

"There is *nothing* wrong with you. No matter how much hate and anger exist in your heart, you don't just wake up one day and become an executioner. That's the only reason I've been stressing to you, this entire time, that you *have to* start training. You have to be ready for violence. Not because I want bloodshed. Not because I'm hoping for it. But because it is undeniably, unquestionably inevitable. One day, you will need to kill, if for no other reason than your own survival."

She turns Unisa's hand over, palm-up, and places the hilt of the sword in it, then closes Unisa's fingers around it. "One day, you will have to make the difficult choice of taking someone's life, Unisa."

CHAPTER 53

"Past and Future"

***Theocracy** SunSide*
***Date** Unknown*

"I DON'T MEAN TO SOUND arrogant," the male Sprite says, examining the memory of the moment they were released from their imprisonment, "but we have come a long way."

"We certainly have, Brother," the female agrees. She turns to Naina, piercing through the wolf with her icy blue gaze. "You were quite disgusted when you saw us emerge."

"If I remember correctly," the male adds, "you vomited."

He saunters to the three crystal thrones and takes a seat to Naina's left, while the female Sprite sits on the throne to her right.

She's sandwiched between the entities who threaten the world, yet they radiate diplomatic sophistication.

The female leans closer to the wolf, causing Naina to shift with unease. "Don't worry. We forgive you." She reveals sharp teeth with a crooked smile, then continues. "It took some time before we were able to build back enough strength to heal. We feasted on forty generations of essences."

The male Sprite looks down at the second pair of arms extruding from the sides of their torsos. "Couldn't seem to rid ourselves of the demon's arms, though." He locks eyes with Naina. "Tell me, little wolf. What answers do you seek?"

Naina hesitates, wondering if she's being led into some kind of trap. She takes a deep breath and cautiously asks, "When will the Three Deaths be released? What's your plan?"

"The first question is an easy one," the female states flippantly. She closes her eyes and utters an incantation. *"Nibera Libera, Ha Daemonia Faelonia, Furusi Ne Lupusi."* Her eyelids part and light bursts from her eye sockets. When she speaks again, her voice echoes all around the void. "You…are…free."

Her eyes close again, and then she turns back to Naina with an expression of satisfaction. "The portal to the demon plane is opened, and the Three Deaths are now released onto Aerthomni. You're welcome, puppy."

Naina's heart sinks. *It can't be.*

"As for our plan," the male begins, "you wouldn't understand what we want, without first knowing what we've lost."

He whispers an incantation and images flash all around her, depicting what the Sprite dictates. "Let's go back over three millennia. My name is Kova. And this is my sister, Elva."

Elva winks at Naina.

Kova continues. "Our parents were the rulers of the largest Sprite tribe, on the continent you now call Panaerth."

The image of two smiling Sprites, a male and a female, clad in lush robes and crystal crowns, appears in the void. Their hands are raised, waving from a stage to a cheering crowd. "Their intention was for me, as their male heir, to succeed them, but when I was a young boy, I fell gravely ill."

"Our parents never called a healer," Elva takes over. "They believed that if Kova's body wasn't strong enough to fight off this ailment on its own, he wasn't worthy. That they would leave it to the gods to decide if he should survive or not. I disagreed and, despite my own youth, learned what I could from old texts and conversations with the healers to save his life."

"Elva came to my aid in ways no god ever did. Once I'd healed, and had returned to my parents' side as their heir, I realized there's no one in this world I could depend on more than my sister. No one who cared about me as much as she did. And this realization was proven correct when, in my late teens, the ailment returned."

The image around them changes to one of a younger Kova, a sickly teen with blood dripping from his nostrils.

Elva sighs and looks solemnly down at her hands, folded in her lap. "With this second bout of illness, our parents grew certain that their gods were trying to remove Kova from the line of succession. They locked him in a dungeon and turned their backs, waiting for him to rot out of existence. When I found out, I returned home from the healer's academy before my training was complete, to find him malnourished and forgotten, clinging to life by a frayed thread."

To her own surprise, Naina's heart breaks for him.

"For the second time, Elva nursed me back to health. Our parents had hoped she would become the Chief Healer of the tribe. Instead, she forsook the remainder of her education to care for me. When we rose from that dungeon, we found a new heir at my parents' side."

Elva scoffs. "The son of a servant. A boy whose sole responsibility had been to clean the latrine pits after we'd used them. In the three years that I spent at the academy, our father had turned him into a sorcerer and promised him the throne in our place."

"I pleaded with my father to drop his foolishness." Kova's tone hardens, mixing anger with desperate supplication. "I reminded him that we were his blood. Asked him how he could insult us in this way, when the boy was nothing more than a servant. And that's" — he pauses, breathing deeply, composing himself — "when he said it."

Elva grits her teeth as she repeats the words her father uttered to Kova three thousand years earlier. "'He may be a servant, but at least he's healthy.'"

Naina gasps, her hand rising involuntarily to cover her mouth.

"I'm not sure what came over me when I heard him say that. I massacred the boy, and then my parents. The moment I wore my father's crown, and Elva donned my mother's, we knew we did the right thing. We had become the rulers of the tribe."

An image flashes around them of Kova and Elva atop a ridge, looking down at a city at the bottom of a canyon. Naina nearly gasps at how different they looked without the additional pair of arms, without the fangs. When there was nothing but hope and triumph in their expressions.

They were enchanting.

"The ruler of the second-largest Sprite tribe was a mage named Vala." An image of another Sprite with gold-colored skin and orange eyes circles in the void around them.

"You mentioned her," Naina says. "In Red-Lo's memory, after your release, you mentioned getting your revenge against Vala."

Kova nods. "We warred for ages. And then one day, it occurred to us that bloodshed was primitive. Pointless. We needed a political alliance. Together, we could conquer all of the Sprites."

"So that's what we did," Elva recounts. "We gave Vala the option to choose Kova or myself as a marital partner, and she chose Kova."

"Vala and I wed, and the three of us became the rulers of the joint tribe. Over time, through countless conquests, we built the Great Sprite Empire, ruling it as the Emperor Mage and the Empress Mages."

"You were all mages?" Naina asks.

Kova nods. "Our culture exalted those who excelled at energy manipulation. Magic, as some call it. The glorious, 'Mage,' title was bestowed on us."

"Shortly after the formation of the Empire, Kova's childhood illness returned for a third time."

An image of Kova lying in bed, his skin dull and translucent, floats around them.

He sighs. "Naively, I had thought that my wife would entrust the Empire and its governance to Elva, leaving the throne to come to my bedside and care for me. I was wrong. While I suffered and deteriorated, Vala proved to be no better than my parents."

Venom seeps into Elva's words. "She starved him of affection in moments we all thought were his last. When she refused to leave her throne, I left mine to care for Kova."

Kova's deep gaze locks with Elva's. "While Vala kept the truth of my illness hidden from our subjects, allowing rumors of abdication to flourish, Elva saved me again. It became clear that no one would ever love me as much as she does. No one, through my entire life, had ever cared about me, except for Elva. Not even my wife."

He turns back to Naina. "The more time we spent together, and the more starved I grew for affection, the more the lines blurred between us. I realized that Elva is all I've ever had. All I ever *will* have. Despite our efforts to stop it, our sibling love evolved into something more."

Elva smiles. "Romance. Intimacy. One that Vala witnessed when she finally decided to leave her precious throne long enough to check on her husband's condition."

Kova taps his chin with his finger. "I believe the words she used were, 'depraved,' and 'deviant.' How dare she?" His fingers ball tightly into a fist. "How dare she condemn us for crossing a boundary, when it was her negligence that blurred the line and pushed us over it?"

"Our magic had grown one-hundred-fold since we began our relations. It was the evolution of our love that magnified our power."

Kova sighs. "And then we invited her to join us in bed, and share in that love. That power." He locks eyes with Naina. "I'm sure you can guess how that went."

"I'd imagine, not well," Naina remarks.

"Correct," Elva says with a nod. "She told the entire tribe what she'd discovered, but she omitted the truth that her failure as a wife drove us together. And when we tried to explain, none but a small group of followers remained loyal. The entire Empire turned against us the moment Vala's great betrayal left her lips."

"We and our followers were banished from the Empire. Vala's deceptions kept the Sprites ignorant to the fact that, despite the enhancements to our magic, my health hadn't fully returned. She was named the Oasis Mage, the highest honor, and became the sole empress."

An image of Vala, wearing the same silver crown that Kova and Elva don now as they sit beside Naina, flashes around them.

Elva continues. "We didn't seek vengeance after the banishment. Only a permanent cure. Vala's usurping of our Empire depleted us of salvers, treatments, resources."

"So we reached out to alternative forms of magic. We tethered this realm to the demon plane and begged them to cure me, which they did. But then they demanded remittance."

"We had nothing to give them, Naina. Vala and her lies had taken everything from us. So we promised the demons the one thing we had to offer: our birthright. The Empire we had built before Vala stripped it from us."

"It was a glorious bloodbath." As he speaks, the images circling the void around them depict a violent struggle, Sprites against demons, under a crimson sky. "All the magic and sorcery of the Sprite Empire couldn't hold the demons back from victory. And as we stood atop that ridge, watching them regain what we lost, Elva and I realized we did, in fact, thirst for vengeance. Retribution. Their surrender was within our grasp when Vala imprisoned us."

"Our followers discovered the location of the prison, but Vala cursed it so they couldn't free us. Instead, they etched guidance into a text that Red-Lo eventually found. He came to us seeking immortality, and in return, we fed on the essences of his descendants. Regained our strength."

Kova takes a deep breath. "Now, we can answer your question. Our plan?"

Elva places her hand, almost affectionately, on Naina's knee, causing the wolf to shudder. "It's very simple, little wolf. Once the Three Deaths have had their fill, and we've sent them back, the surviving citizens of this continent will submit before us out of fear."

"You see," Kova adds through gritted teeth, "an empire is owed to us, just as our parents' tribe was. We pried it from their dead fingers, and we're happy to do the same here on Aerthomni if you stand in our way."

"Aerthomni didn't take your Empire from you," Naina challenges them. "The citizens of this continent have no place in your conquest of vengeance against Vala."

Kova's eyes narrow. "They didn't, but our imprisonment has delivered us to a time when Vala is long dead and Panaerth is a wasteland. We are owed conquest and Aerthomni is all that's left to conquer. Is it unfair? Perhaps, but inequity is a natural quality of existence. Trust me, I know that better than anyone. Your anger should be with Vala for postponing our conquest, not with us for taking what is rightfully ours."

Naina growls. "The Twins will stop you."

"The Twins!" Elva cries out. "So we've heard. They hallucinated victory against us." She turns to the wolf, her gaze solid. "Salessa is on a quest to learn how to resurrect them, isn't she?"

"You must stop her, Naina," Kova urges her. "Elva and I can give you anything. A small, peaceful corner of MoonSide for you and Salessa, where no one will trouble you again. But if you act on this juvenile prophecy—the One Myth—none of the Saviors Six will survive."

Naina raises an eyebrow. "The Saviors Six?"

Elva shakes her head patronizingly. "You don't know much about your own prophecy, do you? The Twins will have four allies on the battlefield, pup. But they will all die." She smiles wickedly. "We have foresight into possible futures. Visions of the many potential outcomes of this war. We see them in dreams, and we've assured our own victory."

"How?" Naina questions them.

"We've already begun breaking one of the Saviors Six down," Kova boasts. "We poisoned her mother's mind."

Naina rises to her feet and backs up from them. "Feathers."

Elva nods. "Her mother is gone. Unisa will continue to break."

"The Saviors Six will all break, Naina," Kova threatens. "Unless you agree to forfeit the resurrection, and accept us as Emperor and Empress."

Naina's fists clench. Rage builds inside her and bursts from her fingers, as she leaps forward. She may not be able to shift, but she can still strangle.

By the time her hands reach Elva's throat, the Sprites, and the thrones on which they sit, vanish. Naina spins, surrounded by nothing but endless white void. She's alone?

No. Off in the distance, maybe yards, maybe miles away, Elva and Kova sit watching her on the crystal thrones. They've transported her, in the blink of an eye, to a distant area of the void.

Elva tugs at the air and, as if an invisible rope is tied around Naina's neck, the wolf is dragged to the ground, choking as she's pulled by her throat back to where the Sprites sit. Gasping for air, Naina's hands reach for the invisible tether, but they find nothing. Nothing to stop the choking.

She finally reaches the Sprites and her body is lifted into the air, paralyzed, hovering before Elva's outstretched fingertips. The Sprite whispers yet another incantation, just as the wolf begins to lose consciousness, and Naina's breath returns to her.

She isn't hovering anymore. The wolf is sitting on the crystal throne between the Sprites again, as if she'd never even moved.

"You stopped strangling me," Naina comments, her fingers softly searching around her throat for remnants of the invisible rope.

"Did we strangle you at all?" Elva questions. "Or did I perform an incantation that changed your perception of reality? Did I make you *believe* you were experiencing something that didn't really happen?"

"You see, Naina," Kova says, leaning forward, "we have power you can't even imagine."

She sits silently, processing what she's experienced, and all that they've told her about their lives, until there's nothing remaining on her tongue but a single question. "If you are so powerful, why haven't you killed any of us yet?"

Elva smiles. "The little wolf has learned to ask the right questions."

"Indeed, Sister." Kova turns to Naina. "The Saviors Six must die on the battlefield. If we kill any of you before that day, all futures lead to our failure."

Elva locks her gaze with Naina's, pouring her words with sincerity. "But we can still take from you, Naina. Anything and anyone. You've seen what we're capable of. Surrender."

Naina shakes her head. She's always been a fighter. "The Twins will be resurrected. The Saviors Six will be brought together. And you will die."

"Don't be foolish. This world gathers its little armies to face the Three Deaths, terrified and unprepared. How will it withstand a battle against us?"

Naina raises her chin. "The Three Deaths. You. We will conquer all."

Elva narrows her eyes, and a wicked half-smile twists her expression. "If you will not *surrender* Aerthomni, perhaps you will *gamble* it."

Naina pauses, hesitates. "What kind of gamble?"

"A game. A wager. I don't believe this world will conquer the Three Deaths. But if it does, we will reward you with a decade."

Kova smiles, pleased. "Excellent idea. If the Three Deaths are killed, we will give you a decade to resurrect the Twins, and to gather the Saviors Six. If they are not, then our conquest begins immediately."

Naina opens her mouth to agree to their wager when the Ancient Ones abruptly become frantic, rising from their thrones to search the void wildly. Naina follows, but she doesn't sense whatever has caught their attention.

Kova growls. "You feel that, too, Elva?"

"I do," Elva says.

"What is it?" Naina asks.

Kova spins, his gaze searching the white void. Then he stops and his eyes widen. "It's her."

CHAPTER 54

"PAIN AND PLEASURE"

Alphocracy *MoonSide*
Date *28th Day of Month 7, Year 1629 DG*

STUDY SESSIONS ENRAPTURE SALESSA, THE energy transfer rituals bring her to life. Everything at Lover's Plateau is more intense now than it once was.

The texts jump to life for her, images and visions flashing through her mind like she's reading through pictures. She feels the energy in her bones and her blood, and she connects with Afzal more deeply through their newly-formed telepathic connection.

Silhouettes continue to plague their visions. Of the Sprites. Of the six warriors on the defensive side of the battlefield. None but the Twins can be identified.

Lexona grows envious of the falcon's telepathy with Afzal. Despite the boulder of guilt in her chest, Salessa thinks it would be unwise not to foster the connection simply to spare Lexona's feelings. She hopes to forge something similar with the serpent, but what exists with Afzal should be built up to match the strength of her telepathic connection to Naina.

And for the moment, Afzal is very much filling the void in her mind that the distance with Naina created.

As Salessa starts to get ready for bed, after a long day of studying and rituals, there's a knock at her bedroom door. It's late at night and she isn't expecting anyone. A small jolt of curious apprehension sizzles to life in her chest. She rises from the bed and opens the door to find Lexona behind it.

"Lexona?" she says, eyebrows scrunched together. "Is everything alright?"

Lexona nods, her gaze lowered. She speaks almost sheepishly. "Can I come in? I wanted to talk to you about something."

Salessa's heart sinks. Good news rarely follows these words. "Of course." She moves to the side to allow Lexona entry. The serpent takes a seat at the foot of Salessa's bed, bending forward, resting her elbows on her knees.

Salessa takes a seat next to her. "What's wrong?"

The serpent sits upright and takes a deep breath. "You've been spending a lot of time with Afzal and Zoya." It isn't an accusation; she states it as a fact.

Salessa raises an eyebrow. "I have."

Lexona pauses.

"What is it, Lexona? Tell me."

The serpent is quiet for so long, Salessa thinks she may have decided against relaying her thoughts after all. But eventually, she speaks.

"I had the idea that, with all Zoya does for us, she deserves a Devotion Ceremony."

Salessa's eyes widen, as her chest brims with excitement. She lets out a short laugh and claps her hands together. "That's wonderful! I had the same idea weeks ago, after I first arrived. Zoya is more devoted to the Twins than anyone."

Instinctively, Salessa's excitement drives her forth to embrace Lexona, who wraps her arms around the falcon. They hold each other for a few seconds before Salessa pulls away. As she does, Lexona holds onto her and their faces hover in the air, nearly nose-to-nose.

It could've been a single second that their faces were this close to each other, gazes locked, breathing heavy, bodies entangled. Or it could've been a lifetime. Salessa loses all sense of time as a lightning bolt of pleasure shoots through Lexona's gaze and into Salessa's body, erupting a warmth in her core.

Before she can react, Lexona's lips are tight against hers. It's a kiss erected on a foundation of three years of longing, and weeks of intimate energy flowing between them. Lingering looks, small touches, warm embraces, and then the final nose-to-nose gaze that broke the dam to allow something powerful, undeniable, and irresistible to flow around them. The serpent and the falcon kiss again, and again, as Salessa accepts all of the intensity in Lexona's lips and her thin, flicking serpentine tongue.

Lexona leads the dance. She breaks from the kiss to guide Salessa by the hands, around the bed and onto her back. The serpent lies down next to her, so close that her mouth is directly over Salessa's.

And then the kiss resumes with all the passion with which it began. Salessa is drowning in the ecstasy of having regained something she'd lost so long ago. The boundless joy of being able to love someone who loves deeply in return. She kisses Lexona with a fervor that makes up for all of the kisses they've lost over the past three years.

Not just on her lips, but she finds the patches of leathery serpentine scales on her cheek, down her neck, and along her collarbone, and kisses her there, too. She gently traces the fangs inside Lexona's mouth with her tongue.

While her hands remain wrapped around the serpent, Salessa can feel one of Lexona's move to the elastic waistband of her shalwar, and slip under it. Salessa's breath hitches as she realizes what's happening.

She isn't ready.

Her hand flies down and catches Lexona's wrist. She smiles and shakes her head. "Kiss me. That's it for now." She presses her lips against Lexona's again and they continue for some time before Lexona's hand again slips under the waistband, and Salessa catches her wrist again.

"Lexona, please," she whispers into the serpent's mouth.

Lexona kisses her again, and then pulls back and says, "We've waited so long for this. We deserve it. Please, don't take this from us."

Salessa meets her gaze and there's a moment of war within her. Her mind begs her to stop where they are, knowing there are stairs she isn't ready to ascend, while the aching heat in her core insists she grow wings and soar with Lexona's desire.

Her heart is torn through the center between the two.

She shakes her head, "Lexona, I-I don't know."

"Trust me," Lexona says. "This is what we need. Please, Salessa."

"Lexona, I—"

Lexona kisses her more passionately than before, diverting Salessa's attention from her slithering hand. It finds its target.

Salessa gasps so loudly she thinks others may hear. "Lexona, wait!" She starts to rise, but Lexona, stronger than her, gently wraps her fingers around Salessa's throat, presses her lips to Salessa's and pushes her back down.

"Don't make me beg," she breathes between kisses, removing her hand from the falcon's neck and slipping it back down to where it was. "I need this. You need this. Stop thinking for two seconds and just feel."

The kissing doesn't stop. The attention Lexona gives between Salessa's legs doesn't stop. The falcon accepts what's happening quietly, continuing to kiss Lexona and drowning deeper into the confusion cast forth between her mind and her moans. The sounds she makes are exactly what Lexona is looking for, but everything behind them begs for Salessa to put an end to it.

"Call me 'Lexi' again," Lexona begs. "Please."

Obeying the instruction, Salessa moans out "Lexi" and Lexona releases a moan herself, kissing Salessa even more passionately than before.

"Again."

"Lexi!"

Lexona releases another moan, louder. "I've waited so long to hear that in your voice."

The serpent's service brings Salessa to a heightened climax, the falcon's first one in her life. As they continue to kiss, Lexona presses her fingers into Salessa.

"You enjoyed yourself," she comments. "I love you."

Salessa, arms still wrapped around the serpent, freezes and whispers back what she knows Lexona wants to hear. "I love you, too."

They lay this way, Lexona on Salessa, limbs entwined, silent. Salessa thinks the serpent may have fallen asleep but she herself lies awake, staring at the ceiling, somehow feeling the throbbing ache of pleasure and the burdensome disgust of invasion simultaneously.

Finally, Lexona rises, kisses Salessa a final time, and exits. After she's gone, Salessa sits up on the bed, her back resting against the headboard. She brings her knees to her chest and her vision blurs with tears. A battle continues to rage inside of her: the mind that cries out in pain, against the aching pleasure in her core.

Her heart remains torn, still.

She sits this way, tears streaming from her cheeks until she hears something in the bathing area, as if someone is there behind the curtain. Salessa wipes her cheeks dry and clears her stiff throat, hiding her weeping.

"Lexona?" she calls out with a broken, distressed voice.

From behind the curtain, a familiar face steps forth. Deep purple cheeks, gray eyes, and pointed ears.

"Zakia," Salessa addresses her. She looks exactly as Salessa remembers her from the year prior.

The purple pixie strides through the room and sits next to Salessa on the bed. "I've missed you."

"I've missed you, too," Salessa admits. "This must be another vision. I had one of Ray-Mi a few weeks ago."

"And what did he tell you?"

Salessa swallows and wipes her eyes again, making certain they're completely dry. "To give Lexona a chance to atone. To forgive her the way we forgave him."

Zakia tilts her head curiously. "And did you forgive her?"

Salessa nods.

"Then maybe I'm here to give you some guidance as well."

The falcon smiles. "What guidance do you have for me?"

Zakia's spirit drops her gaze for a moment, pondering, before she raises her gray eyes and smiles. She reaches forward and places a hand affectionately on Salessa's cheek. "It wasn't supposed to happen this way. And that isn't your fault."

Tears break from Salessa's eyes again, and the sobs return, as Zakia sits with her, quietly allowing her time. Finally, Salessa whispers, "I never got to properly say goodbye to you."

Zakia smiles. "Then say goodbye now."

Salessa takes a deep breath. "I will never forget you. Goodbye, Zakia."

The vision smiles and fades away, leaving Salessa alone again. The war continues, pain against pleasure, mind against body.

And a heart, still torn between the two.

CHAPTER 55:

"STONE AND FIRE"

***Court Democracy** EverEmber*
***Date** 28th Day of Month 7, Year 1629 DG*

THE ENCAMPMENT PLANS HIGHLIGHT THE isolated area along that coast that the Court designated for the defense efforts. Kyoko and Ovida, leaning over the plans laid out on a table, examine with frustration.

"They want us out of sight," Kyoko growls through gritted teeth. "Like children told to play outside."

"We need more weapons," Ovida adds. "A fortress. Warships. Not temporary installations on a closed-off public beach. The Court was willing to inconvenience anyone but tourists."

Kyoko shifts her gaze to a map of EverEmber. "The Death can come from any side."

As she assesses the most probable direction from which the beast would come, Ovida taps the tanto sheathed to the igni's hip, and chuckles. "You tried to attack me with that once."

Memories of her journey with Rafael from the previous year flood Kyoko's mind; the journey that led them to SunSide where she met the General of the Revolutionary Forces.

She turns to Ovida. "I tried to *defend myself* with it. You had just blown up a carriage we were in and nearly killed Rafael."

"I never apologized for that."

"It was a long time ago. I wouldn't want you to feel remorseful. Nothing was lost, but"—she puts her hand on Ovida's shoulder—"so much was gained."

Ovida gestures to the badge of the New SunSidian Guard on her breastplate. "It's different. Leading an underground revolution and leading an organized, formal military. I felt confident about how I handled the former. Not so confident about the latter."

Kyoko is taken aback by her candor. "You're an excellent commander, you know that. The Revolutionary Forces respected you, as do the Guard. And Symin respected you."

A smile widens on Ovida's face, touching her pointed ears. "Rafael told me you were hesitant to take on these duties. To lead these soldiers on this mission. But they respect you just as much as the Guard respect me."

Kyoko's gaze falls to her shoulder.

Ovida continues. "The fire I saw in you, on that day last year, that's the Kyoko who leads these warriors today. Nothing"—she gestures to Kyoko's injury—"can put those flames out."

Kyoko smiles and nods gratefully, internalizing the praise, hoping to live up to the respect of her colleagues and subordinates. She turns back to the map to continue evaluating the many pathways from which the Death can arrive.

And then, it hits her.

She lifts the small metal marker she placed on the map and moves it to sit directly on Mount Mother. "Ana's translation implied it would enter our realm *through* EverEmber, not *to* it."

"What do you mean?" Ovida asks.

Kyoko opens her mouth to elaborate when her gaze catches the marker rattling on the paper. She picks it up, examines it for defects and then places it back onto the map. It continues.

"What's wrong?"

The ground trembles beneath her. The rattling grows harsher. "Do you feel that?"

Ovida's eyes widen as the rattling intensifies further. Items on a shelf nearby fall off and shatter on the ground.

Ana enters the tent. "Kyoko! Ovida! We need you out here, now!"

The two generals simultaneously draw swords—Kyoko with her uninjured hand—and follow Ana out of the tent. The encampment is abuzz with soldiers gathering to catch the sight.

The volcano at the center of EverEmber appears active, after having spent millennia dormant. It roars so loudly, the entire island shivers beneath it. Warriors, salvers, and laborers alike grab onto as many stable pieces of infrastructure as they can to remain steady, but it's of no use. Cracks start to form as the very stone they stand on shatters like glass.

They can hear screams from the townsfolk and villagers at the base of Mount Mother. People hurriedly scurrying like ants around a hill of dirt. If the volcano erupts, all three islands would be doomed. No one is safe. But in the moments that follow, it becomes clear that Mount Mother isn't erupting.

Something is coming out of it.

A single thought races through Kyoko's mind. One day, she is going to talk about what she witnessed here. And no one is going to believe her. *She* can barely believe what she's seeing. The mouth of the volcano cracks into jagged boulders that, from the rumbling and trembling, fall down the sides of Mount Mother and land at the base.

We have to evacuate the area, she thinks.

An object appears from the mouth. Black, stone, pyramidal in shape. It rises slowly from inside until Kyoko realizes what she's looking at.

An avian beak, pointed up at the sky. The beak lowers to reveal the head of a massive stone bird, adorned with shimmering emerald eyes that stare back at them.

"Is that—" Ana begins.

"Yes," Kyoko answers her before she can get the question out. "It's a swan."

After the head erupts from the volcano, a long neck covered in sharp fins appears, followed by a round body and gargantuan wings. The entire swan is made of stone plates, like armor, with glowing orange lava flowing in the cracks between them. It roars loudly; a piercing cry that forces everyone to cover their ears, then opens its mouth to project lava from its throat and onto the buildings below.

More screams follow from the innocents around Mount Mother. Ana and Ovida turn to Kyoko.

"On your command, General," Ovida says to her.

"Raise me up!" Kyoko commands. The Mega uses the Radiance to slowly raise Kyoko up into the air, where most of the warriors from around the encampment can see her.

"Igni!" she yells, and every warrior, exoskeletons and pointed ears alike, stand at attention. "Death has come for your Mother! Prove your fidelity to her!" She points to the volcano and releases a bellowing battle cry. "SEND! IT! BAAACK!"

Every warrior in the encampment raises a weapon into the air and cries out.

"Companies One through Seventeen, evacuate everyone in the vicinity, around the base of Mount Mother." The group of warriors rushes out of the encampment to follow the order. "Companies Eighteen through Twenty, assist the salvers in assembling their triage centers closer to the battlefield." The soldiers grunt in affirmation and do as they're told.

Kyoko addresses those remaining around her. "Companies Twenty-One to Fifty, all of you"—she turns to the stone swan, still rampaging around the base of the island, regurgitating lava at civilians—"bring me its head."

The remaining warriors charge forth from the beaches, collapsing into the island and heading straight for the volcano. Ovida lowers Kyoko, then withdraws her own weapon and charges with the rest.

Kyoko draws the tanto from the sheath, tightens her injured arm in the sling, and follows behind the charging military.

"You're going to fight?" Ana asks, her tone dripping with concern.

Kyoko responds, continuing forth, "I'm going to do whatever I can. Fight. Strategize. Lead."

"Kyoko, wait! The swan is made of stone and fire."

The igni stops and turns back around to face Ana, a smile on her face. "So am I."

***Continent of Panaerth** Nysabaan Desert*
***Date** 28th Day of Month 7, Year 1629 DG*

"THIS IS THE HOTTEST PLACE on the planet," the Mega guide states. "I've brought you this far, but even I don't go any farther. And I'm not mari."

Rafael nods, stepping down from a stone ridge to the cliff where the guide stands. He pulls the head covering he's wearing further forward, hoping to shade more of his face and protect it from the sand in the wind. His loose, beige top waves with the mountain breezes, and his protective boots snuggle tightly against his toes.

The outfit is a far cry from the disrobing that accompanies a swim.

"I appreciate your guidance. I'm not sure I would've been able to navigate the FeatherKnife Mountains without it."

"Well"—the guide laughs and taps the three brimming pouches on his hip—"I've never been paid this much for one expedition before, so I couldn't refuse." His smile fades. "Sincerely, I don't think you should do this. Whatever you're trying to do here can't be worth more than your life. You're going to roast out there."

It is worth more than his life. The lives of innocents hang in the balance. And this journey can save them. The guide departs and Rafael continues down from the mountains and into the dunes.

Alone.

The scorching heat is immediate. The suns rule overhead, like tyrannical monarchs beating the citizens down into the sand. As far as he looks, dunes and desolation are all he sees. There's no right, no left, no forward, no backward, no up, no down.

Just sand, all sand.

He's meticulous with the limited water he's packed with him. It won't be enough if he gets lost, but if he does find an oasis, if such a place exists, he hopes it'll come before the sand claims him.

Wind kicks up unexpectedly and pricks Rafael's face. Tiny needles. His hand pulls the head covering over his mouth and nare slits until it dies down. A small respite until the next one pops up unannounced. The winds are cunning and cruel. They time these outbursts with enough distance to lull Rafael into a false sense of security before battering him again.

At some point, the dunes disappear, but the aridity remains on cracked, dead soil, made up of clay and compacted minerals. Towering stone walls birth canyons through which Rafael continues his travels. The environment is unforgiving. Despite his periodic sips, his throat grows dryer. His fins crack, his lips bleed.

The world grows hazy around him.

Animals exist here. True animals, not Doruh. Hyena pups roam, their mother nearby. Scorpions trickle about as Rafael avoids them. Ibex atop the stone outcroppings. And meerkats searching for food, trying to survive. He doesn't know everything about deserts, but he knows it certainly hasn't rained here in months.

It feels like hours on his feet when he finally drops to his knees, collapsing on the wavering ground beneath him. At first he thinks it may be some natural disaster trembling the soil, but when he pulls out every container and flask he's packed and finds them empty, he realizes the unsteadiness, the disaster, is likely internal.

He's reaching the end of his limits, sitting on his knees on this dry, hard ground, in the middle of a landscape he has no business visiting, searching for a destination that likely doesn't exist.

It's time to go home, he thinks. *The Temple of the Oasis Mage is long gone. Vala is unreachable.*

This was pointless.

As he swivels his head around in circles, trying to figure out which way he came, to begin the journey home, he sees something. The only thing he's seen, in what feels like ages, that isn't made of stone or living under it.

It's far, and the heat radiating from the dry soil makes it wave unsteadily, but when he squints, he recognizes the glint of metal. It's circular, with something shimmering within. His eyeballs nearly pop from their sockets when he recognizes it.

It's a fountain.

He nearly cries out in relief, but his throat is so dry that no sound erupts. He pushes himself onto his feet, but his legs tremble and he drops face first onto the scorching ground. With what little strength he has left, he digs his forearm fins into the cracks of the soil and drags himself toward it.

Is this the Oasis of the Sprites? Have I found it? he thinks as his body scrapes along what feels like stone and fire.

He reaches the fountain and pulls his upper body onto the ledge. Had he the strength, he would've flung himself into it. Breathed the cool, shimmering water into his gills. But all he can do is cup his hands and dip them under the surface.

His cupped hands fill up with liquid life, and he brings them quickly to his lips, but just before he can sip, he hears it. A sound.

A familiar voice.

He turns to his left and lying on the ground, with her back against the fountain wall, is Kyoko. She's unwell, looking more dehydrated than Rafael feels. Her stone exoskeleton is cracked and bloody.

"Rafa," she whispers, clearly unable to speak much from her exhaustion and malnourishment. "I need water, Rafa."

Rafael nods and, without thinking, brings the water from his trembling, cupped hands down to her lips. As she drinks and regains her strength, he remains confused.

How did she get here? I came on this journey alone.

When she finishes drinking, she meets his gaze and begs, "I need a little more."

He nods and brings his cupped hands back to the water, filling them and turning back to Kyoko. But when he returns to her, she isn't there. Someone else lies in her place. An elderly, igni man Rafael doesn't recognize.

A complete stranger.

Who is he? Where did he come from? Where did Kyoko go?

"Help me, young man," the man whispers through withered lips. "I need water."

The man grows blurry as Rafael's vision starts to fade. "I will help you, but I need to drink first."

"No," the man shakes his head, "give it to me first, or I'll die."

Rafael looks from the water in his cupped hands to the dying man, then back again. He's torn between the heat oppressing his fading consciousness and the pleas of a dying stranger. Though no tears form, Rafael is weeping from the agony of decision.

But in the end, there is only one right answer.

He leans forward to feed the water to the elderly man, but before the igni can even drink, the world goes dark and Rafael's consciousness gives out.

The last thing he remembers is landing hard on stone and fire.

CHAPTER 56

"The Warrior and the Traveler"

Court Democracy *EverEmber*
Date *28th Day of Month 7, Year 1629 DG*

FRESH OXYGEN FILLS THE AIR bubble around Kyoko's head, finding its way into Kyoko's lungs when she inhales. She presses her back against a stone wall that once supported housing, but is now reduced to a pile of rubble with a mound of cooled lava on top. Her face and armor are covered in blood, sweat, and soot, the stench of burning stone and flesh polluting the air.

"Is it working?" Ovida asks, catching her breath beside the igni.

Kyoko nods. "I can breathe now."

"Good. I gave the order to every soldier left who can access the Radiance. Excellent idea, General."

Kyoko continues to breathe from the air bubble, wiping the sweat from her stinging eyes. "You learn a thing or two about ash and volcanic gas living in EverEmber."

"What's the next move?"

"How many have we lost?"

Ovida hesitates. "More than half."

"Not many left, then."

"Not many to begin with."

Kyoko shakes her head. "It doesn't matter. We'll kill it with whoever's left."

"What's the plan?"

Another wave of lava soars overhead, followed by a roar that cracks the world. Ovida and Kyoko duck and cover their ears until the Death's attention turns again.

The igni general peers around the side of the broken wall to where the stone swan stands. It's moved from the base of the volcano and is now roaming the streets, razing the infrastructure. Warriors from the encampment continue to attack, but it fends them off with its lava spray, stone armor, and mighty beak.

Kyoko turns back around, rests the back of her head against the wall behind her and closes her eyes. *Think, think. It's made of stone. What weakness does stone have? We're made of stone. What weakness do we have?*

The igni opens her eyes and her gaze falls to her shoulder. Where Vy-Ro found a weakness and took her shoulder mobility from her. It was a spot that even the stone couldn't protect.

"A spot that even stone can't protect," she says aloud.

"What?" Ovida asks.

Kyoko peers around the wall again and examines the swan. Stone from beak to tail, except for the glowing cracks between the hard plates from where lava seeps and flows. She turns back to Ovida.

"Tell them all. Aim for the glowing fissures between the plates."

"Are you sure it's vulnerable there?" Ovida asks.

"You asked for a plan," Kyoko responds decisively. "This is the plan. Go, now!"

Ovida nods and rushes back into the fray. Kyoko comes in from the other side, moving from one pile of rubble to the next, avoiding as many lava blasts as she can. Between piles, she avoids the corpses of her fallen. She leaps, weaves, dodges, and somersaults, keeping her shoulder tucked and protected.

She reaches another fallen building and is immediately hit with a gust of hot volcanic gas emerging from a hole the swan created in the ground. The bubble protects her from the scorching scent of sulfur, not one she ever wishes to smell again in her lifetime.

The base of Mount Mother had once hosted a memorial garden for Courtman Tomohiro, the igni leader who lost his life to the Ore Monger. Now the memorial is nothing but flames and burnt soil.

Rage burns in Kyoko's chest. Just as she readies herself to dart to the next shattered pile of bricks, she feels something slither at her ankles. Startled, she leaps back and holds the tanto out, ready to attack, until she registers what she's looking at. A hand rising from beneath the broken rocks under her feet.

A child's hand.

Kyoko sheaths the tanto and digs, revealing a girl of about six. She's bloody and covered in ash, her dark hair matted, and her expression contorted in horror and agony. She doesn't cry, but from her wide-eyed fright, Kyoko recognizes she's in shock.

At least she's breathing.

Kyoko wraps her arm around the girl and lifts, but as soon as the child moves, she screams. Her leg is still trapped under a boulder, one too large for Kyoko to move on her own with an arm tightly in a sling against her chest.

Panic sets, sweat breaks heavier, as she watches the girl's breaths become labored; as she watches blood color the rocks below. Heart slamming against her chest, Kyoko rises to her feet and surveys the area until she sees a group of warriors some yards away behind another mound of cooled lava. She shouts to them, but the warriors' focus on the stone swan is ironclad.

She bolts forward, rolling to dodge the swan's fury, and sliding between two pillars of unsteady brick remains. She makes it to a Mega soldier.

"Can you teleport?" she asks. The soldier nods. She gestures with her head to the fallen building where the girl lies. "There! Now!"

Without hesitation, he teleports them.

Kyoko steps up to the boulder on the girl's leg. "Help me with this. We have to free her." With his assistance, the girl is freed and Kyoko passes her into the soldier's arms. "Get her to a salver, now!" Before Kyoko can blink again, he and the child have teleported off of the battlefield.

The girl is safe. She'll survive.

Another deep breath. A quick reset. Then Kyoko bounds forward again, continuing her agile assault. She may have one arm tightly strapped to her body, but she can still out-maneuver the beast. The igni hops onto a bench, runs the length of it, and then leaps off the end, landing onto the pedestal of a towering statue, safe from the flowing lava below.

Scorching air cradles her. The bubble defends against odors, but the roasting is unbearable as she's swaddled with the might of molten rock.

Ovida's order has evidently reached all warriors. Armed igni and Radiance-users alike aim for the lava-soaked cracks between the stone plates of the Death's skin. The swan is quick, and the fissures are thin; it's like trying to strike a strand of hair with a dart from fifty yards away.

Ovida is visible from the pedestal, blasting at the beast with Radiant energy. Like her warriors, she's sweating profusely, soaked in blood, quivering with exhaustion. Yet the glowing red energy beams blasted from her eyes persist.

The swan roars every time a blast strikes its fissures. It doesn't sound injured, it sounds furious. The beast retaliates quickly with a river of lava from its throat. Ovida teleports away to the opposite side of the beast, and blasts again.

Pride rises in Kyoko's chest, between the pounding drum beats of her heart. The General of the New SunSidian Guard attacks with calculation. Strategy. Her skill is evident, her training unmatched. The creature is nowhere near as fast as Ovida's teleportation. However, something abruptly becomes devastatingly apparent.

They underestimated the creature's intelligence.

It recognizes a pattern, or it develops an intangible sense of foresight. Either way, when the General teleports again, the swan predicts where she will reappear. The Mega materializes, and the swan's beak finds her and clamps down. Ovida struggles to get loose, and in her exhausted, arrested state, can no longer teleport.

Kyoko's heart sinks. *Come on, Ovida, break free!*

There's a moment when the swan nearly releases her, when Ovida's resilience conquers the beast's jaw strength. But the relief is short-lived. Ovida forces the beast's beak open by standing upright in its jaw, then composes herself enough to teleport once more.

But the Death predicts once more where Ovida will appear, and launches its lava at the spot. When Ovida materializes, she instantly burns alive.

"NOO!!" Kyoko bellows out from the pedestal, her stomach turning in knots as she watches lava and flames devour Ovida. Every muscle, every cell, every fiber of her existence freezes as she watches a dear friend turn from powerful General to flaming corpse in a matter of seconds. Memories flood her mind as the former revolutionary, the warrior, leaves this world.

It takes a few short moments for nothing to remain of her but ash and scorched bones.

The igni shuts her eyelids tightly, containing the rage and agony building within. Bile bubbles up her throat, so she tightens her jaw to swallow it back. Ovida would want Kyoko to continue without missing a beat. And that's what she does.

The fucking thing dies. Now.

She evaluates her next line of advancement. If the swan *is* intelligent, it's paying attention. Kyoko will have to surprise it. Overwhelm it.

She inhales again, resets, and assures that the sling is still tight. She then leaps forth off the pedestal and onto a trail leading up the base of Mount Mother. Traversing jagged stone outcroppings along with narrow mountain paths, she ascends to a point that is halfway up the mountain and taller than the swan. Without a second thought, without a pause or hesitation, without a moment's reflection, Kyoko reaches the end of the trail…

And keeps running.

She launches herself off of the mountain and drops. She isn't sure how many feet or yards she falls but she's in the air for a few seconds before she lands hard on the swan's stone back. It roars, bellowing as loudly as when it emerged, causing everyone to cover their ears.

Kyoko's vision blurs as the air is pushed out of her lungs. She can feel the cracks forming in her ribs as she coughs, spraying blood across the swan's back.

It's angry, but it can't see her.

There's no time for recovery. Trembling, she gathers her wits and pushes herself up onto her knees. She reaches for the hilt of the tanto, withdraws it, and then plunges it into the glowing hairline fissure on the swan's back. It roars again, but this one is different. It isn't a bellow of anger, it isn't a display of dominance, it isn't trying to strike fear in the hearts of its enemies.

It's in pain.

In the swan's lapse of attention, the warriors charge inward, finding as many of the glowing fissures as they can. The swan continues to cry out as the cracks between its stone plates, one by one, start to solidify. Registering its own mortality, it shakes violently to deter the warriors, but they continue on.

Kyoko, still reeling from the fall, is tossed into the air. As her body limply falls from the stone swan's back, the world goes dark around her before she even hits the ground. As everything fades away, the only thing left in her thoughts are the echoes of Rafael's sentiments toward her.

Your shoulder didn't make you a warrior, your fiery spirit did.

The fiery spirit that, she hopes, honors Ovida's memory, and avenges her friend.

Continent of Panaerth *The Sprite Oasis*
Date *28th Day of Month 7, Year 1629 DG*

THE RETURN OF CONSCIOUSNESS BRINGS with it painful lights, a hammering headache, and blurry colors. Rafael battles violent disorientation.

"Please, do not move, traveler," a female voice nearby rings.

Rafael pops up into a seated position and raises his hands to defend himself, but as soon as he opens his eyes, the headache returns and he's forced to close them again.

The voice enters the air again, this time far more irritated. "What did I *just* say? Do. Not. Move."

"Who are you?" Rafael asks through the darkness.

"Lie back down and I'll tell you."

Cautiously, Rafael does as he's told.

"My name is Eela, and I'm caring for you."

"You're a salver?"

"We have our own titles, but yes, I am a healer. I care for those who are ailing or in need of treatment. Or, in your case, nourishment."

"Why can't I see?"

"It'll pass. You were severely dehydrated, and your body has just received a lot of fluids quite quickly. It needs a few minutes to adjust."

Severely dehydrated. "I hallucinated the fountain, didn't I?"

"No, you didn't."

"So it was real?"

She pauses. "It was. And it wasn't."

The ache in Rafael's head grows.

Eela explains. "It was an illusion, intentionally projected to those who reach our gates. Two tests, you passed both. You nearly gave your life to save a loved one *and* a stranger. So you were approved for entry."

"Entry? To where?"

"Open your eyes, traveler."

Rafael does as he's told. It's blurry for a few moments, but then his eyes finally begin to focus and he finds himself in a long room lined with cots. He's in a vast stone hut, with a small table next to his cot, on which sit a number of empty containers of water.

"Did I drink all of those?"

"I'm not sure if 'drink' is the right word. I forced them into you."

Rafael turns and nearly jumps from his skin. Standing before him is a lilac-skinned woman with pointed ears, brown pupils, and voluminous curls flowing down her back. She's clad in vibrant, colorful robes that reach the floor, but the most striking feature about her are the massive butterfly wings coming from her back.

If it weren't for the wings and pupils, he'd have thought she were Mega.

"You're—" he can't bring himself to say the word, but he knows from history lessons what these features indicate.

Eela nods. "Yes, I'm a Sprite. No, I'm not extinct. Yes, you've found the oasis. Did I answer all of the questions?"

"Not even close," Rafael remarks.

Eela laughs. "What's your name?"

"Rafael."

Eela gestures to the door of the hut. "Come, Rafael. Take a walk with me and I'll explain everything."

Rafael follows her out of the hut and into a utopia he could never have imagined.

The oasis is built around a single, natural pool of water in the desert. A vibrant community: smaller stone huts closest to the water and towering clay megastructures around the outer rim. Between them, lush, fecund gardens and parks, stone walkways.

Rafael and Eela sit together under the shade of a towering oak tree, on a hill that overlooks much of the oasis, and she explains everything to him.

She begins with the history of Vala and the Ancient Ones. Eela outlines the marriage of Kova and Vala, the breakdown of their relationship after Vala's discovery of Kova and Elva's incestuous relationship, the banishment, the return of the Ancient Ones and their demon army, as well as their imprisonment.

She then goes on to confirm that Ana's translation of the Sprite text is accurate: after the construction of the Temple of the Oasis Mage, Vala imbued a part of her essence, her consciousness into a statue within it, in the hope that if the Ancient Ones are ever released from their imprisonment, someone will come to seek her out.

But she never told anyone *how* to reach her consciousness in the statue. The Sprites, Eela included, have tried to reach her over many generations, and no incantation or any magic has worked.

"Our species never went extinct. After the imprisonment of the Ancient Ones, Vala used a powerful incantation to hide the oasis, and the Sprites within it, from the outside world. So the outside world assumed we were all dead. In three millennia, many"—she pauses to stress her next words—"*many* have found the oasis, but so few have actually *entered* the oasis, because most fail the illusion."

Rafael's gaze turns to where the spiritual structures congregate. "Will you take me to Vala's temple? I want to convene with her statue."

Eela frowns. "Rafael, I told you. We've tried. For generations."

"I haven't."

Eela looks at him quizzically. "Why is this so important to you?"

Rafael's eyes widen as a realization drops on him. "You don't know, do you?"

Eela shakes her head.

"The Ancient Ones are free."

CHAPTER 57

"The Oasis Mage"

Continent of Panaerth *The Sprite Oasis*
Date *28th Day of Month 7, Year 1629 DG*

THE TEMPLE OF THE OASIS Mage houses statues, shrines, monuments, portraits, paintings, and all manner of art and memorials dedicated to Vala. Rafael wonders, as he travels alone through the holy site, which of these statues is the one in which Vala imbued her essence. The confusion clears quickly when he reaches a wide, carpeted chamber with the largest of them all at the far end.

Eela escorted him to the front gates of the temple, then hurried off to meet with the Sprite Emperor to inform him of the Ancient Ones' release. She seemed certain that Rafael's attempt to convene with Vala would be unsuccessful, and told him she'd return to escort him to the Emperor's palace when he's done.

In a vestibule lined with shelves, a small sign requests for him to remove his shoes, so he does, entering the carpeted area barefoot. The mari sits cross-legged before the magnificent monument.

How does one convene with the spirit of the Oasis Mage?

Generations have failed at this task. But none have had what Rafael does: human Radiance. The Radiance evolved from the energy manipulation techniques wielded by the witches, warlocks, and sorcerers of Vala's time, but that was long after her death. It couldn't be the form of magic that is required to convene with her.

But it's all he has.

He closes his eyes and starts with basics, channeling the Radiant energy through his body. It bubbles in his chest, soars through his veins, swims in his mind, and burns through his extremities.

No contact with Vala.

He then attempts to push it outward, from his body into the floor, and through the floor into the statue. He can feel the weight of the heavy stone on his shoulders, as if he's lifting it. He breaks out into a sweat and then pulls the Radiant energy back.

Nothing.

The last idea he has is to enter the black void. The void was a place he, and all new users of the Radiance, entered to become one with the Radiance; to draw Radiant energy from the source. It's the most magically-powerful place he can think of. He closes his eyes and allows the spiritual energy to carry him to the void. He reaches it, opening his eyes and calling out to Vala. But he is alone there, so he returns to the physical realm.

And he is alone here, too.

He channels energy for some time until he hears footsteps approaching him from behind. Eela's returned to escort him to the Emperor's palace. He sighs dejectedly, as she sits down cross-legged next to him.

"You were right," he says. "Vala's spirit is unreachable."

"I wouldn't say that," responds an unfamiliar voice.

Rafael turns and his heart nearly stops. A glowing, gold-skinned Sprite, with stunning orange eyes, and magnificent butterfly wings sits beside him, clad in colorful robes. A comforting grin widens on her face.

"Vala," Rafael whispers.

Vala nods. "And what is your name?"

"Rafael."

Vala's gaze travels up and down, assessing Rafael's anatomy. "And what exactly…are you?"

Unsure of how to respond, Rafael states, "Human?"

Vala raises an eyebrow. "I see. Humans don't have noses anymore? How long has it been?"

Rafael takes a deep breath. "Over three millennia."

Guilt overtakes him when he sees the look on Vala's face. She almost looks frightened as she turns away from him.

"Three thousand years," she whispers, her eyes on the ground. She keeps her gaze fixed as she continues speaking. "I'm going to assume you're reaching out to me for the reason I imbued my spirit into this statue in the first place."

Rafael nods. "They're free."

The Oasis Mage turns and looks up at him. "Then we must imprison them again. After three thousand years in that tiny clay pot, they must be extremely weak. I can give you an incantation that will work, as long as they don't regain strength."

Rafael holds her eye contact quietly, uncertain how to relay the truth.

She senses his discomfort. "What's wrong?"

"Vala"—he hesitates—"they were released eight hundred years ago, and have been building strength ever since. I don't know how strong they are now, but they're strong enough to connect to the demon plane and release terror onto the world."

Vala's mouth drops open and she buries her face in her hands. "Rafael, their exhaustion, their weakened state, it was a big part of why I was able to imprison them in the first place. If they are at full power, nothing can stop them."

"Not even the Twins?"

Vala's face contorts with confusion. "Who are the Twins?"

Rafael realizes his timeline is off. "The Twins came after your death. They're a pair of siblings, born around sixteen hundred years ago, who had visions of Kova and Elva's conquest, and believed they would one day be resurrected to defend the world against them."

"If they think they can protect this world from Kova and Elva, resurrect them. Now. Do whatever it takes, Rafael, you cannot let them succeed."

Rafael sighs. "Is there *nothing* you, the Oasis Mage, can do to help us?"

Vala's eyes abruptly widen and she starts to look around, as if she senses something Rafael can't.

"What's wrong?" he asks.

"There may be something I can do to help after all."

Rafael's heart ignites with hope.

Her gaze meets Rafael's. "They're on a mental plane. Right now. Talking with someone. I can hear them, feel them."

"What are you going to do?"

Vala shakes her head. "Not *me*. We." She holds her hand out. Hesitantly, Rafael places his into her palm. "Let's go have a chat, shall we?"

CHAPTER 58

"A MEMORIAL OF ITS OWN FAILURE"

Theocracy *SunSide*
Date *28th Day of Month 7, Year 1629 DG*

POLITICIANS. LEADERS. RULERS. HOW OFTEN do they find time to stand by and witness the fruit of their commands coming to fruition?

Standing in an open field of grass and dandelions, on the outskirts of Ward's Fall, watching the cities she ordered rising into the clouds, Saila doesn't feel like a politician, leader, or ruler. She feels like an observer, watching history remove its bandages.

Soon, faeries will live in these homes; faeries that once occupied the settlements in MoonSide. The walls have almost entirely come down, the land almost entirely returned to the Doruh.

It's about time.

"A stone for your thoughts?" Tund-Ra steps up from behind her.

She smiles, her gaze still on the city ahead. "I'm impressed. In two weeks, the prisoners have erected what my crews couldn't in months."

"They're grateful for your mercy."

"No one's going to be executed in Larso for a very long time."

Tund-Ra turns to her, eyes wide. "What do you mean?"

"'Execution after execution after execution.' Those were your words. I don't know what makes a good leader, Tund-Ra. But I know SunSide's history. We've never offered prisoners rehabilitation. We've never reduced crime by bolstering social services. We've never addressed the failures of our justice system, when evidence exonerates those who no longer had their heads."

The Chief Member meets his gaze. "I've submitted a motion to the New Assembly. It's called the Tund-Ra Decree, and it will abolish executions in SunSide."

Tund-Ra's mouth falls agape. "I'm not sure what to say."

"Say nothing," Saila responds. "I'll let you know when it passes." She pulls a small rolled up paper from her pocket and places it into Tund-Ra's violet palm. "One more thing, before I forget: Pina would like to come here. To visit you. I grant you permission for visitors."

Tears escape the prisoner's eyes and he whispers, "Thank you, Saila."

They turn to watch the construction continue, to listen to the loud clangs of metalwork. But it isn't long before a different sound, a far less familiar one, rumbles through the air like thunder. It roars from behind them, from the south.

From Larso.

Saila turns and sees it. Gray and massive, weaving through the sky, between clouds, fins and teeth and gills and all. The eyes are small, the body wide, the rows of teeth bare; it's an animal from which she'd flee if they were in the open ocean. But how does one flee from a storm?

"What in the world is that?" Tund-Ra says, staring at it, his expression contorted.

Saila's mouth falls open. "It's a shark."

"But it's…in the sky."

"Then it's a sky shark."

Sounds erupt from Tund-Ra's throat. Half words, half syllables, all attempts to ask questions that never come to fruition.

Saila knows exactly what she's looking at. *A beast from the sky.* The Three Deaths have been released. And this one is headed straight for the mountains.

She turns to Tund-Ra. "It's going to PeakHaven. It's going to destroy the city. And if it succeeds, it's coming for Larso next."

He waves his hands at her as if hurrying a strolling child along. "Go! Use the Radiance. Teleport to PeakHaven. I'm sure you can do it from here."

He has more faith in my abilities than I do.

She turns and visualizes her destination: the war room of the Generals that lead the city. The pixie closes her eyes and draws all the Radiant energy she can from the grass and the soil and the dandelions, and finally from the PeakHaven mountain range itself. When she's channeling more energy than she ever has before in her life, when she's glowing like a sun, she focuses all of it on her teleportation and—

The entire world around her goes dark for a moment. Shapes, sounds, smells, it all disappears and she hovers in the void. And then it reforms. She's on a stone paved street between two rocky mountain walls. Men, women, and children with wings, clad in colorful outfits made from the traditional angi cloth, turn to her with wide-eyed surprise, as if she's just appeared out of nowhere.

Which she has.

Her heart starts to slow and she grabs her chest, dropping to her knees and realizing she hasn't accounted for the altitude of PeakHaven. Thinking quickly, she creates an air bubble around her mouth and nose, and her heart slowly returns to a normal pace.

She rises to her feet, excusing herself to the confused angi onlookers, battling a tremble from the cold, and follows the mountain path to the city square, at the center of which she finds the magnificent, towering stone building housing the Generals' war room. Surrounded by a mighty metal fence, its gates are manned by guards armed with long, sharp spears and powerful shields.

She approaches the front gate, but the guards place their shields in front of her and shake their heads.

"Please!" She injects urgency into her tone. "PeakHaven is in danger. I have to warn them!"

"Chief Member?" Aissa, the angi Member of the New Assembly whom Saila had sent up to PeakHaven to prepare for the oncoming threat, stands on the other side of the gate.

Saila exhales relief, finding the familiar face. "Aissa, it's here. Tell the Generals."

Aissa nods and darts into the stone building, returning some minutes later with the Generals of PeakHaven at her heels.

"Let her through!" Commander Gumbu orders the guards, who pull their shields back and allow Saila passage.

"Please accept my apologies for coming unannounced, but it's here. The moment you've been preparing for."

The beast's roar rattles the mountains, and it erupts from behind the clouds.

Commander Gumbu turns to the other Generals. "Mobilize them. NOW!"

Saila had heard of the elite PeakHaven military before. Their singularity. Their excellence. But until one sees how they move through the air in almost theatrical waves, a dance of perfect rows and blocks and arrangements, they don't understand how unparalleled these warriors are. Weapons extended, they fly forth, charging at speeds Saila didn't know angi could reach, striking the sky shark both up close, and from a distance.

The beast is formidable. It rains terror on the mountaintop city for hours. Hundreds of winged warriors are sent to their doom, and so many stone structures are collapsed by its tail, fins and jaws. Buildings, neighborhoods, districts.

Homes with civilians who didn't have time to evacuate.

Saila employs the Radiance to teleport with a frequency she never has before. She teleports beneath crumbling buildings and homes to hold them steady as the residents rush past, or she teleports into them to retrieve the civilians before they collapse.

She'd much rather launch herself into the fray, contributing the Radiance to the assault on the sky shark. But it becomes apparent quite quickly that she's most needed in the evacuation efforts.

Though it causes damage that'll take years to repair, the beast is eventually conquered. The winged warriors celebrate as its body drops onto the side of the mountain, hardens into stone, and becomes part of the city it once sought to destroy. A stone sculpture.

A memorial of its own failure.

The angi civilians rejoice, shouting cheers of celebration, despite having lost so many citizens, so many warriors, and so much infrastructure. They hold one another and gather at the Holy Summit to offer gratitude that PeakHaven still stands.

That their beloved city will only need bandages, and not caskets.

Aissa comes forth and wraps her arms around Saila, who thanks the Four that the Generals trusted in Aissa's preparation plans. She prays that Kyoko, Rafael, and Ana have a similar victory celebration in EverEmber.

As she prepares to teleport back to SunSide, a hand falls on Saila's shoulder. She turns to find a teenage girl, perhaps seventeen or eighteen, with deep umber skin and twinkling brown eyes, smiling at her. The Mega recognizes her amongst those she teleported to safety today.

"Thank you," the girl says. Her home is destroyed, but she smiles because she's alive.

Saila accepts her gratitude, and as she takes in the teenager's face, she finds it eerily familiar. "Do I know you?"

The girl shakes her head, but as she walks away, the truth of the familiarity dawns on Saila.

The girl strikingly resembles Unisa.

CHAPTER 59

"REUNION"

***Theocracy** SunSide*
***Date** Unknown*

NAINA RAISES HER CHIN. "THE Three Deaths. You. We will conquer all."

Elva narrows her eyes, and a wicked half-smile twists her expression. "If you will not *surrender* Aerthomni, perhaps you will *gamble* it."

Naina pauses, hesitates. "What kind of gamble?"

"A game. A wager. I don't believe this world will conquer the Three Deaths. But if it does, we will reward you with a decade."

Kova smiles, pleased. "Excellent idea. If the Three Deaths are killed, we will give you a decade to resurrect the Twins, and to gather the Saviors Six. If they are not, then our conquest begins immediately."

Naina opens her mouth to agree to their wager when the Ancient Ones abruptly become frantic, rising from their thrones to search the void wildly. Naina follows, but she doesn't sense whatever has caught their attention.

Kova growls. "You feel that, too, Elva?"

"I do," Elva says.

"What is it?" Naina asks.

Kova spins, his gaze searching the white void. Then he stops and his eyes widen. "It's her."

The whiteness of the void splits to birth two individuals. The first to enter the mental plane is the gold-skinned, orange-eyed Sprite from the images that flashed through the void during Elva and Kova's history lesson.

Vala, the Oasis Mage.

The man who follows brings relief and comfort with him. A friendly, familiar face is the antidote to fear and isolation.

Rafael doesn't appear much older than when Naina entered Red-Lo's mind. He's thinner and the jagged lines across his face, the swollen circles under his eyes indicate he's endured a grueling journey, but he doesn't appear to be an elderly man.

She breathes easier knowing that she hasn't lost a lifetime in Red-Lo's mind. That she'll return to a world, and a sister, that is not too dissimilar from the one she left behind.

"How?" comes Kova's voice in a stressed whisper, his wide eyes focused on his former wife. He steps forward toward the Oasis Mage, ever so slowly, as if she's a ticking explosive that will detonate if he moves too quickly.

"I am a memory, Kova," Vala explains. "Three thousand years later and I exist only in the mind of he who has freed me." She gestures to Rafael.

"Freed you?" Kova's eyebrows come together in the middle of his forehead. "From where? For what purpose?"

"From the imprisonment of my consciousness. I kept my essence alive all this time, in case you were ever liberated. Rafael has freed me to come and intercede with you. To parley. To remind you that you have the power to prevent violence. Innocents do not have to die for my mistakes."

Elva's hand leaps to Kova's cheek and pulls his face toward her. "Do not listen to her. Remember who cared for you." She kisses his lips and then whispers into his mouth, "She betrayed us, stole from us, insulted us, then imprisoned us. She banished us without healers when she knew you were dying. And now she comes holding the hands of our enemies." The sister's finger rises to Rafael. "*He* is one of the Saviors Six."

"Elva," Vala calls to her, "I beg of you. I will do anything you ask. Apologize, atone. But let this world go, the transgression was not theirs."

"We have heard this before! We will not be fooled again. An empire is owed to us." Her eyes narrow and a wicked smile forms on her lips.

Naina's heart drops. She's seen this look on Elva's face before.

Kova's sister-wife continues."You're correct, Vala. The transgression was not theirs. It was yours. Aerthomni became the target of our arrowheads when we were led to believe that the Sprite species was extinct. That your progeny, the descendants of your followers, were gone, and there was nothing left on Panaerth to conquer. Clearly, that is not the case."

She turns back to Kova. "Do you understand, my love? Rafael freed her, but from *where* has she been freed? Under whose protection has her essence been safeguarded all this time?"

Elva's wicked smile is mirrored on Kova's lips, and Vala's expression contorts in an agony that confirms Elva's train of thought.

"My sister, my wife is brilliant," Kova hisses. "She's drawn the truth from behind your words like honey from the hive. The Sprite species lives on, and you've hidden them somewhere. Our vengeance thrives."

As the scene unfolds before her, Naina's mind reels with a heinous thought. A selfish thought. A wicked thought. One that Salessa would never have. One that no good person would ever have. One that Naina is almost ashamed to vocalize.

Almost.

But the survival of her people, the safety of her continent, dangles from life by a single, frayed thread. If there's any chance to save innocents, and if it means sacrificing other innocents, this is the moment to do it.

"Your vengeance lies with the Sprites," she addresses Kova and Elva directly. "With Vala and her descendants. Conquer them, claim your empire, do what you will. But your business with Aerthomni is concluded."

Rafael and Vala both take a step back in wide-eyed astonishment.

"No," Elva responds. "Have you forgotten the Twins? Your prophecy? It is about to become self-fulfilling. The Doruh deities believe they and their allies will face us in battle. Well then, if a battle is foretold, a battle will be fought. The Sprite revelation does nothing but ensure that our conquest will span multiple continents."

"Elva is correct," Kova agrees. "The Twins' visions are a direct challenge to our power. Do you think your sister and the Twins' followers will simply abandon their quest to resurrect them? No. The Twins *will* be resurrected. The Saviors Six will come together. And then," he faces Rafael, "we will turn them to ash and dust."

Like the flash of a lightning bolt, the tip of Elva's finger ignites and a beam of light extends forward. It all happens so fast, Naina can barely react. The beam shoots out and strikes Vala in the chest. The Oasis Mage takes a deep breath, eyes wide. From the site of contact, from the center of her chest, the essence begins to fade away.

"They will all die," Elva proclaims, locking eyes with Vala. "The Twins. The Saviors Six. The Sprites. The casualties will be incalculable. And those who survive will serve us. I want you to know that. I want your consciousness to melt away into oblivion knowing that the final, ragged breaths of every sentient creature in this world…is on your hands."

She turns to Naina. "Remember, little wolf: you have a decade. Resurrect the Twins. Gather the Saviors Six. Prepare for our conquest."

There's a final lingering look between Kova and the fading Vala, in which her lips quiver and she mouths "I love you, too."

And then, the Ancient Ones vanish.

Vala's knees buckle and her body drops limp. Rafael catches her and Naina strides forward to the Oasis Mage's side. When she reaches, drowning in shame from the plea she made to the Ancient Ones, two sincere words drop from her tongue.

"I'm sorry."

When Vala responds, her voice echoes as if it's a distant memory in an empty cave. "It doesn't matter. You, the Sprites, you're all in danger." Her gaze shifts to Rafael. "You are on your own now. My consciousness is being torn from the statue." She swallows as a tear escapes from the corner of her eye. "I'm truly dying now."

"What are we going to do, Vala?" Rafael begs, his tone frantic. "How do we stop them without the Oasis Mage?"

A sad smile curls the edges of her lips. Vala places the fingers of her fading hand onto his cheek. "They named me the Oasis Mage, not because of who I was, but because of what I represented: someone willing to stand up for others. The Oasis Mage is not an individual, but an idea."

Her fingers fade and all the remains of Vala is a floating neck and head. The head turns to Naina. "Are you willing to defend this world?"

Naina nods, her guilt anchoring her resolve to protect anyone who might face the Ancient Ones' wrath. Sprite. Doruh. Anyone.

Vala continues as her ears, chin and forehead fade, leaving only her eyes, nose, and mouth. "You are the Oasis Mages now. The embodiment of that idea."

The fading consumes her, and the Oasis Mage's final words echo into the collapsing void around them. "I believe in you."

White turns to black and the void trembles. As if a giant has grabbed hold of them, and is tugging her and Rafael apart, she feels the pull of the mental plane launching her out of Red-Lo's mind.

"I knew you'd find your way out!" Rafael exclaims.

She offers a smile. "Looks like you were right." Their surroundings darken and they're pulled further apart as the mental plane disintegrates. "I'll see you outside!"

The wolf sits upright, back in Red-Lo's cell in the physical world, and draws in a breath as if she's been holding it for years. She coughs up and gags trying to get air into her lungs, but her body is in shock. She's sweating profusely and has clearly lost an incredible amount of weight. Unable to get her breath in quick enough, she chokes, turns over and vomits next to her, on the cold stone of Red-Lo's cell.

With her eyes closed, vomiting painfully, she feels a hand rub her back, and another pulls the hair from the side of her face.

"Easy, now. You're alright. You're back home." Kruga's voice soothes her.

Naina spits and then wipes her mouth clean on the back of her wrist. She finally takes in a few steady breaths, then asks, "What's the date? How long was I there?"

"The Twenty-Ninth of Month Seven. You were there for fifty-eight days. How long did it feel like you were there?"

Naina shakes her head, partially in disbelief at how long she's spent in Red-Lo's mind, partially relieved it wasn't fifty-eight years. "Not more than a couple hours." The Ancient Ones' threat echoes through her ears and she turns to Kruga. "Have the Three Deaths been released?"

The nymph nods.

"What happened?" Naina asks. "Did we defeat them?"

"We did," Kruga responds, "but not without heavy losses. PeakHaven and EverEmber are standing, but they'll still need years to rebuild."

"And SeaBed?"

He hesitates. "They didn't heed the warning. More than half their domed communities and villages have been wiped off the ocean floor. The waves have turned red with the blood of their population. Including every General that leads the city. They'll need longer than a few years to rebuild."

Naina holds his gaze steadily as she says, "They have ten years. We all do. Not a day longer."

CHAPTER 60

"Crimson Sins"

Sovereign City-State *The Library*
Date *29th Day of Month 7, Year 1629 DG*

EVERY BREATH, REGARDLESS OF DEPTH, is useless. Futile. The hammering of Unisa's heart doesn't slow. The perspiration on her palms doesn't dry. The anxious thoughts in her mind don't quiet.

The dread doesn't wane.

Silence fills the Nest. She, Juhi, Yuki, and Maksi spent the night planning. There isn't much else to say until Konni arrives in the early hours of the morning, before the suns have awoken. She's clad in casual clothing, mirroring Juhi and Unisa: linen tops and loose trousers, in the darkest shades they own.

"Ready?" Unisa asks her.

Konni nods, but the sheer panic in her eyes betrays her.

"I don't like this," Juhi remarks, noticing the Mega's expression.

"You don't have a choice," Maksi reminds her. "There are Cicada eyes on the Loops, the Stream, the Catacombs, and the street. We can't use the air, the water, the land, or the underground. This is your only option."

"But she's never done it before. The last time she tried something she's never done before, she almost turned Uni into an omelette."

Unisa massages her temple with her fingertip, remembering the night they attempted to break Maksi's bonding.

"Just because I've never teleported before," Konni defends herself, "doesn't mean I'll fail. Plenty of nymphs and pixies do it. It just takes practice."

"Did you practice?" Juhi asks her.

Konni rolls her eyes. "Of course. I've been practicing all day."

"Where?" Unisa asks.

Konni swallows. "In my apartment."

Juhi sighs. "So you teleported from one room to another. Were you at least successful in doing that?"

Konni hesitates, then nods. "Definitely." She pauses. "Mostly."

"Mostly?" Yuki questions.

Konni slowly kicks off her shoe, and her gaze falls. Everyone else around the table leans over to see four indigo-skinned toes, and one heavily bandaged space where her smallest once was. "During my first teleportation attempt, I went from the bathroom to the kitchen. Most of me followed to the kitchen, except for a toe."

Juhi shakes her head. "Mission cancelled, I'm not doing this. Whatever is in that safe, is not worth losing body parts."

Unisa draws Juhi's words from her memories and presents them to the hawk. "You said you were prepared to die for this cause."

Juhi pauses, then sighs. "Fine."

"Nobody is going to die tonight," Konni reassures them. "This is an easy mission. We teleport into the Prime's office, find the safe, gather the location of the Fully Broken prison, and then teleport back here."

"Maksi and I will be here with bandages when the three of you get back," Yuki teases Juhi.

Unisa, Konni, and Juhi stand together in a circle, hands clasped, eyes closed, as Konni teleports them out of the Nest. The sensation is unlike anything Unisa has experienced before; it's as if she's turned into rubber and stretched through a tiny hole, and then there's nothing beneath her feet, no solid ground.

She's falling.

Instinctively, the angi's wings kick into action and start to flap, lowering her gently onto the stone surface below her. Konni uses the Radiance to lower herself as well, while Juhi simply drops and lands on her back.

"Am I dead?" the Doruh asks.

"No, we're all alive," Konni informs her.

Juhi starts to feel around her body. "Am I missing anything?"

"I was a little off in my aim," Konni admits, examining their surroundings. "We're on the rooftop of the Center."

"Which means," Unisa begins to explain, as she assesses where on the top floor they're standing, "the Prime's office should be right about"—she walks gingerly over to the spot where she believes the Prime's office is below them—"here."

"How sure are you?" Juhi asks.

"Unfortunately, I've been in it enough times to be completely certain."

Konni leads Juhi to where Unisa is standing, and the three women grasp hands again. "I can phase us through the rooftop." She turns to Juhi. "I've done this many times before."

"Later, I'd like to know why," the hawk responds.

The phasing is far more pleasant than the teleportation was. After the sensation of walking through warm mist, they're standing comfortably in the Prime's office.

As comfortably as one can be, trespassing in a dangerous man's quarters, in darkness.

"Brimah said the safe was under the desk," Juhi says, searching. "I don't see anything."

Konni closes her eyes, then pops them open. "Under the tiles." She uses the Radiance to raise the tile and together, Unisa and Juhi get down on their knees and lift the heavy safe out of the ground. Konni replaces the tile where it was.

"Can you phase your hand through it and retrieve what's inside?" Unisa asks.

Konni examines it, then shakes her head. "Look at what it's made out of."

Unisa taps the surface of the safe and the realization dawns on her. "It's ore."

Konni nods. "It isn't enough to disrupt my access to the Radiance, luckily. But I won't be able to phase through it. We'll have to get it open."

"*We*"—Juhi gestures to Unisa and herself—"will have to get it open. *You* need to keep an ear to the door. If you hear the Gatekeeper's door open, get us out of here."

Konni nods and follows the instructions, moving to the office door and placing her ear on it. Juhi and Unisa turn to the safe. The hawk unsheathes her sword and maniacally tries to pry and slice it open, but neither work.

"I've never seen a lock like this," Juhi says, dipping her sword back into the sheath on her hip.

Unisa continues to stare at the unusual locking mechanism on the door of the safe. It's a square frame, with some smaller, metal squares that are moveable within it. She doesn't know how to unlock it, but she identifies what she's looking at.

"It's a puzzle. You have to solve the puzzle in order to unlock it."

"Of course it is," Juhi sighs. "We shouldn't have expected anything less from a man who truly believes himself the cleverest entity on the planet. Let's just go."

Unisa shakes her head. "No, wait."

She brings her face eye-level to the puzzle as recognition starts to set in. Something inexplicably familiar jumps out to her. Employing nimble fingers, and the extraordinary memory that earned her entry into the Library as a young child, she shifts the metal squares throughout the frame until they're in a specific orientation. The locking mechanism clicks, and the safe opens.

Juhi's mouth falls agape. "How did you—"

"It's the orientation of bedrooms in Prime Palace," Unisa explains. "The hole in the center of the frame where there are no squares is the vestibule from which the hallways branch out, and then each square is placed where there's a bedroom."

The two women lean down to look into the safe. At the very rear, against the back wall, are pouches of stones and gold coins. In front of these is a stack of documents that Unisa withdraws to examine.

At the very top of the stack are hand-written profiles of a number of high-status individuals around the continent. The Prime's close business associates, his political rivals, other Librarians and politicians, intracontinental monarchs and rulers. Their personal information, important data that could be used against them, observations the Prime has made about them, along with a picture that was clearly taken when they didn't know they were being photographed.

Unisa shudders at the thought of the Cicadas following them around, not only within the Library, but around the continent.

She puts these to the side, revealing further documentation underneath that makes bile shoot up into her throat. That makes her blood run cold.

Sitting on the desk between her fingers are identical hand-written profiles to the ones she just found, but these are for the young women and girls in the Inner Catacomb. Regardless of age, from those that are in their mid-twenties, to the teenagers, the Prime has a profile on each one.

But what disgusts her most are the pictures attached to the profiles. Of these young women and girls, entirely unclothed. Some are smiling, while others are sleeping and don't seem to be aware the photographs are being taken.

The room starts to spin and Unisa's knees grow weak. She stumbles slightly, and Juhi catches her.

"We can put it back and leave," the hawk suggests.

Unisa shakes her head, determined. "No, I'm alright. I have to see this." She takes a deep breath and steadies herself, then continues to thumb through the profiles.

"Why would he have these?" Unisa thinks aloud.

"Brimah once mentioned the Oath Master's guarantees," Juhi reminds her. "The moment one of these girls steps a toe out of Prime Palace, he'll show them these images, and threaten that if they don't come back, every citizen in the Library will receive a copy."

A glaze of clarity drips onto Unisa's mind. She now understands why these women and girls stood silently by as Unisa screamed and wept. As time slipped away like sand through fingers.

As Lyla died in her arms.

Because speaking up would have been dangerous for them. That's what the Prime has done, not only to the members of the Inner Catacomb, but to the citizens: he's made the sound of their own voices a harbinger of danger. An omen of defeat.

She finds Lyla's profile, an image of her attached from before she was pregnant. Clearly, she was a fifteen-year-old girl in this image.

She also isn't wearing any clothes.

Unisa folds the paper up and places it into her pocket with the photo, hoping to return home and burn it. She looks to the next profile and her heart stops so quickly, she thinks she may be experiencing cardiac arrest.

It's a profile of her. Identical to the others, it has her personal information, the Prime's notes about her—outlining his suspicions of her intentions, though not giving any indication he knows about the Hawks—as well as a photograph of her. The image is a side profile of her bathing, and from the angle, Unisa can tell it was taken from her window when she was unaware.

Again, she breathes deeply to steady herself as the room spins, then she takes the page, folds it, and places it into her pocket with Lyla's.

The next set of documents are copies of the Prime's own personal identification, and some pictures of Alba. She's younger, a teenager, and she's clothed. The mari appears in good spirits.

Despite there being at least four images of Alba, there are none of Ana.

Finally, after all other papers and images and documents are emptied, Unisa gets to the last page in the safe: a construction order commissioning the building of a detention center in the Dissolved Nations for the rehabilitation of the Fully Broken. It was signed one hundred years earlier by the Prime Librarian who held the title two terms prior to Alvaro.

It's called, "The Forge."

"This is it," Unisa says, showing it to Juhi, pointing out the section that outlines the exact location of the construction site. "This is where he's keeping our army. The Forge."

Juhi smiles and meets Unisa's gaze. "We did it." She hands the page back to Unisa, who folds it delicately and puts it into her pocket with the other pages. While Unisa packs the safe back up, Juhi calls out to Konni.

"You can take your ear off the door now."

Konni takes a step away from the office door. "You found it?"

Juhi nods, smiling in satisfaction. "We got it. Once the safe is packed up, we can—"

It all happens so fast.

Unisa's adrenaline spikes. Time slows to fractions of a second. In the first fraction, the Prime's office door lock clicks open. Konni, who'd removed her ear from the door, didn't hear anyone coming through the Gatekeeper's area.

In the second fraction, Konni's eyes widen as she realizes the door is opening, and then they dart to Juhi. In the third fraction, Juhi mouths a small, simple command to the Mega.

"Go."

In the fourth fraction, Konni, standing just beyond the widening office door and too far to reach Juhi or Unisa, obeys the command and teleports out of the office, saving herself. In the fifth fraction, when Unisa is finally able to perceive what's happening, Juhi attacks her. The attack isn't light or reserved. With every ounce of strength in her fists, Juhi begins to pummel Unisa.

The angi falls backward behind the desk as the hawk straddles her body and continues the assault. Unisa's blood bursts forth from her nose and mouth, pooling on the floor. She's hardly able to see anything as the adrenaline in her veins numbs the pain of the blows, but Unisa is certain from the sounds she hears that Juhi has broken her nose, and maybe her cheekbones.

Unisa's arms rise to protect her face, and Juhi's mighty fists begin to slam into her forearms. It feels like ages and eons before someone pulls Juhi away from Unisa, subdues her, and places metal shackles around her wrists, bound in front of her. A hand reaches down and helps Unisa stand. Her entire face and neck are throbbing. She spits a mouthful of blood onto the floor and a tooth comes out with it.

"What in the world is happening here?" the Prime demands, standing next to Unisa. It was his filthy hands that helped her to her feet.

Juhi sits a few feet away, on her knees, wrists shackled, a Cicada behind her with his sword extended toward her.

The Prime turns to his desk and gasps. "My safe." It comes out in little more than a whisper.

Juhi begins to laugh. A diabolical, wicked laugh Unisa has never heard before. It frightens her. "I knew it."

"Knew what?" the Prime asks.

"I knew you'd have gold and stones in a safe somewhere. And I would've had it, too, if your little angi bitch here hadn't stopped me."

The Prime turns to Unisa, who takes great pains to erase the confusion from her expression.

"Thank you, Unisa," the Prime breathes out, his mouth agape, as if he can't believe what he's heard.

"Fuck you, flyer," Juhi spits, then turns to the Prime and injects gallons of venom into her tone. "And fuck you, Alvaro. You disgust me."

Somehow, Unisa feels the sincerity of Juhi's last statement, despite all the other lies. Panic starts to set in as Juhi's quick planning dawns on the angi. *No, Juhi, don't do this.*

But it's far too late. The hawk's plan is well into motion. And it's successful.

The Prime turns back to Unisa. "How did you know she was here?"

Unisa tries to speak, blood dripping down the corners of her mouth, but she stumbles through an explanation for a moment before Juhi comes to her aid again.

"I should've been quieter. If Unisa weren't so addicted to her work, perhaps I would've left here quite wealthy."

"You were still working?" the Prime questions, an eyebrow raised. "At your desk? Here? In the middle of the night?"

Unisa nods. "I was. What are you doing here?"

The Prime's jaw shifts, as if he's gritting his teeth. "It's my office, Unisa, I don't need a reason or explanation for coming here."

Unisa holds his gaze for a moment before nodding again. "You're right, Great Prime." She turns to Juhi. "What will happen to Juhi?"

The Prime sighs, looking down at the shackled Doruh on her knees. "Clearly, she's Fully Broken."

An idea sparks in Unisa's mind. Hope that Juhi can one day be freed and rejoin the army in the Nest. "Where will you send her? Where do the Fully Broken become rehabilitated?"

The Prime shakes his head. "She tried to steal from me, Unisa. And the only reason she wasn't successful is thanks to you. But Juhi is too dangerous for rehabilitation. It'll never work."

Unisa's heart drops so quickly she thinks it may never rise again. "What are you saying?"

"Juhi must be executed."

"No," Unisa says, too quickly to stop herself. The angi turns to Juhi, whose expression hasn't changed. Either she's a masterful actress, or she's truly unafraid.

"No?" the Prime responds, turning back to her. "Unisa, I know you've grown close to Juhi working with her the past year, but she's committed too grave a crime."

"I understand, Great Prime, and for that she should stand trial."

The Prime sighs again. "Getting caught in the act was her trial. Confessing was her trial. Striking you was her trial." He walks over to the Cicada standing behind Juhi and takes the sword from the warrior's hand, then begins to walk back to Unisa. "The trial is over. I've given her a sentence. Execution." The Prime places the hilt of the sword firmly into Unisa's hand, wrapping her fingers around it tightly. "And now, you will carry it out."

Bile rises into Unisa's throat again, as her knees begin to tremble, and the room spins. She grows lightheaded as only a few words trickle from her rebellious tongue. "I can't."

"You can," the Prime encourages her. "And you will. Now." He turns to Juhi. "I'm so disappointed in you. Do you have any last words?"

Juhi is silent for a few moments, gathering her final thoughts, before she says, "Long burn the flames that raze the lies. Long feast the Hawks."

The Prime's face contorts. "Flames? Lies? Hawks? What does any of that nonsense mean?"

Juhi smiles. "I'm a hawk. And you're a liar."

The Prime's back stiffens as his cheeks glow crimson. "I will not stand here and be insulted by a criminal." He turns to Unisa and commands her. "Do it."

Unisa shakes her head. "Great Prime, please. Is there anything else—"

His volume climbs, his tone hardens. "Do it, Unisa. The Inner Catacomb rests on this for you."

"Great Prime, I—" Before she can complete her sentence, Juhi is on her feet again. The Cicada loses track of her, and Juhi charges forth, attempting to attack Unisa again. The Prime catches her charging toward them and his instincts kick in. He shrieks like a coward and moves aside, clearing the path for Juhi to land blows on Unisa.

The two women scuffle again, as Juhi backs Unisa's wings into the wall behind her. When the hawk's mouth is by Unisa's ear, before the

Prime or the Cicada can pull her away, Juhi whispers to Unisa, "Avenge me, Uni. Make me proud."

Juhi maneuvers her body so that the point of the blade in Unisa's hand is against her stomach, and then she pushes herself forward, driving the blade through her torso. The Cicada reaches them and pulls Juhi back. The hilt still tight in Unisa's hand, she withdraws the now-bloody blade from Juhi's body.

The Cicada forces the hawk back down onto her knees again, as she coughs and blood springs from her mouth.

"Finish it, Unisa!" the Prime commands, now yelling. "Quickly!"

Unisa holds Juhi's eye contact. The hawk smiles weakly and nods to the angi. There's no time left to delay. Juhi's words from the night before ring in her ears.

One day, you will have to make the difficult choice of taking someone's life, Unisa.

Unisa swings the blade and takes her first life. Juhi's life.

The blade splits her through the neck. Her torso falls forward, and her head rolls backward along the office floor.

The shock of what has just transpired, and what's transpired over recent weeks—Ora, Lyla, Juhi—empties Unisa's mind of everything, but three questions.

Who am I? What have I become? How much more will I have to lose?

The Prime opens his mouth wide at the sight of Juhi's body and wicked laughter erupts from her his throat.

The sword hangs limply from Unisa's hands, her fingers loosely clutching the hilt. She feels defeated, though Juhi's plan was successful in keeping Unisa's involvement, and the Hawks' existence, a secret from the Prime.

He still doesn't know anything. And as long as he doesn't know, he doesn't hold the power.

The Prime's laughter echoes through the room as Unisa's crimson sins drip from the tip of the blade and splatter on the floor, washing away the Unisa that once was.

CHAPTER 61

"SUCCESS REQUIRES SACRIFICE"

Alphocracy *MoonSide*
Date *29th Day of Month 7, Year 1629 DG*

SALESSA HASN'T LEFT HER ROOM in twenty-four hours. Zoya came by in the morning to escort her to breakfast, but Salessa had asked to be alone.

Soon after, a young Doruh boy arrived, carrying a message from Lexona. Salessa's mind wondered why the serpent didn't deliver it herself, while her heart filled with relief that she didn't have to interact with her.

The message requested that Salessa refuse to attend Zoya's Devotion Ceremony if the horse invited her. *Request* is a light term that eases the truth of the situation: It was a command. It wasn't about a mutual, consensual agreement. It was about control.

Everything is about control. The request. Lexona's actions the night before. Salessa had obeyed and acquiesced because she thought she was providing Lexona with something the serpent spent years craving, yearning for. Something Salessa herself craved and yearned for.

But Lexona had turned it into something else entirely. Every time she opened her mouth, it wasn't love and intimacy that poured out, it was commands and control.

Sometime in the afternoon, Lexona must have told Zoya about the Devotion Ceremony. As predicted, Zoya knocked on Salessa's door and invited her to attend as a special guest. And as commanded, Salessa thanked her, then refused the invitation.

She could see the light dim from Zoya's eyes and it broke the falcon's heart.

Throughout the day and into the evening, Salessa grows suspicious of the hastily-planned Ceremony. Lexona schedules the Devotion Ceremonies weeks in advance. How could she have made the decision to give Zoya a Ceremony last night, and then planned and scheduled it for tonight? And why did she ask Salessa to refuse the invitation?

As night falls, two things become clear to Salessa.

The first is that her time here at Lover's Plateau has come to an end. Despite all of the rituals she still needs to participate in, all of the resurrection secrets she still needs to uncover, all of the work that still needs to be done, the events of the previous night have done a great deal to show that she has spent too much time away from her life, away from SunSide.

Away from Naina.

She's allowed herself to drift too far into a fantasy. One where Lexona is the girl she fell in love with, and not the one she'd turned out to be later on. Not the woman she proved herself to be last night.

It's time to go home, and to go back to the Salessa that arrived here. She packs a travel bag full of her belongings, but doesn't pack any of the elegant sarees Lexona had gifted her. They are nothing but a reminder of the person she became while she was here.

The second thing that's become clear to her is that she can't allow Lexona the control she seeks. The control she believes is hers, naturally and inherently. She dresses in a plain, cotton, light blue shalwar kameez and white dupatta, hoists her travel bag onto her shoulder, and heads to the Devotion Ceremony chamber to attend Zoya's celebration before she leaves Lover's Plateau.

Forever.

When she gets to the door of the chamber, she can hear chanting from inside. It's quite loud. She places her travel bag down outside the chamber door and slowly pushes it open, entering the room and closing the door behind her.

She stands before the towering altar where she, Lexona, and Afzal sit to perform their rituals. The illumination is dimmer than she expected.

The chanting echoes off of the walls and strikes Salessa's ears at an almost painful volume. There are members of the O'Raha standing in a circle, all the way around the perimeter of the altar, facing in. There must be something happening there that Salessa can't see with all of the people between her and the event.

Zoya must be there, it's where the honorees of the Devotion Ceremonies stand.

The O'Raha members chanting and surrounding the altar are clad in long red robes. Salessa has never seen these garments before; they feature hoods, gloves, and masks, comprehensively covering the wearer from head-to-toe. The falcon listens closely, trying to make out what they're chanting. She isn't able to, but she recognizes it's in Nysabaani, and the cadence makes her believe it's a hymn or some kind of spiritual ode.

She steps toward the altar and the two cloaked chanters furthest out from the altar, at the very edge of the perimeter, notice her. They separate, making a path. With every step the falcon takes, the O'Raha members part to make room, continuing the chorus unfazed.

Finally, the innermost members forming the perimeter separate and Salessa ascends the stairs until she is on the altar. She doesn't see Zoya but something is lying on the ground. With the dim lighting, and the distracting, incessant chanting assaulting her eardrums, Salessa has trouble making out what it is.

She takes a step forward and her sandals stick to the ground. Something wet splashes under her steps and moistens the sides of Salessa's foot. She kneels down and realizes the liquid is all over the altar, but she can't make out what it is. The falcon kneels and places two fingers onto the stone floor of the altar, then lifts them up to find a crimson liquid.

Ice fills her veins. The chanting is suddenly drowned out. The entire world comes to a standstill as Salessa realizes what's on her fingers.

Blood.

Salessa's breath catches in her throat and her eyes widen. Her gaze travels the entire stone altar platform. It's everywhere. The object lying a few feet ahead of her is a person. And they're bleeding out.

Heart beating out of her chest, ears ringing in sheer panic, she crawls forth to the body and turns it over. Nausea grows in her stomach as she makes eye contact with Zoya. The horse is still alive, still warm, but she's indescribably weak and has lost more blood than Salessa has ever seen anyone lose.

Half of her face is covered in it, as Zoya's been lying face-down on the platform. There is a thick gash along her throat. Instinctively, though her mind knows it's far too late, Salessa pulls the dupatta off of her own shoulders and holds it to the wound. She looks around at the still-chanting O'Raha members and screams for help. She screams over and over again until her voice is hoarse and her vision has blurred entirely with her frustrated and devastated tears. But the chants are too loud. They drown out Salessa's cries. Her pleas.

Her desperation.

Salessa looks back down at Zoya's throat and, predictably, the once-white dupatta is now soaked. The horse is fading quickly. She makes delirious eye contact with Salessa, raises a hand to affectionately touch the falcon's cheek, and then her head drops back.

And just like that, Zoya dies in Salessa's arms as the falcon's tears drip off of her chin and land on the young woman's face. As Salessa's heavy sobs are drowned out by the chanting around her.

They sit this way, Salessa cradling her friend's body at the center of the chanting perimeter, for some time. The falcon isn't sure what to do, where to go, what's happening. She's lost in a cyclone of confusion. She places Zoya's body down gently, lovingly, then spreads the dupatta out to cover her face.

And then the falcon rises to her feet in search of answers.

She spins in circles trying to get the cloaked O'Raha to cease the chanting and pay attention to her, but they don't. Many of them have their eyes closed and don't even seem to recognize that Salessa stands before them. The chanting has placed them into a trance.

As Salessa turns, taking in her surroundings, searching for refuge from the mounting pain in her ears and temples, she realizes there's another group of O'Raha beyond this one, also cloaked and chanting. They're facing the back wall, as if there's something happening there, as well.

Salessa steps forward and the O'Raha part for her, making room for her to descend the altar steps and approach the chanting semi-circle facing the back wall. The falcon reaches them and, as if they're expecting her, they part to make room for her without even turning to see her approach. When she's through the rows of cloaks blocking her view, she finally lays eyes on what they're all watching.

It takes every ounce of strength in her legs not to collapse when she sees it.

Afzal and Lexona stand against the back wall, completely unclothed. Afzal sits on his knees, sweating profusely, eyelids fluttering. He barely has the strength to remain upright. There are bloody cuts all over his body, and an expression of pure agony on his face.

Lexona stands facing him, her back to Salessa. The serpent doesn't realize she's entered the semicircle. In one hand, Lexona grasps a small dagger with a serpent design on the hilt.

"Lexona," Salessa breathes out and, despite the chanting, despite the whispered volume, the serpent senses her. She turns around, eyes wide, and raises her arms sharply into the air. All chanting in the room stops instantly and Salessa reels from the jarring shift in noise.

"Salessa, what are you doing here?" Lexona asks. "You weren't supposed to see this. I asked you not to come to the Devotion Ceremony."

"Devotion Ceremony?" Salessa responds, her mouth falling completely open. "Lexona, what the *fuck* is happening? Zoya is dying, Afzal is bleeding." Her voice cracks and tears break from her eyes.

Lexona pauses, then says, "Zoya has been honored and celebrated. She happily offered her life for the resurrection. For the Twins." She spreads her arms wide. "For us, her god and goodesses."

Salessa is lost for words. She nearly stumbles forward as she moves closer, her chest breaking into heavy sobs. "Wh-what are you doing, Lexona? Y-you killed Zoya? And what are you doing to Afzal?" There are so many questions and Salessa is frightened more of the answers than anything else.

"I didn't kill her," Lexona shakes her head, genuine confusion in her expression. "Success requires sacrifice. Sometimes a human sacrifice."

Salessa buries her face in her hands and drops to her knees, wishing more than ever before that she has never left Naina's side.

"Do you remember the conversation we had in the library about blood?" Lexona asks. Salessa keeps her face buried in her hands as she sobs. Lexona repeats the question, louder this time.

"Yes!" Salessa screams back, raising her face from her hands and sobbing louder. Her suffering mutates into rage. "I remember the fucking conversation. What does that have to do with any of this?"

"It has everything to do with this." Lexona turns and in a sight that disgusts Salessa as much as anything else she's seen in this room, the serpent flicks her tongue out and laps up blood from one of the dripping wounds on Afzal's chest.

She then turns back to Salessa. "As I said that day in the library, blood is divinity. It cleanses and purifies. It's there at birth; it's there at death. All at once, it is both a small part of who we are, and the entirety of who we are. And we must share that blood in order for the resurrection to take place."

Salessa shakes her head defiantly. "I won't. I can't."

"You can, Salessa. This is a merging ceremony, and we all need to merge in order to resurrect the Twins."

Salessa's tone hardens and she rises to her feet again, her skin growing hotter. "If this is what it takes, then fuck the Twins."

Lexona's eyes narrow. "You say that now, but wait until the Sprites come and this world needs saviors. Are you going to let innocents die because you weren't strong enough to—"

"Enough to…what?!" Salessa interrupts her. She gestures to Afzal. "This is your *brother*, Lexona, why don't either of you have clothes on?"

Lexona sighs, as if an ignorant child requires an explanation. "Salessa, why are the Sprites so powerful?"

Salessa's mouth falls agape again, lost for where this connects to what she was doing to her brother.

"Their power comes from how intimately bonded they are. They are brother and sister, sure, but the true source of their power comes from a powerful love that they only achieved when they brought their bodies together. The only hope we have to stop them is to show up on the battlefield with equal power. We have to mimic the patterns of their success. Afzal didn't understand at first, so I had to shackle him, but now"—she gestures to the leopard-man, who appears ready to fall to the ground at any moment—"he's learned not to resist. I had hoped you would support me. One day, you and Naina will also have to—"

Bile rises in Salessa's throat and she puts a hand up to stop Lexona. Before she can respond, Salessa's eye catches Afzal's defeated gaze. He uses their telepathic connection to convey a simple, but desperate message.

Help me.

Salessa deciphers tones and emotions from the telepathy. She always feels Naina's fury in much of what she conveys. Afzal's cry for help is filled with suffering. Loneliness. Despair.

She steps forward to approach Afzal, but the cloaked O'Raha members come between them to block her path.

"They won't let you through unless I allow it," Lexona says from behind them. "I am their goddess."

Since the moment she stepped into Lover's Plateau, Salessa has been hesitant to accept her role as a goddess to these people. She's rejected their desires for servitude, and eluded their worship. But now, a time has come to assert her claim. The elders have accepted her divinity.

And now, she must accept it.

Salessa raises her chin, inhales deeply to puff up her chest, and speaks in the most dominant tone her throat can conjure. "I am your Falcon Goddess. I *command* you to allow me through."

There is a moment of hesitation before the O'Raha members exchange glances and part, clearing the way for Salessa to step past Lexona, ignoring her furious protests, and kneel down beside Afzal. She helps the half-leopard sit back onto his rear, so he's no longer putting all his weight on his bloody knees, and then slowly lie down until his back is against the stone tiles.

Salessa speaks in a soft, soothing tone. "Afzal. I'm so sorry. But there is no way I'll be able to support your weight. You'll have to walk. You can lean on me a little, but I need you to walk, alright?"

Afzal nods. "I can try."

"Look at me."

The leopard turns his head weakly and makes eye contact with Salessa.

"I'm going to be by your side every single step of the way," she reassures him. "I promise."

He nods again. "Thank you, Salessa. I just need a minute."

"I understand. Lie here and catch your breath. Where are your clothes?"

He tilts his head, gesturing to a corner of the room where Lexona has discarded his clothes. When Salessa rises to get them, she realizes she had tuned out Lexona's shrieking and ranting about how Salessa is getting in the way of the resurrection and dooming the planet to the end of times. But the falcon isn't listening anymore. Her tears have stopped, her panic has subsided, her fear has died.

There is only one mission at this moment, and that mission has consumed her physically, mentally, and emotionally: get Afzal to safety.

Salessa reaches the clothes and gathers them in her hands, but when she turns back, Lexona is standing an inch away from her face.

"Salessa, I know you're upset."

Salessa gasps. "Upset? UPSET?!"

"This is all a big surprise to you, I understand." Lexona raises her hands defensively. "Please, leave Afzal here and go back to your room. When we're done, I'll come by and we can talk about this. By morning, everything will be cleared up and we can go back to normal."

Salessa is at a sincere loss for words. She stumbles through a response. "Lexona, y-you're truly not understanding what's happening here. I'm not going back to my room. I'm going home."

Lexona takes a step back. "Home?"

"Yes! Home. SunSide. And I'm taking Afzal with me."

"But…but"—Lexona's eyes trace the ground as she seems to search for words herself—"you're leaving me? What about us?"

Salessa hesitates, unsure how to deliver the news. The serpent's gaze is frenzied. Distraught. Unpredictable. "Lexona. There is no 'us.' After what you've done to Zoya. To Afzal. To me."

"To you?" Lexona's expression overwhelms with confusion again. "Salessa, I love you." She reaches for Salessa's hand. "You know I've never loved anyone as much as I love you. You'll always be mine. Last night—"

"Last night was a mistake."

Lexona nearly falls back, as if Salessa's words were a mighty wave. The serpent's eyes fill with tears and her voice breaks. "Don't…don't say that, Salessa. Please."

Salessa's throat tightens, her heart shatters, witnessing Lexona in such turmoil. She can see in Lexona's expression that the serpent truly has no idea what she's done wrong. "I made excuses for you, Lexona.

I believed in you. I tried to forgive you and give you chances to atone. But last night was just as much a betrayal as the one from three years ago." Tears break through Salessa's eyes. "Last night, all you did was prove that Naina was right. And I was wrong."

Lexona releases a broken sob. "W-why are you sa-saying this, Salessa? I was trying to show you love."

Salessa shakes her head. "I wasn't ready. I *told you* I wasn't ready and you did it anyway."

"I-I'm sorry, Salessa. I thought you wanted me to."

"It doesn't matter now. It's too late." Salessa tries to step past her, still clutching Afzal's clothes to her chest, but Lexona grabs her wrists and pulls Salessa toward her.

"Call me, 'Lexi.' Please, Salessa, call me, 'Lexi.' I'm begging you."

"Lexona, let go of me." She tries to jerk her hands away, but Lexona is stronger.

"Call me, 'Lexi.' Tell me you love me." Her grip tightens, pressing into Salessa's skin.

The falcon winces. "Lexona, you're hurting me. Let go!"

Lexona's fingers dig deeper into Salessa's wrist and the falcon think blood might be drawn if they get any tighter.

Heavy footsteps tremble the stone tiles beneath them as Afzal walks up to Lexona and gently places a hand on her shoulder.

"Let Salessa go," he pleads.

Lexona's eyes dart from Salessa to Afzal and back. Slowly, she loosens her grip and then backs away. Salessa hands the clothes over to Afzal and then wraps her arms tightly around his thick bicep, using it to help stabilize his weakened gait.

As the two broken Doruh tread past the cloaked O'Raha, past the altar where Zoya's body lies, they hear Lexona's screams echo from behind them.

"This is a mistake! Afzal! Salessa! The One Myth…the prophecy must be fulfilled! You're sabotaging the fate of the world! You'll regret walking out of here!"

Salessa's feet stop in their tracks at her last statement. She turns around to face Lexona one last time.

"For three years, I regretted walking away from you because there was always a lingering thought. A 'what if' that made me wonder if we could've been something more if I had forgiven you. But what you said, all those weeks ago in the gardens, is still the truth, and will always be the truth, Lexona." She swallows, holding back the pain erupting in her words. "I will always see you as a serpent and nothing more. Because that's the only side of you that you continue to show me."

Not waiting for a reply, Salessa turns back, tightens her grip around Afzal's upper arm, and they continue to exit the chamber together.

Lexona continues to scream, but her final plea isn't to Salessa, it's to Afzal. "What are you going to do without me, Afzal? Huh? I'm the only thing keeping the human side of you alive! Without me, you're an animal. Do you hear me, Afzal? You're nothing but an animal without me!"

By the time they reach the chamber door and Salessa hoists her travel bag over her shoulder, Afzal is sobbing. Salessa closes the door behind them while Afzal gets dressed.

"I'll take you to your room," Salessa offers, "to gather your things for the journey to SunSide."

Afzal shakes his head. "I just want to leave, Salessa. There's nothing here I want to keep. Please. Just take me away from here."

Salessa nods and places a gentle hand on his back. "Of course. I understand. Let's go home."

CHAPTER 62

"I Am Not An Animal"

***Alphocracy** MoonSide*
***Date** 29th Day of Month 7, Year 1629 DG*

THE JOURNEY BACK TO SUNSIDE is not easy. No cart, no horse, no means of getting down the mountain from the entrance of Lover's Plateau. It takes them hours by foot. The journey down the mountain begins at sunset. By the time they reach the base, it's long after midnight.

The first two or three hours, Salessa listens uncomfortably as Afzal sniffles and sobs, but pretends he isn't. The remainder of the journey, his eyes have dried but the silence remains thick. The two Doruh say nothing, as they listen to the sounds of the mountain fauna around them.

Finally, when Salessa's feet feel like they're bleeding from walking so far and so long, they get to the base of the mountain trail at the villages of the Northern Hills. They find a carriage here, a small one built for only two passengers at a time.

It's all they need. Salessa offers the driver a hefty bag of stones, the only one she has left, to take them home.

Afzal climbs up and into the carriage. He crosses his arms over his chest and stares out into the vast openness of the path ahead of them, his thick feline lips still tightly pressed together. The bright, talkative man she'd grown close with doesn't seem to be here with her now.

The silence continues as they watch the residents of the Northern Hills passing by, distracting themselves from thoughts of what they've been through. Finally, Salessa hears Afzal's sad, broken voice emerge from his hoarse throat.

"Thank you, Salessa," he says. "For rescuing me."

Salessa offers him a friendly smile, though her heart is weighed down with guilt. "Don't thank me. I should have figured out what she was doing to you a long time ago."

Afzal shakes his head. "You couldn't have known. I didn't tell anyone."

He looks down at his feet and a gut-wrenching realization strikes Salessa. She takes in his feline muzzle, his massive paws, the rosettes on his skin, and the patches of fur sprouting around him. The truth of his condition is clearer now than ever before.

"It was a lie, wasn't it?" Salessa asks.

Afzal meets her gaze, an eyebrow raised. "What was a lie?"

"Lexona would ask you, every day, if you're an animal. I questioned her as to why she did that and she said it was to remind you of your human side. That was a lie."

Afzal remains silent, confirming Salessa's realization.

She continues, "And you lied. When you said you don't shift your paws back to human hands because it would be an insult to the Twins. You're physically unable to shift back, aren't you? Because it isn't the merging rituals or the resurrection, or anything having to do with the Twins that's turned you into a half-leopard."

Afzal's bottom lip quivers and he nods, turning back to his feet. "It's Lexona. It's all of the things that were done to me when I didn't want them done to me. Those actions, against my will, robbed me of my sense of self, and turned me into the only thing Lexona saw me as." His voice breaks. "Some animal for her to toy with. For her to control. I don't even remember who I was when I was fully human. And now I have to live with"—he raises his paws—"the effects of her actions. She's changed me and I don't know how to get back to who I was before what she did."

He buries his face in his paw pads and breaks into sobs again. Salessa places her arm around his shoulders to comfort him, but he shudders, so she pulls it back.

"I j-just don't want to be touched right now," he says apologetically.

Salessa nods. "I understand."

After a few moments of regaining his composure, Afzal pulls his face from his paws but keeps his gaze on his feet. "I can still feel her. All over me. No matter how much I bathe or wash, I never feel clean after. It feels like—"

"She's touching you? Dirtying you over and over again, all the time?" Salessa's chest tightens as Afzal looks up at her, his eyes wide.

"You, too?" he asks.

She nods, biting her lip to control her anguish.

"When?"

"Last night," Salessa's voice breaks in a whisper. She turns to the road ahead, and she says something that she hopes will reassure him. "She's committed a crime whose filth doesn't wash away with water, but may wash away with time."

Afzal nods, taking her words in. "She told me if I left, the resurrection would fail, and it would be my fault. I couldn't let innocent people die because I couldn't handle the"—he pauses—"ritual. So I let her do it to me. Over and over again. For years. While my body betrayed me and gave her what she wanted."

Salessa leans down. "Your body reacted to a physical stimulus, independent of your desires. You have to remember: none of this is your fault." She nearly gasps aloud. As soon as the statement ends, she realizes she should probably be reciting the advice in the mirror.

But it's harder to wash one's own hands of blame than it is to wash the hands of others.

They sit silently again for some time, the residents of the Northern Hills still bouncing happily past their cart as it makes its way toward SunSide. With silence filling the air between them again, Salessa has a chance to focus on these individuals and couples and families. They all seem peaceful, joyous. Oblivious to the terrors from which these two travelers have just come.

Some of the residents carry portraits and sculptures and other pieces of art. Others gather around small podiums and stages and theaters to listen to individuals making speeches or reciting something. Families with children stop to buy the young ones food or play games. When she hears explosions overhead, Salessa looks up at the night sky and sees fireworks.

She realizes what's happening around them.

"This is it, isn't it?" she asks Afzal, recalling something Zoya said to them two weeks earlier during poetry night in her room. "This is the Poetry Festival of the Northern Hills. The one Zoya invited us to. She wanted us all to come attend this festival together."

Afzal swallows hard and nods. "Lexona said she was the only thing keeping the human side of me alive. But that wasn't true. The only thing that kept me human"—his voice strains—"was Zoya."

Salessa takes the smiles of the joyous passers-by in and has an idea. "Share a poem, Afzal."

The leopard turns to her, eyebrow raised. "What?"

"Share a poem. It's Poetry Night tonight." She points to the starry skies above and Afzal looks up. "Zoya is with us. Up there. The three of us are together to celebrate Poetry Night again." She lowers her gaze to meet Afzal's again. "And it's your turn. Recite something in Zoya's honor."

"I don't have anything written," he responds.

"Just recite it from your heart. You've done it before. She's listening."

Afzal nods and takes a deep breath. He turns his gaze up to the stars and whispers, "I love you, Zoya." And then, with the fireworks overhead, and the love of friends and families and couples flowing around them, he recites from the heart:

As I drift off from the safety of shore,
Casting into an oblivion evermore,
Swimming into a new life unsure,
Possibly into a bed beneath the soil floor,

I ask them: Am I an animal?

Animals choose not the motion of fate
They live to eat, to drink, and to mate
Is it futile to sit and ruminate,
When I'm a man for whom no good awaits?

Does that mean I am an animal?

I wept until these bones were dry,
And begged until blood filled my eyes,
Yet, you still went on to die,
I loved you when I said goodbye,

But, somehow, they are certain I am an animal.

Animals have no life after death
They do not feel this much regret
They do not walk after sunset
They simply fade with their silhouette

And yet, I am an animal?

Muzzle and whiskers, fur and claws
Tail and teeth, ears and paws
Innocence torn from my jaws
I was a man…I was, I was

But now, am I an animal?

I soar high on a falcon's wings,
I warn intruders with bites and stings,
I roar just like the jungle king,
I may be all of these things,

But, I promise, I am not an animal.

I am not an animal.

EPILOGUE

"RED-LO AND DROF-FA"

Theocracy *SunSide*
Date *50th Day of Month 7, Year 1629 DG*

NAINA HATES THE LONG DESCENT down to the dungeons. It's dark, smelly, and the moist stone steps make her feel unsteady.

But she makes the trek nonetheless to do what she must.

She reaches the chamber that holds his cell and enters, closing the iron door behind her. Casually, almost instinctively, she walks up to the bars of his cell, pulls out the key, unlocks it, and enters, taking a seat on the floor next to him.

"What's the date?" Red-Lo asks her.

"The Fiftieth. Month Seven."

"Twenty-one days since we've been back."

Naina nods. "Three long weeks."

"They still don't know you come to visit me?"

Naina chuckles. "How in the world would I explain this to them?"

"Fair point." The faerie turns and his gaze traverses Naina's body. "You've gained the weight back. Congratulations."

Naina flexes her bicep. "Yeah, my muscles seemed to remember what they were *supposed* to look like, so when I started eating and exercising again, they just sort of popped back into place."

"Any other updates from above?" He's curious, as always.

"I don't remember what the last thing I told you was," Naina admits. "Lessi, Afzal, and I have been practicing the rituals they taught me when they got back from Lover's Plateau. He and I haven't been able to form a telepathic connection, yet, but we're still trying. Rafael is still trying to get news from SeaBed, to find out if his mother survived, but they've gone dark on communication since over half the city was destroyed. Saila's new legislation, outlawing executions, passed through the Assembly. Feathers is"—she pauses, sadness filling her chest—"not really herself these days, but she's been through a lot. She'll come back around."

"Does she know she's one of the Saviors Six?"

Naina shakes her head. "I haven't told her yet. I don't think Rafael has either."

Red-Lo lifts his hands and starts counting. "Six champions to face the Sprites on the battlefield. The Twins. Rafael. Unisa. That's four. Who are the other two?"

Naina shrugs. "I guess we'll have to find out."

"You have ten years," he reminds her. "Make them count."

Naina chuckles. "Oh, I will."

"The Ancient Ones gave you a lot of information. It makes me wonder if they're overly confident, or overly stupid."

"Probably the first one." She turns to him. "You were frozen. Like paralyzed or turned into stone or something. When they showed up in your mind and spoke to me. Were you able to hear anything?"

Red-Lo nods. "I heard everything. But that's the last I'll ever hear of them. They've left my head."

"Do you remember what we were talking about before they turned you to stone?"

Red-Lo meets her gaze. "I do."

"You asked me to send you to your wife. To deliver on the promise that Saila and Feathers made to you a year ago."

Red-Lo nods. "I did."

Naina swallows, hesitating. "But, in order to send you to see your wife, I would have to—"

"I understand."

Naina pauses, contemplating whether or not she should make the offer. "So…do you still want me to?"

Red-Lo chuckles. "Of course I do. Nothing has changed."

"So you're ready? Now?"

Red-Lo breathes deeply and smiles. "I'm ready now. Yes."

Naina rises to her feet, then turns to face Red-Lo. "Goodbye, Red."

"Goodbye, Naina. I'm sorry, for so many things."

Naina nods. "I know you are. I was in your head."

Without another word, with only a monstrous growl, Naina shifts into her wolf form. Her mighty lupine jaws envelop his neck, and with one righteous pull, tears his throat out.

Within seconds, the Ore Monger dies with a smile on his face.

***

Endless bliss cradles his essence as a loving parent cradles a newborn. It lasts only for a moment, until his eyes pop open again. He sits up quickly as his senses return. His body is whole, no wound, no ache. In fact, his turquoise skin glows youthfully like an ember in a dark room.

The faerie's essence is clothed in a white outfit; light, airy material covers him from the shoulders down, wrapped around his body. He rises to observe the surroundings. A verdant forest, more stunning than he's ever seen before. It feels alive, breathing around him.

He's in a clearing, filled with spirit and brilliant life. At the very center is a girthy tree with so many branches and leaves, it would take a millennium to count. It features colors Red-Lo has never seen before, and the interconnected roots expand out to every tree in this section of forest.

From behind this tree, an entity appears. A grotesque, deformed figure with thin, raven hair that appears unattached to her scalp. Crimson eyes sunken in, sharp teeth, and a serpentine tongue. Her magenta skin is wrinkled, flaking off and blistery. She is covered in a black garment that flows around her, like a dark cloud trying desperately to cling to her.

Despite her appearance, he recognizes her and his throat tightens. Words escape him, so all he can do is call to her. After eight-hundred-and-forty-six years, he's able to speak to his wife for the first time.

"Drof-Fa." His voice is a whisper. Gentle. Loving. "Is that you?"

The entity steps forward until she is directly in front of him. "It's me, Red."

His breath hitches in his throat. "Drof-Fa, I asked them to send me here to you. I didn't know what happened to you. What the Sprites did to you. I thought they killed you that night. In the cave. Had I known you were here I would've—"

"Would've what?" she demands, her tone hardening. "Died to come here?"

His expression contorts in confusion. "Yes, Drof-Fa. I would have. You're my wife. Are you angry?"

"Do you have any idea how insulting that is?"

Red-Lo's mouth falls open. "I-I don't understand."

Drof-Fa sighs. "Red, we were happy. Everything was perfect until the night we..."

"I know," he says, nodding. "Until we lost her."

"Yes, until we lost her. And then we grieved, and eventually, I had to take up ruling in your place. While you dragged me onto this quest for immortality. To seek out the mighty Sprites who would bless you with it."

Her volume rises. "Well, here we are, Red. I am immortal, and I didn't even want it. Do you know what I wanted? I wanted to die. I wanted to live a normal life span, and die with you in a warm bed. But you didn't want that, so forgive me if I don't believe you when you say you would have died sooner had you known it would bring us together. You had the chance to die with me, and you chose instead to become their puppet, and damn me to this godsforsaken existence."

After waiting so long to see her, he hadn't expected her to be so angry with him. "Drof-Fa, I love you. I've always loved you. Even when I made the mistake of freeing the Sprites, I thought I was doing what was best for us both. I kept SunSide's throne for eight hundred years. For you."

She raises a finger. "Don't. I saw it all, remember? You did *not* keep the Doruh enslaved, for me. You did not invade MoonSide, for me. You did not take their land and slaughter their people, for me. You did not abduct citizens, and drain their essences, for me. You did not hunt two young Doruh girls for twelve years, for me. You did not share your bed with thousands over those eight hundred years, for me. You did not murder igni and use their exoskeletons to make ore, for me."

She takes a deep breath. "Most of all, you did not doom the planet to the wrath of the Sprites, for me. So many will die, and it is not my fault, Red. It is yours."

The depth of Red-Lo's crimes against himself, his wife, innocents, and entire societies and communities strikes him. For eight hundred years, he's done nothing but harm others. His gaze finds the golden light emanating from an opening between two thick trees.

"That's it, isn't it?" he asks. "The World Beyond."

Drof-Fa nods. "That's it, yes."

"What happens to essences like mine? The ones that didn't spend their life enjoining good in the world? The evil ones?"

"That depends on the deities they worshipped in this life. Their deities will either have mercy on them, or they won't."

"And what if you spent eight hundred years not believing in any deity?"

Drof-Fa turns to him. "Then may someone else's deity have mercy on you."

Red-Lo nods. "I really do love you, Drof-Fa."

"I loved you, too, Red. But that was a long, long time ago."

"I wish I had just listened to you. And we had died as you described. In a warm bed, over eight hundred years ago."

"So do I, Red."

He steps forward and as the golden light swallows him, he says, "I'm sorry, Drof-Fa. For everything."

Once he's gone, and Drof-Fa the TreeKeeper is alone again, she whispers to herself, "So am I, Red. So am I."

Glossary

Terms marked with (F) relate to fictional characters, settings, concepts, or items.

Terms marked with (NF) relate to non-fictional concepts or items.

The Academy of Librarians / "The Academy" (F) – institution of study and training for Student Librarians

Adera (F) – both a gerontocratic village and the pixie for whom the village is named / the village is governed by an elderly Headwoman / pronounced *a-DAYR-a*

Aerthomni (F) – one of the two known continents of the All-Sphere / pronounced *air-THOM-nee*

Afzal (F) – 21 years old / Salessa's twin brother / Doruh / animal form is a leopard / has been living amongst the O'Raha for the past three years / pronounced *uh-f-zull*

The Agrarian Townlets (F) – federation of small towns governed by local farmers and those who cultivate the land

Aissa (F) – late thirties / angi / Member of the New SunSidian Assembly from the inner districts of Larso

Alba (F) – deceased / mari human / Alvaro, the Prime Librarian was her uncle / Ana was her younger sister / was Kyoko's mentor / regarded by other Librarians as a paragon of the Library's teachings / shared common mari anatomy: fins on the forearms and down the spine, piscine nare slits in place of a human nose, webbed fingers, and organs that allow for breathing underwater

Alba's Plan (F) – during the events of *The Ore Monger*, Alba and Unisa devised a plot to overthrow the Prime and destroy the modern iteration of the Library, hoping to rebuild it with the ideals of the original Library / at the dawn of the Library, and for many generations after, the founding Prime Librarians were moral and wise, wanting nothing more than to accurately and transparently catalogue the history of the continent within the Library's catacombs / over time, political alliances and societal control corrupted those who held the position, creating a shift in the nature of the Prime's role / modern Primes became willing to alter the records of the Library to glorify their allies and vilify those whom their allies oppress / they also committed heinous crimes against their citizens, emboldened by their control over the collective societal narratives and the lack of accountability this afforded them / Unisa now hopes to enact Alba's Plan

The All-Sphere (F) – planet on which the story is set / has two known continents: Aerthomni and Panaerth

The Alphocracy of Moonside (F) – government headed by Alphas in MoonSide / original iteration formed in 784 DG, until 1381 DG / now being reinstated/reestablished after the expulsion of SunSide's military occupation in MoonSide

Alvaro / The Prime (F) – ninth and top rank of the Librarian hierarchy / political, social, and spiritual leader of the Library / uniform is black silk tunic / title currently held by a mari man: Alvaro, Alba's and Ana's uncle / late fifties / shares common mari anatomy: fins on the forearms and down the spine, piscine nare slits in place of a human nose, webbed fingers, and internal organs that allow for breathing underwater / his most unique feature is his eyes; they are somehow warm and cold at the same time / at the dawn of the Library, and for many generations after, the founding Prime Librarians were moral and wise, wanting nothing more than to accurately and transparently catalogue the history of the continent within the Library's catacombs / over time, political alliances and societal control corrupted those who held the position, creating a shift in the nature of the Prime's role / modern Primes became willing to alter the records of the Library to glorify their allies and vilify those whom their allies oppress / they also committed heinous crimes against their citizens, emboldened by their control over the collective societal narratives and the lack of accountability this afforded them / Alvaro is no exception to this

Ambassador Librarians / Ambassadors (F) – seventh rank of the Librarian hierarchy / uniform is yellow silk tunics / lead groups of Recorder and Vice Ambassador Librarians around the continent to witness historical events and record them for the Library's Catacombs

Amma / Headwoman of Adera (F) – village elder who governs Adera

Ana (F) – 30 years old / mari human / accomplished Nysabaani translator and researcher / Alba's younger sister / shares common mari anatomy: fins on the forearms and down the spine, piscine nare slits in place of a human nose, webbed fingers, and organs that allow for breathing underwater / since the events of *The Ore Monger,* she has left the library and has been living with Rafael and Kyoko in SunSide, while searching for clues in ancient Sprite texts as to the location and timing of the release of the Three Deaths

The Ancient Ones / The Sprites (F) – two Sprites released from imprisonment millennia after, what was believed to be, the extinction of the Sprite species / not much is known about them other than their threat to release the Three Deaths should Red-Lo not provide them with an essence, as agreed upon at the time of their release from imprisonment / with Red-Lo in Saila's custody, he won't be able to hold up his end of the bargain, so it is expected that the Three Deaths will be released / the time and location of the Three Deaths' release is unknown, but Rafael, Kyoko, and Ana have been working on finding this information in ancient Sprite texts

Andres (F) – mid twenties / mari / has taken over the position of Prime's Gatekeeper after Rafael left the Library at the end of *The Ore Monger*

Angi (F) – one of three human clans / possess wings whose feathers appear silver and polished, resembling steel / built the city of PeakHaven atop the highest mountains of the PeakHaven mountain range / governed by a Super-Montane Stratocracy: headed by the military / pronounced *aan-jee*

Arlun (F) – capital city of MoonSide / founded at the time of the first Alphocracy's formation in 784 DG / connected to SunSide's capital city, Larso, by PeakHaven Pass / pronounced *ar-lin*

Ashiyu (NF) – a Japanese public bath in which the feet are dipped / common in EverEmber, as the development of the fictional igni culture was influenced by Japanese culture

Bravers (F) – disbanded SunSidian military and law enforcement who served the now-dissolved monarchy

Bravers United (F) – former Bravers who've joined together to form a rebellious force within SunSide / led by Tund-Ra / responsible for violent uprisings in the capital city, Larso, that led to the deaths of innocent civilians

Braver General (F) – former head of the Braver organization / last held by Vy-Ro, before the disbandment of the organization

The Bridge Tree (F) – spiritual location that connects this world to the World Beyond / watched over by the TreeKeeper / girthy tree with so many branches and leaves, it would take a millennium to count / interconnected roots expand out to the other trees in the Forest of Essences / where essences arrive in order to be ushered into the World /beyond by the TreeKeeper

Brimah (F) – captured Cicada Librarian / angi

The Bunker (F) – a track-proof safe house Zakia built in SunSide / where Rafael, Kyoko, and Ana have lived for the past year, since the events of *The Ore Monger*

Captain General Francisco / Francisco (F) – one of the Generals who govern SeaBed / leads SeaBed's stratocracy

The Castrum (F) – complex of buildings and structures in Larso through which all SunSidian government functions operate / the Assembly's Forum, the Head Salver's clinic, and all government administration lies within the Castrum

The Catacombs / The Library's Catacomb Network (F) – system of tunnels under the city connecting large chambers called "sections," in which the Library houses and catalogs the entirety of Aerthomni's written history / also connects all of the sections to the Center: the Library's hub for government and administration / the records and documents held within the Catacombs are the most valuable artifacts in existence

The Center (F) – the Library's hub for government and administration / the top floor of the Center is a wide, open chamber filled with sturdy, metal desks and flimsy, wooden partitions between them / this is where the Prime's office is

CereCenters (F) – educational epicenters constructed and governed by the Library / there are a total of fifty-six CereCenters / Educator Librarians are sent to CereCenters for the academic season to teach human, Doruh, and Mega students about the continent's history, along with various other subjects / at the end of the academic season, the Educators return to the Library until the following season, during which they are assigned to a new CereCenter / the Prime seeks out impoverished villages to which he can offer economic and architectural rehabilitation in exchange for building the CereCenter / pronounced *seh-ra-sen-ters*

Chai (NF) – a popular tea throughout the South Asian subcontinent / *chai* is the full name of the beverage, and it should never be called "chai tea" / popular Doruh beverage, as the development of the fictional Doruh culture was influenced by the culture of the South Asian subcontinent

Cicada Librarians / The Cicadas (F) – undercover faction of Librarians who work in secret, following the orders of the Prime

Corazón Azul (F) – largest of the domed communities, in the center of SeaBed / home to commercial districts, government buildings, the homes of the wealthiest residents

Court Democracy (F) – form of government in which seven elected officials, known as the Mother's Court, governs the city / officials are given the title of Courtman or Courtwoman / this is the only human government that is not led by the military, as both SeaBed and PeakHaven are Stratocracies

Currency / Stones (F) – polished stones used as currency / a circular blue stone, a triangular green stone, and a rectangular red stone / dominant form of payment across the continent

Deepweed (F) – large farming municipality in the Agrarian Townlets, northeast of West Wine and southeast of Soil King

The Dissolved Nations (F) – once dominated by prosperous kings and queens, ministers, councilmen, and presidents / now empty land that others do not settle, as it is believed to be cursed / each nation in the region was named for the most common occupation of the residents there: Merchant, Bard, Cobbler, Courtesan, and Smith

Doruh (F) – species of shapeshifters / shift into animals using energy from the Radiance / their animal forms are typically hereditary / Doruh twins, whether identical or fraternal, will always shift into the same animal form / have two essences: one human and one animal / the term "animal" is used as a slur to refer to this species / most Doruh worship the Twins / pronounced *doe-ROO*

Doruh Genesis (F) – current calendar era / noted as "DG"

The Doruh Uprisings / Doruh Liberation (F) – Liberation originally planned for 767 DG, but was stopped by the usurping of the SunSidian throne by Red-Lo, Drof-Fa, and the Faerie Empowerment Forces / this led to the Uprisings in 784 DG, which freed the Doruh and set up the Alphocracy / the Doruh were free until 1381 DG, when SunSide invaded MoonSide, assassinated the Alphas, and set up their military occupation

Drof-Fa (F) – faerie / General of the Faerie Empowerment Forces until 767 DG / MegaMother of SunSide from 767 DG to 783 DG, when Red-Lo asked her to join him on a quest for immortality / this led to them inadvertently liberating the Ancient Ones from their imprisonment, and Drof-Fa subsequently being cursed to live on as the TreeKeeper / wife of Red-Lo the MegaFather / pronounced *DRO-fa*

Dupatta (NF) – a long shawl-like scarf traditionally worn by women in the South Asian subcontinent to cover the head and shoulders / most commonly as part of the women's shalwar kameez outfit / common Doruh attire, as the development of the fictional Doruh culture was influenced by the culture of the South Asian Subcontinent

Educator Librarians / Educators (F) – fifth rank of the Librarian hierarchy / uniform is red linen tunics / teach courses at both the Academy and the CereCenters

Eela (F) – Sprite / healer

Eloa (F) – small village on the northern coast of SunSide / where Saila grew up and where her mother resided prior to her death / pronounced *eh-lua*

Elva (F) – one of the Ancient Ones / "the female Sprite" / imprisoned with her brother/husband Kova by Vala

Era of the Nysabaan (F) – original calendar era of recorded history / noted as "EN" / era during which ancient inhabitants of the All-Sphere, known as the Nysabaan, were the dominant species / Nysabaani was the dominant language / runs until 2165 EN, the year during which historical records indicate the extinction of the Sprite species, and evolutionary divergence of the human and Mega species / pronounced *NEE-sah-baan*

Essence (F) – soul

EverEmber (F) – one of the three human cities / governed by Court Democracy; only human city without a military-led government / populated by the igni human clan / comprised of three islands: Roba, Sila, and Tusa / Mount Mother is at the center of the city and the igni culture - historically, spiritually, socially, politically / heat from the volcano rises into the air, then descends and covers the waters around the island, forming a natural defense / the igni do not display any particular organization in religion or spirituality, yet they do "feed" their dead to Mt. Mother, so that their stone exoskeletons can be liquified and become part of the volcanic rock

The Everlasting Journey (F) – a journey in search of immortality taken by Red-Lo the MegaFather and Drof-Fa the MegaMother in 783 DG, which leads to them inadvertently liberating the Ancient Ones from their imprisonment, and Drof-Fa subsequently being cursed to live on as the TreeKeeper / with the help of his Head Salver, Red-Lo penned an autobiography and titled it after this event

Evic (F) – small village on the farthest edge of MoonSide, directly to the east of Red-Lo River / this is where Naina and Salessa settled after escaping Arlun at 8 years old / they lived here until the events of *The Ore Monger* when they were 20 years old / Salessa's entire original relationship with Lexona occurred in the years they were living in Evic / pronounced *EE-vik*

The Facilitator (F) – advisor and confidant of the monarch, prior to the dissolution of the SunSidian monarchy / position last held by Saith (Saila's father, now deceased)

Faeries (F) – one of the three Mega clans / evolved from the Sprites toward the end of the Era of the Nysabaan / originally possessed the ability to access and harness the energy of the Radiance, though that ability dwindled as the faerie reliance on technology increased and they used the Radiance less and less / present-day faeries can no longer access the Radiance at all / share the common physical traits of all Mega: pointed ears and solid-gray eyes with no pupils or irises / led the Mega campaign to enslave the Doruh after their creation in 1 DG / prevented Doruh Liberation in 767 DG by usurping the SunSidian throne / invaded MoonSide in 1381 DG and assassinated the Alphas / created the Braver organization and used it to set up a military occupation in SunSide / built settlements in MoonSide in 1422 after capturing land that belonged to MoonSidians and driving them from their homes / drove most of the nymphs and pixies out of Larso and into Nivyan Hollow / introduced the ore to SunSide, and later to the entire continent, severing any remaining nymphs and pixies in Larso from the Radiance / most faeries are followers of the Four, the dominant Mega religion / faerie familial naming conventions hyphenate a family name to the first name (e.g. Red-Lo and Zar-Lo; Hay-Ro and Vy-Ro)

Faerie Empowerment Forces (F) - faerie warriors who came together to oppose the policies of MegaMother Picana, as she attempted to liberate the Doruh and instill equity amongst the species and clans of SunSidian society / started by Zif-Lo, father of Red-Lo

/ when Zif-Lo dies in a clash with MegaMother Picana's forces, Red-Lo takes over and Drof-Fa becomes the general / they eventually assassinate MegaMother Picana (depicted in the prologue of *The Ore Monger*) and Red-Lo usurps the throne

Faolan (F) – 17 years old / nymph with skin the color of reddish autumn leaves / Member of the New SunSidian Assembly from the villages of the north

The Forum (F) – vast chamber in the Castrum where the Members of the New SunSidian Assembly hold their sessions / a magnificent stage rests on one end of the chamber, tall windows line the walls, and polished stone, embedded with gems, covers the floor

The Four (F) – the four suns, deities of the dominant Mega religion / the Four are Ona, Lona, Throna, and Frona; this is the order in which they rise from the horizon, as well as how they are ordered in strength and age / Ona is the oldest and the strongest while Frona is the youngest and weakest / Ona and Frona are typically referred to with feminine pronouns, while Lona and Throna are typically referred to with masculine, though there is no certainty of gender from scripture / they are praised often with the phrase "Glory to the Four!" / statues, monuments, and shrines to the Four are featured in designated areas all around the vast compound of the Temple Complex in Larso

Francisco / Captain General Francisco (F) – one of the Generals who govern SeaBed / leads SeaBed's stratocracy

Frona (F) – Frona is the youngest and weakest of the Four, deities of the dominant Mega religion / she is the last to rise from the horizon, after Ona, Lona, and Throna / she is typically referred to with feminine pronouns, though there is no certainty of gender from scripture / pronounced *FROE-nah*

Fully Bonded (F) – an ideal that the Prime commands all Librarians to strive toward / he uses this ideal as a way to manipulate and control the citizens

Fully Broken (F) – an ideal that the Prime warns all Librarians to avoid / the Fully Broken are promptly arrested and taken for rehabilitation or exile / these are the individuals who've seen past the Prime's lies

Gatekeeper Librarians / Gatekeepers (F) – third rank of the Librarian hierarchy / uniform is gold cotton tunics / oversee the intake and outtake of records, documents, and artifacts from their assigned sections within the CataCombs

Gerontocracy (NF) – a form of government led by elders

The Gerontocratic Villages (F) – federation of small villages governed by local elders

Halving of SunSide (F) – battle at the end of *The Ore Monger,* one year prior to the start of *The Oasis Mage,* in which the SunSidian Revolutionary Forces stormed the Castrum, defeating the Bravers, killing the Facilitator, and bringing the Ore Monger (Red-Lo) into custody / after this, the theocracy abolished the SunSidian monarchy, making SunSide a sole theocracy again

Hassan (F) – Educator Librarian / angi human / shares trait common to the angi: wings that look like steel in color and texture / religious; prays facing the Holy Summit / fluent in Nysabaani / stationed at CereCenter Forty-Two for the current academic season / was good friends with Alba for many years / part of the conversation that began Unisa's disillusionment from the Prime's teachings (in *The Ore Monger*)

Hay-Ro (F) – faerie / originally a salver in Larso, joined the Faerie Empowerment Forces as a warrior / became Head Salver during Red-Lo's and Drof-Fa's reign as MegaParents / assisted Red-Lo later in life in writing his autobiography / had a strong friendship with Drof-Fa, but Red-Lo regarded him with disfavor / ancestor of Vy-Ro, former Braver General / pronounced *HAY-roe*

Headman (NF) – male chief or leader of a tribe or village

Headman of Deepweed (F) – village elder who governs Deepweed

Headwoman (NF) – female chief or leader of a tribe or village

Headwoman of Adera / Amma (F) – village elder who governs Adera

The HearthBark (F) – dense forest at the south of the continent / some describe it as a maze, or a prison if a traveler gets lost

Hemmar (F) – late seventies / nymph / Member of the New Sun-Sidian Assembly from Nivyan Hollow

The Holy Summit (F) – sacred angi temple constructed on a mountaintop in the PeakHaven mountain range / the angi face the Summit during their daily prayers

Igni (F) – one of the three human clans / possess stone exoskeletons / built the city of EverEmber on three islands surrounding the volcano, Mount Mother / governed by Court Democracy / seven members to the elected Court / do not display any particular organization in religion or spirituality, yet they do "feed" their dead to Mount Mother, so that their stone exoskeletons can be liquified and become part of the volcanic rock across Roba / in *The Ore Monger,* Red-Lo committed a genocide against the igni people to use their exoskeletons to make the ore / pronounced *ig-nee*

The Inner Catacomb (F) – a small circle of young women and girls who are given preferential treatment, affection, and attention from the Prime / Kanako revealed its existence to Kyoko in *The Ore Monger,* who then explained it to Unisa / part of Alba's plan, and Unisa's plot, is to free the members of the Inner Catacomb

Joaquina (F) – 17 years old at the time of her death / mari human / Rafael's sister / gave her bracelet to Rafael before she died / shares common mari anatomy: fins on the forearms and down the spine, piscine nare slits in place of a human nose, webbed fingers, and internal organs that allow for breathing underwater / in *The Ore Monger,* Rafael was able to convene with Joaquina's spirit at the Bridge Tree and resolve his guilt over her death, so that she could pass into the World Beyond

Juhi (F) – 27 years old / Doruh / animal form is a hawk / Unisa's Vice Ambassador

Kanako (F) – 33 years old / igni human / Kyoko's sister / Natsumi's mother / came to the Library with Kyoko when she was 16 and Kyoko was 12 / groomed by the Prime until she left the Library / estranged from Kyoko until the events of *The Ore Monger,* when they reconciled / shares common igni anatomy: stone exoskeleton

Konni (F) – 56 years old / indigo-skinned pixie / almost-retired Librarian / long-time acquaintance of the Prime and friend of Alba's / Alba was once Konni's Vice Ambassador / alluded to having had a romantic relationship with the Prime in their youth

Kova (F) – one of the Ancient Ones / "the male Sprite" / imprisoned with his sister/wife Elva by Vala, his ex-wife

Kura (F) – igni human / owner of Kura's Kitchen, a dining stall in the Library's marketplace

Kurti / Kurta (NF) – a kurta is a loose collarless shirt or tunic worn in many regions of South Asia / a kurti is a short hip-length kurta worn traditionally by young women and girls / common Doruh attire, as the development of the fictional Doruh culture was influenced by the culture of the South Asian Subcontinent

Kruga (F) – 36 years old / crimson skin / shares common Mega features: pointed ears and solid-gray eyes with no pupils or irises /

formerly a scientist and member of the SunSide Revolutionary Forces / now Counselor to the Chief Member (Saila) / has spent the last year teaching Rafael how to use the Radiance / pronounced *KROO-ga*

Kyoko (F) – 29 years old / former Vice Ambassador Librarian and Alba's protege / igni human / her sister is Kanako / has been living with Rafael and Ana in SunSide for the past year / during the Halving of SunSide, in *The Ore Monger*, the Braver General Vy-Ro injures her shoulder severely / she now deals with chronic pain in her shoulder that prevents her from being able to use one arm in battle the way she used to / shares common igni anatomy: stone exoskeleton

Larso (F) – capital city of SunSide/ connected to MoonSide's capital city, Arlun, by PeakHaven Pass / where the Castrum is / was covered in ore by the Ore Monger, but Saila is now working to return the ore to EverEmber / pronounced *lar-soe*

Lexona (F) – 21 years old / Salessa's ex-girlfriend / Afzal's twin sister / Doruh / animal form is a sea serpent / was in a romantic relationship with Salessa from the age of 16 to 18 / relationship ended when Naina walked in on Lexona attempting to steal the twins' escape funds / a physical altercation ensued in which Naina thought she had killed Lexona, but Lexona survived and subsequently found her twin brother and birth family / has been living amongst the O'Raha for the past three years / pronounced *LEXA-na*

The Library (F) – sovereign city-state in the northwestern corner of the continent / built with the sole purpose of housing and cataloging the entirety of Aerthomni's written history / this history is preserved in a system of tunnels under the city called the Catacomb Network, which connects various parts of the city and large chambers called, "sections" / for ease of transportation, also has a Stream Network and Loop Network built into the city's infrastructure / Stream Network is interconnected canals, intricately woven under bridges, around buildings, and through tunnels for those who wish to travel by water / Loop Network is a framework of multicolored hoops that direct and manage the airborne traffic throughout the Library / many of the Library's citizens desire to become Librarians: the Library's primary military, law enforcement, government officials, and healers / individuals find themselves in the Library in one of four ways: (a) born in the Library, (b) accepted by the Library under refugee or exiled status, (c) accepted by the Library for the youth education program and assigned to a Librarian for care and upbringing, or (d) accepted by the Library to train as a Librarian after displaying a high level of skill or intellect in a particular field / had strong political ties and allyship with SunSide's monarchy until its dissolution after *The Ore Monger* / governed by the six Supreme Librarians and the one Prime Librarian / protected by golden gates, and surrounded by a nearly impenetrable forest / at the dawn of the Library, and for many generations after, the founding Prime Librarians were moral and wise, wanting nothing more than to accurately and transparently catalogue the history of the continent within the Library's catacombs / over time, political alliances and societal control corrupted those who held the position, creating a shift in the nature of the Prime's role / modern Primes became willing to alter the records of the Library to glorify their allies and vilify those whom their allies oppress / they also committed heinous crimes against their citizens, emboldened by their control over the collective societal narratives and the lack of accountability this afforded them

Librarians (F) - the Library's primary military, law enforcement, government officials, and healers / devote their lives to the history recorded and preserved in the Catacombs, as well as the wisdom and teachings of the Prime / the various ranks dutifully collect, defend, or manage the information, but their focus remains the same regardless of where in the Library's hierarchy they fall: protect the history, protect the Catacombs, protect the city / Librarians are extensively trained in combat and weapons skills, and have some level of fluency in speaking and understanding Nysabaani / the ranks in ascending order are: Student, Scribe, Gatekeeper, Recorder, Educator, Vice Ambassador, Ambassador,

Supreme, Prime / each Librarian rank is associated with a different color tunic as a uniform, and performs a specified function or duty / the only Librarians with a duty or function that differs from that of their colleagues are the Prime's Gatekeeper, who acts as a personal and professional assistant to the Prime, and the Librarians who guard the gates

Lily Beach (F) – island that was situated on Ardev Ocean between the two known continents / the Ore Monger was using the island to commit a genocide against the igni people, turning their exoskeletons in ore / destroyed in *The Ore Monger*

Lona (F) – Lona is the second sun and deity of the Four / considered oldest and strongest after Ona in the Mega religion / typically referred to with masculine pronounce, though there is no certainty of gender from scripture / pronounced *LOE-nah*

The Loops / The Library's Loop Network (F) – a framework of multicolored hoops that direct and manage the airborne traffic throughout the Library

Lover's Plateau (F) – home base for the O'Raha / said to be an ancient ruin or to have never existed at all / 'Lover's Plateau' is a misnomer; intentionally inaccurate to mask its location / city built within a mountain / the Twins housed the O'Raha here, but they enchanted the entrance with their divine energy / after they died, the O'Raha were locked out / reopened by Lexona and Afzal

Lyla (F) – 16 years old / pregnant / part of the Inner Catacomb

Maksi (F) – late 20's / formerly Uni's coworker / carrot-colored skin / shares common Mega features: pointed ears and solid-gray eyes with no pupils or irises / likes writing poetry and vegetable stew in a corn bowl / dislikes breaking the rules / Fully Bonded / pronounced *max-ee*

Mari (F) – one of the three human clans / possess anatomy that assist in sub-oceanic travel and existence: fins on their forearms and down the spine, piscine nare slits in place of a human nose, webbed fingers, and organs that allow for breathing underwater / built the city of SeaBed at the bottom of Ardev Ocean / the city consists of domed communities with interconnected walkways as well as tubes through which mari can swim from one community to the next if they are in a hurry / the domes allow for their vast agricultural production / governed by Sub-Oceanic Stratocracy: an underwater government led by their military / largest of the domed communities, in the center, is Corazón Azul; home to commercial districts, government buildings, the homes of the wealthiest residents / pronounced *ma-ree*

Mega (F) – humanoid species, said to have evolved from the Sprite species toward the end of the Era of the Nysabaan / divided into three clans based on internal anatomical variances and differing levels of connectivity to the Radiance: the pixies, the nymphs, and the faeries / common traits amongst all Mega: pointed ears and solid-gray eyes with no pupils or irises / skin colors occur from all over the color spectrum / pixies tend to have the strongest connection to the Radiance, with nymphs having a lesser connection; present-day faeries have lost their connection to the Radiance as their dependence on technology has grown / *Mega* is both the singular and the plural / pronounced *may-ga*

MegaParents / MegaMother / MegaFather / SunSidian Monarchy (F) – formerly one-half of the SunSidian government until the dissolution of the monarchy after the events of *The Ore Monger* / referred to as "Father" or "Mother" / greeted with a circled fingers placed over the center of the forehead

Monarchy (NF) – a form of government in which an individual, a monarch, is head of state for life or until abdication

MoonSide (F) – capital city is Arlun / largest state on the continent after SunSide, directly west of PeakHaven Mountains /

encompasses all land between the PeakHaven Mountains and Red-Lo River / inhabited by the teri human clan through the Teri Age, though their numbers dwindled as human exploration led the teri to PeakHaven, SeaBed and EverEmber / SunSide invaded MoonSide during the War of New Clans and turned the remaining teri humans into the Doruh, marking the beginning of the new calendar era, Doruh Genesis (DG) / many Doruh captured and removed from MoonSide; brought back to SunSide and enslaved until the Doruh Uprisings in 784 DG / Alphocracy (government of Alphas) formed to govern MoonSide until they were assassinated / after the events of *The Ore Monger*, the SunSidian military occupation is expelled from MoonSide, along with the faerie settlements, and a new iteration of the Alphocracy is being established

Mount Mother (F) – the volcano around which the igni settled during the Teri Age / Mount Mother is at the center of the city and the igni culture - historically, spiritually, socially, politically / heat from the volcano rises into the air, then descends and covers the waters around the island, forming a natural defense / the igni do not display any particular organization in religion or spirituality, yet they do "feed" their dead to Mount Mother, so that their stone exoskeletons can be liquified and become part of the volcanic rock

Naina (F) – 21 years old / Salessa's twin sister / Doruh / animal form is a wolf / black hair cut just above shoulders / formerly professional cage fighter in Evic's underground fighting ring known as the Pit / since the events of *The Ore Monger*, has been employed as a member of the New SunSidian Assembly and a liaison to MoonSide / pronounced *NAN-na*

Natsumi (F) – 3 years old / igni human / Kanako's daughter / Kyoko's niece

New SunSidian Assembly (F) – theocracy of the SunSidian government / govern with the goal of establishing and enforcing the will of the Four over SunSide / Members are greeted with four fingers placed over the center of the forehead / meet in a vast chamber called the Forum / formed as the sole leadership and government of SunSide after the dissolution of the monarchy at the end of *The Ore Monger*

New SunSidian Guard (F) – SunSidian military and law enforcement / many warriors of the SunSide Revolutionary Forces went on to become part of the New SunSidian Guard after the Halving of SunSide, at the end of *The Ore Monger*

Nivyan Hollow (F) – large forest forming the southern border of MoonSide / paths run through the forest from Larso to the docks / powerful epicenter of Radiant energy / named after a minister who designed the legislation that became Doruh Liberation / pronounced *nih-VY-in*

Nymph (F) – one of the three Mega clans / can access and harness the energy of the Radiance, though they tend to have a weaker connection than the pixies do / share the common physical traits of all Mega: pointed ears and solid-gray eyes with no pupils or irises / nymph familial naming conventions build names within families around a common vowel (e.g. Symin, Syma, Zynima, Nypa)

Nysabaan (F) – name for the ancient inhabitants of Aerthomni and Panaerth during the Era of the Nysabaan (EN) / largely made up of Sprites and the ancient humans / spoke an ancient language called Nysabaani

Nysabaani (F) – ancient language that was the *lingua franca* during the Era of the Nysabaan (EN) / modern-day Librarians are taught to understand, translate, and converse in Nysabaani during their training / some national mottos are written in Nysabaani

Nytra (F) – a young nymph and war refugee raised by a pixie family who gave her life to defend those who raised her / a small SunSidian village, north of Larso, called Ward's Fall, is named to honor her sacrifice

The Oath Master (F) – alias of the Prime Librarian when he is working with his underground faction of Librarians, the Cicadas

Occupied Territory (NF) – a political territory placed under the authority of a hostile military

Ona (F) – the oldest and strongest of the Four, deities of the dominant Mega religion / she is the first to rise from the horizon, before Lona, Throna, and Frona / she is typically referred to with feminine pronouns, though there is no certainty of gender from scripture / pronounced *OE-nah*

The One Myth (F) – another name of the Resurrection Prophecy that foretells the resurrection of the Twins, their battle with the Ancient Ones, and the four Doruh who will physically and spiritually merge to bring the Twins back to life:

One from the land, one from the seas
One from the skies, one from the trees
Two sets of twins will be conceived
Their souls and bodies will be weaved
The God and the Goddess will be retrieved
And peace on the All-Sphere will be achieved.

Ora (F) – retired Librarian / Unisa's assigned mother / pixie / celadon-colored skin / suffering from a neurodegenerative disease

O'Raha (F) – group of devotees of the Twins and the One Myth / the O'Raha continued to keep oral (and later, written) records of visions the Twins had, passing them down through the generations / eventually disbanded, though they continued to pass down the oral and written records until the present day, when Lexona and Afzal reopened Lover's Plateau

Ore (F) – thought to have been a mysterious black stone or mineral discovered by the Ore Monger / he initially manufactured ore weapons and armor, later including it in roads, buildings, and Larso's infrastructure / also began to distribute the ore to political allies / interrupted the Mega connection to the Radiance, though the size of the ore, the distance from it, and the strength of the Mega's connection to the Radiance all played a role in how each individual was affected by it / during the events of *The Ore Monger* it was discovered that the ore was produced from a genocidal campaign in which the igni people were slaughtered and their exoskeletons were harvested to manufacture the ore / Saila, as the new Chief Member of SunSide, has vowed to return all of the ore the EverEmber, so that the igni people can properly mourn

Ovida (F) – former Co-General of the SunSide Revolutionary Forces / orange skin / shares common Mega features: pointed ears and solid-gray eyes with no pupils or irises / now the General of the New SunSidian Guard / pronounced *oe-vee-dah*

Panaerth (F) – one of the two known continents of the All-Sphere / pronounced *pahn-AIRTH*

PeakHaven (F) – one of the three human cities / governed by Super-Montane Stratocracy: headed by the military / populated by the angi human clan / built atop the highest mountain of the PeakHaven mountain range / built a temple called the Holy Summit

PeakHaven Pass (F) – built through the narrowest part of the PeakHaven mountain range / connects Arlun and Larso, the respective capital cities of MoonSide and SunSide.

Picana (F) – MegaMother during the time of Red-Lo's and Drof-Fa's usurping of the throne / opposed by the Faerie Empowerment Forces, led by Red-Lo's father / said to have been the most just of all MegaParents, fighting for equity amongst the clans and species of SunSide's citizenry / planned to liberate the Doruh before the regicide in 767 DG / her assassination was featured in the prologue of *The Ore Monger* / pronounced *pee-KAH-nah*

Pina (F) – Tund-Ra's daughter

The Pit (F) – Evic's underground fighting ring where Naina made her living

Pixie (F) – one of the three Mega clans / can access and harness the energy of the Radiance / tend to have the strongest connection to the Radiance of all Mega clans / share the common physical traits of all Mega: pointed ears and solid-gray eyes with no pupils or irises / pixie familial naming conventions build names within families around a common initial phoneme (e.g. Saith, Saila, Saimiza; Zakia, Zabeza, Zalona)

The Prime / Alvaro (F) – ninth and top rank of the Librarian hierarchy / political, social, and spiritual leader of the Library / uniform is black silk tunic / title currently held by a mari man: Alvaro, Alba's and Ana's uncle / late fifties / shares common mari anatomy: fins on the forearms and down the spine, piscine nare slits in place of a human nose, webbed fingers, and internal organs that allow for breathing underwater / his most unique feature is his eyes; they are somehow warm and cold at the same time / at the dawn of the Library, and for many generations after, the founding Prime Librarians were moral and wise, wanting nothing more than to accurately and transparently catalogue the history of the continent within the Library's catacombs / over time, political alliances and societal control corrupted those who held the position, creating a shift in the nature of the Prime's role / modern Primes became willing to alter the records of the Library to glorify their allies and vilify those whom their allies oppress / they also committed heinous crimes against their citizens, emboldened by their control over the collective societal narratives and the lack of accountability this afforded them / Alvaro is no exception to this

Prime Palace (F) – the estate of the Prime Librarian / palatial in its magnificent architecture and grand views / teeming with stunning fountains and vibrant flora, rests atop a hill that overlooks the busiest intersections of the Library / positioned above the citizens, rising like a guard tower from which the Prime can survey and scrutinize the population

Pyr-Sa (F) – early fifties / faerie / Member of the New SunSidian Assembly from the outer districts of Larso

The Radiance (F) – energy fields emitted from organic matter / Mega possess the ability to access and harness the energy for any purpose (dependent on the strength of the Mega's connection to the Radiance and their personal skill level) / in present continuity, faeries have lost their ability to access the Radiance, while the nymphs and pixies have retained it / Pixies tend to have the strongest connection to the Radiance, of all three clans / ore blocks the nymphs' and pixies' abilities to connect to the Radiance / Doruh cannot actively harness the Radiance, but do use Radiant energy when shifting / humans were able to access and harness the Radiance prior to 1 DG, but lost it when the human teri clan was transformed into the first generation of Doruh / during the events of *The Ore Monger,* after over 1600 years, Rafael reignited the ability for humans to connect to the Radiance / for the past year, he has been training with Kruga on how to use the Radiance and has now become quite skilled at it / he is currently the only human in the world who has access to the Radiance

Radiance-Return (F) – the Mega religion dictates that the Four use energy from the Radiance to build essences prior to life / after death, the essences become energy again and return to the Radiance / funeral rites are performed by a loved one during a Radiance-Return burial

Rafael (F) – 24 years old / formerly the Prime's Gatekeeper / mari human / exiled from the underwater city of SeaBed at the age of 15 / wears a bracelet that originally belonged to his sister, who gave it to him prior to her death / skilled archer / shares common mari anatomy: fins on the forearms and down the spine, piscine nare slits in place of a human nose, webbed fingers, and organs that allow for breathing underwater / during the events of *The Ore Monger*, after over 1600 years, Rafael reignited the ability for humans to connect to the Radiance / for the past year, he has been training with Kruga on how to use the Radiance and has now become quite skilled at it / he is currently the only human in the world who has access to the Radiance / has been living with Rafael and Ana in SunSide for the past year

***Rayga* (F)** – early thirties / pink-skinned pixie / Member of the New SunSidian Assembly from Ward's Fall

***Ray-Mi* (F)** – deceased / faerie / cornflower-blue skin / former Braver / fought alongside Symin, Kruga, and the Revolutionary Forces against the Ore Monger / gave his life during the escape from Lily Beach in *The Ore Monger* / pronounced *ray-mee*

***Recorder Librarians / Recorders* (F)** – fourth rank of the Librarian hierarchy / uniform is purple cotton tunics / duties include: accompany Ambassadors on missions to record historical events for the Catacombs, supervise Gatekeepers, record testimonies, managing the intake of those entering the Library, etc.

***Red-Lo* (F)** – faerie / took over from his father as the leader of the Faerie Empowerment Forces / usurped the SunSidian throne from MegaMother Picana and became the MegaFather / started the Red-Lo Royal Dynasty / husband of Drof-Fa / widowed in 783 DG, during the Everlasting Journey / built the Temple Complex in Larso, using land when nymph and pixie communities once stood / thought to be an ancestor of MegaFather Zar-Lo, but the events of *The Ore Monger* revealed that he took a journey in search of immortality with Drof-Fa the MegaMother / this journey lead to the inadvertent liberation of the Ancient Ones from their imprisonment, and Drof-Fa's subsequent curse to live on as the TreeKeeper / Red-Lo, in exchange for immortality, promised to feed the essences of his descendants to the Ancient Ones, allowing his essence to live on, generation after generation, in their bodies / after the events of *The Ore Monger*, Red-Lo is now in Saila's custody and, unable to fulfill his end of the bargain by providing an essence to the Ancient Ones, has doomed the planet to the release of the Three Deaths

Red-Lo River (F) – named after Red-Lo the MegaFather / forms the western border of MoonSide

Saila (F) – 36 years old / theocrat; Chief Member of the New SunSidian Assembly / pixie / green skin, inherited from her father, Saith / powerful connection to the Radiance, also inherited from her father / Alba and Sonali were like sisters to her / killed her father during the Halving of SunSide, in *The Ore Monger,* when she learned he had given the order for Alba's assassination / pronounced *SY-la*

Saimiza (F) – former Head Salver / pixie / Saith's aunt / Saila's great-aunt / was killed by the Ancient Ones when attempting to enter Red-Lo's mind in *The Ore Monger* / pronounced *sy-MEE-za*

Saith (F) – deceased / formerly the Ore Monger's Facilitator / pixie / lost one arm years prior while protecting the MegaFather / Saila's father / Saimiza's nephew / killed by Saila during the Halving of SunSide (at the end of *The Ore Monger*) / pronounced *sy-th* (like "scythe")

Salessa (F) – 21 years old / Naina's twin sister / Doruh / animal form is a falcon / light brown eyes / mid-length hair, dyed auburn / taught at the village schools and orphanages during the daytime, then worked the evening and night shifts at Sultana's Chai Palace / since the events of *The Ore Monger,* has been employed as a member of the New SunSidian Assembly and a liaison to MoonSide / received an anonymous note at the end of *The Ore Monger* to search for the author of the note in Lover's Plateau / has now gone on a journey to find the author of the note / pronounced *sa-LESS-sa*

Salvers (F) – healers

Saree (NF) – a garment consisting of a length of cotton or silk elaborately draped around the body, traditionally worn by women from South Asia / common Doruh attire, as the development of the fictional Doruh culture was influenced by the culture of the South Asian Subcontinent

Scribe Librarians / Scribes (F) – second rank of the Librarian hierarchy / recent graduates of the Academy; initial rank out of training / uniform is pink cotton / duties primarily revolve around assisting Gatekeepers, be that with copying, filing, general tasks, etc.

SeaBed (F) – one of the three human cities / governed by a Sub-Oceanic Stratocracy: headed by the military / populated by the mari human clan / at the bottom of Ardev Ocean / the city consists of domed communities with interconnected walkways as well as tubes through which mari can swim from one community to the next if they are in a hurry / the domes allow for their vast agricultural production / largest of the domed communities, in the center, is Corazón Azul; home to commercial districts, government buildings, the homes of the wealthiest residents

Shalwar Kameez (NF) – shalwars are trousers, common in the South Asia subcontinent, which are atypically wide at the waist but which narrow to a cuffed bottom / the kameez is a long shirt or tunic that often accompanies the shalwar / common Doruh attire, as the development of the fictional Doruh culture was influenced by the culture of the South Asian Subcontinent

Sofia (F) – Rafael's mother / one of the Generals who govern SeaBed

Soil King (F) – both a small village near the border of the Agrarian Townlets and the Gerontocratic Villages, and the leader/ruler of this village

Sonali (F) – deceased / Doruh / animal form was a bald-faced hornet / executed for aiding the Revolution during the Siege of the Castrum / buried in the Northern Hills of MoonSide with her parents

Sovereign City-State (NF) – an independent city with its own sovereignty

Sprites (F) – extinct species who, toward the end of the Era of the Nysabaan, evolved into the Mega / not much else is known about them, other than what was left behind in the ancient texts and records they kept / the Ancient Ones are commonly referred to as, "The Sprites," as they are the only known living Sprites

Stratocracy (NF) – government led by the military

The Stream / The Library's Stream Network (F) – interconnected canals, intricately woven under bridges, around buildings, and through tunnels for those who wish to travel by water / the Stream and the Loop reach the outer neighborhoods of the Library

Stones / Currency (F) – polished stones used as currency / a circular blue stone, a triangular green stone, and a rectangular red stone / dominant form of payment across the continent

Student Librarians / Students (F) - first rank of the Librarian hierarchy / study and train at the Academy / uniform is white cotton

Supreme Librarians / Supremes (F) – eighth rank of the Librarian hierarchy / uniform is blue silk / six Supremes / responsible for lawmaking, governance, and general administration along with the Prime / also responsible for managing the mission assignments of the Ambassadors

Sultana (F) – owner of Sultana's Chai Palace / formerly Salessa's boss / not fond of Naina or Lexona

Sultana's Chai Palace (F) – where Salessa worked as a chaitender for the evening and night shifts after her breakup with Lexona

SunSide (F) – capital city is Larso / largest kingdom and political entity on the continent / governed by a sole theocracy, the New

SunSidian Assembly, after the dissolution of the monarchy in *The Ore Monger* / encompasses all land to the east of the PeakHaven mountain range / originally settled by a community of Sprites who evolved into the Mega / these Mega further split into the faeries, nymphs, and pixies during the Teri Age / SunSide invaded MoonSide during the War of New Clans and turned the remaining teri humans into the Doruh, marking the beginning of the new calendar era, Doruh Genesis (DG) / many Doruh captured and removed from MoonSide; brought back to SunSide and enslaved until the Doruh Uprisings in 784 DG / SunSide invaded MoonSide again in 1381 DG, assassinating the MoonSidian Alphocracy and forming the Braver organization to set up a military occupation / in 1422 DG, more Doruh were driven from MoonSide, as their land was further captured and faerie settlements built / the occupation and settlements began dissolution and expulsion after the events of *The Ore Monger,* with Saila and the New SunSidian Assembly hoping to return the stolen land to the MoonSidians and reestablish the Alphocracy

SunSide Revolutionary Forces (F) – formed in 793 DG after Red-Lo drove the nymphs and pixies out of Larso / disbanded in 1621 DG after the failed Siege of the Castrum / reestablished for a brief time in 1628 DG to conduct the Halving of SunSide, the battle at the end of *The Ore Monger* / many former Revolutionary warriors went on to become part of the New SunSidian Guard

Symin (F) – deceased / lost his daughter, Zynima, in 1613 / joined the Revolution until its disbanding in 1621, then set out with a group of warriors to continue the fight by attempting to find ways to rid the MegaFather of the ore / gave his life fighting in the Halving of SunSide during *The Ore Monger* / pronounced *SY-min* (like "Simon")

Tanto (NF) – a type of Japanese short sword / common in Ever-Ember's military, as the development of the fictional igni culture was influenced by Japanese culture

Temple Complex (F) – massive complex of shrines and temples, devoted to the Four / no greater symbol of SunSide's devotion to its theocracy exists than the Temple Complex / tall buildings house chapels, feast halls, council chambers and classrooms / towering statues, monuments, and shrines to the Four are featured in designated areas all around the vast compound / the outer rim is guarded by gates and pylons, and an ablution river runs around the center courtyard

Theocracy (NF) – a system of government in which religious leaders rule in the name of a god or gods.

The Three Deaths (F) – demon beasts that the Ancient Ones, have threatened to release before the final battle / the Twins will take on the Sprites, but before then, the world must survive its first test: a beast of the sky, a beast of the soil, a beast of the sea / the time and location of the Three Deaths' release is unknown, but Rafael, Kyoko, and Ana have been working on finding this information in ancient Sprite texts

Throna (F) – Throna is the third sun and deity of the Four / considered the youngest and weakest after Frona in the Mega religion / typically referred to with masculine pronounce, though there is no certainty of gender from scripture / pronounced *THROE-nah*

The TreeKeeper (F) – a grotesque, deformed figure who carries essences to the World Beyond / keeper of the Bridge Tree / it was revealed in *The Ore Monger* that during the Everlasting Journey, MegaMother Drof-Fa, wife of Red-Lo, was cursed by the Ancient Ones to live immortally as the TreeKeeper

Tund-Ra (F) – late fifties / leader of the Braver's United / former Braver/ Pina's father / responsible for violent uprisings in the capital city, Larso, that led to the deaths of innocent civilians

The Twins (F) – deities of the Doruh religion / a brother and a sister who were the first naturally-conceived Doruh / born to Adera, a pixie, and her human lover, Anhum / the Twins are prophesied to be resurrected one day to battle the Ancient Ones / the time of their resurrection is said to be identified by the birth of two sets of Doruh twins who will shift into four different animals / genetically, all Doruh twins must shift into the same animal, so the varying animal forms of two sets of twins will signal the return of the Twins / one of the sets of twins is Naina and Salessa, who shift into a wolf and a falcon, respectively

Unisa (F) – 24 years old / formerly Gatekeeper Librarian in the Catacomb section *Witness* / at the end of *The Ore Monger*, she was promoted the Ambassador Librarian / her Vice Ambassador is a Doruh shifter named Juhi / angi human / shares common angi anatomy: wings that look like steel in color and texture / accepted for the Library's youth education program at the age of four / raised by an adopted mother, a pixie named Ora / pronounced *oo-NEE-sa*

Vala (F) – The Oasis Mage / ex-wife of Kova / former sister-in-law of Elva / imprisoned the Ancient Ones

Vice Ambassador Librarians / Vice Ambassadors (F) – sixth rank of the Librarian hierarchy / uniform is green linen tunics / assist Ambassador Librarians in preparation of, during, and after their missions to witness historical events and record them for the Library's Catacombs

Vinino (F) – mid eighties / lavender-skinned pixie / Member of the New SunSidian Assembly from Nivyan Hollow

Vy-Ro (F) – deceased / former Braver General / descendent of Hay-Ro / killed by Kyoko during the Halving of SunSide, at the end of *The Ore Monger* / during the battle, injured Kyoko's shoulder severely / pronounced *VY-roe*

Ward's Fall (F) – a small SunSidian village, north of Larso, at the base of the PeakHaven mountain range / named after Nytra, a young nymph and war refugee raised by a pixie family who gave her life to defend those who raised her

Witness (F) – section of the Library's Catacomb Network in which primary historical records and eyewitness testimonies to historical events are stored / Unisa was one of the Gatekeepers assigned to this section / Maksi still is

The World Beyond (F) – final resting place of the essences of this world

Yuki (F) – 20 years old / igni human / neighbor of Ora and Unisa / helps Unisa care for Ora in the evenings

Zakia (F) – deceased / pixie / royal purple skin / joined Symin's group at the age of thirteen / gave her life in the escape of Lily Beach during the events of *The Ore Monger* / prior to her death, had started to develop a romance with Salessa / pronounced *za-KEE-ah*

Zar-Lo (F) – descendant of Red-Lo whose body was used as a vessel for Red-Lo's essence, in the same manner that all of his descendents bodies were used / last MegaParent of the SunSidian monarchy and of the Red-Lo Royal Dynasty (though it was revealed in *The Ore Monger* that all of the monarchs of the dynasty were Red-Lo, as the Ancient Ones were feeding on their essences and passing Red-Lo's essence down into their bodies

Zoya (F) – late twenties / Doruh / animal form is a horse / member of the O'Raha / has dedicated her life to the One Myth and the resurrection of the Twins / enjoys poetry

ACKNOWLEDGEMENTS

If it takes a village to raise a child, it takes a nation to publish a book. Those named in this section (and perhaps others I may forget – forgive me) played an important role in getting *The Oasis Mage* out of my head and into your hands/e-reader. I owe a vast debt of gratitude…

To my wife, Seenu. The luckiest man in the world is he who has a loving, supportive wife. And because I have you, I am even luckier than he. I love you more and more each day, my darling.

To my parents, whose constant support means the world to me. I am only able to do anything in life because you've given me the confidence to be myself, unapologetically. It's a gift I rarely thank you for (so I put it in the Acknowledgments section…now you have my gratitude in writing).

To my brother and sister-in-law, Bilal and Anusha. It is in the interactions we have that I find inspiration for some of the most poignant scenes of siblinghood that I write. Thank you for always supporting me.

To my nephew and niece, Ayaan and Aleeza. Chachu now has *two* books you can read when you're old enough! (in shaa Allah). At only five and three years old, you both hold a vocabulary more advanced than my own (ma shaa Allah). I cannot wait to see the wordsmiths you may become yourselves (if you want, no pressure). Chachu loves you so much!

To my grandparents, aunts, uncles, cousins, and other extended family members. The outpouring of love and support I received after the release of *The Ore Monger* is appreciated in ways I fail to articulate beyond a simple, "Thank you."

To my good friend, Daniel Tilley. Dan, I don't think I'll ever be able to release a book without first acknowledging the profound impact you've had on my life by casually asking one day, "Hey, do you want to join a writing group?" I joined it, and here I am. Thank you, Dan!

To my beta readers: Katrina Lewis, Rose Thomson, and Ana Španović. Thank you for all of your time and efforts, and above all, thank you for the endless support! All three of you have made a significant difference in empowering me to write with courage and conviction. And I owe you a huge debt of gratitude for that.

To the consultants of my world-building, again: Gee Rothvoss, Maseeha Seedat, Ryota Ochi, and 凌危贊 of Shiranui Editorial. The igni and mari cultures could never have been constructed, based on the beautiful cultures of Japan and Spain respectively, without your authentic input and collaboration. Thank you!

To my editor and friend: Emilie Mortati at Glitterpenned Edits. There is a significant paralysis and anxiety that comes with switching from one editor to another between books, and I was terrified. But it took *moments* of interacting with you to realize my fears were unfounded. Emilie, you are a light in this world, and *The Oasis Mage* would never have been able to be published if it weren't for your expertise and your unshakable professionalism. Thank you so much for all you did for me.

To all of the authors, writers, editors, artists, and readers who make up the loving and inviting place that is Bookstagram. I may not be able to name each and every one of you, but if you've ever been in my DMs, the comments of my posts, or anywhere else we've interacted, just now how important a role you've played in getting me here. Thank you!

And as I ended my last Acknowledgements section, I do the same again, with the two most wonderful book besties an author can ask for: Ciara Hartford and Essie Rowley.

We tell each other all the time, but I'm going to say it here, too: sincerely, none of my books would have been published without you two. I find myself, almost every single time I sit down to write, sinking deeper and deeper into the trenches of imposter syndrome and self doubt and technical confusion and overall frustration, and it is only in seeing your hands reaching to pull me out from above, with the light of the sun shining through, that I am able to escape.

Please know how sincere I am when I say that there is no one on this planet quite like the two of you. You're brilliant and selfless and I am better simply for having spent a short time interacting with you. From the bottom of Elixabeth's heart, thank you!

About the Author

ZAID HASAN IS AN AUTHOR who enjoys crafting epic Science Fantasy stories. He's written many books throughout his life, none of which you've read because they're buried in a box somewhere in his storage unit.

In 2021, however, Zaid started to outline a story that he felt could be worthy of publication one day, and that epic tale became his debut novel: The Ore Monger.

Outside of storytelling, Zaid is a happily-married husband, a Muslim, a devoted cat dad, a loving uncle, a tattoo enthusiast, a comic book collector (DC Comics), and an obnoxiously proud New Yorker.

Follow Zaid Hasan's projects on his website and his instagram. Or reach out to him at his official email address below, he would love to hear from you.

www.hasanfantasy.com
instagram.com/hasanfantasy
contact@hasanfantasy.com

OTHER WORKS BY INDIE AUTHORS

Ciara Hartford – @ciarahartford.author and @dark_zephi_art
The House of Starling
The House of Amfithere
Blackwarden

Essie Rowley – @essierowley
Papercut

AG Rodriguez – @agrwrites
Stone Feather Fang
Space Brooms

Emmie Hamilton – @authoremmiehamilton
The Destined Series
When Stars Become Shadows

Luke Courtney – @lukecourtneyauthor
The Girl Who Sings to Dragons
The Wolf and the Swan

Jordan Smith – @jordansmith.author
Mourn Not the Mortals
Read Not the Runes

Roger Sandri – @roger_sandri_wordslinger
The Den of Stone
The Nightmare Path

Nimmi Sheikh – @n.s.chaudhury
Frostbyte

Genesis Bird – @writergenesisbird
Forget the Feckin' Wellies
Fast Times at Excellent Yonago

Malika D — @malikadauthor
Shadows of Innocence
Entangled Shadows

Paula Elisa Menz — @mayaseranawriter
Easy Guide to Escape Hell

Sarah Vespertine — @writersarahvespertine
Forged in Crimson
A Grave of Chains

Amanda Slоothaak — @amandasloothaak
Fire Fox
Ice Wolves

KV Meadows — @authorkvmeadows
Dance of the Copsewood

Gigi Zarbi — @gigi.zarbi
Broken Wings & Tangled Webs

www.ingramcontent.com/pod-product-compliance
Lightning Source LLC
LaVergne TN
LVHW100500110826
845146LV00002B/467

* 9 7 9 8 9 9 1 4 4 6 7 2 3 *